THE START OF THE DEAL

The Devil doesn't tempt you with something you don't want.

He grins at you, licks his scaly lips, then reaches into his sack with long bloody fingers and pulls out the one treasure you cannot live without.

You snatch for it, but—too quick for you—he steps back and holds it tauntingly beyond your reach. Not so fast, he says. He'll give it to you only when you agree to give him something in return. Then he leans toward you, bringing his face so close to yours all you can see are his flat yellow eyes, whirling and glinting like flaming discs. They burn into you as he reads everything you are. He whispers soothingly that what he wants from you is of no value. You won't miss it.

When you hesitate, he shrugs and turns away. It means nothing to him, he says. Perhaps he'll offer the treasure to your sister instead. She won't refuse.

With a cry, you reach out imploringly. *"I must have it!"*

You'll give him whatever he wants.

And so the deal is done.

He'll return another day to claim what you've promised, as he always has. Only then will you know what you've lost. But by then it will be too late.

I see you smirking. You don't believe in the Devil. You think you're safe, that the world was born this morning, fresh and uncorrupt. You think the Devil is a Halloween costume.

You don't know history.

The Devil is real.

And he's here now.

THE DEVIL'S CRADLE

KATE STEWART

ZEBRA BOOKS
KENSINGTON PUBLISHING CORP.

ZEBRA BOOKS

are published by

Kensington Publishing Corp.
475 Park Avenue South
New York, NY 10016

First printing: July, 1992

Printed in the United States of America

To Peter, Peggy, Carey and Tom:
I know no fruit as sweet.

Prologue

The Devil doesn't tempt you with something you don't want.

He grins at you, licks his scaly lips, then reaches into his sack with long bloody fingers and pulls out the one treasure you cannot live without.

You snatch for it, but—too quickly for you—he steps back and holds it tauntingly beyond your reach. Not so fast, he says. He'll give it to you only when you agree to give him something in return. Then he leans toward you, bringing his face so close to yours all you can see are his flat yellow eyes, whirling and glinting like flaming discs. They burn into you as he reads everything you are. He whispers soothingly that what he wants from you is of no value. You won't miss it.

When you hesitate, he shrugs and turns away. It means nothing to him, he says. Perhaps he'll offer the treasure to your sister instead. She won't refuse.

With a cry, you reach out imploringly. *"I must have it!"*

You'll give him whatever he wants.

And so the deal is done.

He'll return another day to claim what you've promised, as he always has. Only then will you know what you've lost. But by then it will be too late.

I see you smirking. You don't believe in the Devil. You think you're safe, that the world was born this morning, fresh and uncorrupt. You think the Devil is a Halloween costume.

You don't know history.

The Devil is real.

And he's here now.

PART ONE

Dorothy

Chapter One

Dorothy Kite was a gentle person with a soft voice and long elegant legs, but she wasn't the kind of woman men's eyes followed. Her gaze was often on the pavement in front of her and because she was shy she had trouble making friends.

She'd spent most of her adult life caring for her sickly mother and working as a librarian at the New York Literary Library, an obscure branch of the public library system located on West 44th Street. She seemed much too ordinary to harbor a secret yearning.

But nobody is ordinary. Each of us has a secret. The Devil knows this. Look again at Dorothy Kite.

Her mother was dead at last.

Probably the cancer killed her, but she'd had so much bad luck, so many disabilities, the doctor didn't say exactly which disease finally carried her off. High blood pressure and heart palpitations were the first afflictions Dorothy remembered—that must have been during seventh grade. Diabetes then, and something wrong with her thyroid. Arthritis. Bursitis. Emphysema. Graves' disease and kidney stones. A bad gall bladder. Endless pills, nostrums, elixirs, capsules, bottles of bad-smelling medicine, little jars of ointment.

She could throw them all out now.

The funeral was pathetic. If Dorothy hadn't been so numb

and tired, the bitter evidence of the wasted life might have made her cry. There weren't even any real flowers, just the dusty plastic ones the mortician set around the dingy room. And the grand total of six people showed up. Madelyn Kite had three relatives: Dorothy, Dorothy's brother Spark and his wife Jeannie. They'd flown in from Portland, Oregon.

Then two old ladies, each gripping an imitation leather pocketbook, materialized as the service began. As they peered at Dorothy they blinked membranous lids over their bulging eyes like a pair of ancient fish. They confided to her that they'd gone to grammar school with Madelyn. Heaven only knew how they'd discovered she'd died, or why they'd come. Perhaps they hadn't known her at all. They might have been a pair of those old women Dorothy had heard about who liked to read obituaries and attend funerals of people they'd never met, ghoulish imposters pretending to mourn.

It gave her the creeps.

The sixth person at the funeral was Henry Small. He was the other librarian at the library where Dorothy worked. He was a middle-aged bachelor with an Adam's apple the size of a plum, and he left as soon as the ritual ended, even before the taped organ music concluded. Dorothy didn't have a chance to invite him to dinner afterwards, to meet Spark and Jeannie. When she stood and turned around, he was gone, vanished with the old women without a word.

"I wish you could have met him," Dorothy told her brother and sister-in-law. She saw them exchange looks, as if Henry and she had some kind of romantic relationship, which of course they didn't. Henry was terribly nervous— he fidgeted, cracked his knuckles, sometimes ran out of air as he talked, and gasped at the ends of his rapid sentences. The world he viewed came to him through a quirky prism of irreverence and he made Dorothy laugh. Yet their friendship existed only at the library.

She knew he'd been too shy to meet Spark and Jeannie.

"Do you have to go back to Portland tonight?" she said, once she was seated with them in a noisy neighborhood restaurant. "Maybe Henry can come for supper tomorrow. You could meet him then."

Jeannie shook her head.

12

"You wouldn't believe the Simon Legree Spark works for," she said. "It's lucky the funeral was on a Saturday so we could get back without missing a single day of work. I must say it's one of the few thoughtful things your mother ever did, dying so her funeral could be on a weekend." She smoothed the lapels of her bright jacket. "I'm afraid there wasn't much love lost between us," she admitted.

"What are you going to do now?" Spark asked Dorothy, moving in quickly to change the subject as he did whenever Jeannie's frankness veered too close to tactlessness. Spark hated scenes. Dorothy noted with a twinge that he'd lost much of his hair. He'd taken to drawing the part low, next to his ear, and combing wisps separately across his pink scalp. She remembered when he couldn't force a comb through the tangle of curls. How handsome he'd been. Her big brother.

"I don't know," she said. "I haven't made any plans."

Jeannie clucked her tongue noisily against her teeth and looked intently at Spark.

Nodding at the none-too-subtle reminder, he said to Dorothy, "Why don't you come and stay with us for a while? You'll like Portland." He frowned. "It isn't dirty and depressing the way New York is."

Jeannie agreed eagerly. "There's nothing for you here now," she said.

"Of course you may be too busy to get away," Spark said quickly, implying Dorothy's life was crammed with important activities.

She avoided his probing gaze by looking down quickly and straightening the napkin across her lap. It had been her choice to stay home to look after Madelyn. She wished he understood that. Nobody had forced her. She resented his pity.

"Oh, but you have to come," Jeannie insisted. "You can stay in the spare room until—" She stopped and looked at Spark. "Can we tell her now?"

He nodded.

Dorothy glanced uneasily at him and back to Jeannie. "What?"

"We're going to have a baby," Jeannie said. "In November."

13

Dorothy's eyes widened and Jeannie reached impulsively with both arms across the table to hug her.

"Careful," Spark said, grabbing the sugar bowl. "You'll knock everything over." But he was clearly pleased and rose halfway as Jeannie turned back and hugged him exuberantly too.

Dorothy's stomach tightened as if kicked but she tried to smile.

"We want you to come out and help us get ready," Jeannie said.

Dorothy took a painful swallow of ice water. Her throat had closed as if she were about to cry.

"Or you can pull up stakes entirely," Spark said. "Move out west where your family is."

"Go west, young woman," Jeannie said, waving her butter knife.

Dorothy shrank back, sick with jealousy.

Jeannie leaned toward her, her eyes shining. "There's nothing to hold you here," she said. "Not any more."

"Let me think about it," Dorothy murmured, feeling cornered. "Everything's happening at once."

"I knew it," Jeannie said, looking forlornly at Spark. "She doesn't want to move. She wants to stay here with her boring job."

Spark laid his knife and fork carefully across the top of his plate. "You may not want to make plans yet," he said. "But at least you can come out and visit, to see if you take to the great Northwest."

Jeannie banged the table. "I *need* you," she said. "I'm scared to death. You know I'm such a klutz. My gosh, I'm thirty-six. I'll be older than everybody else in the maternity ward. They'll think I'm the visiting grandmother."

Dorothy clenched her hands in her lap.

She was two and a half years older than Jeannie.

She watched her sister-in-law tear a roll apart and butter it lavishly on every side, then take a big bite. Chewing silently, Jeannie looked imploringly at her. At this moment she seemed hardly older than when Spark first brought her home from college. "This is Jeannie," he'd said quietly, so much in love he could say nothing more, certain his sister would love her as he did, wonderingly, instantly. Dorothy never forgot the desperate hurt she'd felt looking at her brother standing in the center of the living room holding hands with a stranger. She'd wanted to hate the tall eager girl, with her wild hair and badly bitten nails, who'd stolen him away. But hating her had proved impossible.

Soon Dorothy learned that Jeannie's openness brought floods of tears whenever she was hurt or disappointed. But the honesty also allowed uninhibited laughter, searching questions, self-deprecating stories told with gestures. Dorothy was enchanted too.

Unsurprisingly, Madelyn disliked her instantly. She preferred to be the center of attention herself, and didn't approve of intruders. So despite Jeannie's several clumsy attempts to make friends, her mother-in-law pouted and resented her. But Spark had learned long before to ignore Madelyn. He and Jeannie eloped shortly before he finished graduate school in Michigan. After that they visited New York only occasionally, spending time with Dorothy and keeping out of Madelyn's way. In fifteen years she'd never forgiven them and barely spoke to Jeannie.

Unrepentant, Jeannie and Spark concentrated on advancing Spark's career (he was a C.P.A.). They lived in five different cities in ten years on his carefully planned corporate ascent. But when they settled in Portland, Jeannie confided to Dorothy that she was finally going to devote herself to having a family.

And—after several false alarms and frantic midnight phone calls ("Oh, Dorothy, I just know my body doesn't know how to make a baby!")—here it was.

Dorothy stirred herself to make the expected response. "Of course I'll come and help you get ready," she said, flushing as she smiled. "I'm the *aunt.*"

Jeannie beamed. "I knew you would," she said.

"But first I have to settle things here."

Jeannie agreed. She chattered on about how excited she was and never noticed the pain on Dorothy's face.

After dinner Spark and Jeannie kissed her goodbye and took a taxi to La Guardia. Once settled on the plane, her legs cramped sideways in the insufficient space between her seat

15

and the one in front, Jeannie listened to the hum of the engines and stared out the black window. Finally she looked back at Spark, who slumped next to her with his eyes closed.

"I'm worried about Dorothy," she said. "She's so thin."

Spark opened his eyes and sighed, making it clear he'd rather nap than talk. "She's all right," he said and closed his eyes again, hoping the conversation was finished.

"It doesn't seem fair," Jeannie said.

"What doesn't?" he asked patiently, opening his eyes.

"She older than I am but I'm the one who's pregnant."

He crossed his arms and turned away. "You're the one who's married," he said with finality.

Jeannie looked out the window again. After a while she reached for his hand and fit their fingers together. His skin felt cool and dry.

"It makes me sad, thinking of her, all alone, with nobody to talk to," she said. "What kind of a life is that?" She glanced back to search Spark's face for a reaction. But he'd fallen asleep. His mouth sagged and he snored imperceptibly. She smiled at her balding husband, usually so self-contained and dignified, as a puddle of drool collected on his shirt. A wave of affection washed over her and she squeezed his hand. His head rolled toward her and he sighed shudderingly. Soon he'll be a father, she thought with relief. She wasn't going to fail him after all. Joy from the knowledge brought tears to her eyes. She patted her stomach in secret greeting to its new inhabitant.

Turning her gaze back to the window, she nestled into her seat and pictured Dorothy going home. She saw her climbing tiredly the four flights to the empty apartment. She watched her put her coat away and turn on the lights, one by one, each of them flickering insufficiently against the enveloping darkness. She imagined the silent rooms. The loneliness.

Looking toward her husband again, Jeannie lay her cheek against the headrest, watching him and wondering that he slept so easily on the night of his mother's funeral.

After helping Spark and Jeannie into a taxi, Dorothy

walked along upper Broadway through a mist that settled on her cheeks like tears. The street lights shed a wavering silvery beam onto the sidewalk and she picked her way carefully between pedestrians, keeping close to the curb, hugging the oblong cardboard container she carried, looking at other people without seeing them, and at the shuttered stores she passed. When she got home she put away her hat and coat, as Jeannie had imagined her doing. But before she turned on the lights she pushed the oblong box containing her mother's ashes up onto the closet shelf between the boxes of jigsaw puzzles.

She could hardly believe her mother wasn't here to greet her, that she would never again be sitting in the big chair by the window looking up expectantly as Dorothy came in. "What's up?" she'd said every night, demanding a full report as soon as Dorothy entered the living room. And Dorothy told her what she wanted to hear, describing herself as heroine, as sidekick or even dupe, sometimes making her mother laugh, sometimes making her angry at some unfairness or other. ("Let's write a letter to the Mayor!" Madelyn would say, and they'd put their heads together and write it.)

Madelyn wanted Dorothy to stand up for herself, to get ahead in the world. She never understood what interested Dorothy about her job and the "useless" old books she was always dragging home. What good was reading stuff written by people you'd never heard of? Who cared about what ordinary people thought about anything? Madelyn had no interest in ordinary people. Her fascination was with the lives of the rich and famous. She didn't care what it had felt like to wear a long heavy dress and walk on cobblestones in thin-soled buttoned shoes, as Dorothy did, or to ride in a horsedrawn carriage behind a man in a silk hat with a whip in his hand. Madelyn didn't wonder about the way it was in some long-ago time, what it had felt like to open your front door and step out into 1783.

So Dorothy read the old books privately, after Madelyn had gone to bed. And in response to her mother's insistent questions she portrayed herself as an active participant in her own life, a forthright, modern woman. In this way she deflected Madelyn's criticism and, additionally, enabled her mother to participate in a life beyond their apartment.

Every morning Dorothy had caught the bus on the corner, gone to her job, done her work, ridden the bus home again. Sometimes when Henry said something funny at work she reported it to Madelyn, imitating his indignant long-armed gestures and earnest expression. Acting out stories about Henry invariably made Madelyn laugh. Henry liked to hear about her, too. "What's your mother up to these days?" he asked sometimes, chuckling at Dorothy's response, whatever it was. Madelyn and Henry were acquaintances who'd never met. Dorothy was the go-between who presented one to the other in the best possible light. All knowledge of the other was selected by her in her role as information-manager of what they knew of each other.

She couldn't invent her mother for Henry any more, or make him up for her.

Nor was there need for her to construct her own life in an acceptable version for her mother. She didn't have reason to pretend any longer.

It was time to look at her life as it was, not as a story she was making up to please somebody else.

She stood irresolutely in the center of the room looking at Madelyn's empty chair. Finally, hesitantly, she sat in it. She removed her shoes and set them neatly on the floor. Then she lifted her feet wearily onto the hassock and leaned back with her hands on the chair arms.

"I've left you plenty of money," Madelyn had said matter-of-factly not long ago. "After I'm gone you'll be able to do whatever you want. For heaven's sake, get your hair done." (Madelyn disapproved of the way Dorothy wore her dark hair in a thick braid, pinned in a coil on top of her head.)

Now she could wear her hair any way she liked. She could shave her head if she wanted to. She was free to do as she wished. But recognition of this new autonomy brought no surge of exhilaration, no desire to make plans or change the familiar pattern of her life. Instead, she felt lonely and frightened.

She hastily turned her mind to practical matters.

The closets must be sorted out, decisions made about what

she wanted to keep, what she should throw away. Madelyn had favored frilly nightgowns and bedjackets decorated with ribbons, bows and lace, as if she'd expected callers.

But no caller ever came.

Undoubtedly the ladies' auxiliary at some hospital thrift shop would jump for joy at the unexpected gift of boxes full of silky lingerie.

And no matter what Madelyn had said, there couldn't be much money, she'd never had two pennies to rub together. She'd often told Dorothy and Spark how she'd foolishly run off with Anthony Kite against her parents' warnings. In 1950 he'd taken her dancing under the swirling amber and lilac lights at the Roseland Ballroom. "He danced like an angel," Madelyn told her children. "He swept me off my feet." She claimed her elopement had killed her mother—who'd sensed the irresponsibility behind the handsome swagger—and her alcoholic father had "drowned in his own evil juices" a few months after that.

Madelyn pointed out grimly that of course her mother was right about Anthony. Scarcely two years after the marriage he walked out, just like that, went for a pack of cigarettes and never returned. He left behind an upright piano only he could play, a bank account containing twenty-seven dollars, and two babies, Anthony Adam Kite, Jr. ("Spark"), and Dorothy.

She often told her children you had to look out for yourself, nobody was going to do it for you. "Learn from my bad example," she said. And when Spark wasn't around she told Dorothy: "Never trust a man."

Dorothy didn't remember her father, of course. All she knew of him was what Madelyn had told her, and Madelyn was certain he'd come long ago to a bad end. "Probably stabbed to death in a barroom brawl," she said. "He told me his grandmother was a full-blooded Cherokee, and you know Indians are all drunkards."

After her husband left, Madelyn continued to work at the telephone company, arranging to trade off child care with a neighbor, whose senile mother required constant attention on the weekends.

But Madelyn's chronic illness forced her early retirement

19

not long after Spark and Dorothy started high school. She was a difficult patient. Through the years, as she became sicker and less able to care for herself, she complained, she wheedled, she got mad, she schemed, planned, worried, bullied. She made herself the center of attention. She puttered around the kitchen experimenting with recipes, leaving disorder and dishes caked with goo behind. ("Her own private slum," Spark said, referring to the mess that followed her from room to room.) She cut items from the newspaper and taped them to the door of the refrigerator and to the wall in the bathroom. She wrote letters to daytime television personalities and wrote them again, rudely, if they didn't answer the first time. She called up radio talk shows and bawled people out. She was excitable, bossy, opinionated.

For thirty-eight years the apartment rocked with the rich vitality of her personality.

Dorothy sighed. She wondered if people became ill on purpose. She'd read somewhere that getting sick was a way neurotics coped with unsatisfactory lives. "All illness, including death, is psychosomatic," she remembered reading. She had to admit that Madelyn's diseases and infirmities had provided her with another lifelong companion after her first choice had abandoned her. It might have been unintentional, but it had certainly been convenient. For her.

From early childhood Spark had avoided spending time at home, first with odd jobs after school, then working nights and weekends. He gave his mother everything he earned, but he left for the University of Michigan—on full scholarship—the day after his graduation from high school. ("Without a backward glance," according to Madelyn. "Like the ungrateful son in *The Glass Menagerie*.") Dorothy remained at home.

She liked thinking about how Madelyn had been in love with her father. She hadn't always been bitter and sarcastic. Once she'd been a romantic girl with secret hopes and dreams. When Spark left home Dorothy couldn't abandon her too. That would have meant leaving her behind too many times, breaking her heart once and for all. Dorothy loved her mother. She loved her passion and her spunk, the queer perversity that made her eager for news from outside but resisted going past her front door. Dorothy knew her mother was frightened of life and she sympathized with her. She understood Madelyn's stubborn romanticism that preferred television families to real ones and needed to remain within the safe boundaries of familiar walls because independence, with all its demands and excitement, was something Dorothy herself had felt unready to face at eighteen. So she went to library school at City College because she loved books and stories of other peoples' lives. When the job opened at the Literary Library, and she was hired, she couldn't believe her good luck. She became her mother's protector, and her mother's needs overwhelmed her own.

Many times she'd told herself her own turn would come, later, and that when it came she would be ready for it.

In this way years had slipped by.

Light from the street lamp angled through the window, falling across her face, illuminating the high-bridged nose, the slightly flared nostrils, the wounded dark eyes. A few loose strands of hair escaped from the braid on top of her head and fell softly across her forehead.

Now that her mother was dead, Dorothy knew she'd lost her usefulness, her focus. It felt as if there was nothing but blankness stretching endlessly ahead of her. She could no longer justify her life.

She moaned, bringing her knees to her chest and hugging them.

Why didn't she know how to live? Why didn't she know how to make friends and talk to people? She lifted her head and stared into the darkness. "Why did I grow up so afraid?" she whispered. She wanted a life but didn't know how to have one. She knew only stories, how to weave them for Madelyn, to make a cocoon for them both, to keep away the terrible suspicion of mutual failure. But Madelyn had deserted her, just as her father and Spark had done. There was no one left for her to cling to. She was all alone.

Her shoulders hunched as she started to cry, missing her mother and giving in finally to her oldest, most persistent yearning.

21

She wanted a baby.

She'd wanted one since childhood, when she'd wished for one on every wishbone, every evening star, every meteor she saw arcing across the purple sky.

It was all she'd ever wanted, a baby of her own, not Spark and Jeannie's child to visit and croon to and then give back. She wanted her own child, and she wanted it with a desperate, hopeless ache born from years of need.

She didn't need freedom. She didn't know what to do with freedom. What she needed was to be connected to another human being, as she'd been connected to her mother. She needed somebody waiting for her when she came home, somebody who loved her without reservation, somebody who'd smile and stretch out her hands in greeting, who'd fall asleep in her arms, somebody she could love with all her heart.

Without her mother, or a baby, her life was pointless.

Chapter Two

The New York Literary Library was a three-story granite structure located next to a warehouse on West 44th Street. Dorothy had been a librarian there for nineteen years.

Estates of Manhattan residents dying without debt or heir came automatically to the City. Proceeds of property auctions and funds from unclaimed bank accounts were awarded to its General Fund. Those unbequeathed items without dollar worth yet retaining unassessable personal, historical or literary value were assigned to the Literary Library.

Nobody wanted the stuff that ended up there, which included lengthy unpublished novels, geneological charts of early New York families without distinction or descendant, unproduced plays, handwritten epic poems.

Dorothy and Henry Small, who shared a small office, called their workplace the Library of Broken Dreams. After her mother died Dorothy felt safest here—among the dusty manuscripts and other useless residue of failed ambition. She had no place else to go. Several autobiographies, not all of them typed, had to be read, catalogued and filed, so she did these things, because it was her job, silently, hopelessly. Henry didn't bother her. In fact her dark face frightened him and he kept his distance. He didn't know what to say to her, but he hoped his presence would comfort her.

One afternoon when she got home from work she opened her mailbox with the key dangling with other keys on a chain she wore around her neck. (Once Henry had teased her:

"You're the oldest living latchkey child." But lately he didn't dare make jokes.) The mailbox contained a knitting magazine and a flyer announcing the opening of a neighborhood discount pharmacy. There was also a letter from an insurance company which she opened absent-mindedly, leaning against the tiled wall of the entry.

"Dear Ms. Kite," she read. "Please accept our condolences for the recent loss of your mother, Madelyn Makepiece Kite. She was our valued customer for many years. Your bereavement is ours as well.

"Enclosed please find our check for $183,000, which is the total amount of the insurance policy your mother maintained with our firm. As you probably know, you are her sole beneficiary."

Flabbergasted, Dorothy reread the letter. Then, blankly, she studied the check. $183,000 was stamped in italicized blue numbers under the name of a large New York City bank, and an illegible signature was scrawled at the bottom. Stuffing the letter and the check into her pocketbook, she unlocked the heavy entrance door and climbed the four flights of creaking stairs, using the banister to pull herself up. Her knees were suddenly wobbly and she couldn't catch her breath.

Once inside her own door she double-locked it, moved into the living room and removed the check from her purse. After she'd turned it slowly and examined both sides, once again satisfying herself as to its authenticity, she folded it and placed it in her wallet, in the compartment where she kept bank deposit slips. She put the wallet in her purse and laid it carefully in its accustomed place in the corner of the sofa. Then, unexpectedly, she raised her fists above her head and spun on her toes. "I'm rich!" she cried, laughing, radiant. "I'm rich!"

She threw herself dizzily onto the couch, grabbed her pocketbook and held it tightly against herself. She remembered Madelyn saying often that men knew how to take care of themselves. Spark would be able to stand on his own two feet, she'd said (even though she resisted and grumbled at every step he took toward independence). And she'd been right. He *was* a survivor. But if it turned out there wasn't

24

going to be a man in Dorothy's life after all (and surely it looked that way by now), then there'd be money she could use to take care of herself. Madelyn had had the foresight to reach across the years—and her own death—to protect Dorothy in this immensely practical way.

And she'd never said a word.

How had she managed to pay the premiums year after year? It couldn't have been easy, even before she'd gotten sick there'd never been enough money for the simplest pleasures. Going to the movies had been something to consider carefully. Yet she'd done it. She'd kept up the payments.

"For me," Dorothy whispered. She took out the check and rubbed it against her cheek. Madelyn had given her this gift so she'd get her chance—at last—to construct a life.

Her mother hadn't deserted her after all.

The following morning Dorothy deposited the check in her money market account. She added it to the $8,011 already there, a tiny sum which had taken her nineteen years to accumulate.

After she left the bank, she walked slowly along the west side of upper Broadway, looking into store windows, thinking about her money and what she'd do with it.

She entered a bakery and bought a glazed doughnut. On the street again she took a neat bite, chewed it thoughtfully and wiped her mouth with the waxed paper. After a few seconds she impulsively stuffed the rest of the greasy pastry into her mouth and closed her eyes with gluttonous pleasure. She didn't care if anybody were watching. Nobody was going to tell her to mind her manners. She was rich. She could do whatever she wanted.

As she waited for the light to change she watched a ragged woman rummage through the contents of a trash basket. She pulled out a ripped tassled object which might have been a pillow and crammed it into her shopping cart. A heavy, unwashed smell throbbed visibly in the air around her.

Dorothy strolled on, past a corrugated tin newsstand. Its narrow side door swung open to reveal a fat man sitting on a

25

stool inside who impatiently pulled it shut with a hand the size of a platter. She crossed the street and moved toward a beggar with splayed shoes sprawled on the sidewalk. He stretched toward her with a dirty paper cup. As she hastened past he spat at her, a glob of mucus splatting in front of her shoe. Then he leered up at her, took his hand and hitched it insinuatingly over his filthy crotch. She tightened the grip on her purse and quickened her pace.

She passed a store selling maternity clothes and found herself studying the window display. One of the dummies, in a colorful dress gathered in wide flounces, rested her hands crookedly on the handle of a baby carriage. Her wooden face gaped at passersby, the eyes as black and hard as onyx. Dorothy hurried on, impatiently pushing back the familiar ache.

At the next store, an avant-garde boutique, the window was entirely empty except for a manikin exploding stiff strings of witchlike hair. It slouched against a broken pillar wearing an arrangement of purple burlap carefully draped from one shoulder and hiked at the knee. A shining silver spike dangled from an ear. Dorothy studied the display. She realized she could afford a dress in this store. Carefully wiping her hands with a paper napkin, she folded it with the sticky waxed paper, put the square in her purse and entered the shop.

Half an hour later she emerged carrying an elegant red silk dress carefully packed with tissue in a big black and gold box.

The sunshine was bright in her eyes as she made her way through the crowds toward a shoe store on the next block.

That night she attended a performance of *Tosca* at the Metropolitan Opera. For her first opera she wore her new red dress and carried a beaded handbag found wrapped in ancient tissues at the back of her mother's dresser drawer. She washed her hair, stood in front of the bathroom mirror and brushed it until it glistened. Finally she made a long braid and swept it up, coiling it across her head, holding it in place with an arrangement of tortoiseshell combs. Getting

26

ready took longer than she expected. She was unused to elaborate preening, felt conspicuous and undignified in the wobbly new heels.

From West 96th Street she took a taxi to Lincoln Center, stuffed a ten-dollar bill into the fare box and told the driver to keep the change. He couldn't hear her through the plexiglass shield and she had to shout her instructions several times.

After she bought her $100 ticket, she went outside again and stood in the huge courtyard looking up at the fountain as the water cascaded from giant plumes. Couples around her walked arm in arm, talking quietly. Some of them held hands. The women were dressed in diaphanous stoles and glittering jackets decorated with rhinestone sunbursts or medallions made from clusters of brilliant gems.

After a while she joined the festive crowd walking across the marble plaza into the opera house. People jostled one another in the lobby under the three-story Chagall paintings, moved under them past towering columns. A bearded attendant selling librettos stood against a semi-circle of polished wall glistening with tiny gold names. Giving her ticket to an usher, Dorothy climbed the sweeping scarlet staircase and passed through gilt doors to her seat in the front row of the parterre.

As she opened her program she glanced up and saw the huge crystal snowflake chandaliers dim and rise toward the mighty domed ceiling a hundred feet above her. She watched their stately ascent. When the rustles and whispering subsided in the darkened auditorium, she looked down to see the conductor spotlighted at the rear of the orchestra pit. He made his way rapidly past the harpist and several rows of violinists. As the applause died he turned crisply to face the orchestra, spread his arms and began to call forth the opera's first crashing chords.

Dorothy gasped at the sight of the massive church interior revealed when the majestic gold curtains puckered and rose. A famous tenor appeared and climbed a scaffolding hanging in front of a large painting mounted high on the stone wall. When he began his passionate aria, Dorothy's eyes filled with tears.

She wept throughout the performance. Nothing in her life had prepared her for the experience. Sitting as one of the audience but floating somewhere beyond and above it, everything filled her—the colors, the vastness and grandeur, the scores of people on stage and—above all—the glorious, heart-swelling music. She'd never imagined pain and pleasure might exist simultaneously, exquisitely, shutting out everything else. She'd not known herself so vulnerable, ready to burst with unaccustomed, overpowering sensations. It was as if she *became* the music as she heard it, so naturally did each chord follow another, so liquidly and easily did the melodies erupt and fade and pulse again from somewhere else, in some other voice, all of it touching and holding her in some deeply yearning and unsuspected place. She felt herself awakened, quivering, ready.

Nothing else existed for three hours.

She remained in her seat long after the performance and the curtain calls ended, past the time when the house lights came up and everybody stood, putting on their coats, laughing and talking, and left. In a few minutes the only people with Dorothy in the hall were attendants who moved up and down the aisles collecting discarded programs. Finally she stood and began edging toward the exit, unwilling to disturb the glorious echos still reverberating within herself.

Suddenly the force of a violent cramp made her cry out and grab her midsection.

"You all right, lady?" asked a man in a black uniform with gold buttons. He stood three rows above her and held a whisk broom in his hand.

"Yes," she gasped, straightening cautiously. "It's nothing. I'm all right."

"Maybe you should sit down," he said. "You look a little rocky."

She didn't think so, but thanked him for his concern. She picked her bag up from the floor, crammed the program into it, hurried up the aisle two steps at a time. She knew she had about thirty minutes. Then the hemorrhage would burst from her, the hot clotted blood washing like high tide down the insides of her thighs and legs, rivers of it streaking her stockings and skirt, filling her shoes. Her menstrual period always came upon her like this, excruciatingly, explosively, like a punishment. She had no excuse for forgetting, it had happened this way exactly every twenty-five days since she was thirteen. It was as if she'd forgotten today's date on purpose, to ruin her evening.

She raced down the lobby escalator, trotted uneasily through the empty tunnel beneath Lincoln Center, hurried past the bulletproof plastic enclosed change booth, stuffed a token into a slot and boarded a car just as the train lurched to a halt and opened its doors. As the subway started again, she sat with her knees pressed together, blind to the jumbled grafitti scrawled on the walls and ceilings and across the windows. A man hunched and staring across from her was the only other occupant of the car.

There was no reason for her to go through this every month, she thought miserably. She wasn't planning to have any children, not when she faced her situation realistically. She was an almost thirty-nine-year-old spinster. Her sister-in-law was pregnant. She had a husband. Dorothy had no husband and no prospect of finding one.

That was reality.

Maybe Madelyn's gift could count for something besides new dresses and opera tickets. She smoothed the lustrous folds across her lap and allowed herself to consider having a hysterectomy: Then she'd never have to go through this monthly agony again. What a relief!

But even as she tried to persuade herself that she wanted relief, a terrible grief rose in her. If she were sterilized she'd never be able to give birth. There'd never be anybody to complete her life, no little person to hold, to sing to, no hand reaching trustingly for hers, nobody to play with and read to. There'd be no whispered secrets, no clatter and disorder, no tears, no laughter, no love in her empty house. For the rest of her life. No child.

She ached for that vanished person, and for herself.

She couldn't abandon the fantasy. She knew the idea was foolish. She wasn't going to get married, she wasn't going to have children. Her nice neat life was all she could expect. But—for now, knowing all of that—for now she'd keep herself ready. She sensed something about to happen. She felt again the powerful emotion she'd experienced at the opera, the feeling of doors opening, of a journey beginning.

When she got off the train and climbed the steps to get outside again she tensed her shoulders and walked quickly, intent on getting home and taking care of herself. Her high heels distracted and delayed her, making it difficult to take long strides.

It was after midnight. Nobody was on the street. The silly clatter of her shoes rang in the empty air as she tightened her coat and looked ahead.

She watched anxiously as two dogs moved from a doorway and advanced toward her. They were large, ugly animals, their coats dense and slick in the smoky beam from the streetlight. She wondered where their owner was. They seemed unaccompanied and she moved toward the curb to get out of their way. Another large dog joined them, coming at a trot from around the corner. As Dorothy looked toward them apprehensively she banged her toes against the edge of a pothole. Straightening awkwardly, she tried to quicken her pace despite the sharp pain. The dogs faced her as she approached. Their massive jaws hung open and when she saw their long pink tongues hanging out, she was suddenly frightened.

Just as she turned to escape into the street, the biggest of the dogs broke away from the others and ran toward her. Before she could push him back he jumped on her, circled her shoulders clumsily with his front paws and began dancing and rubbing against her. She felt the creature's rancid breath on her face, felt its claws in her back and the insistent, rhythmic pressure of the swollen red penis. He jumped and writhed on his hind legs, encircling her, pulling himself closer, panting.

"Ugh, no," she said, pushing against the huge animal with all her strength, staggering back, buckling from the weight and crashing onto the pavement. As she thrashed and twisted, trying to sit up, the friction from his body forced

30

open her coat and she felt the moist heat of his pulsating underside.

The other animals stood by silently, watching, their yellow eyes glinting like gold coins.

She squeezed her hands in front of herself and wrenched her head to escape the suffocating stench, tried to pull her knees up to force the animal sideways, but he was too heavy. He easily rolled over on top of her, drooling onto her face, grinning humanly.

As he pressed his haunches against her, rocking and pumping, her skull cracked against the sidewalk. She screamed.

Suddenly the dog's movement stopped and he lifted his head, curling his lip to show many sharp teeth. As he growled she watched him turn his head, listening. Then he laid his ears flat against the sides of his head, like spoons.

The moment he shifted his weight she pulled herself out from under him and clambered to her feet. The other dogs joined in a frightened whining. He took no further notice of her, but instead thrust his tail between his legs, wriggled and minced backwards, then turned and scrambled away, yelping, all three animals vanishing northward.

Dorothy didn't care what had frightened them, she began to run clumsily toward her apartment building, alone on the street except for an old woman making a bed of newspapers in a doorway.

As soon as she reached the entrance Dorothy groped for her keys, found them in the zipper compartment of the beaded bag, opened the heavy glass door and slammed it. Bending to remove her shoes, she turned and raced in her stocking feet up the stairs. She double-locked her own door and frantically pulled the chain across. Safe at last, she stood panting, her cheek pressed against the door's scratchy surface. She clenched her eyes and saw the dog again, his terrible eyes, blank and hard as marbles, felt his throbbing hairy body, her own fear. She covered her mouth with her hands. In the bathroom she fell onto the cold tiles next to the toilet and vomited into it repeatedly, on all fours. Finally she sat back, wiped her mouth with a handful of toilet paper, and examined the scratches on her throat and palms. Her stockings were ripped and shredded. Thick ribbons of warm menstrual blood were smeared over her legs, caked in her crotch and on the insides of her thighs. Her underwear was soiled with it, torn and stained from the dog.

She rose and began undressing slowly, leaving her ruined clothes in a pile on the bathroom floor. She felt dazed.

"I'm all right," she said, calming herself, turning the shower faucets on all the way. She stepped into the stall and stood naked with her face pointed toward the jetting hot water.

"It's the curse," she told herself. "I wasn't hurt." She took a washcloth and began soaping herself carefully. The rushing water washed away her tears.

Chapter Three

When Dorothy arrived at the library Monday morning Henry was already there. He squatted in the corner of their office rooting in a cardboard box filled with grimy papers and notebooks. His hands were covered with strands of cobwebs.

"We really have to get a computer," he said resentfully. "We have to confront Mrs. Blietz and tell her we can't go on this way."

Mrs. Blietz, their boss, worked in the main library at 42nd Street. Her cavernous office was cluttered with sagging leather chairs and glass-topped tables holding her coin collection. Once she'd hired Henry and Dorothy and posted them to the 44th Street branch—Henry in 1967, Dorothy in 1972—she'd had little to do with either of them. They were on their own, with only their required attendance at an annual meeting to remind her they existed.

"There's no reason for us to be treated as second-class citizens simply because nobody cares about this ridiculous archive," he said. "If it exists we should be able to care for it properly." Standing, he brushed off his trousers and went to the sink in the corner to wash his hands.

Dorothy hung up her coat and sat at her desk. "Maybe I'll buy us one," she said mysteriously.

Henry raised his eyebrows. "On our combined salaries we couldn't afford a new filing cabinet," he said. "Much less a computer."

She grinned. Her eyes were dancing.

"What are you smiling at?" he said. "You look demonic."

"You'll never guess what's happened," she said.

"I can't imagine," he said. "You haven't smiled in weeks."

"Henry, my mother left me $183,000," she blurted out.

His mouth dropped comically. "Egad."

"She never told me about it," she said. "It was a complete surprise."

He repeated the figure incredulously, sitting on the edge of her desk. "What are you going to do with it?"

She glanced toward the dirty window. "I don't know yet," she said. "I went to the opera," she added. "The ticket cost $100."

"You probably sat next to Mrs. Rockefeller."

"*She* sat next to me." They laughed and returned to work.

Toward noon Henry glanced up from a pile of newspapers he was clipping. "Here's something," he said. "It's quite a coincidence."

She interrupted her typing on the rickety Smith-Corona. "What's that?" she said.

"According to the *New York Times*," he said, clearing his throat and reading, "a sociologist at Yale University has declared that a child born to a middle-class family today will cost its parents $183,000 to raise."

Very calmly, she took her hands from the typewriter and put them in her lap. "$183,000?"

"Yes," he said, scanning the article. "Isn't that something? The same amount you've inherited!" He smoothed the paper on his desk. "She lists various child-rearing expenses like shelter, clothing and schooling." He quoted several figures, then laughed. "You could have a baby!"

"Let me see."

He leaned across to hand her the paper. "Little Dorothy, Jr.," he said, getting up and standing behind her to read over her shoulder. "Of course there wouldn't be any money left for you. You wouldn't be able to move to Pago Pago."

"It's not so farfetched," she said, sitting back and looking up at him. After a moment she admitted cautiously, "I'd like to have a baby."

He went to the sink. "You can't be serious," he said as he

rinsed out his mug. "It would drive you up the wall. At your age."

But she thought of little else the rest of the afternoon.

It had been realistic to suppose she'd use her money to travel, to see the pyramids, ride a camel, look out over the Great Wall of China. Move into a safer neighborhood. Buy a subscription to the opera. Take a course. Sleep late. Eat out. Plan for her retirement.

But all the pictures of herself she'd conjured were exactly that: pictures of herself. Her and nobody else. Somebody going through life alone, an old maid, somebody's sister, somebody's aunt—sipping coffee alone, taking books out of the library and returning them. A tired woman standing in line at the supermarket with a container of milk, a can of tunafish and a box of lightbulbs in her shopping cart. She'd made herself believe nothing else was possible. This new knowledge—that she had the tools to change her life—astonished her.

She had enough money to raise a child.

When she got home that night she walked through the familiar apartment, inspecting it. There were two bedrooms and a small windowless dining room (once Spark's bedroom) next to the kitchen where the ironing board and a folding table for the laundry had been set up for years. The cluttered living room faced the front of the building, its grimy windows shut to keep out the city grit and noise.

She pulled up the sash impatiently, stood back and watched the curtains flare into the room. She'd have to put a rail across.

She grinned happily.

She'd decided to have a baby.

Now she must figure out how to manage it.

The next afternoon she and Henry strolled together to the coffee shop around the corner from the library for lunch. Marcus, the middle-aged luncheonette owner, handed them menus and smiled as they slid into their usual booth. The smile was a token geniality signifying their status as regular customers. It disappeared as soon as it appeared, like a tic.

After Marcus left them Henry jerked his head to indicate something unpleasant behind Dorothy.

"What is it?" she whispered, turning to look into the room.

"Shhh," he said, leaning forward. "Look at Irene," he whispered. "She has a black eye."

Irene was Marcus's teenaged wife. Since their marriage less than a year before, she'd worked in the coffee shop, sometimes as cashier, sometimes as waitress. Often Marcus, who was at least thirty years older than she, hovered near her smoothing his hand down her rump or squirming and insinuating himself against her backside. Other times he yelled at her from across the room, ridiculed what she was wearing, yanked or pushed her savagely. Often he accused her of flirting with the customers.

This afternoon she was wearing a short black skirt, heels with ankle straps and black mesh stockings, a zebra patterned blouse made from chiffon cut tight and low enough to reveal her rigidly uplifted cleavage. Heavy makeup caked her complexion, several shades darker than her neck and chest. Dorothy saw an unmistakeable purple swelling beneath her right eye. The lid was puffy and nearly closed.

"It's none of our business," Henry hissed as Dorothy beckoned her to join them.

"What happened to your eye?" she asked as Irene neared their table.

Irene shrugged and glanced at Marcus, who was standing at the counter conferring with a man in a dark overcoat so long it brushed the tops of his shoes. "Marcus got mad at me," she said, picking listlessly at a cuticle.

"Jesus," muttered Henry.

"He's not so bad most of the time," Irene said. "But he has a short fuse."

Henry met Dorothy's gaze and raised his eyebrows skeptically.

The sullen girl pulled her order book from her waistband and licked a stumpy pencil as she carefully wrote out their orders. She looked up, sighing hugely to elicit even more sympathy.

"It's just that I'm pregnant," she said. "I said I didn't want a baby and he got a little upset."

"The man's a monster," Henry said.

"It's against his religion for me to have an abortion."

"So he gives you a black eye instead," Henry said. "To demonstrate his Christian sentiments."

She shrugged again. "I told him I'm too young to have a baby but he says it'll keep me in line." She turned and navigated languidly between the crowded tables to a place behind the counter where she pushed their orders through a small opening into the kitchen.

"That's it," Henry told Dorothy. "We can't keep coming here. It's too depressing."

Dorothy watched as Irene bent to straighten one of her stockings. She licked her finger and tugged at a thread dangling from the fabric. Her self-absorption was childlike and pathetic.

Henry observed Dorothy disapprovingly. "Don't start crying," he said. "It's a mess and we can't do a thing about it."

"I wish we could help her."

Dorothy imagined Irene's apartment, filled with cheap ornamented furniture, her husband criticizing and brutalizing her whenever he felt like it. Why was this pathetic girl having a baby when she didn't even want one? It would ruin her already awful life and the child was doomed to a similar fate.

Dorothy sighed, and looked at the clock hanging above the counter. A photograph of the Parthenon was pasted on its face. The numbers were concealed, making it difficult to read. But she could hear the loud ticks above the noise of the restaurant. The second hand jerked up the stately pillars, into the blue sky and down again into greenery.

Glancing back at Henry she swallowed, struck with the simplicity and power of her idea. "I can adopt her baby," she said.

"What?"

"Remember that newspaper article yesterday?" she said. "The sociologist who said it cost a hundred and eighty-three thousand dollars to raise a child?"

37

"What does that have to do with anything?"

She set her glass quietly on the table top. "That's the answer," she said. "I'll buy Irene's baby."

"Slow down," he said.

"I'm serious." She studied her turkey sandwich, thinking quickly. "If I offer enough money, Marcus will make her sell the baby to me, I know it," she said. "He's an awful man. And she doesn't want it."

They both looked across at Marcus. He was slicing a cantaloupe with a long knife, throwing the pieces into a plastic bowl. As they watched he sneezed hugely, filling the air with tiny flakes of phlegm. He wiped his nose with his knuckles and continued cutting.

"Ugh," Henry said, looking unhappily at his dish of fruit, then pushing it away.

"I wonder how much I should offer," Dorothy said. "Do you think eight thousand dollars would be enough?"

Henry rolled his eyes in disbelief. "Any amount is too much," he said. "You don't want a baby from that couple. Look at them, Dorothy. The father ought to be in a zoo, he's a throwback of some kind, half human—half gorilla. And the mother—" He waved his hand. "I'm sure she's on drugs. Or has AIDS."

"Don't be absurd," Dorothy said. "She's perfectly healthy."

"I can't believe what you're saying!" he said. "Think about the gene pool, for god's sake."

Dorothy didn't respond.

"What's the matter with you?" he said. "You're usually so sensible."

"I'm tired of being sensible!" she cried hoarsely.

"All right, all right," he said, patting her hand. "Don't make a scene. I had no idea you were keen about having a child."

"It was a secret," she said. "I thought you'd laugh." She looked away, embarrassed by her confession, and by letting him see her passion, if only for a moment.

"I'd never laugh if something were important to you," he said gently. "You should know me better than that."

"I'm sorry for biting your head off," she said.

He crossed his arms. "And there are other ways to have a baby, Dorothy," he said.

When she didn't answer, he added insistently, "Promise me you won't act impulsively."

"I don't have to promise you anything!" she said, out of control again, angry and helpless, resenting him for having heard her deepest secret. "This is none of your business."

Stung, Henry stood and reached for his coat. He shouldn't have allowed his natural sympathy for her predicament to cloud his usual reserve. He never should have said anything. But she didn't have to attack him. He'd only been trying to be her friend. He felt wronged, misunderstood. "I beg your pardon," he said with dignity. "I certainly didn't mean to interfere."

She stood too, and pulled on her coat. He looked so hurt. She was ashamed of her outburst. She told him so. "Henry, you know you're my best friend. I couldn't have gotten through these last few months without you."

He relaxed, forgiving her. "Well, you're my friend, too, Dorothy," he said. "I hate to see you so troubled."

"Before I make them an offer," she added, placating him, "I'll talk to a lawyer."

"Promise?"

She nodded, moving toward the door, wondering where she'd find one, and what she'd say when she did. She was certain people did this sort of thing all the time. A respectable attorney would help her understand what she was supposed to do, what her rights were. He'd advise her what to say to Marcus and Irene. Perhaps he could handle the whole thing and she wouldn't have to confront them at all. That would be preferable.

Henry followed a few paces behind her, looking disapproving despite himself. She was opening a bucket of worms. He just hoped she knew what she was doing.

Chapter Four

That evening as the bus drew up to her stop, Dorothy began pushing past the other passengers on the way to the exit. Surprisingly, a woman grabbed her arm. "Don't get off," she warned, nodding urgently toward the window.

Dorothy pulled back, startled. "Why not?"

Other passengers crowded in front of the windows trying to glimpse what was outside.

"The dogs," said the old woman, her milky eyes wide with fear.

Dorothy looked outside. Five huge black dogs stood menacingly on the sidewalk at the bus stop, their glittering eyes fastened on the front door of the bus. As it opened the animals edged forward, growling. In front of Dorothy the elderly man with a cane who'd been concentrating on preparing to exit looked up from his careful descent, saw the dogs and gasped. Clumsy and frantic, half falling, he scrabbled backwards, pushing his wife who was following him. "Get back!" he screamed. Several other voices shouted to the driver. "Close the door!"

One of the dogs, a male with bared fangs, leapt against the door just as it folded shut. The passengers heard the sound of claws grating against the metal exterior of the bus. Then the dogs started barking. They threw themselves against the side of the bus. It rocked slightly at the impact. There was a hush inside. People looked at one another, hardly understanding what was happening. The driver stood at his seat, seeking a view of the dogs through the crowd of passengers. "My god," he breathed, looking ahead then and wrenching the large steering wheel. The bus moved rapidly away from the curb and swung into the street.

Dorothy bent toward the window and watched as the dogs, galloping and leaping alongside the speeding vehicle, gradually fell behind and out of sight. Finally only the largest one, the lead male, remained, loping beside the rear wheels. But the bus careened down the avenue and even that strong animal couldn't keep up and it too disappeared. Dorothy recognized it as the same animal which had attacked her Saturday night after the opera. A chill of foreboding radiated from her spine and down her legs.

By the time the bus heaved to a halt it had covered twenty blocks and there was no trace of the dogs. After he pulled up, the driver reached to adjust the large rearview mirror protruding from the outside of the window frame by his seat. He peered cautiously into the glass.

"They're gone," he said finally. "We outran them. It's safe now."

The passengers shifted uneasily.

"They're probably making a movie," a teenager suggested loudly. "I'm getting off."

Faces turned toward her. "It's not safe," somebody said.

The girl set her jaw. "It's one of those dumb TV movies," she said. "I have to meet my boyfriend."

"I'm coming too," Dorothy said, hearing the words and knowing she'd said them without meaning to. She felt compelled to leave the bus. It was as if she had no choice.

Soundlessly the other passengers made a path for them. The old man and his wife stood back as Dorothy and the girl climbed down the steep steps. His chin still trembled with fear. "Good luck," said his wife, a shriveled woman in a stiff woolen coat.

The doors banged shut behind them. Alone together on the quiet street, Dorothy and the teenager watched the bus drive off.

The silence was eerie. There were no cars, no people on the sidewalks. They heard the traffic light click as it turned from green to red. In both directions the stores were deserted, although it wasn't yet six o'clock. A hazy yellow, as if the air

41

were filled with invisible chemicals—sulphur?—gave the setting an unreal, nightmarish color. The streetlights glowed weakly through flickering circles of nimbus and Dorothy held her breath. Something terrible was about to happen. Her heart thumped and skittered. Why had she left the bus?

The girl grabbed her hand. "Let's go over to Amsterdam Avenue," she urged. "The dogs are on Broadway, they won't be on Amsterdam. We can turn south there."

They trotted together for a block, then turned right.

"See?" the teenager said triumphantly. "They're gone. I knew it was a movie."

But there was no traffic on Amsterdam Avenue either. No pedestrians, nothing. They walked faster, their quick breathing and thudding shoes the only sounds on the usually bustling avenue.

"Seems like somebody should be around," the girl—whose name was Marge—said nervously. "It's weird."

Dorothy was too frightened to talk. They crossed another empty intersection, looking up and down apprehensively.

"This is my street," Marge said. "I'm turning here." She shook Dorothy's hand energetically. "Thanks for coming with me," she said. "I was really scared at first."

Feeling abandoned, Dorothy watched the brave girl hitch her backpack and hurry off. At the far corner she turned and waved. Dorothy lifted her hand in a weak salute, then watched her disappear around the corner.

I have to get home before they catch me.

She hugged her purse against her chest, like a fullback, and starting running. Covering two blocks, then three and four, she took heel-pounding strides, the wind whistling past her ears. She didn't look back. She willed herself to get to the corner, across the empty street, past the shuttered grocery store and to the street light and beyond it, further, further, faster, faster. Suddenly she heard a bark behind her, half a block away, then another, then a wild chorus of them, close.

Here they come!

Next she was running in the middle of the pack. They loped along, surrounding her, as tall as her chest. She breathed a musty, rancid odor. Dead things. They smelled like dead things.

She tried to run faster but couldn't. Her breath came in painful gasps and she was afraid of losing her footing, of falling and being trampled. The dogs slowed beside her as she slowed, surrounding her, carrying her along, easily pacing themselves to her. But while they pushed her from behind and jostled against her, they didn't attack her. They were accompanying her.

Unable to keep up her pace, she slowed to a jog, then stopped running altogether. She walked as fast as she could, hopping, scurrying forward, gulping, trying to control her terror, to breathe, all the while remaining at the center of the pack. The largest male positioned himself at her side. An escort. She turned the corner. The dogs turned with her. As she neared her apartment house, she sensed their mounting excitement. They began to yelp and then to howl, sounds unlike any she'd ever heard. Their pace quickened and they pushed her along. It was as if they knew her destination and were taking her there. At the base of the steps leading to her building's entrance, they stopped—as if commanded—and moved apart, permitting her a path between them. Incredulous, she understood they weren't going to harm her. She fumbled with the top buttons of her coat and managed to pull off the chain of keys from around her neck. As she went up the steps to the front door, staring ahead and hardly daring to exhale, the dogs remained on the sidewalk behind her, snuffling and prancing, nipping savagely at each other. She unlocked the heavy door, pulled it open and slammed it behind her.

When she was finally safe in her apartment, she clasped the keys in her fist and made her way rapidly down the hall, through the dark living room to the double windows. In her haste she knocked over a small table, cracked her shin against it as it fell. But she paid no attention. When she reached the window, she grabbed the curtains and ripped them back. She looked past the fire escape and down into the street.

People walked by, hurrying home to dinner. A boy in a windbreaker threw a tennis ball against the wall of the building across the way. He threw the ball, it bounced back, he caught it, he threw it again. He played at a relaxed, measured pace, as if he'd been standing there for hours.

There was no sign of the dogs.

Had it been some kind of hallucination?

Had the dog Saturday night been a nightmare too?

Both times had seemed real. Terrifying.

But had they happened?

Willing herself calm, she switched on the light, picked up the telephone book, looked up the number for the A.S.P.C.A. Of course what had happened was real. She'd stuffed her ruined silk dress into a paper bag which lay—right now—on a shelf in her closet. That dress had cost a lot of money. She wasn't crazy. She'd call and report this latest incident. Wild animals roaming the streets of New York, something should be done. They could have killed her. They must be caught, rounded up, impounded. Injected with lethal serum. She dialed the number, got a busy signal. Replacing the receiver, she moved again to the window. Probably somebody else was already calling in a complaint. There'd been many people on the bus. They'd seen the dogs. So had Marge. And there must have been a witness to what had happened to her. Perhaps somebody had been looking out the window as the pack of animals had brought her home. That's why the line was busy, somebody was reporting the incident at this very moment.

Suddenly hungry, she closed the drapes, turned and went into the kitchen to find something to eat.

The dogs had made her forget her plan, but now it came flooding back to her. As she started thinking about it again she began to whistle softly.

She was going to have a baby.

And nobody was going to stop her, not even the hounds of hell.

44

Chapter Five

That night she dreamed of a scary man in a cape who emerged from swirling fog and pursued her past many closed doors down an alley. As she fled around a corner she found her way blocked by a marble wall rising skyward as smooth and cold as a tower of ice. She turned back desperately but her pursuer lunged closer, his face hidden in the shadows. He loomed huge in the alley and there was no room to push past him, no way to escape. She froze as he leaned over her, his hand materializing to scrape her cheek with fingerlike claws. His scarlet hood fell aside and as she shrank from him she saw the wide head of a dog protrude from its folds. His great jaws opened so close to her that she could see past the quivering uvula deep into his moist red throat and the blackness beyond.

She exploded awake, sat up and looked into the corners of the dark room. She lay back, shivering, uncomforted by the familiar surroundings. Cold sweat glistened on her chest and shoulders. She couldn't stop her chattering teeth. It was as if the nightmare awaited her, watching, breathing softly, hidden among the shadows—as real as the chair in the corner—ready to grab her as soon as she relaxed.

When she fell asleep again she saw herself standing among endless rows of iron cribs stretching away from her—like spokes in a wheel. Dust hung in the air like smoke. A little girl sat primly in a wooden chair facing away from her. A feeling of doom and hopelessness knotted Dorothy's stomach as she watched the child open a cardboard box and take from it a large paper doll, which she carefully examined, then placed in her lap. She selected another doll from the box and scrutinized it. There was something peculiar— unchildlike—in the child's measured manner, but Dorothy was mesmerized, and she felt herself moving closer, unwillingly, until she stood in front of the child. As Dorothy stood looking down at her, the little girl, whose plump hands were as smooth and colorless as porcelain, looked up. Dorothy recoiled. She wasn't a child at all. Her eye sockets were empty. The lashless wooden lids blinked and clacked. Her painted doll's eyebrows raised and lowered with mechanical jerks. The brightly painted cupid's mouth, hinged at the corners, opened, revealing tiny bright squares of teeth, and she seemed ready to speak. Dorothy looked around frantically. All the babies were dolls. They lay silently in their cribs on starched sheets, motionless, their dimpled wooden hands reaching like pincers toward her. Their blind eyes spun like prisms, reflecting hundreds of terrified Dorothys.

She fled, stumbling and frantic, across another great space toward a three-story building in the distance, one vaguely familiar but unrecognizable in this setting. As she neared, huge scarlet and orange flames burst silently from the windows, licked up the brick facade toward the roof. A plate glass window shattered—without a sound, in slow motion— blasting shards of glass and smoke into the sky. She heard faint shouts coming from inside the building, unearthly cries for help.

She wanted to reach toward the structure but her arms hung limp. There was nothing she could do.

With a desperate lunge that felt like a scream, she tore herself from sleep. Awake in her bedroom the fear continued pressing against her. There was no safety. She feared closing her eyes again, feared looking into the shadowy corners of her room or even toward the windows. She felt herself a child, alone and unprotected.

She still smelled smoke.

Turning on the light by her bed she sat up tensely holding the blankets against her chest.

Her teeth ached from grinding. She brushed her hair back

and inhaled.

Was she losing her mind?

The dogs . . . the nightmares. The smell of smoke, even now. She squeezed her palms against her temples and clenched her eyes. There was a dark world inside her having nothing to do with what went on around her. A kind of private, terrifying vision shared by nobody. She was afraid to go back to sleep.

She cleared her throat gruffly, threw her legs over the edge of the bed and stood.

"This is crazy," she said, reassuring herself. "It's only a dream."

She went to the window and, hands on hips, looked up and down the street. All was silence. It was the middle of the night and all over the city everyone else was asleep.

Moving quickly into the living room, she turned on every light, even the one in the hall by the front door, which she relocked. The carpet felt gritty under her feet. She turned on the television, went to the linen closet and with a great clatter took out the vacuum cleaner and all its attachments.

Mary Tyler Moore laughed with Ed Asner on the television, but Dorothy paid no attention. Instead she screwed one snakelike tube energetically into another and kicked on the machine.

She vacuumed the rug and each of the chairs, between and under the cushions, the grimy place where the overstuffed arms attached to the back of the couch. She scrubbed the woodwork and dusted the bookshelves, removed a dozen books, wiped each of them with a damp cloth. At dawn she fell across her bed and slept, exhausted and dreamless, until the jangling alarm clock awoke her.

Chapter Six

Fire had destroyed Marcus's luncheonette and gutted the three-story brick structure housing it. Just as Dorothy had seen it in her dream, it had happened. Early the next morning she and Henry stood in the street with a crowd of onlookers watching as firefighters entered and exited the smoldering building. Three red engines with blinking lights blocked the avenue, their huge hoses uncoiling from the hydrants and crisscrossing the pavement, curving into the charred doorways and windows like giant tubes in a failed life-support system. The firefighters stepped busily across the debris carrying smoking fragments of furniture, water-soaked paraphernalia, pieces of doors and windows, table tops and seat cushions, throwing it all into a steaming pile on the sidewalk.

Dorothy and Henry edged through the crowd to a uniformed man who stood assessing the scene and writing with a tooth-marked pencil in a notebook. When Henry identified himself and Dorothy as workers in the library around the corner, the burly man asked if they knew anyone who'd lived in the building.

Henry told him about Marcus and Irene. "It was his coffee shop," he said. "But I don't think they live here. They always drive up in the morning." He pointed to a vacant place at the curb. "That's where they park their car. A big black Cadillac." He asked what had caused the fire.

The tired man shrugged and pushed back his cap. "It's hard to tell," he said. "Nothing's nailed down yet. It started in the kitchen—of course it might have been accidental, the wiring's way substandard." He shook his head. "But we found a trail of gasoline and greasy rags. Typical of arson. And then the bodies—"

"What bodies?" Dorothy asked sharply.

The man squinted up at the building. "Around 4:00 A.M. we found the remains of a man and a woman on the second floor," he said.

Henry put his hand on Dorothy's back to steady her. "They must have been a pair of vagrants," he said. "Drug addicts who sneaked in to get out of the cold."

"Yeah," the man said. "That's what we think." He shrugged. "Funny thing, there were reports of dogs barking—a hell of a racket—for an hour or so before the fire was discovered. But there aren't any guard dogs registered in the area. Nobody knows what happened to the dogs after they made all the noise. No trace of them." He tucked his notebook under his arm, removed his sooty spectacles and wiped them with his thumb. Then he moved off, answering the order of a woman in uniform who'd just arrived in an official car, its lights flashing.

Dorothy stood tensely, clenching and unclenching her fists. The dogs again. Where did they come from? They had something to do with the fire. "Irene and Marcus should be here by now," she said.

Henry didn't think they were coming. "Maybe he set the fire himself," he said, pulling at his eyelid cautiously and removing a cinder with his forefinger. "I wouldn't put it past him. Probably went to the bank yesterday and took out all his money in preparation for the flight to South America." He blinked rapidly, then frowned. "Probably robbed his partner, too. He and Irene could be in Brazil by now, celebrating the bonanza of their ill-gotten gains. Let's go back to the library. You look like you could use a hot cup of coffee."

"Henry," said Dorothy quietly, "I dreamed this."

He took her hand and pulled her away. "It's familiar because you've seen the same scene on TV a thousand times," he said.

"I dreamed it," she insisted as they hurried up the street.

49

Then she added: "They're dead."

They climbed the library steps and Henry unlocked the door. He suggested they look up Marcus's address in the phonebook. "They probably live someplace in Queens," he said. "Next door to Archie Bunker."

But Dorothy didn't laugh. Instead she slumped at her desk, her coat collar sliding up around her chin. "They're dead," she repeated.

Henry bent over the sink while he filled the coffee pot. Setting the pot on the hotplate, he measured several spoons of Sanka into the coffee filter.

"It's my fault," she said. "I wasn't suppose to get her baby."

"What are you talking about?" he said, exasperated, turning toward her.

She gazed toward the window as he pulled his chair from behind his desk and set it emphatically in front of hers. He put his arms across its back and straddled it, facing her. "That's crazy," he said.

She looked at him. "I'm not supposed to have her baby," she said. "That's why it happened. I killed her."

"Look," he said earnestly, tipping his chair forward, "this isn't about you. A couple of homeless characters got careless and died in a fire they set themselves. It's an indictment of the times, and it's tragic—but not because of some dream you had. Try to look at it that way. It has nothing to do with you."

She sighed, not listening. "She died because I was going to buy her baby."

He glared at her. "I'm calling the fire department to find out whose bodies they found," he said, getting up, swinging his long leg over the chair. "It couldn't have been Marcus and Irene. They never stay there all night, that's totally uncharacteristic. People you *know* don't get burned to death anyway, not even in New York." He paused, reflecting. "I think this baby thing has temporarily unbalanced you," he said, picking up the phonebook and leafing through it.

After many calls and referrals to several different city departments, early in the afternoon he was finally connected to someone who gave him the names of the persons burned to death in the fire at the building on the corner of Eleventh Avenue and 44th Street. They were Irene and Marcus Kansakos. The blaze had swept the room above the luncheonette where paper supplies had been stored. The windows were padlocked—against fire department regulations—as was the steel door leading to the fire escape. Marcus's next of kin in Athens was being notified. Apparently Irene had no relatives.

Henry replaced the receiver in its cradle, his eyes wide with surprise as he repeated what he'd learned.

Dorothy lowered her eyes. She was not surprised.

After a minute Henry said, "He must have killed her to get the insurance. He was tired of her, maybe there was another woman in the picture. We knew he was disgusted that she was pregnant. Men like that don't have any tender paternal feelings. My god, he gave her a black eye when he found out she was pregnant! After hours he got her upstairs somehow, knocked her unconscious and lit the fire. But it got out of control. He couldn't get out fast enough." He swallowed, picturing the scene. "A flash fire. With him clawing at the padlock." He looked across at Dorothy. "I'll bet that's how it happened. It was probably double indemnity if his wife *and* his restaurant were destroyed."

Dorothy rubbed her fingers across her desk blotter, back and forth, saying nothing.

Henry returned to his desk, clicking his tongue. "Poor Irene," he said. "What a wasted life."

He fell silent, and began looking through the papers.

But Dorothy couldn't stop thinking about Irene. Her pathetic attempts at being sexy. Marriage to an evil man, old enough to be her father. Her pregnancy. Dorothy couldn't shake the ominous feeling that she was responsible somehow for the girl's death. She didn't know what she'd done, only that the grisly death was her fault.

After a few minutes she stood nervously and began stacking papers. "I'm going home," she said.

"Are you all right?" Henry said. "You look terrible," he added, then paused. "Do you want me to come with you, see that you get home okay?"

51

It was a generous suggestion. Except for attending Madelyn's funeral, he'd never volunteered anything so intimately tied to their friendship. "I'm all right," she said, impulsively putting her hand on his arm. "Thank you."

"Get some sleep," he said, shyly squeezing her hand. "Go to the movies. Forget about it. You're not responsible for what happened."

Dorothy nodded. "I know," she said, not believing it.

After she left the library, she walked carefully up the street, her eyes fixed ahead. She could see Irene's pretty face, her straight eyebrows and large dark eyes, the lavishly applied lipstick on her wide mouth. Her plump arms, dimpled at the elbows. Dorothy thought of the day before, when Irene had chewed absent-mindedly on the end of her pencil as she stood talking, and later, when she twisted to straighten her stocking and pull the dangling thread. Dorothy could imagine the girl looking at herself in the ladies' room mirror yesterday morning, pleased with her reflection and thinking about how sexy she looked. Unaware she would be dead within twenty-four hours.

She pulled open the large wooden door of a church and went inside. Nobody was sitting in the several rows of wooden pews. A ray of sunshine pierced a stained glass window high in the center of the rear wall and cast its yellow beam on the altar and the first several pews. The wood glistened in the light as if rubbed by invisible hands. Dorothy sat quietly at the back of the church. She wanted to hide here, never to go out again into daylight. Thinking about Irene and her horrible death left her numb and empty.

Her own greedy need for a baby had caused Irene's death. Dorothy was certain of this, and the knowledge confused and frightened her.

As she sat in the quiet church she tried to push away her overwhelming feelings of culpability. She wanted to remember Irene, to feel sorry for what had happened to her without grappling simultaneously with this deep and inexplicable sense of having caused it. She wanted to ignore the ugly voice that kept telling her what had happened was all her fault. She wanted to pull back from the tragedy to regain her sense of reality and perspective. She wanted comfort.

Finally she stood up and went to the side of a church where a large aluminum stand held many rows of white candles. She took a long match and lit one of them, placing it carefully in one of several holders jutting from the stone wall. The small flame flickered cheerfully. Dorothy looked at it for a long time. Then she closed her eyes. "Please let her find peace," she whispered, bowing her head, picturing Irene walking along a road somewhere, laughing, and free at last.

Later, during the ride home on the bus she pressed her face against the window, searching for the dogs. But there was no sign of them. The streets were full of people hurrying this way and that. The only dogs she saw were small, and on leashes.

At home a letter from Spark awaited her. She turned the envelope, studying the unfamiliar handwriting. He'd never written her, in all the years he'd been away. Usually it was Jeannie who wrote.

Her stomach sank. The letter must be about her inheritance. She'd written Spark and Jeannie with the news, not wanting to talk about it on the telephone, afraid he'd disapprove, that his feelings would be hurt when he learned he'd been left out. But she couldn't put off learning his reaction, even if it were, as she feared, disapproving and a little jealous. She had to face it sometime. She slumped on the couch and opened the letter. "Dear Sis," she read. "I've been thinking about your inheritance." She sighed—how well she knew him—and went on. "I must admit I was surprised. I never guessed Mother would take care of you in that way. You were probably as astonished as I was."

Dorothy pictured him sitting at his desk, adjusting his glasses, composing the letter with care, crossing out sentences and starting over. Probably he'd written several drafts before he'd settled on this one.

She continued reading: "I admit I was disappointed to learn she hadn't included me as beneficiary along with you. We could certainly use the money, especially now with the baby coming.

"But since she didn't, I have to assume she was thinking of you and not me. I've thought about it and I'm not bitter. Or—to be truthful—not *very* bitter. When I left home,

53

everything got dumped on you. You were a good soldier, you never complained, you didn't blame anybody, and I want to tell you I noticed.

"I guess Mom did too."

Dorothy stood and took the letter to the window, where, slanting the page toward the afternoon light, she finished reading. "Mostly I want to say I hope you use the money in some way that will make you happy. If you want to blow it all on a trip around the world (some trip for $183,000, less taxes!)"—Dorothy smiled at the accountant's interjection—"then do it. Listen to your heart, Sis, that's what I'm saying. For once put yourself first. If you spend it all on something foolish, remember that you'll always have a home with us, wherever we are.

"Jeannie sends her love too."

His name was written neatly at the bottom of the page, with a period after the *k*.

She replaced the letter in its envelope and held it tightly as she laid her cheek against the glass. Her quiet breath fogged the pane. She stood back and wrote his name in the condensation: "Sparkie."

She hadn't thought about the nickname for a long time. It came from a book Madelyn had read to them before either of them could read, *Sparkie and the Talking Train*. Spark had loved the story so much Madelyn borrowed it from the library again and again, and she'd teased him, calling him "Sparkie" until it became his name. Finally, one Christmas— was he six?—Madelyn gave him his own copy. Dorothy remembered lying with him on the living room rug, studying the pictures in the large book as he read to her the paragraphs he'd painstakingly memorized. She could see again the drawings of the redheaded boy in striped jersey and short pants, the illustrations of his perfect parents, the father smoking a pipe in his green easy chair. "I'm worried about Sparkie," Spark had said, his voice pitched deep, like a father's—Dorothy could hear it now. Then, imitating the mother, lighter, higher: "I'm worried about Sparkie too." Turning the page, a drawing showed the little boy silhouetted against a hillside someplace incomprehensibly pastoral—Ohio? Montana?—watching as an engine chugged

54

into the distant hills, sending up cheerful clouds of smoke. "G-o-o-d-b-y-e, S-p-a-r-k-i-e," Sparkie had read gruffly, sounding the way a train would sound if it could talk. The back of Dorothy's neck prickled at the memory, the way it had then.

Sparkie and the Talking Train. Her brother. Spark.

He'd given her permission to do anything she wanted with her money. Solemnly, she drew a heart around the name on the glass. She told herself she was a grown woman who didn't need his permission, but now that she had it she found her determination strengthened. A baby of her own was what she wanted. Nothing was changed. If she couldn't have Irene's baby . . . Her stomach tightened at the memory of the smoldering building, the blackened windows, the broken glass.

The bodies.

She turned from the window, pushing back the image.

She'd find another baby. She had the money from her mother. Now Spark had given his okay. A baby was what she wanted most.

Perhaps Henry could help.

Chapter Seven

The next morning, her head bent against the unseasonable wind, Dorothy hurried to the library and arrived several minutes before Henry. She hung her things neatly in the closet by the front entrance, went into the office and brewed a pot of coffee. Then she fidgeted, waiting for him, planning what to say. When he finally appeared, he slammed the front door jarringly and stamped on the mat while complaining about the weather. She interrupted impatiently. "You said there were other ways I could get a baby," she blurted out, forgetting her careful preparation. "I was too much of a smart aleck to listen but now I want to know what you were talking about. What other possibilities did you mean?"

"My god, Dorothy," he said, unwrapping his scarf, "don't you even say good morning?"

"Good morning," she said.

He nodded, pulling his gloves off and stuffing them in his pockets. "That's better," he said. "Irene's body is hardly cold, if you'll pardon the expression."

"I made some coffee," she said, changing the subject hurriedly. She went to the counter and poured some into his mug. "And I bought some coffee cake. Your favorite kind."

He looked at her suspiciously.

"It's a cold morning," she explained lamely.

After he hung up his coat he took the mug and stirred milk and sugar into it, returned the milk carton to the small refrigerator on the table against the wall, cut himself a large piece from the pecan roll and placed it on a square of paper

56

towel. She watched as he finally pulled out his chair and sat.

"Now can we talk?" she said.

"Go ahead," he said ungraciously. "I can't stop you."

She wished she hadn't brought the matter up so soon. She'd forgotten to consider his usual morning grumpiness. It was a tactical mistake. But she couldn't backtrack now, so she smiled warmly to encourage his good nature. "It's just that I remembered you mentioned something about knowing another way I could get a baby," she said. "Were you talking about an adoption agency?"

He glanced at her uneasily. "You certainly have a steel trap memory," he said.

"I want a baby, Henry."

"Yes," he said. "I've noticed." He frowned. "I thought you were ranting about something—or someone, I'm not clear which—being against your having one," he said.

"I was mistaken," she said firmly. "What happened to Irene was awful. But you were right. Marcus probably killed her for the insurance, just as you said—and then got caught by his own carelessness. Her death had nothing to do with me." She'd permitted herself to get spooked, she thought. The nightmares and the dogs. But nightmares weren't reality and the dogs were a grisly coincidence. Nothing more.

He took a big bite of sweet roll and chewed it thoughtfully. "I'm glad to hear you say that," he admitted, wiping his mouth with a paper napkin. "You were behaving very oddly."

"I'm over it now," she said.

He glanced nervously toward the doorway. "Look," he said finally, turning back to her. "Are you sure you still want a baby?"

"Yes," she said.

"It's crazy, you know," he said. "You could do something much more sensible with your inheritance."

"I don't care."

His voice lowered. "I wasn't talking about adoption," he said. "If you're so set on it, I think it's better if you know who the parents are."

She watched him silently.

"And if you're certain it's what you want, there's a way I

can help you. I've thought about it and it would be okay. Unorthodox but okay."

She wanted to scream with impatience. Why was he being so slow and deliberate? "What are you talking about?" she said. "I can't read your mind."

He crossed his arms and tipped back in his chair. "You could have a baby yourself," he said.

She'd thought of that, of course. Nothing could be more obvious. But if she were going to have a baby in the usual way, she couldn't do it by herself. She needed a father.

She looked at him suddenly, widening her eyes.

"No, no, not that, not what you're thinking of," he said hastily, flushing to his ears and holding up his hands. "I'm talking about artificial insemination. With me as the *donor.* I'd be willing to do that."

She stared at him uncomprehendingly. "Artificial insemination," she repeated stupidly. Then, considering, letting the notion settle in, "I never thought of that."

"It's almost the twenty-first century, Dorothy," he said. "People do it all the time."

She laughed, clapped her hands. "That's a wonderful idea," she said. "It never occurred to me."

"But I wouldn't want to have anything to do with the baby afterward," he added. "I hate babies. Once you were pregnant, and then, when you'd given birth—all of it would be entirely your responsibility, nobody would ever know I had anything to do with it. You'd be on your own, you'd have to agree to that." He cleared his throat. "The child would never know."

"Of course," she said. That was precisely what she wanted, single parenthood in every sense.

"We could go to one of those sperm bank places," he said. "Everything on the up and up. Nothing sordid or dangerous."

"That would be wonderful of you, Henry."

"You sacrificed a lot so your mother could end her days in contentment," he said. "It's about time you got what you wanted. I'd like to help you get it." He paused, swallowed, then admitted quietly, "I care about you, Dorothy."

She looked with confusion into her lap, unable to find words for her gratitude.

58

After a moment he stood, came over to her and patted her shoulder with embarrassed little taps. "There now," he said. "Don't cry. It's only fair."

That evening Dorothy looked up names and addresses of family planning clinics and sperm banks in the phone book. Finally she located a facility on the Upper West Side not far from her apartment. It catered to "private clients" and promised anonymity. She phoned and made an appointment for them to come in together on a Thursday night two weeks away. She didn't know how many interviews or applications the process would take, but she did know that in two weeks she'd be ovulating.

Chapter Eight

On a Thursday evening two weeks later, Dorothy met Henry in front of the clinic at 7:30. The offices were located at the head of a flight of stairs, on the second floor of a small stone building. Except for "O'Hara Clinic," typed discreetly on a card slipped into a slot next to the bell, there was nothing to indicate to passersby what went on inside. Dorothy and Henry entered hesitantly by way of a solid mahogany door and found a large waiting room furnished with chairs and sofas upholstered in tangerine Naugahyde. Copies of *National Geographic* and *Money* magazine were scattered on the tables.

Henry had gone home after work and changed into a festive striped tie and a shiny blue suit with unfashionably wide lapels. Dorothy was touched.

They sat together, each pretending to read a magazine. Dorothy glanced surreptitiously at the other people waiting. A young couple sat talking gloomily in the corner, the woman, all in black as if in mourning, twisting her hands. Stiff in a straight chair a lone woman stared stonily into space. Two teenage boys lounged by the window playing with the venetian blinds.

When Dorothy's name was called, she and Henry jumped up, collided, and laughed nervously, feigning nonchalance.

The nurse led them into a small room with doctors' diplomas and certificates in narrow black frames on the walls. They sat facing a desk covered in walnut veneer.

"The doctor will be with you in a moment," the nurse said,

then bustled through another door. Dorothy looked up and saw an old man in a white jacket with a stethoscope around his neck watching her through the window in the door. His eyes glistened, bright as glass. A string of hair was brushed across his yellow forehead and other fine strands fell behind his ears and along his collar like oily threads.

"Who's that man?" Dorothy whispered, but in the moment it took Henry to look up, he'd vanished.

She felt the skin on the back of her arms stiffen as if something unpleasant were standing behind her. She turned uneasily but nobody else was in the room.

"What man?"

"He's gone now," she said, turning back.

"Are you losing your nerve?" he said.

She frowned impatiently. "I saw a man in the next room. I wasn't expecting to see anyone, that's all."

The door behind them opened, finally, and another man hurried in and sat at the desk. He was young, looking scrubbed and benign, like a proper doctor, and Dorothy exhaled with relief.

He said his name was Dr. Thomas and asked their names and addresses, writing in a folder he'd brought with him. Then he asked, "What can we do for you, Ms. Kite? Mr. Small?"

Dorothy replied in a low, uncertain tone. Dr. Thomas cupped his hand to his ear and asked her to speak up.

"I want to have a baby," she repeated, hearing her own quaking voice but unable to do anything about it. "I'm thirty-eight years old, but I'm quite healthy. My menstrual periods are strong and regular." She glanced at Henry, whose arms were crossed across his chest as he stared intently at the floor, his face a flaming red. "I'm not married," she continued. "I don't plan to marry."

"You want to bring up a child as its only parent?" Dr. Thomas asked.

Dorothy nodded. "I know it's unusual," she said. "That's why I came here." She explained haltingly about the inheritance making it possible for her to raise a child.

"And what about Mr. Small?" Dr. Thomas said, indicating Henry with his pencil.

61

"He's agreed to be the father," Dorothy said.

Dr. Thomas glanced expectantly at Henry, who said nothing. "Mr. Small?"

Henry looked up defensively. "Yes?"

"You intend to father Miss Kite's child?" Dr. Thomas asked.

"That's what she said, wasn't it?"

Dorothy smiled at him nervously. "Don't lose your temper," she said. "He has to ask these questions, it's part of the procedure."

"Well, then let's get on with it," Henry said.

"How old are you, Mr. Small?" Dr. Thomas asked, looking at the form.

"I'm forty-eight," Henry said.

"Have you ever donated sperm?" Dr. Thomas said.

"I most certainly have *not*," Henry said.

"It's a perfectly respectable thing to do," Dr. Thomas said. "Many men do it without ever knowing the recipient or their issue."

Henry refolded his arms. "That seems tawdry," he said. "And irresponsible."

"My impression was that Miss Kite planned to raise a baby by herself without further assistance from you." He turned to Dorothy. "Isn't that correct?"

"Oh, yes," she said quickly. "Henry's just doing me this favor now, in the beginning. Then he's going to withdraw from the—er—project. I'm entirely responsible for what happens in the years afterward."

As Dr. Thomas wrote in the folder Henry tapped his foot against the desk. "This is taking longer than I thought," he said.

"These are important questions," the doctor replied. He probed his ear, scrutinized the tip of his little finger, smelled it, then wiped it carefully on the handkerchief he removed from his jacket pocket. "May I ask you why you decided to conceive a child in this manner, instead of in the usual way?"

Henry glanced impatiently at Dorothy, widening his eyes sarcastically.

"It seemed best, under the circumstances," Dorothy murmured.

"I beg your pardon?"

"Best. It seemed best," Dorothy said, louder.

"Umm." The doctor looked at the application. "The request is unusual," he said. "You must know that. Miss Kite, you're at leat seven years over age. We don't ordinarily consider a woman after thirty-one, you know. Statistics work against an older woman bringing a healthy baby to term."

She shifted and cleared her throat. "I'm willing to take all the necessary precautions and tests," she said. "And—and if the fetus is found to be defective, why, I'd—" she paused, placed her hands firmly on her knees. "I'd agree to an abortion."

"That's very modern of you," Dr. Thomas said. "But I'm afraid that's not the point. Many women, much more appropriate candidates than you, want to conceive and bear children. They're the ones who benefit from our programs here." He cleared his throat. "You've let time slip through your fingers, my dear, and now it's too late." He leaned back in the chair, his palms flat on the desk. "I'm afraid I'll have to turn down your application," he said.

"Oh, Doctor," she pleaded, "don't refuse me just because of a technicality."

"My dear girl," he said, "it's hardly a technicality. If you were to bring a healthy baby to term, you'd still be too old. And without the blessings of matrimony—a man to help you in rearing the child," he added, "financially and physically—well, I think it's an impossible task for a single woman." He brushed back a lock of hair, ran his fingers through his bright head of curls.

"Dr. Thomas, I just lost my mother and this may be my only chance for happiness," Dorothy said. "Please don't turn me down, you can't know what this means to me."

He shrugged and held up his hand helplessly. "Please. I know this is difficult for you," he said. "But we can't have whatever we want in this life, you know. I'm sure you can find other more appropriate arenas in which to use your inheritance. Perhaps you can perform volunteer work at an orphanage or charitable institution. You mustn't be selfish." He closed the buff folder and turned to Henry. "As for you,

Mr. Small," he said, "we're always in need of healthy sperm. And we're willing to pay for semen. If you'd allow us to perform some not very complicated tests—"

Henry stood quickly, knocking back his chair. "I wouldn't consider anything of the kind," he said indignantly. "I think the way you're treating Ms. Kite is reprehensible." He pronounced each syllable precisely, to give emphasis. "You asked her all those embarrassing questions without having the slightest intention of granting her request."

"Oh, come now," Dr. Thomas said. "That's hardly fair."

"It's the truth," Henry said. "And then—if that weren't bad enough—you end up patronizing her with sexist attitudes— telling her she's too helpless and dependent to manage it." He turned to Dorothy. "Let's get out of here," he said.

She looked pleadingly at Dr. Thomas. "Can't you reconsider?" she said.

He shook his head. "Those are the rules," he said, glancing irritably at Henry. "Despite what Mr. Small may think."

"I'd like to know why you bothered talking to us once you found out how old Ms. Kite is," Henry insisted. "I think you just wanted me to donate sperm, you only pretended to be interested in her situation." He pulled her sleeve. "Come on, Dorothy, this is a waste of time."

They passed through the empty waiting room, yanked their coats from the hangers in the closet, hurried down the stairs and outside where Henry finally let go of her arm.

"It's all for the best," he told her vaguely.

"But it isn't!" she cried. "How can you say that?"

He edged closer to her, straightening the lapels of her coat and brushing away a thread.

"I wanted a baby so much," she said. "I can't believe it's not going to happen."

"Perhaps there are other places."

"They'll all say the same thing," she said. "I'm too old."

"Would you like a cup of coffee?" he asked gently. "There's a restaurant just up the block. We can decide what to do next."

He guided her into the brightly lit luncheonette. A counter ran along one wall. The rest of the room was large enough for a dozen red vinyl booths. They sat facing each other in

64

the rear and Henry ordered two cups of coffee and a sandwich for himself. "Would you like something to eat? I'm famished."

She shook her head, no, and stared at the heavy ashtray, turning it in her hands.

"Try not to feel sorry for yourself," he said. "It won't do any good."

"Why not?" she flashed. "My life is a wasteland. Irene's life was a mess but at least she was going to have a baby. I can't even do that."

Henry frowned. "Well, *I'm* not going to feel sorry for you," he said firmly. "You're healthy, you're intelligent, you have a steady job, and now you have some extra money. You'll never end up with a husband who beats and murders you." He cleared his throat. "You're a very attractive woman, Dorothy. And you're young enough so that most of your life is still ahead of you. I don't blame you for being depressed after your mother died. You were wonderful to her, and you sacrificed a lot for her. But—my gosh—you have a lot of choices! You have plenty of time to change your life into something you want." He wiped his mouth carefully with his napkin. "And you've got me," he said. "I'll help you. We'll figure something out."

But she hardly heard him. *I don't need his sermon,* she was thinking. *What does he know about my pain?* She was gripped by it, unable to hear the sense of what he was saying or even to respond to his warmth.

"If only I had a baby," she moaned, looking past him. "I'd do anything to have a baby. *Anything.* Oh, god, it isn't fair."

A heavy odor of decay was suddenly so strong that Henry covered his mouth and nose with his napkin, fighting an impulse to gag. He looked up as an old man slid swiftly into the seat next to him.

"Forgive me for intruding," he said to Dorothy. "You're Miss Kite, aren't you?"

It was the old man she'd seen in the clinic. He'd changed from the white jacket into an expensively tailored Italian suit and burgundy silk tie.

"Who are you?" Henry said through his napkin.

At close range Dorothy could see the wisps of white

eyebrow hairs that bent like whiskers above his drooping eyelids. The skin under his eyes sagged in discolored creases and circles, dangled from his jaw in hundreds of tiny wobbling pleats. But despite his obvious age, the old man's voice was strong and deep, his movements vigorous. He was old but he carried himself with the confidence of success.

"I apologize for my rudeness in joining you without warning," he said, smiling easily. "But I had to act quickly. I followed you here from the clinic."

Henry pursed his mouth with distaste and moved into the corner of the booth, as far away from the old man as he could get. "What do you want?" he demanded. Surely the smell meant there was something dreadfully the matter with him, some disease or debilitating condition. Henry shifted his glance uneasily to Dorothy. But she seemed unaware of the smell. She was asking the stranger how he knew her name.

"I'm with the O'Hara Clinic," he said. "I was witness to what happened to you there tonight."

As the waiter brought Henry's sandwich Dorothy admitted she'd seen him there.

He introduced himself. "My name is Shaw," he said. "Elmo Shaw."

"You still haven't said what you want to talk to us about," Henry said testily. "We didn't invite you to sit down, you know."

"On the contrary. I heard Miss Kite imploring me to join you," Mr. Shaw said.

Henry looked at Dorothy, expecting her to disagree. But she was looking with curiosity at the old man, who was still smiling at her. "I have a proposition for you," he said. "I won't beat around the bush," he added taking a business card from his breast pocket and handing it to her. She examined it as he continued. "Since you seem to desire it so much, there is a way you can have a baby."

Henry bent forward to retrieve a piece of sandwich from his lap. "What are you talking about?" he said, wiping his trousers with his napkin. He glanced at Dorothy and held out his hand for the card. "May I see it?"

Without taking her eyes from the old man's face, Dorothy

66

handed Elmo Shaw's business card to Henry. Henry saw his name was engraved in gently sloping letters in the center of the stiff card, with "O'Hara Clinic," its address and telephone number appearing discreetly in the left corner.

"Dr. Thomas's rejection of your application was heartless," Shaw said emphatically. He leaned toward Dorothy. "I'm certain you would make a much better mother than most of those silly young girls the clinic panders to," he added, then grinned. "Of course you understand my bias tends toward older women. It's in my self-interest to promote the many advantages of maturity, you see. But then most progress springs from enlightened self-interest, don't you agree?" He shrugged good naturedly. "Forgive me. One of the *disadvantages* of age is that one tends to ramble. Permit me to climb down from my soapbox. I'm sure you'd rather hear my proposal."

"No we wouldn't," said Henry instantly. He couldn't believe Dorothy was listening to this strange old man. "I don't see how any of this is your business." He glanced worriedly at Dorothy. But she wasn't paying attention to him, her eyes were riveted on the old man's face.

"What proposal?" she said.

His tone was conciliatory as he turned to Henry. "Mr. Small must hear it too," he said. "Are you willing to listen and consider it?"

Henry gestured, palms up. "If Ms. Kite wants to listen, I guess I will too." He turned again to Dorothy. "But if you ask me, this isn't the person to help us."

"We're not agreeing to anything by listening," Dorothy said impatiently. She turned back to Mr. Shaw. "Go on," she said, staring in fascination at the old man's transparent nostrils, webbed with patches of hairlike blue and purple veins.

"My employer—who wishes to remain anonymous— desires very much that you have your baby, Miss Kite," he said. "Exactly as you'd planned, using Mr. Small's donation of semen. I've arranged for us to use the clinic tonight so that we may serve you." He looked at Henry. "With Mr. Small's assistance, of course."

Henry said he didn't understand how Mr. Shaw could go against clinic policy. Dorothy said nothing.

"My employer feels it an injustice that because of a technicality a woman so clearly qualified for motherhood is refused the clinic's services," Mr. Shaw said. "He wants to make it possible—discreetly—for you to conceive a child, Miss Kite, and he has instructed me to assist you and Mr. Small in that endeavor."

"Who's your employer?" Henry asked sharply. "I thought you worked for the clinic."

"I do, Mr. Small," the old man said. "The person to whom I refer has ultimate authority over my clinic responsibilities. Rather than making an ugly disturbance and causing unpleasantness with the other staff members—who sincerely believe in the efficacy of their exclusionary policy, unfortunately—my employer feels it best if I make our services available outside of office hours." He folded his arms. "We've done this many times, you see."

"Are you a doctor?" Henry persisted. He remembered that M.D. hadn't appeared on his business card.

Mr. Shaw brushed aside the question with a wave of his hand. "Be assured I'm entirely qualified to perform the procedure," he said. "I've been doing it for years. What do you say, Miss Kite? Are you interested?"

She nodded. "Of course I'm interested," she said, then frowned. "But I'm not sure I understand how you can do this. Aren't you taking a risk?"

"Not when my employer is author of the policy, Miss Kite," Mr. Shaw said. He went on patiently: "Rules are useful, my dear. They order our lives. Sometimes, however, it is necessary to bend rules in order to accommodate human need." He paused to wipe his nose on a linen handkerchief. "And as you so rightly point out, you deserve to be a mother." He refolded the handkerchief and replaced it in his jacket pocket, his steady eyes fixed on Dorothy. "Why don't you both come back with me now to the clinic?" he said. "The whole process will take only a few minutes."

"I think you should wait till morning," Henry said. "Sleep on it, Dorothy. There's no rush." He rubbed his knuckles nervously. "Under the circumstances, I'm not sure I'm willing to do whatever it is I'm supposed to do," he told Elmo Shaw.

"Mr. Small, you're going to do whatever Miss Kite wants you to do," said Mr. Shaw. He narrowed his eyes coldly.

Henry glanced anxiously at Dorothy.

"He's right, Henry," she said. "If I wait even a few hours, it'll be too late. I'm ovulating right now." She reached across the table to cover his hands with hers. "It can't hurt if we go back and find out more about it," she said.

"That's the spirit," Mr. Shaw said. He rose immediately and took his wallet from his breast pocket. It was a folding type made from exquisitely handstitched red Moroccan leather. He removed a twenty-dollar bill and threw it carelessly on the table.

"How much is this going to cost?" Henry asked suspiciously. But the old man had moved ahead of them, out of earshot. "There's something very peculiar about this," Henry said to Dorothy. "This is a rich man, Dorothy. It doesn't look to me like he takes charity cases."

"I'm not a charity case," she said defensively. "I can pay him whatever he wants." Her heart was pounding. Perhaps she could have a baby after all. This was the only clear thought in her head.

"Well, I *know* you can pay him," he insisted. "But who would you report him to if something went wrong? He hasn't told who he's accountable to, not really." He gestured emphatically. "And besides, Dorothy, can't you *smell* him? It's disgusting. I think he's got some awful rotting disease like leprosy. And he's about a hundred years old." He rubbed his chin. "He reminds me of those people in *Gulliver's Travels*—what were they called? The Struldbrugs. That's it. The immortals. You remember, no matter what happened to them, they couldn't die. But instead of getting wiser as they got older, they just got more and more bad-tempered and senile."

"I'm sure he's not a Struldbrug," Dorothy scoffed. "Don't be silly. He's very charming."

Henry sniffed. "He doesn't look normal. I think there's something wrong with him."

"He's just old."

"It's more than that."

Mr. Shaw beckoned to them from the front of the coffee shop.

"Come on," Dorothy said.

Henry followed her outside. She hurried along, two or three steps behind Mr. Shaw, who walked rapidly on long skinny legs. Henry trotted a step behind her. The street lights cast thin beams onto the stores they passed, all of them shut and padlocked. Their footsteps echoed. No one remained on the street except a derelict crouched over a grating.

Mr. Shaw took a key from among many large ones on a round metal ring and unlocked the front door of the clinic. When they got inside he switched on an overhead light and ushered them through the waiting room to the office where they'd met with Dr. Thomas. The other door was ajar, revealing an adjoining small room. Dorothy could see the stirrups of a gynecological examining table in the shadows.

"In a minute we'll leave you and you can disrobe," Mr. Shaw told her. "But first there is a paper you'll have to sign. A formality."

"I knew there was a trick," Henry said.

"There's no trick," Mr. Shaw said. "But my employer has a request. A small favor in return for the large one, since there'll be no charge for the service."

Dorothy sat tensely on the arm of a chair. "What is it?" she said. It was important for her not to mistrust him merely because of how old he was, she told herself. No matter what Henry said. If she thought of him as experienced and wise, his age became an attribute, and his proposal—whatever it was—something to take seriously. A way to help her achieve what she wanted most in the world.

"We guarantee you will carry to term a healthy baby," Elmo Shaw said. "Of whatever sex you desire. It will become yours and yours alone to raise."

Henry raised his eyebrows. "Come now," he said. "Guarantee?"

"But there is a stipulation," continued Mr. Shaw, ignoring him.

"How can he guarantee a healthy birth?" Henry demanded, turning to Dorothy. "Why, even Dr. Thomas said a

70

woman of your age—"

"Hush, Henry," Dorothy said. "I want to hear what he has to say."

With a satisfied nod, Mr. Shaw continued: "My employer longs for a healthy baby, as you do, Miss Kite," he said. "He is willing to guarantee you will give birth to twins—identical twins—one of which you will keep, the other give to me for him, no questions asked."

Henry's jaw dropped. "That's ridiculous," he said. "He can't guarantee you're going to give birth to twins."

"The agreement is not unusual," Mr. Shaw said, the gaze from his penetrating eyes causing Dorothy to blink. "Fertile women are often hired by barren wives to carry babies for them. They're implanted with the husband's semen. Their role is a simple biological function. They are breeders, as you will be. The babies are taken from them at birth and the mothers are paid in cash for the service. It's a business transaction. Everybody is satisfied. I feel we're being especially generous with you, since we will allow you to keep one of the babies for yourself."

Dorothy stared at him. "How can I be sure I'll have twins?" she asked finally. "What if I have only one baby? Would you take that one and leave me with nothing?"

Mr. Shaw smiled reassuringly. "That won't happen," he said.

"How can I be sure?" Dorothy asked.

"Wait a minute," Henry said. "This is ludicrous. It sounds like something out of the *Weekly World News.*"

Dorothy turned on him. "Do you have a better idea?" she snapped. "This may be my only chance. You don't know how much I want a child. In the restaurant I was thinking of killing myself."

Henry looked at her worriedly. "You're not yourself, I can see that. You haven't been yourself for weeks," he added. "But this is madness. Even if he could guarantee you'd have twins—think of giving up one of your babies, for heaven's sake, if you want one so much. Think how difficult that would be for you."

"But if they're identical twins," she said, "then they'll match, like bookends, and it won't be so awful to give one

71

away." She glanced back at Mr. Shaw, who smiled with satisfaction.

"Of course," he agreed soothingly.

Henry glowered. "Now I've heard everything," he said.

"How can I be sure you'll provide a good home for the one I give away?" she said, turning again to Mr. Shaw.

"My dear Miss Kite, the child will have every advantage. An enviable life."

"But why can't I know more about your employer?"

He smiled. "It's better this way." He took a piece of paper from his breast pocket and unfolded it on the desk. "What sex to you prefer?"

Dorothy looked into her lap, at her hands twisting together. "A girl," she whispered. "A little girl."

Yes.

"And so it is," Mr. Shaw said. With a flourish he filled in a space on the paper, then signed his name and pushed the document toward Dorothy. "Sign here, Miss Kite. Under my name. Then we can get the other business over with as soon as possible."

As she took the paper its edge sliced the tip of her forefinger, causing a fine line of blood to appear. She sucked it.

"Don't sign it," Henry said. "You'll regret it."

"Sir," Mr. Shaw said icily, turning to him. "This matter concerns me and Miss Kite. Other than a few necessary details in the beginning, it has nothing to do with you." Henry started to interrupt, but Mr. Shaw gestured commandingly and continued. "You claim Miss Kite is your friend, yet your alleged concern centers on the unconventionality of the transaction. What I propose will help her. Your carping serves only to delay her relief."

"But I'm going to be the father," Henry said. "Surely that gives me the right to ask questions."

"Isn't it true you planned to deposit your sperm in the clinic facility and then wash your hands of the whole affair?"

"Well, yes," Henry said. "But under normal circumstances. I don't believe she's thinking clearly." He lowered his eyes and continued uncertainly. "I think she needs my protection."

"Presumably you will allow Miss Kite to speak for herself," Mr. Shaw said. He looked calmly at Dorothy. "What is your disposition?"

She glanced at Henry pleadingly. "I don't have anything to lose," she said.

"But you do!" he said. "What if you do conceive twins? I'm not saying you will, but what if you do? Why, you'd have to give one of them to—" he hesitated, his eyes round. "To—this—man."

"But one child was all I wanted in the first place," she cried. "If I never even see the other baby, it'll be like I never had it at all. And he's promised it a good home. Oh, Henry—can't you understand what this means to me?"

"I don't think you should do it," he said stubbornly. "I think you're letting yourself in for a lot of trouble. What do you do if something goes wrong?"

"Nothing will go wrong," Mr. Shaw said. He pushed the contract toward Dorothy. "Sign here, where the x is," he said.

Dorothy pretended to read the document, but the neatly typed words swam and jiggled on the page.

"I'd like to look at it too," Henry said.

"Sign it," Mr. Shaw directed Dorothy, ignoring him. She bent forward and signed it. A bloody smudge from the paper cut appeared under her signature, leaving an unmistakable fingerprint.

Henry reached for the document but Mr. Shaw turned from his outstretched hand, took the paper from Dorothy, refolded it and replaced it in his pocket.

"Where's her copy?" Henry said, dropping his hand.

"I'll see that she gets it in the mail," Mr. Shaw said, vaguely. "Now, Mr. Small, if you'll come this way with me, we'll get on with the procedure." He turned back to Dorothy. "Please go into the examining room and take off your clothes. You'll find a hospital gown on the chair."

Henry glanced again at Dorothy as Mr. Shaw placed his hand on his shoulder. "I don't like this," Henry said, drawing back. "I don't want to do it."

"Oh, Henry," she said. "Don't be such an old maid."

He winced as if she'd slapped him. He was acutely aware

of his eccentricities. A middle-aged bachelor was often fair game for people who despised unconventionality, and he was used to the insults of small boys and construction workers as he hurried past them. But he'd never imagined Dorothy allying herself with such bigotry. As he turned away he found himself blinking back tears.

She watched him square his narrow shoulders as he departed with Mr. Shaw. She'd never called him an old maid, not in all the years they'd known one another. He was a fine man, a principled one, and he'd been doing his best to help her. Shame warmed her cheeks and she almost called after him.

But she didn't.

Chapter Nine

Dorothy shut the door, unclasped her beads and laid them carefully on the chair, hesitated, looked around.

That's a window, she reminded herself sternly. Here is a chair with a scratch on one of its arms. These are my shoes, this is my sweater that I'm unbuttoning.

She reached awkwardly to tie the stiff robe over her naked rump, then lifted herself onto the table. As she sat back her feet dangled several inches from the floor.

Mr. Shaw had mesmerized her, it was as simple as that. She'd agreed with him against Henry's sensible precautions and had even enjoyed siding with Mr. Shaw against him, relishing (relishing?—yes, *relishing*) his discomfort. Yet Henry never would have suggested donating semen if it hadn't been for her. He was shy and careful. Maintaining his separateness was important to him. He clung to his privacy. It had taken courage for him to make the offer, but he'd overcome his natural reluctance because he cared for her, had seen her pain and wanted to help her change her life.

She'd repaid him by insulting him, by acting as if he meant nothing to her. And she'd made certain he didn't know she understood what the special offer of intimacy cost him.

Yet he'd allowed her to glimpse a corner of himself that other people didn't ordinarily see. He'd even tried to protect her from her dangerous impulsiveness.

And his resistance made sense! Nobody could assure conception. Technology lagged far behind mother nature, everybody knew that. Women were always getting themselves artificially inseminated without becoming pregnant.

And the old man acting as if he could guarantee she'd have twins!

The whole thing was preposterous . . .

Yet he seemed to know his way around. It couldn't all be an act. He must have experience in a clinic or health facility, although apparently he wasn't a doctor since he called himself "Mr." He was connected here, she'd seen him earlier, peering at her through the glass in the office door. His card identified him as a clinic staff member.

She studied the tray of sparkling instruments on a metal table in the corner, and she squirmed nervously as Mr. Shaw opened the door and smiled at her reassuringly. He went to the sink in the corner and scrubbed his well-manicured hands carefully. Then he pulled on a pair of surgical gloves. He pulled a small plastic container from his pocket and removed from it a vial containing milky fluid.

"This will take only a moment," he told her. "Lie down and put your feet in the stirrups, please."

She lay back, clasping her hands on her chest. "Is Henry all right?" she asked, resting her bare feet in the stirrups, tensing reflexively at the sudden cold.

Mr. Shaw's back was toward her as he busied himself at the tray of instruments. "Of course," he said. "There's nothing to worry about. It's a very simple procedure."

"Is he waiting for me outside?"

Shaw turned toward her. "Really, Miss Kite," he said with slight impatience, "there's no reason for your concern. He's a grown man." He came to her and lifted the gown. She lay exposed to him. "This won't hurt," he said. "Please relax."

He placed one of his gloved hands firmly on her abdomen. With the other he took a long steel instrument with a metal bulb at one end and inserted it into her vagina. She recoiled as he pushed and twisted it inside her, causing a sharp pain.

"Why, Miss Kite," he announced. "You're a virgin!"

What difference can that possibly make, she thought, squeezing her eyes shut and holding her breath. She pulled back from the scalding pain and wished fervently for the procedure to end.

"My employer will be delighted," Mr. Shaw chuckled. "So

rare these days, you know." With his left hand he pushed insistently on her abdomen, scrutinizing the place between her thighs where the metal instrument entered her body. He began undulating his fingers against her, enlarging the vaginal opening with them, thrusting and pressing the tool inside. His mouth fell slack, she heard his rattling breath. "Lovely," he rasped, rocking back and forth, pushing inside her rhythmically, further and further, his tongue curling between his teeth. "Lovely."

What is he doing?

With a tremendous effort she brought her knees together and twisted sideways. She pulled herself up on her elbows and glared at him.

His eyes focused unwillingly and after a moment he sighed, grinned and winked, as if she and he were in collusion. He jerked his hand and the chrome instrument out of her with a smacking sound. When he took it to the sink she saw it was laced with strings of blood.

"That's all there is to it," he said. "We're finished. You'll probably bleed a little tonight, you may want to wear some protection against that. But don't worry, blood is customary for someone of your gentle experience." He chuckled again with unpleasant intimacy.

As he turned away from her the thought occurred to her that he'd wanted to rape her.

"You may put your clothes on and go home now," he said. "You'll be hearing from me a few days after the babies are born."

She sat up and adjusted the gown. "Is that all?" she said gruffly. "Don't I have to notify you if I'm pregnant?"

"No," he said. "You are."

"When the time comes will you be at the hospital with me?" she asked, shuddering at the idea. She never wanted to see him again.

"Don't worry, Miss Kite. When the time is right, I'll get in touch with you."

With a practiced motion he ripped the bloody gloves off and tossed them into the wastebasket. In the doorway he turned back to her and bowed. "Goodnight, Miss Kite. And congratulations."

"Where is Mr. Small?"

But Mr. Shaw left without answering, closing the door softly.

She dressed quickly, pulled on her overcoat, grabbed her purse and dashed through the adjoining office and into the waiting room. She tried not to think about how helpless she'd been, how she'd endangered herself by submitting to the dangerous process. "Stupid," she said to herself as she hurried down the hallway. "Stupid. Stupid."

The waiting room was dark. "Henry?" she said softly. "Hello?"

The room was so still she couldn't even hear noises from the street. She groped along the wall, felt the doorknob, twisted it and pulled open the door. She blinked at the bright light from the hallway and rushed down the stairs, her shoes making thumps on the uncarpeted treads.

He was probably waiting for her on the street.

But when she got outside he wasn't there.

Nor was he in the coffee shop where they'd met Mr. Shaw. The waiter was alone, reading the *Racing Form* and leaning against the counter. He looked up as she entered.

"Has anybody been here?" she asked. "Somebody—a nice-looking man in a blue suit—waiting for me? In the last few minutes?"

"Nope," he said, and returned to his reading. She went back outside, took a quarter from her change purse and stopped at a phone booth. After she'd gotten the clinic's number from the information operator, she punched it in. If Henry was still there it was possible he'd answer if she let it ring. Or Mr. Shaw might pick up the phone and she'd demand to know what had happened to Henry.

Nobody answered.

She hung up, took out her address book and looked up Henry's home phone. He lived in Greenwich Village, if he'd gone home it was unlikely he'd be there yet but she'd try anyway.

This time she counted twenty rings.

She imagined the phone jangling in his empty apartment. The image frightened her and she hung up.

She stood uncertainly next to the booth.

Why hadn't they planned to meet afterwards?

78

Perhaps he'd been embarrassed by the indignity of whatever that dreadful old man had made him do. She couldn't blame him if he hadn't wanted to linger, waiting for her. Not after the way she'd behaved.

At this moment he was undoubtedly sitting in the subway on his way home, wishing he'd never agreed to the procedure and furious with her. She nodded uneasily. That was it.

She'd bring a bouquet of flowers to the office tomorrow. She'd apologize and they'd make up, even laugh about the whole ridiculous thing. He'd chastise her for permitting the old man to hypnotize her, but she deserved it.

And she'd tell him she understood what he'd done for her and how grateful she was.

She hurried along the deserted sidewalk, preoccupied, writing the script for the next day's conversation.

Suddenly she heard the unmistakable hiss of a snarling dog. At the sound she stopped instantly, all her senses alert. For a long moment she kept herself motionless. Then, slowly, slowly, she turned her head to look into the shadows. Half-hidden in the darkness a few feet from her a terrified derelict huddled against a corrugated tin door. "Get away," he whispered, pulling back and gesturing ineffectually as a huge black animal approached him menacingly. As Dorothy watched, the dog stretched its drooling muzzle into an almost human grin, as if enjoying the old man's terror. Its growl deepened and it pushed closer to him, trapping him against the door.

"Get away!" the man whimpered, waving his hands. "Shoo."

With a flash of purple gums and bright teeth the animal pounced on him. The old man screamed and pulled away a fraction of a second too late.

Dorothy bolted forward and grabbed the animal's head. it wore no collar and her frantic hands slid down its thick neck.

But the dog paid no attention to her. It shook the man's forearm between its jaws as if her resistance meant nothing.

As if she herself were nothing at all, a flea.

She was filled with wild rage. She reached again, this time to wrap her fingers around the dog's slimy ears—she could imagine herself ripping them off, the dark blood spurting, the dog's howls of pain—but she couldn't get a grip, her

79

hands slid away impotently. She couldn't hurt the creature, she couldn't make it stop or even notice her. She stood back and kicked it mightily in its side. Her foot landed with a resounding thwack, her shoe flew off with the impact and thudded against the building. She hobbled back, her toes hot with pain, wrapped her purse strap around her hand, came forward again and swung the purse with all the strength of her fury, striking the creature between its eyes, which glistened eerily and reflected the yellow beam from the street light. But the dog paid no attention to the blow and continued gnawing the man's arm, pushing against him as he resisted feebly with his free arm. Dorothy saw the animal's small gray incisors, as sharp as razors, and the fangs, curving like rat's teeth into the fabric of the old man's sleeve.

She began shouting incoherently, bringing her pocket-book down again on the back of the dog's broad head. The blow had no effect but she continued pounding, again and again, with furious strength, her rage driving the blows, harder, harder. She wanted to kill.

Finally the creature loosened its grip on the man's arm. The derelict shuffled backward, whimpering. His fingers moved to his mouth and he sucked on them as he watched the dog turn to threaten Dorothy. She took a reflexive step back.

"Keep away from me," she warned, tightening the strap around her hand. The dog planted its mighty paws on the pavement and crouched, ready to spring on her. She looked into the dog's blank eyes and felt her knees lock. She tightened her fists and challenged the animal, leaning toward it in exquisite readiness, the taste of blood in her mouth.

Suddenly the dog sat back with ears pricked and head tilted, listening. After a long moment it turned away from Dorothy and trotted off—purposefully, obediently—as if summoned. She watched, astonished, as it reached the cross street and joined several other huge animals as they appeared from around the corner. Each of them was mastifflike, with powerful shoulders and haunches, a wide ugly face and shaggy black coat. They nuzzled and sniffed one another under the street light, then moved off, starting to run—like a herd of wild creatures thundering across an African plain—gathering speed, stirring up a cloud of city grit and dust, wheeling into the center of the empty avenue. After a block they turned together and swept westward toward the river, their claws scrabbling on the pavement as they galloped away into the darkness.

Unbelieving, licking her bleeding lip, Dorothy watched them disappear. Gradually she released her fists.

The old man groaned. She turned toward him, averting her gaze quickly from a dark stain spreading from his crotch over his ragged trousers. The stench rising from him, of urine, fruity wine and rot made her swallow a wave of nausea.

Why had she risked her life? She'd never done such a thing before. As recently as last night if she'd been confronted with the same terrifying situation she'd have run away, looked for a telephone to call 911, or sought somebody else to help. She'd never have defended the old man and jeopardized her own safety, not before tonight.

And she'd never felt such overwhelming rage. Never in her life. She still felt the power of it smoldering sickeningly at the base of her stomach. It made her sweat. Where had such fury come from?

She gingerly poked the derelict's shoulder. "Are you hurt?"

He groaned again and gestured toward something behind her. She straightened apprehensively and glanced over her shoulder.

An old woman pushing an overloaded shopping car approached. She halted to peer down at the derelict.

"This man was just attacked by a dog," Dorothy told her.

The old woman had seen what happened.

The man made a quarrelsome sound, like a baby.

"We should get help for him," Dorothy said.

The old woman said he was all right.

"But his arm may be hurt," Dorothy said. He might need a rabies shot. She glanced downtown uneasily. "Where are the police?"

Ignoring Dorothy, the old woman bent stiffly to rouse him. "Wake up," she said. "Move over."

"There were five or six other dogs," Dorothy said, needing to talk, wiping a strand of hair from her eyes. Her hand was trembling.

The old woman parked her cart against the doorway and sat heavily on the sidewalk next to the man. He wiped his ragged sleeve across his mouth and leaned against her, closing his eyes and sighing deeply.

"Those weren't no dogs," the woman said to Dorothy. She took a newspaper and spread it carefully over their legs for a blanket, then pulled his head to her shoulder.

"Of course they were," Dorothy said impatiently. "Didn't you see them?"

"I saw them, all right," the old woman said. She leaned back into the doorway. "They was the Devil's own hounds."

"Oh, for heaven's sake," Dorothy said. "What are you talking about?"

The old woman grinned up at her. One of her front teeth was missing and the other was split with a jagged crack. "Nothing you know about, sister," she cackled. "You better go home now."

Dorothy's wallet contained a dollar bill and a five. "Here," she said impulsively. "Take this six dollars. Tomorrow morning you can pay for a taxi and go to the hospital with him. He should have his arm looked at." She glanced at the now peacefully sleeping man. "Or have breakfast, if you like, if he's all right."

Without a word of thanks the old woman took the money and stuffed it into a pocket on her dress, under several sweaters and a baggy overcoat. She buttoned the pocket carefully, then rearranged the layers of garments and newspapers. She folded her arms across her chest and closed her eyes. "Vigilance," she said, settling back.

"I beg your pardon?"

The old woman sank silently into the shadows.

Dorothy sighed and looked around. The street was empty. There wasn't a sign of the dogs, or of any people. She watched a discarded newspaper blow and crumple against a lamp post.

Finally she turned, picked up her shoe and hobbled toward her apartment building. Apprehension crept up her legs like ink in her veins.

What about Henry? Where was he?

Chapter Ten

"But where did you go?" Dorothy demanded the next morning. Henry sat at his desk rattling pencils in a container. "I was worried sick." She stood at the door with her hand on the knob, her bandanna tied tightly under her chin. She'd forgotten to bring him flowers as an apology for what she'd put him through, so eager had she been to get here and see him safe this morning.

He looked at her. "I wanted to get out of that place as fast as I could," he said.

"You might have told me you were going to rush off like that," she said. "I didn't know where you'd gone. I thought he might have murdered you or something."

He didn't smile. "That possibility occurred to me, too," he said.

While he watched quietly she put away her scarf and coat, unlocked and opened the bottom drawer of her desk and deposited her pocketbook. She closed the drawer and sat. Her heart swelled with shame as she looked into his gentle, sober face. She noticed he hadn't shaved. There was an uncharacteristic shadow of stubble on his chin and cheeks.

"Henry," she began, hesitated, then blurted, "Oh, Henry—can you forgive me for the way I behaved?"

"You were beside yourself," he said. "I can't blame you."

She shook her head. "You're a much better person than I am. I don't deserve you for a friend."

He smiled. "I knew you'd come flying in here this morning to apologize," he said. "You probably didn't sleep last night any more than I did."

"No," she admitted. It had been a horrible night.

"It's important for us to stand together on this," he said. She wasn't sure what he meant.

"I think we're involved in something . . . queer," he said.

"I'm so sorry you had to go through all that," she said. "I certainly didn't intend—" Her voice trailed away.

He frowned at her. "We have to think carefully, Dorothy," he said. Then, "Did he put my semen into you?"

"Yes." She gave an embarrassed shrug. "He put *something* into me, I assume it was . . . yours."

"Oh, god," he said, continuing to look at her intently.

"Don't worry," she said quickly. "We agreed you wouldn't have to be involved."

"It isn't so simple," he said. "I don't think you realize what's happened."

"What do you mean?"

He studied the tip of his thumbnail as it followed the grain in the oaken desktop. "What do we know about this fellow, Dorothy? Who is he, anyway?"

"I think he could be a rapist," she said. "Or a criminal of some kind. A psychopath. To think I let him near me! I must have been in a trance."

He groaned. "Jesus, Dorothy, how could you have been taken in by him?"

Before she could answer he held up his hand. "No, no," he said. "How could *I* permit it? I'm as much to blame as you. You didn't know how crazy you were behaving, but I did. I should have stopped you, but I let my feelings get hurt. That confused me and before I knew it I was standing outside in the street." He punched his fist into his palm. "We're a couple of fools."

"No we're not," she argued. "And you're not to blame at all, you just put that idea out of your head. I was the one who behaved like a fool, and I was rude and cruel to you. I have no excuse. I was obsessed, that's all there is to it—"

"We're not talking here about your obsession. That's not the point. We're talking about what happened."

She laughed nervously. "Other than my losing my mind? Probably nothing, Henry. With the cold light of morning

84

shining in my windows I saw how ridiculous it all is. Imagine getting taken in that way. He's just some dotty old man who hangs around that clinic place. He's probably the janitor or something. A pervert—" she pushed back her memory of what he'd done to her, of his old face, the sweat quivering in drops around his mouth, the rhythmic pushing, withdrawing, pushing withdrawing. . . . "A pervert," she finished quickly. "Some demented former hospital worker who gets his kicks examining women. And men too, I guess."

"How do you think he can guarantee your giving birth?" he said. "To twins? Doesn't that strike you as peculiar?"

"Well, of course it's peculiar. It's insane!" she said. "Don't tell me you actually think I'm pregnant."

She heard how unconvincing her laugh sounded.

"What did the contract you signed say?"

"I don't know," she said. "I didn't read it."

"You should always read a legal document before you sign it," he said reproachfully. "That's just inexcusable, Dorothy."

"I was out of my mind," she said. "You said so yourself. Besides, it wasn't a legal document, Henry. It was just a piece of paper with a lot of mumbo jumbo typed on it."

She pretended to herself she wasn't frightened. She wanted both of them to think she thought the whole business was absurd.

"I want to go back to the clinic and get that piece of paper," he said. "I want to tear it up."

"You're taking it all too seriously."

"Maybe so. But I want it in my hands." He leaned toward her grasping the aluminum arms of his chair. "Dorothy. This—Mr. Shaw—who is he? Why does he go around with a contract like that in his pocket?"

She inhaled deeply, fighting her fear. "He's a nutcase, I told you. An asylum escapee."

"Maybe he is and maybe he isn't," he said mysteriously. "At least we have to go back and tell the people in the clinic what happened. They should know what goes on there after hours."

"Oh, Henry," she said. "You're overreacting."

"Dorothy," he said. "He was a horrible man."

85

They looked at each other. "I'm so sorry for getting you into it," she said finally.

"And what if you *are* pregnant?" he persisted. "It's possible, isn't it?"

"Well, yes, I suppose so."

"And what if he shows up and wants to take your baby, once you've had it? What will you do then?"

She waved her hands. "He said I'd have twins," she said. "I'm sure the agreement would be invalid anyway—it wasn't notarized or anything—but even if—and I'm playing the devil's advocate—even if it were valid, I won't have twins, the odds of that happening are about a zillion to one."

"But it's possible, isn't it?"

"Oh, Henry."

"What if you have twins?" he said.

"I'm not even pregnant."

"But what if you are?" he said. "And what if you have twins?"

She told him there were too many "what ifs."

"How would you like to give your baby to a man like that?" He looked at her pleadingly. "We have to rip up that contract, Dorothy," he said. "That's a debt you don't want to owe anybody."

Her own fear sounded in his voice and she swallowed finally, then nodded. "I give up," she said. "Let's go back. We'll find him and make him give us the paper."

He jumped up and grabbed his jacket from the back of his chair. "Let's go now," he said.

She removed her purse from the drawer. "All right, all right," she said, switching off the light as they hurried out the door. "Let's go now and get it over with."

ght to see of think abut it. She said meekly.
"And what it you get pregnant?" she persisted. "It's
possibility, isn't it?"
"Well, yes, I suppose so."

Chapter Eleven

When they arrived at the clinic building it looked smaller in the daylight, dingier and older. The exterior window frames were splintery with age and too many coats of black paint. Inside, the same nurse who'd greeted them the night before sat at the reception desk. She smiled as they approached, her eyes invisible behind tinted glasses.

"We'd like to see Mr. Shaw," Henry said.

"Who?" she asked, tilting her head.

"Elmo Shaw," Dorothy said. "He works here."

The nurse smiled humourlessly. "There's nobody here by that name," she said.

"Oh, but you're mistaken," Dorothy said. "He was here last night." She spelled his name.

The nurse looked perplexed. "You want to see somebody named Shaw?"

"That's the idea," Henry said, raising an eyebrow at Dorothy, who gave their names quickly. "Last night we talked with Dr. Thomas," she said. "Then Mr. Shaw, later. After everybody else had gone home."

The nurse paged back in her appointment book. "Yes, I see," she said. "Your names are here last night at eight o'clock."

Henry jerked his head up and down but she ignored him and told Dorothy, "There wasn't anybody here last night named Shaw. Are you sure you didn't get the names mixed up? Shaw sounds a little like Small, perhaps that's where the confusion started."

Henry snorted. "I can tell the difference between my name

and somebody else's," he said. "There's no confusion."

"There's no need to get snippy," said the nurse, whose neatly typed name, Lucy Trent, was inserted in plastic and pinned to her collar.

Dorothy smiled nervously, trying to avoid an argument. "Please, Ms. Trent," she said. "We want to see Mr. Shaw."

"I'd like to help you," Lucy Trent said. "But I don't know who you're talking about."

"We saw him last night," Henry said, pronouncing his words slowly and carefully, as if he were talking to a lip reader. "He brought us back here after hours. He had a *key*. Nobody else was here."

"No one is allowed here after hours except the staff."

"He told us he *was* staff."

Lucy Trent folded her arms and stared stonily at Henry. The door behind the reception desk opened and Dr. Thomas bustled in, his clipboard clasped against his chest.

"Why, good morning, Miss—ah—ah—Mr.—"

As Lucy Trent reintroduced them her expression sent storm warnings.

"What seems to be the trouble?" Dr. Thomas asked amiably.

"They claim they want to see somebody—"

"Mr. Shaw," Dorothy said. "We've come to see Mr. Elmo Shaw."

"Who?" Dr. Thomas said.

"Oh, please," Henry said in exasperation. "Not you too."

"We saw him last night," said Dorothy. "We spoke to him after everybody else had gone home. Around ten-thirty. He's an old man. He works here."

"He smells," said Henry, gripping the corners of the desk and leaning threateningly toward Lucy Trent, "like a *decaying body.*"

"Do you know anything about this?" Dr. Thomas said to her.

"Certainly not," she said defensively. "I locked up myself, the way I always do. I think they have this Mr. Shaw confused with somebody else," she said. "Somewhere else."

"Nobody is allowed back here after hours," Dr. Thomas explained to them. "It's a very strict rule, you see. It wouldn't happen except in the gravest circumstances, and only with either me or Dr. Roberts present. She's the only other physician on our staff." He smiled reassuringly. "She wasn't on duty last night."

Lucy Trent removed a manila folder from her middle drawer which she placed on her blotter and opened. "This is a list of all the people who work here," she said, turning the document and showing it to Dorothy. "As you can see there's nobody here named Shaw. Or anything like it."

Henry stepped forward and scanned the list: "Cassidy, French," he read. "Where are the S's? . . . Reade, Roberts, Stein, Thomas, Trent." He looked at Dorothy. "There's no Shaw here," he said. Dorothy picked up the list and studied it, then handed it slowly back to Lucy Trent.

"Let's get out of here," Henry said. "They can't help us."

Dr. Thomas leaned forward to squeeze Dorothy's arm. "We were terribly sorry we couldn't help you last night, Miss Kite. I can understand how disappointed you were. Would you like to go into one of our vacant rooms and lie down for a few minutes?"

Dorothy shook off his hand. "I certainly would not," she said. "Stop acting as if you think we're crazy. Mr. Small and I know what happened, even if you don't believe us."

Henry backed away. "Come on, Dorothy," he said. "Let's go."

"But somebody has to know him," she said.

Henry shook his head. "There's nobody," he said with finality. "Only us."

"We'll be back," Dorothy said to Dr. Thomas. "We're going to talk this over and then we'll be back and get to the bottom of it. And maybe you'll have a lawsuit on your hands."

"I'll just pretend I didn't hear you say that," Dr. Thomas said soothingly. "I know how distraught you are." He handed her a brochure from one of the tables by the door. "Here's a mailer which explains our services," he said, and turned to Henry. "You'd better get her right home," he warned.

Dorothy stuffed the folder into her purse and hurried after Henry, who closed the door firmly behind them. Once on the street he stopped and looked at her. "Dorothy," he said, "I don't understand what's happened, but I think we're in trouble."

"What do you mean?" she asked, her stomach sinking.

He pivoted and began striding up the street. She trotted at his side, barely keeping up with him. "Henry?" she said. "What are you talking about?"

"Don't you think it's strange *yet?*"

"Of course it's strange," she said breathlessly. "But there's an explanation, we just don't know what it is. Perhaps they're afraid of a malpractice suit. Did you see how the blood drained from his face when I mentioned that possibility? Or it could be a case of mistaken identity, Henry, those things happen sometimes."

"Mistaken identity?" he exploded. "Dorothy, what's the matter with you?"

She stopped in the middle of the sidewalk. "Please slow down, I can't keep up."

He slowed his pace but continued glaring at her. "Okay," he said. "Let's go over what happened. You signed a contract with a man nobody's even heard of. Right? And he didn't give you a copy, so all we have to go on is our memory that it happened. As far as we know—and that's not much—you were artificially inseminated with my semen. And according to the mysterious Mr. Shaw you're now pregnant with identical twin girls. Right?"

She nodded. "And it's all ridiculous, Henry. There's nothing to be upset or frightened about."

"Just hold on," he said. "I'm recapitulating."

"Yes, Henry," she said, trying to calm him. "All right." She hoped he wasn't getting into one of his states.

"And when you give birth to these identical twin girls," he continued, watching a man hurrying past with a newspaper under his arm, "you're going to give one of them to Mr. Shaw. At the behest of his employer. Right?"

"Yes," she said. "That's what I remember. But perhaps none of it happened," she added. "Perhaps it's some kind of mutual fantasy. I've heard of that happening sometimes."

He grabbed her arms and shook her. *"When* have you heard of that happening?" he shouted, then looked around self-consciously. He lowered his voice. "When?" he said. "I ask you. We're not on drugs. And this isn't some kind of mass hysteria, that's not what what's-his-name means by

90

mass hysteria. Two people are hardly a mass. Both of us remember what I've described, isn't that so?"

"Yes," she said. "I guess so."

"Don't give me an 'I guess so.' You *know* it, don't you?"

"Of course I know it," she said impatiently, unpeeling his fingers from her sleeves. "I was just trying to be helpful."

"That kind of a statement isn't helpful," he said. "We're the only people who know what happened. And Mr. Shaw, wherever the hell he is." He paused. "*Whoever* the hell he is."

"What do you mean by that?" she said. "Who do you think he is?"

"Jesus, Dorothy." He put his hands on his hips and rolled his eyes. "You usually aren't this dense," he said. "I can only credit it to extreme duress."

"What are you talking about?" she said.

"When will you know if you're pregnant? How long does that take?"

She swallowed. "About a month, I suppose."

"You *suppose?*"

"I'll *know* in a month." She frowned. "Henry, you don't actually believe I'm pregnant, do you? The odds against that happening are phenomenal. People have to try artificial insemination again and again. And I'm old and you're old. The whole thing is ridiculous. We just got mixed up with some thrill-seeking old man, somebody who got into the clinic by stealing somebody's keys. He was a harmless lunatic who thought he was a doctor, you think that, don't you?"

He listened with his head lowered.

"And even if I *were* pregnant, Henry," she pleaded, leaning forward trying to force him to meet her eyes. "Even if I were, there's no way what he said will happen, is there? He can't guarantee that I'm going to have twins, can he? Twin *girls?* That's impossible, isn't it? Henry?"

"I'll tell you what I think in a month," he said, taking her arm. "Until then I don't think anything." He looked nervously over his shoulder, then pulled her toward the street. "We've been gone for hours. I'll split the price of a cab back to the library with you."

This suggestion was so extraordinary Dorothy knew he was taking the whole thing seriously.

She was afraid.

Chapter Twelve

During the next few weeks spring crept inexorably along upper Broadway. Tulips pushed boldly past the last gray patches of snow, through the cigarette butts, discarded wine bottles, slushy fragments of newspaper, used coffee containers, crumpled stubs and receipts cluttering the Avenue's center meridian. The flowers exploded gaily behind the benches where people sat talking to one another or to themselves, from under the waving branches of thorn bushes. Theirs were brave blossoms of pink, coral, yellow, scarlet. Blue and crimson crocuses unfolded and peeped out beneath them, daffodils paraded in separate clumps.

Along the sidewalk, flowershop owners set out pots fragrant with hyacinth, buckets jammed with three-foot branches of magnolias or lilacs wrapped in cellophane and tied with narrow purple ribbons.

The breezes wafted and warmed, forced open windows locked all winter.

Dorothy went back and forth to work every day and kept her eye on the calendar. She sat at her desk and did what she was used to doing. She made lists, catalogued the contents of boxes, typed cards, read manuscripts, talked to Henry—but only about their work. Each maintained an agreement neither spoke of.

Every morning she stood before the full-length mirror on her mother's closet door and studied her reflection. She turned sideways slowly, watching herself.

She wasn't familiar with her body. Its warmth, its color,

its texture, the odor and shape of it were all new to her. It was as if she'd lived inside it all her life, this costume with her name, had moved it around, looked out from inside without knowing it. She'd had no real idea what other people saw, or what they meant when they said her name. Always it had been as if everything of her existed inside, behind her eyes, in the place where she thought about things. In there she lived separately, oblivious to how she appeared to others. Everyone else shared crucial information about which she knew nothing: how she looked, how she sounded, what it was like to see her moving along the street. This information wasn't important to them. To everyone else she was just another stranger walking along.

But what others knew so carelessly was everything to her.

This idea had never occurred to her. It was as if she'd been asleep like the Sleeping Beauty. Her awakening had come, not from a kiss, but from the moment Henry had told her shyly he cared enough about her to help her achieve something she wanted, even though he didn't want it with her.

From time to time she looked across her desk at him and considered this.

It was possible he loved her. In his own unconventional way, with his own cautious delicacy. He'd responded to some importance he saw in her, some special quality she hadn't guessed or valued. He'd gifted her with his connection to it, his awareness of this person he saw who was her.

She wanted to know what he knew.

So she studied her body.

Did her breasts hurt? She'd never scrutinized them as she did now, every morning—so she wasn't sure they felt different. Tight. Were they bigger? It could be her imagination.

She squeezed them and didn't know whether the pain she felt came from the pressure she exerted or from some other pressure exerting itself within them.

Later, walking along the street she sought her reflection in store windows. She bought a small mirror at a pharmacy and kept in in her drawer at work. She began unbuttoning the top two or three buttons of her cardigan because she'd noticed the firmness of her neck. If Henry noticed her doing this, he didn't say anything. But *she* knew she did it and she felt in control of surprising knowledge: Dorothy Kite had nice breasts and an attractive throat. That was part of what people saw when they looked at her.

When the morning she expected her menstrual period dawned, she opened her eyes and knew the day instantly. She felt the familiar cramps, low in her back and abdomen, the pain she'd suffered every twenty-five days since the age of thirteen.

But when she went into the bathroom she discovered there was no blood.

And no mistaking the pain in her breasts.

She flew to the library to tell Henry.

Chapter Thirteen

He received the news with surprising calm.

"Are you sure?" he said. "Couldn't it mean something else?" He asked how old she was and she told him even though she knew he knew her age. "Maybe it's the change of life," he said unpersuasively. "It might come upon you suddenly. You're almost old enough, if you'll pardon me for pointing it out." He blew his nose into his everpresent handkerchief. "Or anxiety," he suggested. "I understand anxiety can throw off the menses."

She tried not to glare. He said it so prissily, "the menses," making it sound like an oldfashioned athletic event, women in bustles pitching horseshoes or wielding croquet mallets.

"You'd better see a doctor," he said after several seconds when they sat looking at one another. He took out his wallet. "Last week I got the name of an obstetrician from my landlady, just in case." He withdrew a piece of paper, handed it to her with a sheepish smile. "You can imagine her excitement when I asked her for the name of an obstetrician," he said. "She kept trying to pretend I meant oculist."

Dorothy accepted it meekly. He'd assumed, correctly, she didn't have her own physician, that she wouldn't want to have anything to do with Madelyn's doctors.

Here was fresh evidence he knew her in ways she hadn't suspected, and knew her better even than she knew herself.

She telephoned the doctor and made an appointment.

A few days later, when she left the library at 5:30 to take

the bus to the doctor's office, Henry stayed behind. "I won't go with you, if you don't mind," he said. "I'm not done here yet. Just let me know what he tells you as soon as you finish with him. If the rabbit dies. Or the stick turns green, whatever it is."

He was involved in a project which required searching through stacks of old papers and records. She didn't know what he was looking for. He'd been behaving mysteriously and wouldn't tell her what he was doing. During the last several days he'd ignored his other duties and instead went downstairs repeatedly, lugged up heavy crates and barrels bursting with ancient manuscripts. Everything he found was covered with scum and mildew, the residue of scores of years in the cellar. After a while even his eyebrows dangled clotted strings of dust. The office was a mess. She had to pick her way through the boxes to get to her desk.

"It's probably nothing," he said when she asked what he was looking for. "Just somethings I vaguely remember from fifteen or twenty years ago."

She stood by the door. "Don't stay too late," she said. "It gets chilly here at night and you know how easily you catch cold."

"I'm on the last batch," he said, looking around. His eyes were thoughtful when he glanced back at her. "Good luck," hesaid.

She thanked him.

"Whatever *that* is," he added, trying to smile.

She hurried off.

Chapter Fourteen

Dr. Blanchard was a kindly man with a large handsome head, glistening hair brushed back modishly from his forehead. He sported a moustache that curved above his upper lip like an eyebrow. Dorothy felt at ease with him and gave her meager medical history without feeling invaded.

She didn't want to admit what had happened—it sounded crazy—so instead she looked him squarely in the eye and told the story she'd concocted: She wasn't married, her beau of many years had been killed in a recent automobile accident. This explained her lack of a wedding ring. She found too that claiming the conventional relationship comforted her. She said her fiancé had lived with his ailing mother, that's why they hadn't married, although they'd been planning to. His mother had been killed in the crash along with him and her own mother had died after a long illness only a couple of months before that.

"Quite a dreadful series of calamities," Dr. Blanchard said sympathetically as he took her blood pressure.

When he'd finished examining her he left her to put her clothes on. Later they sat together in his office.

"It's too early for me to tell for sure from a pelvic examination if you're pregnant," he said. "Although you seem to be in fine health. I'll give you a call as soon as I get the lab results."

"Don't you have any idea?" she said. "You've been doing this for so long, surely you must have a feeling about it. It's so important to me."

He smiled. "Do you want to have a baby?" he asked.

"Yes." Despite everything, she thought.

"It certainly would be an affirmation of life after all you've been through," he said. "And I don't want to get your hopes up, of course." He leaned back, his fingers interlaced across his chest. "But yes. I think—even without a test—I think I can tell you you're pregnant."

She found herself grinning. "I think I am, too," she said.

"But it's our secret until we get the green light from the lab," he said, standing and reaching across the desk to shake her hand. "I'll call you the moment we know." He walked with her to the door. "Why don't you make an appointment to come back in a month," he said. "For good luck. You can always cancel if nothing comes of the test."

"Oh, I will," she said eagerly. "Thank you so much."

"Don't thank me yet," he said. "We've got a lot to go through together, Ms. Kite."

She stopped suddenly. "Is it dangerous?" she asked, remembering Dr. Thomas's admonition. "I know I'm older than most first-time mothers. What are the chances of my miscarrying—or having a deformed child?"

He gripped her shoulder reassuringly. "I think right now we just have to find out if you're pregnant," he said. "We can worry about the rest later. Besides," he added, "you're strong and healthy. You have no history of illness. The chances are excellent for you to carry a healthy baby to term. Why don't we leave it at that?"

She thanked him again, then laughed, abashed—apparently unable to stop thanking him—and left him smiling in the doorway.

Once on the street she sped to a phone booth and called Henry at the library. As she listened to the ringing she glanced at her watch. It was a few minutes after eight, he'd have gone home long ago. She retrieved her quarter, took out her address book, found his home number and punched it in. She let it ring half a dozen times, then hung up. He didn't seem ever to be there when she wanted him.

Probably he'd gone out for supper. He'd be back soon, she'd call him later.

Whoever Elmo Shaw was, he'd known what he was doing.

If she ever saw him again she'd thank him. Perhaps he was a doctor who'd lost his license, some poor old soul who secretly roamed the back rooms of clinics and hospitals to help people the medical establishment wouldn't pay attention to. His was an inspired calling, almost saintly, once you looked at it that way.

She'd tell Henry that, perhaps it would make him feel better.

Of course he'd made her sign that weird contract, and he'd behaved badly. Very badly.

But Henry was mistaken, there wasn't anything sinister about what had happened. They'd talk together about it. She'd help him see he didn't have to be afraid of what was going to happen.

They were finished with Elmo Shaw.

She decided to walk home languidly, swinging her purse, looking into stores and savoring the evening smells and sounds, the velvet feel of air on her face and arms. She was giddy with the joy of her pregnancy. She thought of Henry. He was a fine man. He was intelligent, caring. A person of real strength and integrity—and he cared for her. She was proud he was the father of her baby. Perhaps he would want more involvement with their child—and with her. The thought pleased and excited her.

She couldn't wait to tell him the news, and she stopped at another phone booth to call him again. But there was still no answer, he hadn't got home yet.

Couples strolled past with their children. Next year she'd be walking along with a baby in a carriage too. She imagined people nodding and smiling at her. "What a pretty baby," they'd say. She smiled to herself, enjoying the secret, proud that she was like other women—like her sister-in-law.

As she stood grinning foolishly at her reflection in a shop window, she felt somebody close behind her and the heavy material of a sleeve pressed against her and she heard someone else's quiet breath. In the window she saw herself reflected—her wide face and high cheeks, her purse hanging by the strap slung athletically across her jacket. At her shoulder she saw another woman, smaller, dressed in a high-waisted dress much like the one worn by Andrew Jackson's

99

niece in a portrait she remembered from one of her old books. The woman's sad gaze held hers unwaveringly. Dorothy heard another troubled sigh but when she pulled her eyes from the reflection and turned around there wasn't anybody standing with her. She was startled and looked up and down the street. There was no sign of the woman. She rubbed her forearm, remembering the feel of the wool, the faint scent of lemon. She looked again into the window and saw herself standing alone.

When she got home she telephoned Henry again, but he still didn't answer.

She made a peanut butter and jelly sandwich, poured a glass of skimmed milk and turned on the television. She put the plate on her lap as she lifted the receiver, dialed Henry's number again and listened to it ring. Finally she hung up, went to the kitchen and opened a box of gingersnaps. Returning to the living room with it, she turned her attention to the television movie, a rerun of *Klute,* the story of a prostitute stalked by a killer. Dorothy had seen the movie many times but it never failed to engage her, especially the scary early part when the young woman was being watched but didn't know it, when the audience knew more about what was happening than she did, but couldn't warn her.

Donald Sutherland, the detective who fell in love with the heroine, reminded Dorothy of Henry. Henry had the same large quiet eyes, the same sandy hair, the same protective concern. Sutherland was taller and bigger, of course. A laconic Canadian. You felt he *liked* Jane Fonda, that he respected her, that there was a good chance for their relationship.

During the commercials Dorothy permitted herself to pretend that she and Henry had the same good chance for their relationship. Why not? They were already friends, and wasn't that the best place to start? With knowing one another and caring about each other? Perhaps the pregnancy would change her life in ways she hadn't expected.

She ate the cookies slowly out of the box and continued watching the movie. After an hour she'd telephoned Henry a dozen times. If only he'd been there when she first called. Her elation slowly subsided, leaving in its wake a buzz of apprehension.

After the eleven o'clock news she took a long shower, washed and dried her hair. She called him several more times but there was still no answer. Finally she went to bed.

The phone on her bedside table rang after she'd been asleep for an hour.

She picked it up clumsily and peered at the alarm clock. The figures glowed in the dark. It was nearly 2:00 A.M.

The voice was Henry's.

"Are you all right?" she said, hugely relieved to hear his voice.

"We have to find him," he said. "We have to get him to give us back that contract. We have to tear it up, Dorothy, we're in terrible trouble."

His voice was strangely muffled, the usually precise diction sloppy.

"Is something wrong with you?" she said. "Where are you?"

"In a saloon," he said. She heard people talking. Somebody laughed.

"How long have you been there?" she asked. "I was looking for you. I called and called."

"I've been here since eight this evening," he said. "I telephoned you when I got here but you weren't home yet."

He must have called while she was standing on the street corner calling him.

"So I waited for you here," he said. "I've had about fifty martinis."

That wasn't at all like Henry.

"I'm glad you're safe. I didn't know where you'd gone."

"But I'm not drunk," he said. "I can't get drunk."

He certainly sounded drunk.

"Why do you want to get drunk?" she said. "You never drink."

"I found out who he is," he said.

"Who?"

"Elmo Shaw," he said. "Oh, god, Dorothy, it's worse than I thought."

101

"Calm down," she said. She heard him blow his nose.

"I think he killed Irene and her husband," he said. "Just to get them out of the way."

She could hardly understand him. "What?"

"He wanted to deal with *you*, Dorothy. He didn't want anybody else interfering."

She tightened her pajamas around her throat. She'd thought the same thing until she'd pushed it from her mind.

"They were in the way and now they're dead," he said. "Now I'm in the way. I think he's going to kill me too." She heard him take a shuddering breath. "You're pregnant, aren't you?"

"Well, the doctor can't be sure," she said. "But yes. He thinks I am. I'm going to get one of those test things from the drugstore tomorrow and make sure, even before the doctor calls me back—"

"Oh, god," Henry interrupted. "I knew it. What'll we do?"

"Henry, what's the matter?"

"I found out who Mr. Shaw is, Dorothy, I found one of the manuscripts I was looking for. I knew I'd seen it years ago, and I found it." His voice trailed off, she heard him mumbling.

"What manuscript?" she said. "What are you talking about?"

"I hid it," he said, suddenly sly. Then she heard a thump, as if he'd hit the telephone. "Oh, Dorothy," he cried. "I'm so frightened."

"Henry, I want you to come over here, right now. Leave that saloon."

"No way," he said. "I'm not leaving here until it's light. I'm not going out in the dark. Not with him out there someplace."

"Don't be silly," she said firmly. "You'll be a lot safer here than in some terrible barroom. I can make you some nice hot coffee—"

"You're not my mother, Dorothy," he said, and she could see him straightening and scowling at her. "And I don't want to get sober, I want to get drunk." He made a bleating sound. "But I'll come over as soon as it's light. We can plan what to do."

102

There was a series of loud clicks on the line. "Deposit twenty-five cents, please," a recorded voice directed him. "Or else your call will be interrupted."

"Oh, god," he said.

"What's the number there?" Dorothy asked. "I can call you right back."

"I don't have any change," he said. "I've spent my last quarter."

"The number, Henry, tell me the number."

"Damn telephone."

The line went dead.

She replaced the receiver and waited for him to call her back. Surely someone at the bar would give him a quarter. She heard the clock ticking. A minute passed. Another thirty seconds. Two minutes. Three.

He didn't call back.

He wasn't going to.

But it was all right, he'd said he'd come over first thing in the morning.

She crawled back into bed, lay on her side and pressed her palms tightly together between her thighs.

He'd be safe. There was nothing to worry about.

Chapter Fifteen

When she awoke she lay on her stomach, shivering. During her restless sleep the comforter had fallen to the floor and her arms and back were icy. Rain poured through the open window and formed rippling puddles on the rug. She twisted herself upright, put her feet on the floor, picked up the phone and dialed Henry's number. By this time she knew it by heart.

He didn't answer.

He'd said he'd come over as soon as it was light but she dialed the library just to make sure he hadn't gone there instead. He didn't answer there either.

He'd be here any minute now.

She slammed the window shut, dressed, went to the kitchen and made coffee and toast. She filled the creamer with half-and-half for Henry, and set it out briskly next to the sugar bowl.

The radio announcer predicted a cold rainy day. She took her umbrella from the closet and leaned it by the front door along with her rubber boots. Hands on hips, she peered out the window. The morning was dark and raw, one of those awful April days, more like February, when spring couldn't seem to get a foothold and reverted to winter.

He'd be embarrassed about being drunk. She'd tell him it didn't bother her at all.

She sat on the sofa with her library book but she turned the pages blindly, unable to concentrate. The minute hand on the mantel clock inched along. Finally she went and picked up the clock, shook it vigorously and replaced it, centering it carefully. She looked toward the door.

He wasn't coming.

She pulled on her boots, donned her raincoat and plastic bonnet, locked the door and set forth. She'd meet him at the library, he'd be sure to show up there sooner or later, he was a creature of habit, as she was. He probably couldn't even remember he'd told her that he had intended to come to her apartment this morning. Sometimes you forgot what you said when you had had too much to drink.

She mustn't worry. Nothing had happened to him.

There was a newsstand on the sidewalk in front of the subway entrance. As she approached she saw a cluster of agitated people huddled around it talking to one another. "It happened right up this street," one of them said, squinting against the rain.

"It was terrible," said another.

"Did you see?" somebody asked the newsstand operator.

He shook his head. "Naw, it was early this morning. I wasn't here yet."

Dorothy approached them. "What are you talking about?" she asked.

A man in a yellow slicker streaming water indicated the front page of the *Daily News*. The stack of newspapers was protected by the corrugated overhang of the tin roof. The huge headline read: "MAN EATEN BY DOGS."

"What happened?" Dorothy said, squeezing the handle of her umbrella with both hands, looking first into one face and then another.

The man in the slicker looked down at her. "This guy was coming out of a bar early this morning, around two A.M.— Casey's right up the block—" he pointed to a shuttered entrance with a faded shamrock painted over the door. "Out of nowhere there was this pack of dogs—"

"Yeah," somebody else said. "A pack of wild dogs. Can you believe it?"

Everybody was looking at Dorothy, watching her reaction. "What happened then?" she said.

"They chased him up the street."

"They say he was drunk. Staggering. Couldn't run."

105

"He was a goner."

"Makes you want to swear off the booze."

A chuckle. "Says who?"

"He didn't have a chance."

"A pack of wild dogs?"

"Can you beat it?"

"What direction was he running?"

"North," one of them said. "He came out of Casey's heading north."

Toward my house.

"Are you all right, lady?"

"What happened to the dogs?" She yanked her arm away as several hands reached consolingly toward her.

The newsstand operator shrugged. "Nobody knows," he said. "Can you beat it? They ran off. A pack of wild dogs and nobody knows where they came from or what happened to them."

"Spooky."

"Does anybody know who he was?" she asked.

"No, the paper says the bartender didn't know him. Said he sat in the corner all night."

"Drinking martinis," said the man in the slicker.

Dorothy moaned. "Where—where is his body?" she said.

"City morgue, I guess," he said. "Wherever people like that end up."

"Not much left of him. Poor slob."

"Hamburger."

"Dog meat," somebody said, laughing nervously.

Dorothy waited numbly under the drooping awning of Casey's Bar and Grill until, around ten, a man in a hooded macintosh appeared, pushed up the latticed gate and unlocked the front door. She followed him inside. Shaking her umbrella and frowning into the dusky light she saw a wooden bar with a brass foot-rail along one side of the long room. A row of back-to-back booths, some with sprung seats, others patched with silver duct tape, stood against the wall facing the bar. Behind the bar hung a splattered mirror stuck with a number of yellowed photographs of Korean War pinup girls, several curling postcards from places with palm trees. Bottles of alcoholic beverages were displayed in graduated rows in front of the mirror. The stale, smoky odor made Dorothy want to cover her face, but she did not.

In the shadows at the rear of the room she saw a public telephone next to a door marked "Men." She turned from it feeling tears constricting her throat. Henry had called her from that phone.

"Excuse me," she said to the bartender, after he'd hung up his dripping coat. He was a heavy man in a checked shirt who stood on the other side of the bar resting his palms on its polished surface.

"Yes, m'am?" Despite his deferential words, he looked her over boldly.

"I'd like to ask you about what happened this morning," she said.

"Are you a reporter?" he said, sighing.

"No."

"Police?"

"No."

"Well, whoever you are, I don't know anything about it. I wasn't on duty." He moved away, opened the cash register, cracked a roll of nickels violently against the edge of the counter, dumped them into the drawer.

"How can I find out what happened?" she asked.

"Read the papers, same as me," he said.

"Who was on duty last night? I'd like to talk to him."

"Look, Missy," he said, approaching her and leaning his heavy arms on the bar, "the less you know about what happened, the better. Believe me."

"I must find out."

"I wouldn't want to if I was you."

"What's the name of the bartender who was on duty last night? Will he be in later?"

He shrugged. "He won't be talking to anybody," he said. "He's taking the rest of the week off. You would too, if you'd seen what he seen." He leaned toward her again, his voice taking on an unpleasant intimacy. "You really don't want to find out the details, sweetheart."

"You don't understand," she said. "I have to know what happened."

He moved away, dusting the bar with what looked like the remains of a dirty undershirt. "Go back to your knitting, little lady," he said. "This isn't any place for you."

Suddenly she was very angry. "Do you know the name of the police officer who's handling the investigation?" she asked, her voice trembling.

"No."

She concentrated on keeping her gaze level. She didn't want to cry, not in front of this person. "Well, what precinct are we in?" she said. "Surely you know *that.*"

He frowned, a flicker of curiosity momentarily clouding his close-set eyes. "Did you know the guy?"

"Yes," she snapped.

"Sorry," he said. "I assumed you were one of those blood-thirsty ditzes that gets off on blood and guts."

"You assumed wrong," she said. "I want information." She paused. "I'm not a *ditz* and I'm not your *little lady,"* she added firmly.

He bowed, but instead of conveying apology or concern, the gesture was insolent. "My mistake," he said. "Don't get on your high horse, I'm only trying to protect you from getting involved."

"I suppose I can decide whether I want to get involved," she said.

He clucked his tongue and winked. "Feisty little thing, aren't we?"

She turned abruptly toward the door.

"Wait a minute, don't take offense, I was only having a little fun with you," he said.

It was enlightening what he called *fun,* she thought furiously, squeezing her hands in her pockets to prevent herself from yelling.

"We're in the twentieth precinct," he said. "Headquarters on 82nd between Amsterdam and Columbus." When she turned back toward him he wet his lips and gazed frankly at her chest. "Can I get you a drink? A beer or a glass of sherry? On the house. You look pretty pasty." His cold eyes met hers. He didn't care about her or what she was feeling. He wanted her to break down so he could continue to feel superior. "A nice lady like you shouldn't get involved in this. You'd be surprised at the newshounds who came around last night, poking and prying. They wanted to take pictures of the corpse. When his own mother wouldn't have recognized him, he was that chewed up." He paused again, studying her reaction. "Makes you wonder about human nature. I mean, they should've left him alone, nobody should have the right to take a picture of what was left of that poor man." He lowered his voice and spoke with emphasis, so she wouldn't miss a word. "Why, his head was hanging by a thread," he whispered. "The dogs ate out his throat. And the blood, all over everything, oozing out. The tendons and the human gristle that was sticking out. Christ."

She clenched her jaw, fought back a wave of nausea. "I thought you weren't here last night," she said in a small, steady voice. "I thought you didn't see anything."

He stepped back and held up his hands, surrendering. "You got my last word on it, lady. I'm not going to say anything else."

Keeping her head high, she turned and strode from the saloon. After hurrying south on the rainy sidewalk for about a block her hands went to her mouth and she staggered, caught herself with an elbow against the side of a building and vomited onto the pavement.

Taking her handkerchief from her pocketbook, she wiped her face and began walking again. Her pace quickened and she began running.

Chapter Sixteen

When she reached police headquarters Dorothy pushed past tall doors under a granite archway reading "Twentieth Precinct" in art deco flourishes. In the reception area she approached a policewoman behind a glass window above an aluminum barrier.

"Excuse me, officer," Dorothy said. "I'd like to find out about what happened last night." She hesitated, her stomach churning. "When that man was—chased—killed by—dogs."

"We're not giving out any information on that," the officer said crisply, examining the papers in her hand.

"I think you should want to talk to me."

The officer raised her eyebrows. "Oh?" she said, looking up for the first time. Dorothy read *you wouldn't believe the nuts we get* clearly in her eyes. But she persisted. "I think I was the last person the—the victim spoke to. On the telephone." She cleared her throat in an effort to steady herself. This couldn't be happening. "I can identify him."

The policewoman looked at her sharply. "Wait here," she said, gesturing toward a golden oak chair padded with a thick plastic cushion. Dorothy sat stiffly and watched her disappear through a door behind the reception area. After a few moments the officer returned and beckoned, opening the gate in the dented fence separating the waiting area from the police desks. Dorothy followed her down a hallway with rooms opening off both sides, into a small office where a man in shirtsleeves and an empty shoulder holster sat behind an untidy desk. He was talking on the phone but as she

110

entered he looked up and pointed to a chair next to his desk. Dorothy sat in it, placing her purse on her lap and gripping it. The policewoman left.

There were no windows. Illumination came from several florescent lights suspended from the water-damaged ceiling. Two of the tubes flickered, another didn't work at all. Hanging on the wall was a huge precinct map with hundreds of tiny red and blue lines squiggling and intersecting like varicose veins. It was the sort of quasi-historical item that ended up in the Literary Library. In thirty or so years, despite its being hopelessly outdated, somebody would claim that such a chart was of possible (though unlikely) interest to city historians. So one day it would arrive without warning at the library. Sitting beside the detective, half listening to his terse conversation, Dorothy imagined herself, a little old woman with wild white hair and a faded smock, protesting in helpless dismay that there was no more room in the stacks for nonliterary material. But nobody would pay her the slightest attention. She would have no ally.

Henry was dead.

The man she'd loved without even knowing it.

"I'm Detective Lieutenant Sam Canaday," the police officer told her, interrupting her reverie, hanging up at last and rising slightly, then falling back again into his chair. His stomach sagged in a relaxed way over his belt. "What can I do for you?"

She studied her knuckles, collecting herself. She must concentrate. There was nobody left on her side. From now on she must take care of herself.

She told the detective quietly that she was the last person to talk to the man killed outside Casey's Bar and Grill.

He tilted his head skeptically. "Our information is the bartender was the last person he talked to."

"Oh," she said. Of course. "What I mean is that he called me from the public telephone there."

"Around what time?"

"Nearly two A.M."

"Why do you think that's important?" he said.

Dorothy noted the midwestern twang in his accent.

111

(Chicago? *City of the big shoulders.* Nelson Algren and Theodore Dreiser.) His blue eyes were direct and sensible as they stared into hers. His jaw was square, no nonsense—Dick Tracy—and his large nose had long, aristocratic nostrils.

She hesitated, considering her answer carefully.

As he waited for her response he glanced at his watch, brought the spectacles resting on his forehead into place and looked from her to a document on his desk. He signed the letter and put it in a stack of others, then looked at her again over the tops of his half-glasses, giving himself a grandfatherly air.

"I'm not sure," she said finally, realizing that the police didn't necessarily care who Henry had telephoned from the saloon. As far as they knew, he was the victim of a bizarre incident involving wild dogs. They didn't know that what had happened to Henry was somehow related to what had happened to Marcus and Irene. They knew nothing about what had happened at the O'Hara Clinic. Now that Henry was dead she and Elmo Shaw were the only people who knew these things.

"You believe yourself to be personally acquainted with the victim?" Detective Canaday said.

"His name was Henry Small."

He looked at her with new interest.

"Is there some reason for you to believe this?" he asked. "His name wasn't released to the press." He pulled at one of his ears. "You're Ms.—?"

"Kite. My name is Dorothy Kite," she said, and hesitated, thinking hard. "He told me where he was. Casey's Bar and Grill," she lied. Then she added, "I can identify his body."

The detective removed a cigarette from a crumpled pack of Camels, tapped it against the desk and began searching through the clutter for matches. "Well," he said, "you're right, that's our tentative identification." After a minute he gave up the search and stuck the cigarette behind his ear. "Are you next of kin?"

"No." She unclenched her hands from her purse. "We worked together. We were friends."

"Are you aware of any relatives he had living here in the city?"

"Not that I know of," Dorothy said. "He was a bachelor. He lived alone as long as I knew him."

Canaday sat back and gazed steadily at her. "We have to have identification before we can release the body for private burial. But if there's no family, maybe it's better if we don't formally identify him."

"Why not?"

He rubbed his wide mouth with the back of his hand. "Frankly, Ms. Kite, I don't think anybody who knew him should have to view the remains," he said. "I've been on the force for a lot of years and—believe me—I've seen a lot of gruesome things. But I've never seen anything like this." His Adam's apple rose and fell.

They stared at each other.

His phone rang and they both jumped. He leaned across the papers and picked up the receiver. "Hold my calls for the next five minutes," he said, then hung up without waiting for a reply. Pulling a handkerchief from a back pocket, he blew his nose noisily, stuffed back the handkerchief and looked at her again. "Were you special friends? Engaged to be married or something?"

"Not exactly," she said. (Would they have gotten married? Had that been a possibility?) "I owe it to him to see he's buried properly." She owed him more than she could ever repay. "Did he have anything else with him?" she asked suddenly. He'd found something at the library, that's what his frantic call had been about, he'd found out who Elmo Shaw was, and the information had terrified him. She had to learn what he'd found. It was her only chance.

"Like what?"

"I don't know," she said, frowning. "Papers. A manila envelope." Maybe he'd brought whatever it was with him to the bar.

Canaday crossed his arms and looked thoughtfully at his phone. "There was nothing on him except his wallet." His eyes moved back to hers.

"Oh," she said, disappointed. He must have hidden

113

whatever it was at the library, then left.

There was a long pause as she collected herself. "Please tell me exactly what happened to him."

He had to lean forward to hear her. "Perhaps we should start with what you know, Ms. Kite."

"I don't know anything except what was in the newspaper," she said. "I didn't see what happened, that's why I'm here, to find out from you."

"I see." He pushed through some papers, found the report he was looking for. "Apparently he—Mr. Small—spent the evening getting pretty well tanked at Casey's." He scanned both sides of the document. "He came in between eight and eight-thirty," he said. "And he sat at the bar not talking to anybody. He wasn't a regular, the bartender didn't know him. There was a ball game on television, but he didn't take any interest in that—"

"No," she said softly. "He wouldn't."

"Around two A.M. he went to the phone and made a call," he said.

"To me."

"Apparently," he said, making a note. "Shortly after that," he continued, "the bartender began locking up. He told him he had to go. Your friend resisted. Strenuously. The bartender practically had to throw him out."

Dorothy remembered the bartender. A man like that would have had no sympathy for a nonmacho man like Henry.

He hadn't even given him a quarter for the phone.

"He paid for his drinks," Canaday said. "He didn't tip the barman, called him—cussed him out. He was pretty drunk."

Good for him.

He glanced up. "Yes?" he said.

She folded her hands on top of her purse. "What happened then?"

"It's not clear. Within a second or two after he left there was this commotion outside—" He began reading. "This horrendous noise, like in a zoo or something, snarling and barking. Shouts." He looked up. "The barman and another patron rushed outside and they saw a pack of dogs, maybe twenty of them—"

114

"Twenty?"

He nodded. "He swears there were that many. I find it hard to believe too."

"Where did they come from?"

"God knows."

They collected outside the bar, Dorothy thought, one by one, waiting for Henry to emerge, like the birds in the schoolyard in that Hitchcock movie. The way they'd waited for her at the bus stop a month ago. But the pack was bigger than it had been. And more dangerous. They were killers now.

The detective's manner remained businesslike. "By the time the bartender and the other guy came out of the bar," he continued, "your friend was staggering up the sidewalk, in the thick of the pack. The bartender says the dogs were black, huge. As big as Great Danes. Bigger. Your friend tried—" he paused, looked at her from under his eyebrows, instinctively censoring the brutality of the story. "He tried to get away from them, the way you would. But there were too many."

She saw him hesitate and immediately insisted he tell her everything. "I can stand it," she said.

"He was trying to climb a wall," he said, quickly selecting the information he'd give her. "He jumped onto a window ledge, then grabbed above it to pull himself up. The bartender said it was as if he were trying to climb up the side of the building and for a minute it looked like he might make it. But he couldn't do it. He was too drunk to get a grip and the dogs were leaping up after him, tearing at him, he couldn't hold on, there were too many of them, he was cornered. When he fell among them they grabbed him and started running again." He removed his glasses, rubbed them with a corner of his shirt. "We figure he was in shock by then. Unconscious." He decided against reading the part in the report describing the dogs running along, tossing the man back and forth in the air as if he were a rag doll. He didn't want to tell her about the horrible screams the bartender said he'd never forget. Her face was pale and he could see she was trying hard to be brave. She seemed so . . . protected. He didn't want to make it worse for her. He cleared his throat.

"By this time there was a crowd of five or six people running after the dogs," he read. "They were yelling and throwing things. Somebody grabbed the lids off a couple of garbage cans and crashed them together like cymbals to scare them off with the noise." He glanced up and frowned. "Do you want a glass of water?"

She shook her head. "No," she said. "Go on."

He continued. "Nothing helped. Finally the victim was lying on the pavement and the dogs were crowded around. Nobody could get near until one of our units arrived. The officers began shooting and the dogs ran off." He adjusted his glasses. "But it was too late by then."

"Were any of the dogs killed?" She heard her voice, hollow, reverberating, as if spoken from a distance by somebody else.

"No," he said. "The officers said they might have wounded a couple of the animals, but they all escaped, every one."

"Where did they go?"

"Nobody knows," he said. "It's the damnedest thing. They didn't go after anybody else, the way you'd expect. Wild animals. They came out of nowhere, attacked, then disappeared. It's almost as if they dispersed so as not to be identified, the way humans might have done." He fingered another cigarette, put it unlit into his mouth, removed it and examined it, then stuck it impatiently behind his other ear. "The gunshots must have frightened them, made them scatter," he said. "That's the only thing I can think of. Once they stopped running together we couldn't recognize them as a pack." He glanced toward the door. "A woman we picked up earlier—pretty badly battered—swore she'd been trampled by a pack of dogs, but we figured she was covering up for her pimp." He pulled his ear again. "And we do have a problem with strays in the warmer weather."

"Oh, Lieutenant Canaday, this isn't a problem with strays," she cried. "You don't really think that."

He shrugged. "Ms. Kite, I don't know what to think."

"And it isn't warm outside, it's cold and rainy," she said. They looked at one another.

"Where do I go to identify Henry?" she asked finally.

"Downtown. The city morgue. But if you want to take

116

charge of the funeral arrangements, let me see if I can get somebody to release the remains to you without your having to look. We do that sometimes, under extraordinary circumstances. I don't believe you should have to go through the ordeal of an identification."

She stiffened. "I have to see what happened to him," she said.

"Isn't there anybody else who can do it?"

"No," she said.

He gazed at her thoughtfully, then at his watch. "Look," he said. "It's almost lunchtime. I'll take you, we'll ride down in a squad car. I don't think you should do this by yourself."

"I can manage."

"Afterward you may not be in any shape to get home on your own."

He removed a revolver from the top desk drawer and slid it into his holster, donned the suit jacket from the back of his chair. Despite his size he swung easily down the hall in front of her.

They left the building through a back entrance leading to a parking lot. Under a drooping tree next to a tow truck he opened a car door and helped her into the front seat. Rain splashed noisily onto the macadam.

Turning to look out the back window and stretching one arm across the back of the slippery seats, he spun the steering wheel expertly and backed the car into the street. Once on their way he bent forward to switch on the dashboard heater. "It'll warm up in a minute," he said.

They drove silently. Dorothy stared ahead in anguish. Why hadn't she made Henry go with her to the doctor's? If he'd accompanied her he'd have been safe. Or she could have arranged to meet him somewhere afterward. Then he wouldn't have gone to a bar to wait for her. Why had she *walked* home, making herself unreachable for all those precious minutes? She'd known something was wrong. There'd been nothing normal about Mr. Shaw or what had happened, why had she been so busy acting as if Henry were crazy? He'd known. She'd known too but she hadn't wanted to face it. She'd wanted to become pregnant more than anything else. She'd never even told him about the dogs. *She*

117

should have warned him about the dogs. Her obsession had caused his death. She'd as good as murdered him.

She looked back at Sam Canaday. "Did the other patron in the bar given a statement too?"

"No," he said. "He didn't stick around."

She watched the windshield wipers flicking back and forth. A frightening idea hovered on the edge of her consciousness. "Did anybody get his name?"

"No," he said, looking over at her. "Why?"

"Was there a description of him?"

Sam Canaday squinted at the windshield. He was becoming increasingly uncomfortable with her sitting next to him. His wife had been dead for several years and it had been a long time since he'd been aware of a woman's body warmth. It made his mouth dry with desire. "The bartender said he was an old guy," he said crisply. "Came in late, all bundled up, sat in a booth at the back nursing a beer for a couple of hours. Kept his muffler around his face. The bartender couldn't get a good look at him but he was pretty sure he didn't know him either." He stepped on the gas and swung the car around a corner as the light changed. "He said he had a world-class case of B.O.," he added.

Dorothy closed her eyes. She knew who he was. If Henry had seen him he might have been able to protect himself. But he hadn't wanted to see. He'd tried to erase what was happening. So he got drunk and destroyed any chance he might have had.

Why hadn't she been there?

The shortwave radio began crackling. Traces of voices struggled through the powerful static. He reached to switch it off, then looked at her sharply. "Are you okay?" he said.

She wiped her eyes with a tissue she took from her purse. "He must have been so frightened," she whispered.

For several minutes the only sound was the clacking of the windshield wipers.

As they rode along she studied his hands on the wheel, the blond hairs and freckles, the blunt fingers. She swallowed, sick with shame. She concentrated on making her mind blank.

"You live by yourself?" he said.

118

She nodded.

"Me too," he said. "My wife died five years ago."

"I'm sorry," she said, turning her face to the window and staring out.

"I miss her," he said.

She nodded again. He meant his wife.

They rode without speaking. Blood pounded in her ears, so loud and insistent she felt sure he must hear it too. She fiddled with the clasp on her pocketbook, clicked it open, rummaged among the papers inside, snapped it shut. She took another deep breath and concentrated on exhaling slowly.

After several minutes he turned the car into an alley behind a sprawling series of gray municipal buildings. He gripped the wheel as they skidded across a wet patch of broken pavement, then slowed and pulled into a small area next to a loading dock. A large van idled next to them. Two men in soaked leather jackets and woolen caps were pulling a heavy plastic bag from the platform through the double doors of the building entrance.

"It's a body bag," Sam explained. "They're making a delivery. Are you sure you want to do this?" He unbuckled his seatbelt. She drew her gaze from the tight place where his shirt met his trousers and looked up to meet his kind eyes. "Nobody's going to think worse of you if you change your mind and decide not to identify him," he said. "I certainly won't and I guess I'm the only one who'll know."

She opened the door on her side and got out. "You don't understand," she said. "I have to do it, I have no choice."

He frowned. "It's like a penance," he said thoughtfully.

She looked away. "Yes."

He took her hand and helped her up to the dock. Shouldering aside a man who leaned against the building with his hands in pockets, Sam said, "Make way for the living, for Chrissake."

A burst garbage bag spewed across their path, its torn side exploding pieces of rotten grapefruit, several half-eaten rolls, handfuls of greasy paper toweling, a squashed milk carton, cottage cheese and yogurt containers. Several small plastic boxes filled with decaying remnants of salad spilled onto the pavement.

"Rats," he commented, kicking at the tear in the sack. "Get this into another bag," he directed the loiterer. "It's disgusting." Still glaring, he guided Dorothy through the doorway. They entered the building, turned and immediately descended a staircase, then pushed past an unmarked door which opened onto another set of stairs leading down to a brightly lit corridor with a single door at one end. He pulled open the door, stepped back and allowed her to precede him into the room.

The man sitting at a large oak table in front of a wall of filing cabinets rose and came forward. He greeted Sam, who named him to Dorothy. "This is George Hall," he said.

She found she couldn't speak.

"She's here to identify the victim of the dog attack this morning," Sam said.

Hall frowned. "Somebody already did that," he said.

Sam looked quizzically at Dorothy, then back at Hall. "What's that?" he said.

"We released the body to some guy this morning."

Sam brushed back his hat irritably. "When?"

"Early. Before I got in. An hour or so after they brought in the body. The night man had hardly finished the paper work," George Hall said. "The guy had a hearse."

Sam raised his eyebrows at Dorothy. "I thought you said there wasn't anybody else to identify him."

"But there isn't," she said, turning back to George Hall. "Are you sure?"

He shrugged. "Sure I'm sure," he said. An insinuating grin spread across his face. "I was disappointed. I didn't get to see anything. I hear it was really something."

Sam moved forward quickly to shield her. "Shut up, George," he said. "This is a friend of the deceased."

Hall blinked stupidly. "Sorry."

"Who was it?" she said. "Who took the body?"

Hall turned to an outbasket on the table, pulled off the top sheet and handed it to Sam. "See for yourself," he said.

The detective scanned the form. "Shaw," he said. "Somebody named Elmo Shaw."

"Let me see that," she said, reaching for the paper.

It was as he said. There was Mr. Shaw's signature in black ink, as clear and distinctive as she remembered on the contract in which she had agreed to give him her baby.

She grunted, as if kicked, and rocked on her heels.

"Are you all right?" Sam said, putting his arm protectively around her. Hall grabbed the paper as it fluttered to the floor.

"I have to get out of here," she said, her eyes rolling wildly, as if she were an animal in a trap. She pulled away from Sam and lunged for the exit.

"Wait," he said, hurrying after her.

She must get to the library. Henry had hidden whatever he'd found there. She must find it.

What had he known?

Chapter Seventeen

In the car again Dorothy asked Sam to drive her to the library on his way uptown.

Henry had made his discovery there. In that collection of unwanted and forgotten documents, he'd found something crucial. He hadn't had time to take the information anywhere else. He'd gone straight from the library to the saloon. He'd said so.

Whatever he'd found was still at the library.

She stared into the rain and tightly enclosed her thumbs within her fists.

Sam didn't seem to notice her turmoil. He drove casually, his large hands resting lightly at the base of the wheel. "It's none of my business," he said sympathetically. "But whatever work you have can wait until you're on your feet. Believe me. I've seen what happens to people when the shock wears off."

She didn't answer him.

After several minutes of driving he leaned forward to wipe the fogged windshield with his handkerchief. "I can't help thinking there's more to this than meets the eye," he said, probing gently. "Your friend's death seems staged somehow. Like an execution." He stretched to stuff the handkerchief into his pants pocket and glanced keenly at her, then returned his gaze to the road ahead. His face remained carefully blank. "I'd lay odds you know what I mean," he added. "And I don't even know what I'm trying to find out or what questions I should ask."

She pressed her knees together. "What?" she said.

"Never mind," he said, flexing his hand and placing it at twelve o'clock on the wheel. "For the time being let's just say it was a one-of-a-kind attack by wild dogs. In New York City in 1990. Mysterious but accidental."

He halted the car in front of the library. "I'd like to stay in touch anyway," he said, clearing his throat. "Nothing personal."

She twisted to tug at the door handle, then drew back to avoid his arm as he leaned across her to snap up the lock. He smiled at her with his face inches from hers, then withdrew abruptly, still grinning sheepishly. She got out of the car. "I'm lying," he said, stretching across the seat to look up at her as she stood on the sidewalk. "It *is* personal. I'd like to take you to lunch sometime. Or dinner. If it's all right with you," he added. "No strings."

She tried to nod politely, remembering her manners as if it mattered. "That would be nice," she mumbled. Using both hands she pushed the door shut, then stood back. After a moment the blue and white automobile moved off smoothly into the rain. As the back lights disappeared, she turned and hurried into the library.

When she entered and switched on the office light she found chaos. An ankle-deep morass of papers surrounded Henry's desk, overflowed the wastebasket, stretched from one wall to the other. Ancient barrels and crates had been wrenched open and upended, their contents strewn haphazardly. A dozen card catalogue drawers from a long unused cabinet were thrown upside down and sideways against the wall. Hundreds of the faded cards had been ripped out and scattered.

Henry had spent his last hours here in a frenzy.

The smell of mildew lay heavily in the air. She cupped her hands across her mouth and looked around. Whatever he'd found he'd hidden here in a place nobody would think to look, even her.

He'd planned to come back for it himself.

The panic swelled again. With a moan she pushed it back, made her way across the room to hang her coat in the closet. She must control herself. She had to empty her mind in order to concentrate on the steps she must take to protect herself.

She tried to think as Henry would have thought. She

heard him muttering to himself as he threw things around. She imagined his impatience, the obsessed light in his eyes.

But once he'd found what he was looking for he'd have been cunning, no matter how frightened he'd been. He'd have located a good hiding place.

She stopped behind her desk. Stuck in her blotter was a sheet torn from a yellow pad. Her chest tightened as she read Henry's handwriting: "Dorothy—check out one of the 7 sisters. Historian? Geneticist?" She turned the paper over but nothing more was written on it. What had he meant? She folded it carefully into eighths and replaced it in her blotter. She'd look into whatever it meant later. There must be a connection.

She opened a desk drawer, looked blindly inside, closed it and went to the closet, tiptoed to see onto the shelf. She bent to run her hand along the bottom of his desk, then her own, thinking he might have taped something out of sight. She pulled out the framed graph on the wall behind her desk and peered under it. Then she rolled down the window blinds, releasing a cloud of grime that floated benignly into the air. She sputtered and turned away. After she probed cautiously along the wall behind the filing cabinets, she shoved her chair on its casters across the papers on the floor, kicked off her shoes and climbed to examine the inside of the light fixture, as Ray Millard had done in *The Lost Weekend*.

Nothing.

She stood unsteadily on the chair and looked around the room. Where could he have put it?

What was it?

She glanced uneasily toward the door leading to the stacks.

Perhaps he'd stashed it somewhere in there.

She jumped from the chair and raced into the warehouse. As she ran along the familiar brick wall she punched the light switches and the huge room brightened weakly. It was jammed with rows of iron bookcases, each stuffed with books and documents, the towering structures forming a labyrinth of floor-to-ceiling pathways.

She'd always felt so safe in here.

She rubbed her arms to dispel the chill and scanned the shelves, wanting to find a category suggesting fertility or longevity, maybe something about the conception of twins, even papers on enchanted animals—"the hounds of hell"— or scientific experiments having to do with artificial insemination. Her imagination raced. Identifying possible classifications challenged her all-encompassing knowledge of the Dewey decimal system, even her familiarity with the musty collection here.

If only she had some idea of what Henry had found. . . . But how would Elmo Shaw be categorized? What part of him had been catalogued here?

If only she had an idea of what she was looking for! Henry had remembered something from long ago, but she had no such memory. She needed to be lucky.

She didn't feel lucky. She was dizzy with dread and fear.

At a shelf near the rear of the gigantic room she paused, rubbed her handkerchief across the backs of the books so she could read the titles. Here was a thick volume in blue binding stamped "Cyril Siebert/Among the Pygmies" in faded gold lettering. Stuffed next to it a squashed cardboard container was tied with rotting string. A sprinkling of dust stood undisturbed along the edge of the shelf. She recognized her own neat printing across the boxtop: "The Life of Missionary Muriel Stacey/Saintly Sinner/In Her Own Words." But there was nothing in Anthropology under *S* written by or about anybody named Shaw.

Medicine?

She looked hurriedly into several volumes and folders in that section but found nothing.

She moved into the section on the occult, carefully scanned the area to see if anything was out of place, if there were telltale evidence of disturbance, footprints or other signs of recent activity. Then it occurred to her that if Henry had found what he was looking for in the stacks, he'd have hidden it elsewhere. He'd never have replaced it where he'd found it. (He *said* he'd hidden it.) But there was no indication here that anything had been moved or even touched. Dust lay everywhere, inviolate as fresh snow. The petrified army of bookcases marched silently into the dark, the deep silence following, undisturbed and patient, like death.

If Henry had found something on one of these shelves, he'd have had to float in and out. The only footprints she saw were hers.

With a final desperate look around, she turned off the lights and returned to the office, where it was warmer and brighter.

She pushed away a stack of crumpled folders from her chair and sat numbly. With her elbow on the chair's arm and her clenched jaw in her palm, she stared at Henry's desk opposite hers. For nearly twenty years she'd looked across at him like this. How well did she know him? Could she predict where he'd hide something? Deliberately, she pictured him again: A tall, neat man dressed in dark slacks and a blue sweater vest, standing in the middle of the room clutching something against his chest, wondering where to hide it, in this mess. He wanted to leave, to escape from something frightening him dreadfully.

She straightened.

In this mess.

One corner of his desk stood slightly higher than the others and the only thing preventing his blotter and calendar from sliding off was the back of his chair which had been hurriedly tilted against the drawers on the left side.

Something was pinned under one of the legs. She leaned forward to look. The stiff corner of a bookkeeper's ledger was visible in the debris under the desk. Its marbled cover was discolored and mottled with age. Piles of paper were strewn everywhere around and on top of it, she was almost unable to see it.

But the ledger—and nothing else—was stuck *under* the leg.

He'd had to lift the heavy desk, position the notebook on the floor and replace the desk on top of it. The book was too thick to have slid underneath accidentally.

He'd hidden it in the middle of the mess, where nobody would think to look.

She jumped up and hefted the desk with one hand, kicked the ledger free and set the desk down again. Then she bent and picked up the notebook, returned to her own desk, clicked on the gooseneck lamp, sat and opened the old journal to its first page.

Chapter Eighteen

The date of the first entry was July 9, 1820.

"I do not know what prompts me to set down the story of my life," Dorothy read. "Nothing in it is suited for commemoration. One failure after another has been my fate. I have no money. I am forty years of age and respectable men scorn me. I am married to a woman without grace or prospect, an evil creature who tricked me into wedlock. My children represent nothing to me but her fertile womb; in fact I despise them. They require endless attention and have replaced me in her affection. Unless I toil from dawn to dark for the rest of my days I will end a starving pauper because of their constant need.

"She does not care. She is slovenly, ignorant, too good at breeding. She neglects her duty to me.

"I have not the money even to seek manly pleasures elsewhere."

Several brittle pages followed. Stains and discolorations ruined many of them. Dorothy examined the next legible entry, scratched in the same hasty, cramped handwriting and slanting down the page in uneven lines of thin black ink.

"Only bad luck marks and sets me apart," she read. "Others of ordinary gifts and preoccupations succeed and their successes fill me with despair. My destiny is inferior. Ignominious misfortune plagues me.

"None of this is my fault. From my earliest, most innocent days everyone has conspired against me.

"My father neglected and abused me, gifting my undeserving sister with showers of presents and affection. That he preferred her to me became clear even before I was able to read and do sums. I was made to sleep in the garret, alone and forgotten. No one came when I cried. The fire in the grate was never tended (a metaphor for my own pitiable existence). She, with the face of a horse, the disposition and requirements of an opera singer, the intelligence and personal hygiene of a fly—*she* was doted upon by my father even as he beat and locked me away.

"My mother died before memory begins."

Dorothy turned the page. "There are two worlds," she read. "There is the world of squalor and meanness, where I reside without ability to meet my most basic requirements. In this hell I am imprisoned with a bad-smelling population of barely human scum who snatch crumbs from each other, chatter and scurry like rats, who sleep in ordure and constantly wheedle and complain."

Dorothy shivered and moved the lamp closer.

"But the other world!" she read. "In that enviable place exist velvet carriages, fine horses, magnificent buildings, fringed draperies, expensively appointed and ample apartments warmed by fires never permitted to go out. There men of no finer sensibilities than I—but far luckier—adorn themselves in fashionable clothing which they casually discard and replace every season. There life is celebrated without obsessive pandering to the whims of others. Each man is permitted to reflect quietly on life's abstract and intellectual aspects without the intrusion of women nattering ceaselessly about petty details. In this Paradise a man's every need and inclination is served instantly, without harrassment. Order prevails.

"O that I could inhabit that world of quiet opulence instead of this inferior one where the noise of disordered humanity bombards my ears with unending cacophony. To be let alone! To languidly taste and savor every pleasure, to be provided whatever I desire without thought of utility, to feel silk against my skin, to kick the ugly rabble from around my chair and breathe for once the free air!"

Dorothy turned the stiff page, scanned it, then the next, and the next, reading the story of a man who'd recorded his

128

bitter thoughts when James Monroe was president.

Another entry was dated in December of 1820.

"I am an apothecary," she read. "I wanted to become a physician. But there was no money for my use." The corner of the page was carefully (recently!) turned down, a flag from Henry. She read quickly, an anecdote about a little boy who died as a result of surgery the writer performed, apparently while drunk: "It was a bitingly cold night, there was no money for coal in the dismal hovel, it was necessary for me to fortify myself before undertaking the ordeal. None of the city's legitimate physicians would bother with this meager family who now say they can pay me only a few cents, spread over several months. 'Well, he died,' mewls the mother into her filthy apron, as if that has anything to do with my just recompense!

"No one else would have treated the child under such conditions. But the family are not grateful, they treat me as they would an ignorant peddler hawking kitchen pots."

On the next page: "My lack of financial success is entirely due to the inadequacies of my wife. She is slow-witted and altogether unsuitable, having long ago lost her looks and any ability at making pleasant conversation, a ladylike skill worldly patients require from the wives of their physicians and importantly governs their selection of same." His wife did nothing to curtail or discipline her ever-increasing number of offspring, whose names he never mentioned and whose births he did nothing to prevent.

Dorothy read with tense absorption. The circle of light from the desk lamp spilled weakly onto the ledger but the rest of the cluttered room was obscured in imperceptibly lengthening shadow. The quiet rustle as she turned the pages were the only sounds in the room.

She read a description of the meeting between the journal writer and a stranger—"a traveler"—in a tavern where the writer had gone to escape his wife's nagging. After several such late-night encounters, the writer's self-pitying tone changed to jubilation as he confided to his journal, "He says if I do as he instructs I will become a grand success. The wealthy infirm will flock to my door, battling each other for an hour's consultation with me, paying huge sums for the privilege. My home will be a mansion, my clothes will reflect the latest in taste and elegance, each day's costume cut fashionably and sewn from the most expensive fabrics. I will ride with rich men and talk as their equal about the new philosophies. Our conversations will address edifying concepts such as the errors of the compassionate (who give away our wealth to the unworthy), the modern idea recognizing greed as integral to progress and positing the control of inferiors as society's primary objective—weighty matters reflecting on the very purpose and vision of civilization. I have yearned to speak of such ideas but of course have no competent person with whom to discuss them, certainly not my wife. Her limited interests focus on the trivia of her children and their eternal need.

"The traveler promises for performance of a single task I will earn this reward.

"Can it be true?"

Dorothy turned the page.

"At the time of my wife's next confinement, within a few weeks' time, as I estimate," he wrote, "I am to take the newborn from her and give it to him. He promises the infant will have an enviable life."

She reacted with a start. Mr. Shaw had enticed her with the same oily phrase.

"It is a small price for me to pay for worldly success, which I so richly deserve," she read. "What prevents me from doing this? I will not miss the creature. There are so many others, all of them encumbrances, each with the same needy face. Who are they? I care not."

The next entry was dated January 1, 1821.

"I should have known she would do her best to betray and destroy me," he wrote. "The damned woman has bolted the bedroom door and refuses to let me enter or come near her and the new infant. She has closed and fastened the shutters, which prevents me from setting a ladder to the windows and entering the chamber even in that undignified way. Without my knowledge she has sent the other brats to her aunt's, a journey of three days by coach, and the oldest but twelve years of age! The packing off of these innocents, unprotected on a dangerous journey, demonstrates conclusively she is

130

cruel and uncaring, unfit for God-given proprietorship of guileless children. She deserves nothing less than having them taken from her.

"She did not permit me access to her during the delivery, insisted on going through the ordeal alone, in the locked bedroom, without even brandy to numb her senses, pigheaded creature. I could hear her horrible screams and was forced to numb my own senses with spirits so I could sleep peacefully, without having to listen to her caterwauling. Having no medical instruments to assist her in the diabolical undertaking, she bit through the umbilicus herself, like an animal. Disgusting. Now she claims from the other side of the door I plan to steal the new child from her. How can she know? I keep this journal from her, hidden in a cupboard to which only I have the key.

"She cannot read anyway. (Unless she has taught herself secretly, like a witch.) Her father wisely forbade her that dangerous frivolity, in the same way I have protected my own little daughters, preventing them from filling their heads with dangerous ideas. Their husbands will take care of them, as I have taken care of her, undeserving wretch though she be.

"She accuses me of having made a pact with the Devil. Such is the sentimental nonsense with which women fill their heads. The man with whom I have made this arrangement is a traveler whose clothes are worn and unmodish. Surely Satan would pay greater attention to his appearance!

"She will soon starve to death for she stupidly refuses food when I offer it, wildly calling this charity my 'ruse' to gain entry.

"I think she drinks her own urine.

"If only the infant survives until I can take it from her. I beat on the locked door but she cries out she would have them both die rather than release the child to me—*her lawful husband*. Has any other upright man suffered such castigation and rebellion? I rue the day I met her. I lie on my couch planning to rid myself of her. I will snatch the baby from her undeserving arms and leave her to die, the sniveling hysteric. She has many children, one more or less will not be marked, especially when its absence will win me untold

131

pleasures. Unworthy wife!

"I console myself that without food or water she cannot sustain herself."

The entry for the next day read: "And still she lives! She cares only for herself and does not see how selfishly she interferes with my glorious destiny."

With a rush of pity Dorothy read the entry describing the morning when at last his wife didn't answer the writer's threats and curses, when he could no longer hear her moans from behind the door, or the baby's faint cries. Then he stole an axe from a neighbor's shed and broke down the door. In the foul-smelling, airless room he found his wife on the floor beneath the shuttered window holding the baby tightly against herself. When he wrenched back her rigored arms he discovered the naked child was as dead as its mother.

"Ruined!" he scribbled.

He described stuffing both shriveled bodies into a burlap sack and dropping it off the end of a Hudson River pier in the middle of the night. In the days afterward nobody asked him what had happened to his wife or the children. He claimed to his journal that it was as if she'd never lived. "Her existence was abomination," he wrote. "She is lucky to be dead. Yet my grotesque life continues, an endless tragedy."

He didn't send for his children but instead moved his belongings to a room in another part of the city and left no forwarding address. "I am well rid of them," he wrote. "Let her aunt's husband be pulled by them into the stinking pit of drudgery. I am finished with them at last.

"But I was foolish to hope I would be spared. Even in death she has foiled my hopes. I hate her still.

"And sweet success within my grasp! Woe is me."

Several unreadable pages followed, then another entry in a bolder hand.

"Praise God, the stranger has reappeared—as if by magic—and says he will forgive me for defaulting on our bargain if I will but sign a paper in which I agree to secure other babes for him. As with our prior agreement his part of the arrangement will be to arrange a medical practice for me. My new specialty will center on the scientific treatment of infertile women. In this prestigious practice I will be advantageously situated to secure newborns since multiple births will occur as a result of my treatment. At the time of the mother's lying in I will carry away one of her issue in my satchel without anyone interfering. He guarantees the mothers will be so grateful for my therapy they will promise me anything in order to secure achievement of their desires, even their offspring—*if they are permitted to retain others.*"

The phrase brought Dorothy upright, frozen. Mr. Shaw must be directly related to the man who'd written the journal for her performed the same task with the same persuasive words. Smoothing and fastening her hair with trembling fingers, breathing deeply, she forced back the panic and began reading again.

"My mentor confides—unsurprisingly—he has no use for squalling infants. I am not to give him the child I have obtained until it reaches its majority. Unlike our former agreement, when I was to award him my wife's newborn, he now trusts me to keep the child with me until—in twenty-one years—he is ready to accept it for his purposes. I am proud he trusts me. He understands that my failure to produce an infant for him was entirely due to the rebellion of my unlamented wife and has nothing to do with my commitment to him.

"He assumes—correctly—I have no interest in children. So while I am to have responsibility for the child until he is ready to accept it, it will never be permitted to interfere with my life. During the two-decade interim he will provide inobtrusive, obedient caretakers who will carry out my orders and adhere strictly to my rigorous philosophy of child care. The child will not be spoiled, indulged or allowed to interrupt my pleasure, as in the recent and unmourned past. It will be sternly prepared for bondage to my benefactor. Then, after I have given over the grown child to him I will locate another child-hungry female and repeat the procedure. The steadiness and dependability of my employer's need insures my ongoing prosperity.

"He promises I can do with each child whatever I want short of murder until it is time to award it to him. An interesting prospect.

"He is a generous and perceptive man who understands

females and their curious yearning for children. While I have observed this phenomenon in my own wife, I cannot comprehend it. I am, however, grateful for the peculiar hunger because it will help me achieve my own more laudable and sophisticated objectives."

The rest of the journal contained several badly decomposed pages without another readable entry until the last page. There Dorothy found a carefully compiled list. She studied it carefully, noting the last dates with a sick tightening around her heart.

Jan. 1, 1822, Female twins. Emily Bellman, mother, d. Jan. 5, 1822

Jan. 1, 1843, Female twins. Lillian Butterworth, mother, d. January 5, 1843

Jan. 1, 1864, Male twins. Ruth Sloan, mother, d. Jan. 5, 1864

Jan. 1, 1885, Female twins. Marian Trask, mother, d. Jan. 5, 1885

Jan. 1, 1906, mother, d. Jan. 5, 1906
Jan. 1, 1927, mother, d. Jan. 5, 1927
Jan. 1, 1948, mother, d. Jan. 5, 1948
Jan. 1, 1969, mother, d. Jan. 5, 1969
Jan. 1, 1990, mother, d. Jan. 5, 1990

Numbly, she turned to the last leaf of the journal. Her eyes fell to the bottom of the page. There the journal writer had written a single sentence—"I grow stronger"—and under it inscribed the date he'd completed his journal—April 13, 1893.

His signature appeared below the date, gaudily flourished. It was the only place his name appeared in the document.

Dorothy's hands flew to her mouth and she screamed.

His name was Elmo Shaw.

Chapter Nineteen

In a single motion she raised herself from her chair and hurled the ledger against the wall. Its spine split with the impact and the broken notebook thudded in pieces to the floor.

Then she stood and leaned on her fists against the desktop. Her eyes darted from one corner of the room to the other.

Elmo Shaw was two hundred years old.

His power was magical.

This was the knowledge that had sent Henry flying, terrified, into the night.

She'd made a pact with the Devil.

That's who Mr. Shaw's "employer" was.

If she didn't do what Elmo Shaw wanted, his dogs would get her too. They knew where she was at this moment. So did he.

And even if she kept her side of the bargain and awarded one of her babies to him, she was going to die on January 5th anyway.

The telephone jangled on her desk. She jumped as if she'd heard a gunshot and stared at the instrument as it rang again.

With a quick defensive movement she picked up the receiver and put it cautiously against her ear. "Hello?" she whispered. "Who is it?"

It was Dr. Blanchard telling her she was pregnant.

Chapter Twenty

She snatched up the broken ledger, stacked the pieces clumsily and secured them with a grid of rubber bands. Then she shoved the untidy parcel into her shoulder bag and fumbled with the clasp until it snapped shut.

As she pulled on her coat she looked around warily at the overturned filing cabinets, the boxes spewing dusty folders and envelopes, at the jumble of barrels and file drawers, cards and musty manuscripts strewn everywhere. "I have to get out of here," she said, ducking her head and moving from the room, wanting to run away, to vanish, to live someone else's life in another place where she'd never heard of Elmo Shaw.

Once outside she found she couldn't run. Her legs jerked and wobbled as if they were connected by strings. Tears ran down her face and into her mouth. She wiped her cheeks with her palms as she tried to hurry.

When she arrived home she jerked her mother's vanity chair across to her closet, pushed it inside and climbed up to claw at the shoeboxes and aged pocketbooks on the top shelf. Behind the clutter, wedged into the corner, she found the big leather suitcase Madelyn had kept but never used. She tugged at it and finally it gave way with a loud scratching noise and thudded onto the floor. She clambered down and dragged the huge valise to her own room where she hoisted it onto the bed. Unbuckling the frayed straps, she threw it open, rushed to the dresser and back again as she dumped the contents of her drawers inside. She didn't know what she

136

was packing because she had no thought except escape.

She was going to Oregon to hide at Spark and Jeannie's.

Dr. Blanchard had told her her baby was due New Year's Day. If she stayed in New York she'd give birth, then die on January 5th, just like Mr. Shaw's earlier "patients"—every twenty-one years since 1822.

As if from a distance she watched her fingers cram the bag shut and rebuckle the straps. After a moment of indecision— terror made her forget what she was doing—she grasped the bag with newly frantic energy and lugged it, thudding and bumping, to the front door. She slumped against the wall as she retied her scarf, fastened her coat and then made her way with difficulty down the four flights of stairs.

Once outside she squeezed the fingers of both hands through the suitcase handle, hoisted it in front of herself, bending backward for balance. In this way she lurched to the corner, set the bag on the pavement, hailed a cab, opened its door, lifted the bag again with a grunt and pushed it inside. She climbed in after it, shoved it across the seat and pulled the door shut.

The driver's gum crackled as he watched her exertions through the rearview mirror. With a sigh that was half sob, she cowered into the upholstery and directed him to take her to La Guardia. As the car moved into the crosstown traffic she put her hands over her eyes.

Seven hours later she trudged with seven or eight rumpled passengers into Portland airport's quiet waiting room. Huge color photographs of city sights lined the walls but she hardly glanced at them. Her tired pace quickened when she saw Jeannie asleep in one of a row of look-alike plastic armchairs, her legs thrust out and her purse dangling from a hand.

Dorothy leaned to kiss her forehead. Jeannie's lids fluttered open and she focused slowly. "Welcome to the city of roses," she said finally, then settled back and closed her eyes again. "Wake me when my sister-in-law gets here."

But it was only a joke. In an instant she exploded from the chair, threw her long arms around Dorothy and gave her an extravagant hug and many kisses.

When Dorothy's suitcase tumbled onto the baggage treadmill, Jeannie leaped in front of her to pull it off. "My god," she said, stepping back and clutching her back in mock agony. "What do you have in that thing? Dumbbells?"

Dorothy hastened forward and dragged the bag from the conveyor belt. They found a baggage cart against the wall and together loaded the suitcase and made their way through the glass doors to the parking lot.

"Does the huge grip mean you're planning to stay forever?" Jeannie suggested hopefully.

Dorothy sighed. "We'll see," she said, noncommittal until she felt calmer. She didn't want to blurt out what had happened and she was afraid she would if she started talking before she was ready. Jeannie and Spark must never know what had happened.

The ride home in the battered Plymouth was a guided tour.

"There's Mount Hood," Jeannie said, the car swerving across the yellow line as she held the wheel with one hand and twisted across Dorothy to point with the other. "And over there, off to the west, Mt. St. Helens, do you see it rising out of the clouds?" Jeannie sat back and steered the car to its own lane on the empty highway. "I try not to think about it, burbling away, ready to let go again. Last time it erupted the city was covered with ashes for weeks. And all those poor people living on the side of the mountain who refused to leave. . . ." Her voice trailed away. Dorothy stared ahead into the soft morning light, letting go of herself one aching joint at a time. She turned to study Jeannie as she negotiated a left turn, her arm waving defiantly out of the window.

"Move over and make way!" Jeannie shouted at a lone vehicle approaching from the opposite direction. As they swerved in front of it the driver rolled down his window and shook his fist angrily. "Road hog!" he yelled.

Dorothy laughed without a trace of hysteria.

Chapter Twenty-One

That afternoon when she woke from her nap Dorothy crept into the darkened master bedroom where she found Jeannie still asleep on the big double bed, her arms flung across the pillows. Picking up the quilt that had slid to the floor, Dorothy gently covered her, then tiptoed from the room to explore the house. With its openness and comfortable clutter the house was a reflection of Jeannie's personality. Dorothy felt surrounded and warmed by it—safe at last.

At supper she sat quietly as Spark and Jeannie talked. She didn't need to participate in the conversation; instead she half listened while she studied the woven mats and brightly painted plates, looked across at the big windows and white cotton curtains tied with strips of yellow fabric. After the meal she joined Jeannie on the porch while Spark finished the dishes in the kitchen. A black and white kitten lapped milk from a saucer, then rolled over displaying its fat tummy, and promptly fell asleep. One tiny paw rested trustingly on Jeannie's ankle. The porch light went on across the street and a screen door slammed. Dorothy watched a boy run down the steps, pick up his bicycle from among the bushes at the side of the house, jump on it and wobble up the winding sidewalk and around the corner.

Elmo Shaw was thousands of miles away in New York, in another life. When she closed her eyes she couldn't even picture his face. He was a fading nightmare. She'd escaped.

That night she slept as if painted on the bed. Nothing

disturbed her. She didn't even dream.

On Wednesday morning she borrowed a pair of Jeannie's overalls to help ready the baby's room. Busy painting the woodwork around the leaded windows, she smeared yellow paint in her hair and had to wash it out with turpentine.

That evening at supper Jeannie looked at her suspiciously. "You've been acting strangely," she announced, then glanced at Spark. "Don't you think so? She's been quiet and mysterious ever since she got here."

Dorothy fingered her water glass. Jeannie had always been able to read her thoughts. "I'm thinking about the insurance money," she said evasively, setting the tumbler at a right angle to her knife and plate. "About how I'm going to spend it."

Jeannie shook her head emphatically. "It's more than that," she said. "You haven't given me one straight answer since you arrived." She crossed her arms. "I know what I think," she announced, her eyes bright. "I think you're going to tell us you're in love."

Spark sputtered, his mouth full of meatloaf. "What?" he said. Then, turning to Dorothy with surprise. "Are you?"

She blinked, hurt by his astonishment. "No," she murmured. "I'm not in love." With their eyes on her she must say something more. She couldn't pretend everything was the same, when Jeannie sensed the change. "I wasn't going to tell you for another couple of weeks," she admitted, and swallowed. "But I'm pregnant too."

"What?" Spark said again, his fork—speared now with a neat piece of baked potato—suspended inches from his open mouth.

"I knew it!" Jeannie jumped up, pulled Dorothy from her chair and hugged her. "You devil! Did you think you could keep it from me?" After a final rib-crushing squeeze she returned to her seat and replaced her napkin on her lap. She looked again at Dorothy. "You couldn't fool me with that nonsense about wanting a change of scenery." She took a bite and chewed it energetically. "I knew there was more to it than that."

Spark's face was earnest. "When do we meet the father?"

140

he said. He cleared his throat nervously. "Are you getting married?"

"No," Dorothy said quickly. Then, "I was artificially inseminated."

Spark was flabbergasted. He glanced again at Jeannie, then back to Dorothy. "Isn't that dangerous?"

"Of course not," Jeannie said.

He shook his head and concentrated on buttering a slice of rye bread. "But what do you know about the father?" he insisted.

"Very little," Dorothy said. She wiped some crumbs from the tablecloth into her palm, then deposited them carefully on her plate. "I'm told he had blue eyes." Slightly more green than blue, she remembered. With specks of gold around the iris. And dark brows arching above his eyes like wings.

He'd made her laugh.

Spark frowned. "Pardon me for saying so, but eye color is hardly important," he said. "It doesn't indicate what kind of gene pool you're dipping into," he added, sounding so much like Henry that Dorothy almost told him so. Instead she quietly sipped her water and wondered that she'd never noticed the similarity.

"There might be insanity in the donor's family," Spark continued. "Or hereditary disease of some kind."

Jeannie winked at Dorothy. "He might even be a *Democrat,*" she said.

Spark glanced at her disapprovingly. "This isn't a joke," he said, turning again to Dorothy. "You can't have a baby just because you feel like it."

"Oh, Spark," she pleaded, "don't scold me. It's done. Please be happy for me."

"It's not so simple," he said stubbornly, pouring more water from the crockery pitcher.

"You wrote me I should use the money for something I really wanted," she said. "Didn't you mean it?" Despite everything she still felt like his baby sister and wanted to please him.

He hesitated and looked at Jeannie, whose expression clearly signaled whose side she was on. "I don't want to be

141

a wet blanket," he said.

"Then stop acting like one," Jeannie muttered.

He turned back to Dorothy. "But we wanted children too—ever since we were married. For *fifteen years,*" he emphasized, reminding Dorothy of their extraordinary patience, as if she couldn't count or didn't admire the virtue of it. But she wanted him to stop talking about how difficult it had been for them, to consider instead how patient she'd been, how laudable her choice to stay with their mother. Why did he assume that's all she'd ever wanted? She wanted him to approve of her, to applaud, to jump up and hug her, as Jeannie had. But that wasn't his way. First he must tell her all that was wrong about what she'd decided, why his decisions had been superior to hers (even though hers had benefited him). With all his successes he was still competitive with her. The endless story of sibling rivalry. It made her tired.

She wrenched her attention back to what he was saying. "For years," she heard him droning, "we couldn't afford it. Then, when money wasn't a problem, job security was. We wanted to find just the right job, just the right place—which we did, here in Portland. Just the right house, just the right time. We planned everything very carefully."

Jeannie interrupted him. "Lucky I wasn't sixty-seven years old when the time was finally right," she said. "Then I'd have needed more than artificial insemination. I'd have needed the heavenly choir."

"You shouldn't jump into this impulsively," Spark continued, his voice deep and sonorous, like a radio announcer. "Wanting something badly isn't a good enough reason."

"Oh, honey, relax," Jeannie said impatiently. "She's a grown woman, for heaven's sake." Then she grinned at Dorothy. "Now you have to move out here," she told her. "We'll have our babies together. They'll be friends all their lives." She leaned back in her chair and folded her arms. "I think you're very brave," she said.

After a minute Spark reached across and patted her hand. "Of course you are," he said. "I'm a fuddy-duddy."

Her heart warmed with gratitude.

Late that night she was awakened by violent sounds of thunder. She rolled onto her stomach, squashed the pillow over her head and tried to go back to sleep but the explosions crackled and ripped through the air, shaking the house. She lay quietly and listened. Surely lightning wasn't usual this time of year? And there was no accompanying rain. Lying there for several minutes, she realized she didn't hear spatters on the roof.

She padded across to the window and pulled back the curtains.

Flashes of lightning were so bright she could easily see the yard. She recoiled at another brilliant flare and instantaneous crash. In the brightness she saw something—a figure?—beneath one of the trees. She leaned forward, steeling herself against the next burst of light and noise. Was somebody there? It was impossible to see. But the lightning came again, and—simultaneously—a jolting explosion. In that moment she saw a woman standing quietly under the tree. She was dressed in an old-fashioned dress falling in straight folds to the ground, caught up behind with a bustle. Her figure was ample in the tight vest, even matronly, and she held her hands patiently across her stomach. As Dorothy watched she looked up and their eyes met. The woman's expression was one of infinite sadness. Dorothy saw her lips move and then it was dark again. But Dorothy knew what she'd said.

"Help me."

When the lightening came again there was nobody under the tree.

Toward dawn, long after the storm had subsided, Dorothy lay in her bed and watched shadows flicker and soften across the ceiling. She thought about the woman she'd seen under the tree and remembered the other woman in old-fashioned clothes whose reflection she'd seen in the store window the night Henry was killed.

She covered her face with the inside of her elbow.

Who were they? What did they want from her?

When the dogs came she wasn't surprised, only deeply

tired. First she heard an unearthly falsetto cry, then snarls and barks, finally a chorus of savage howls. She listened to the sounds of many heavy creatures moving and jostling among the bushes beneath her windows.

She hadn't escaped. The Devil was in Oregon, too.

Without looking outside the pulled down the shades and went into the hallway. She sat quietly on the chair next to Jeannie and Spark's closed door, in the dark, guarding them until morning.

Chapter Twenty-Two

After Spark left for work the next morning Jeannie searched for her kitten. "Here, little kitty," she crooned, bending to peer under the sink, tiptoeing to see behind the good china on the top shelf of the cupboard. But the animal was nowhere to be found. Dorothy sat with her hands folded on the kitchen table and watched as she opened the back door and stepped onto the porch. "Here, little kitty," Jeannie wheedled, carefully descending the steps grasping the railing in one hand and a saucer of milk in the other. "Come have your breakfast."

Dorothy knew Mr. Shaw would kill her. A man employed by the Devil for a hundred and sixty years wasn't somebody who'd worry about the number of innocent people he murdered. His hands had been bloodied long ago.

Jeannie screamed.

Dorothy jumped to push open the screen door. Jeannie was crouching in the bushes next to the garage. As Dorothy clattered down the steps she looked up tearfully. "Who would do such a thing?" Jeannie said, reaching out to show what she'd found. The body of her kitten hung from her grasp, its head dangling at a grotesque angle. Dew glittered on the soft fur.

Dorothy kneeled beside her.

"Poor little thing," Jeannie said, rubbing her cheek against the stiffening body. Then, "Maybe some fool thought my poor kitten was what excited those howling dogs last night."

Dorothy had hoped the supernatural racket was meant for her ears alone.

"But did they have to break her neck?" Jeannie said, getting awkwardly to her feet. "You didn't have to kill her!" she shouted.

The morning was unusually quiet. Nobody looked from the kitchen windows facing Jeannie's garden. A lawn mower stood unattended in the middle of the yard next door; no children played on the swing set across the way, although one of the swings—making a steady clicking sound—swung back and forth eerily, as if ridden by a phantom child. The tall trees around them rustled. "Shall we bury her?" Dorothy said, thrusting her fists into her trouser pockets.

Jeannie nodded miserably. "Over there," she said. "Next to the flower bed." She glanced back at Dorothy. "I should have been more careful. I should have kept her locked inside. It's my fault."

"It's *not* your fault!"

Instantly regretting her outburst—Jeannie's eyes had widened in surprise—Dorothy turned and hurried toward the garage. "I'll get the shovel," she said.

After they buried the kitten they sat sipping coffee and facing each other across the kitchen table. Fingering the sugar bowl, Dorothy told Jeannie she would return to New York. "I hadn't planned on staying," she said.

Jeannie scowled. "That's not true," she said. "If you hadn't meant to stay you'd never have brought that heavy suitcase and all your worldly possessions." She wiped a frizzy strand of hair from her forehead.

Dorothy studied the crescent of dirt from the garden under her thumbnail. "It's not a matter of choice," she said finally. "I have to get back. Henry . . ." she hesitated. "The man I worked with?"

Jeannie nodded. "Yes," she said. "You wanted us to meet him after Madelyn's funeral."

"Yes," Dorothy said. "Well. He died. So I have to get back. My supervisor doesn't even know I'm gone."

Jeannie flinched. "He *died?*"

146

Dorothy nodded. Yes, it had been very sudden.

"I'll say it was sudden," Jeannie said. "And you didn't mention a word." She leaned forward and studied Dorothy's face. "Why didn't you say something? You were crazy about him."

Dorothy looked away, shrugged. "I didn't want to burden you," she said. "And we weren't that close, not the way you think."

Jeannie slumped. "I don't understand you," she said. "You pull up stakes, pack every useless piece of clothing you own, hop a plane and come out here, ostensibly to stay forever—"

"I never said that."

Jeannie held up her palms. "I don't care what you *said,*" she said. "Your actions were clear." She stood, carefully placed Dorothy's mug inside her own and carried them to the sink. She let the water fill them, then wrenched the faucet shut. Crossing her arms, she turned again to face Dorothy. "First you tell us you're pregnant," she said. "Next you're saying this man is dead. And I don't care what you say, you were crazy about him, for all I know he's the father of your baby. There's something fishy going on." She jabbed her hair with her fingers. "You burn me up, do you know it? You always act as if you know something nobody else knows, as if you were smarter than the rest of us. So *superior,* damn it. Untouchable." She glared.

Dorothy stood too, facing Jeannie and gripping the back of the chair. Tears at the unexpected hurt stung her eyes. "I'm going home and that's all there is to it," she said.

As Dorothy turned to leave the room, Jeannie hurried to confront her in the doorway. "I didn't mean to hurt your feelings," she said. "But you're hiding something, Dorothy." She hesitated. Then, firmly, "I'm going back to New York with you."

"Oh, no," Dorothy cried, horrified. "You're staying here."

"I'll call the airlines myself," Jeannie said. "You're not going back by yourself. Something's the matter."

Dorothy blocked her way to the living room. "You can't come," she said. "It's impossible." She searched frantically for a persuasive argument. "Spark won't let you. He needs

147

you here."

"He can manage without me for a few days." Jeannie faced her grimly. "Something's gone haywire for you and you're terrified about it. If you won't tell me what it is, I'm going to find out for myself." She rolled down her sleeves and buttoned the cuffs. "Damn it, Dorothy, when are you going to notice you need other people?" she said angrily. "Stop being such a loner."

She pushed past Dorothy into the living room to telephone the airline.

Dorothy stood at the window in the guest room looking across the yard. The house was quiet. Their reservations were on the "red-eye" flight leaving tonight at eleven. Jeannie had telephoned Spark at his office and after she'd explained the reason for the urgency ("Dorothy's in some kind of trouble"), he agreed reluctantly that Jeannie should go with her to New York for a few days. Dorothy knew he couldn't have prevented her journey even if he'd wanted to. Jeannie was stubborn.

So he hadn't even mentioned that bad planning had forced them to pay full fare.

Satisfied all would be well, Jeannie lay now on her bed, deep into the peaceful dreams of her afternoon nap.

Dorothy pounded her fist softly against a pane.

The only two people left in the world she loved were going to die. First Mr. Shaw would kill Jeannie and then when Spark came winging in to see what had happened, he'd kill him too. Or perhaps he'd die here. Geography didn't seem to matter.

She banged her head against the window and bit into her fist to keep from crying out.

Jeannie mustn't come to New York.

Dorothy turned and paced from the window to the bureau, past the neatly made bed, the closed door, back to the window. She pulled her fingers, squeezed them together. *If Jeannie is sick she can't fly to New York.*

But she wasn't sick.

And pregnant women flew all the time, from one end of

the world to the other, nobody said flying harmed the fetus. She moaned again, remembering the stiffening body of the dead kitten.

She slumped onto the edge of the bed and with a bounce fell backward onto the spread, her feet skimming the rug.

She wondered if she could do something to make Jeannie sick. Poison? She rejected the notion at once. Even if she could bring herself to consider it, she knew nothing about toxins and didn't have enough time to learn. She had to do something in the next few hours and it had to be uncomplicated enough for her to accomplish without a hitch.

What if she fell?

She was always falling. She was accident prone. But she never hurt herself. Once a chairlift at a ski resort had dumped her and Spark into a snowdrift concealing a tree. Spark had to wear a back brace and use a cane for the next several months; but nothing whatever happened to Jeannie, even though she'd been hit in the head by a heavy branch. It was the luck of drunks and Jeannie, Spark claimed.

Could Dorothy cause her to fall and injure herself—but not seriously?

She could set a trap on the basement stairs.

It was worth a try. She couldn't think of anything else.

She tiptoed downstairs, opened the basement door cautiously, flinching at the loud series of clicks as she turned the latch.

As she pushed the door open a dank smell confronted her. Taking a deep breath she switched on the light and pulled the door shut behind her. Despite her care it rattled again as she turned the knob. Clenching her teeth, her palms supporting her on both walls, she made her way down the creaking steps. When she reached the foot of the stairs she looked around. The room was neat, bearing unmistakeable signs of Spark's tidiness, but neglected. Two brooms and a mop stood against one wall, their wooden handles covered with slime. Nesting cockroaches or spiders, afraid of the light, scurried soundlessly between the mop strings into the darkness as Dorothy watched. She looked away quickly, at a battered sideboard atilt across the room. Paint cans rested on its speckled surface; yesterday Jeannie had set among them a coffee can holding brushes in an inch of turpentine. The boiler and the hot water heater squatted on the cement floor at one side of the room. Both appliances were glossy with humidity. Behind the furnace she could see a case of wine, resting on its side, and in the middle of the wall behind it a door hung crookedly, a passageway leading to another, darker room. A cobweb swung gently from the frame.

She hurried to the paint cans. Urgently lifting two of them—they were surprisingly heavy—she lugged them to the stairway and set them on a tread, about eight inches apart. Frowning, she looked around again. Her eyes fell on a piece of faded cloth in the corner next to the mop. It had been ripped from a tarp Spark used to collect leaves. She picked it up and shook it gingerly, then folded it and carried it to the paint cans on the stairs. She laid the rectangular piece of cloth carefully across them, pulling it tight and anchoring its ends beneath the cans. She stood back. Yes. If the light were dim you might mistake it for a step. The material was approximately the same color as the wooden treads. And she'd placed the snare on the second to last step. When Jeannie's foot sank in the space between the cans and she fell, she'd hurt herself, maybe sprain an ankle, but she wouldn't harm herself seriously, she wouldn't fall far enough. She'd twist her ankle but she'd be able to grab the railing to keep herself from falling all the way.

Dorothy had no other choice.

Better to break a leg than to be eaten alive by a pack of wild dogs.

She hauled the stepladder from behind the boiler to the center of the room where the floor was indented slightly by a rusty drain. The ladder wobbled as she put her weight on it and she reached unsteadily above her head to unscrew the bulb jutting from the grimy ceiling fixture. Instantly and silently the room went black. She left the loosened bulb in its socket and climbed carefully down the ladder. Jeannie might think she'd left the cans on the stairs herself but she certainly wouldn't presume she or Spark had removed a light bulb without replacing it. They'd know Dorothy had done that and Jeannie would realize it had been a trap.

Whether she was blamed for what was going to happen wasn't the point anyway. Even if they ended up hating her it couldn't be helped.

Better they were alive to hate her.

She dragged the stepladder across the floor and replaced it approximately where it had been. Then she groped her way up the stairs, opened the door and turned to look back. Yes, with only the light from the upstairs hallway you might mistake the tarp for a step. You couldn't see the paint cans under it. It was a perfect trap.

Later that afternoon Dorothy suggested tensely that they get an hour's worth of painting done before leaving for the airport. Jeannie would have to go to the basement for paint. But Jeannie said they didn't have time. "I have to make some meals for Spark to warm up while I'm gone," she said. "Poor dear doesn't know one end of the kitchen from the other."

For the rest of the afternoon Dorothy's mind raced, inventing reasons to send Jeannie downstairs. Maybe she stored jars of homemade jams and jellies in that room behind the furnace.

"Do you ever can?" she asked.

"You can't be serious."

Of course not.

"That's like asking if I weave my own bath towels," Jeannie laughed.

By six o'clock, when Spark's car pulled up the driveway, Dorothy was frantic. There were only a few hours left.

"Are you girls ready for your adventure?" he asked cheerfully as he came in.

Characteristically he pretended nothing was wrong, that Jeannie's sudden plans were a caprice, an adventure on the spur of the moment. His discretion had never been so irritating.

Jeannie stood at the stove stirring the stew. She dipped the wooden spoon, blew on the mixture and tasted it. "Needs some wine," she said.

"Pregnant women aren't supposed to drink," he said.

"Whiskey," Jeannie said. "We're not supposed to drink whiskey." She sprinkled in a pinch of oregano. "The doctor didn't say anything about cooking with wine."

151

He tossed the paper on the table. "I'll get a bottle from that case I bought last year."

Before Dorothy could stop him he opened the basement door, found the light not working. "Damn," he said softly, clicking the switch several times, and thumped down the stairs. She sat at the kitchen table holding her breath.

There was a shout, a crash, and then silence.

Chapter Twenty-Three

Later Dorothy sat by the airplane window and watched the wing lights flashing against the blackness of the night. She'd never imagined *Spark's* injury would prevent Jeannie from coming with her to New York. But Jeannie's famous luck had held. It was Spark who'd fallen and sprained his ankle. He'd have to wear a cast and use crutches for six weeks. Jeannie was fine. But she'd been forced to choose between Dorothy and her husband. He needed her and Dorothy swore she didn't. So she stayed in Portland.

But she hadn't given in easily.

"It's almost as if you planned this," she hissed to Dorothy as they waited for Spark outside a cubicle in the emergency room. Then the resident emerged and they rushed into where Spark lay on a stretcher. "Go ahead to New York," he urged Jeannie, and she almost did. But the thought of him driving back and forth to work—in a *cast*—clumping onto the accelerator instead of the brake, skidding into a tree. . . . She was convinced he needed her.

"I'm not going to ask what your problem is," she told Dorothy later, as they stood on the porch awaiting the airport taxi. "You're obviously not going to tell me."

Dorothy said nothing.

Jeannie apologized again for her harsh words in the kitchen. "But you need to know I'm on your side," she said. "I wish I could make you see that." She leaned closer. "Confiding in me isn't going to make it worse. It might even help."

Dorothy put her arm around Jeannie's bony shoulders. "I need time," she said, squeezing her. "Be patient."

"If only you could give me a hint of what's wrong," Jeannie said.

Dorothy sighed. She mustn't weaken. "It's something I have to take care of by myself," she said. "I'll tell you as soon as I can, believe me."

"I want you checking in at least once a week," Jeannie said. "Is that agreed?"

Dorothy nodded. She studied Jeannie's intense face, the familiar scowl, the messy lipstick, the smudge under her eye. She turned helplessly into her and they put their arms around each other, standing wrapped together silently until the cab pulled up and honked.

"Please take care of yourself," Jeannie whispered, squeezing her one last time. Then they pulled apart, each bending to share the weight of the heavy suitcase as they carried it down the steps to the taxi.

After an hour on the plane, Dorothy shifted, leaned forward and retrieved her pocketbook from under her seat. She squeezed past the sleeping person next to her.

Every seat was filled. She went up the aisle toward the restroom and glanced at the woman sitting directly behind her between a sleeping man in a business suit and a long-haired younger man in jeans and suspenders whose face rested against the window. Dorothy looked away, uneasily moving past.

But she remembered the woman she saw.

She was about forty and wore a curiously outdated dress with a draped neck and short skirt. Jet sequins glittered in the crepe bodice and rows of beads lined the skirt. Her elbows were placed delicately on the armrests and she held an empty cigarette holder in an angry gesture. She was very pale. The mascara on her lashes was clotted with tears. Her intense gaze followed Dorothy as she passed.

Dorothy wondered who she was and why she was watching her with such mournful hostility, as if she wanted to communicate with her. What was the matter? Apparently

154

she was alone—she didn't seem to be accompanying either of the men sitting next to her. And the out-of-fashion garb she wore was like a costume. As Dorothy returned from the lavatory she decided to say something to her. But when she reached the seat where she'd been sitting, the woman wasn't there. Instead a redheaded girl sat in her place, her face nuzzled into the shoulder of the young man in jeans. Their hand were linked on her lap. She wore a sweatshirt with "Boston University" printed in a circle of purple letters.

Dorothy looked up and down the aisle in confusion. Where was the woman in the flapper dress?

She almost woke the young couple to ask them where she'd gone. But she didn't. Instead she returned to her seat. Leaning back and closing her eyes, she listened to the steady engine noise. In her interior darkness clear images emerged: the woman standing under the tree during the storm last night; the despairing woman reflected behind her in the shop window the night Henry was killed.

Now this angry woman in the twenties outfit.

They were coming to her from out of history, and each of them was seeking her help.

Who were they? What did they want from her?

Chapter Twenty-Four

Home again, she picked up her life. But her brain was stuck. Would it rain? She'd need her umbrella. What did she want for dinner? She'd have to stop at the market. She rode the bus back and forth and stared blindly out its window.

She shopped for groceries, watched television, ate her cereal in the morning with a library book propped against the sugar bowl. At the office she set about the monumental task of cleaning up the mess Henry had left. Their supervisor telephoned from the main branch of the NYPL and wanted to know if there would be a memorial service for him.

"No," Dorothy said, ripping yesterday's page from her calendar, wadding it up and hurling it toward the waste basket.

"I suppose that's better," Mrs. Blietz said.

Better than what? Dorothy wondered, suppressing a desire to inform her boss that Henry had kicked his heels together and stiff-armed a Nazi salute whenever he mentioned her name. Now that he was dead she yearned to brag about how original and funny he'd been.

But it was too late.

"And what a shame," Mrs. Blietz went on. "In just four years he could have put in for early retirement."

"Yes," Dorothy said. *He was eaten by dogs,* she wanted to shout. *What's the matter with you?* She'd never noticed how people avoided talking about what confused or frightened them. The reticence didn't spring from good manners. It was fear. Fear of getting involved, fear of emotional connection.

156

Fear of pain. Silence built walls, and behind them you were safe—if alone.

And she didn't want to talk about Henry's death any more than Mrs. Blietz did.

"I can't send anybody to take his place, not just yet," Mrs. Blietz continued. "We're short of personnel right now."

"That's all right," Dorothy said. "There's not enough work for two people any more," she lied, looking around. It would take an army weeks to plow through the mess.

"I'm relieved to hear that," Mrs. Blietz said. "Let me know if you need anything," she added, her voice fading as she hung up without saying goodbye.

Dorothy sighed with relief. Mrs. Blietz wasn't going to bother her.

Nor would Elmo Shaw. She could count on being safe for eight months. As long as she was carrying the baby he wanted he's see nothing happened to her.

Once she'd given birth, of course, then she'd die, just like the other women he'd treated. On January 5th, 1990, as he'd noted in his journal.

But she didn't want to think about that. She told herself when the time came she'd know how to protect herself. Now she knelt, reorganizing the card files, reading through the documents, making marks with a grease pencil, evaluating and stacking the material around her, performing familiar tasks.

She'd pushed Henry's chair against the wall and stuffed his possessions—a cluster of pens and pencils held together with a rubber band, a desk calendar, box of Kleenex, a seat cushion, heating pad, a toothbrush and miniature tube of Crest—in a plastic bag on the closet shelf. She didn't have the heart to throw it out.

It seemed a meager collection, after twenty years.

For weeks she sensed him waiting for her in the next room or rummaging in the basement while she filed cards upstairs. Sometimes she almost called his name. When she unlocked the door in the morning an instant passed before she remembered she wouldn't see his coat hanging on the rack by the entrance. As she undid her scarf she found herself listening for his impatient step.

She steeled herself against these recurrent shocks. But she continued to peer expectantly into the dark office when she arrived. A week later she found herself setting out his mug for coffee and brewing enough for two.

She ached to see his face.

She kept remembering episodes from their years together. Not long ago he'd borrowed her mirror to scrutinize his upper lip when he'd been growing a pencil-line moustache.

"Do you think I look like Ronald Coleman?" he'd said.

"No," she laughed. "More like an aluminum siding salesman."

He chuckled at that—a good sport—snapped shut the compact and tossed it back to her.

But the next morning the moustache had vanished.

She could have said something nice to him. It wouldn't have cost her anything. She was ashamed to remember how sarcastic she'd been.

And that night at the O'Hara Clinic she'd called him an old maid. She couldn't shake the memory of that moment, his quickly concealed expression of hurt as he turned away. Remembering the look in his eyes when she'd said that tormented her most of all.

This was the man she'd loved. And never guessed it. All those years. Gone. Wasted. When she wasn't dabbing at her eyes feeling sorry for herself, self-disgusted rage surged through her. Once she punched the wall behind Henry's desk so hard the skin on the back of her knuckles split and she wore a bandage for several days, reminding her—as if she needed to be reminded—of her own cruelty and stupidity.

During all the years they'd known each other she'd bullied and bossed him. She'd corrected him at every opportunity and tried to be smarter than he was, reveling in his infrequent mistakes as if pouncing on them made her better than he was, as if she never made mistakes, as if making a mistake made you inferior instead of human. (And just who was it who'd seen the danger of dealing with Elmo Shaw? It certainly hadn't been her, she'd jumped in like a perfect dunce. But Henry had suspected. *Why hadn't she listened to him?*)

Yet he'd forgiven even that. He'd cared for her. He'd

warmed to some part of her she wasn't even aware of. Despite everything. She wouldn't forget that. He had seen past the sand she'd been throwing in his eyes. She had to learn to see past the sand too, to accept herself as he had.

She must learn to value herself as he'd valued her. She had to step beyond the self-hatred, the shame and disgust. She had to forgive herself in order to find self-respect. Then she could feel and act as if she mattered. Until then she was powerless—the queen in somebody else's chess game.

And there wasn't anybody left to help her.

Chapter Twenty-Five

One summer evening after she'd showered and dried her hair with a towel, Dorothy crept into bed and lay looking out the window at a sliver of moon. Its light brightened the shadows in the room without warming her.

She became aware of a ripple within her abdomen, a soft breath across a pool. The movement was gentle—like a sigh—and if she hadn't been lying still, she'd not have noticed it.

She turned her face on the pillow and closed her eyes.

It came again.

She opened her eyes, brought her hands across herself and pressed cautiously. There was no response.

After a few minutes when the sensation didn't recur, she closed her eyes again and fell asleep.

At their appointment a few days later, Dr. Blanchard told her the deep ripplings she described were the first stirrings of her baby. "Everything is progressing exactly as it should," he said.

After that, Dorothy concentrated on feeling what was happening to her body. Although the sensations were within her, they didn't belong to her. They were in her but not hers, the same but different.

Unexpected.

Independent.

Days passed and she experienced nothing unusual. She became uncertain she'd felt anything, couldn't remember exactly what she thought she'd felt, couldn't *refeel* it. Then

160

without warning an unmistakable bubbling and skittering occurred, something so fleeting and capricious she laughed and looked down at herself.

Somebody was alive inside her.

She began walking briskly to and from work.

She joined a health club not far from the library. At lunchtime every day she strode the seven blocks to it and went swimming. She swam for half an hour, slowly the first few times, but rapidly gaining strength and speed. At night she tuned her portable radio to a rock station and touched her toes a hundred times in rhythm to the music, shouting numbers as she stretched up and down. She lay on the rug next to her bed and did fifty knees-bent sit-ups, her hands clamped behind her head, then turned on her stomach and did twenty-five push-ups. She rose, stretched her arms and then her legs, stood with her back against the wall and slid to sit on an invisible chair for ten fifteen-second periods. When she finished the exercises she went into the bathroom, made muscles into the mirror, grimaced fiercely like Arnold Schwartzenegger, then measured the firmness in her biceps.

She bought a book on nutrition and followed its instructions carefully, eating only fresh fruit and vegetables, whole grains, broiled chicken and fish. When her ankles swelled in the hot weather, she gave up salt and, regretfully, threw out her store of gingersnaps. The puffiness went away.

After two months she was able to swim steadily for an hour every day, long, powerful strokes that ate up the distance.

As promised, she telephoned Jeannie regularly every Friday, and they compared notes. Jeannie seemed content to permit Dorothy to tell her what she chose. And her own news was envariably cheerful. "I can't zip my skirt any more!" she announced proudly in May. "Can you zip yours?"

Dorothy began telling other women she was going to have a baby. She told cashiers at the supermarket, strangers in line with her at the bank or standing with her at the bus stop. When she told them they smiled with genuine interest.

161

Sometimes she went into stores without any purpose except to announce her news.

She learned other women enjoyed telling about their own pregnancies, describing how their babies had been born on the coldest day of the year, or the hottest, in a taxi or after hours of painful labor, sometimes with hardly any pain at all. One fifty-year-old woman at a cosmetics counter described to a circle of fascinated women how her fourth baby had "just squirted out into the bedclothes" in the middle of the night. She hadn't even known she was pregnant.

Dorothy felt connected to the other women. They cared about one another and shared a common experience. She was interested in their stories and felt the warmth of their interest in her. It was as if she had friends. She felt herself reaching out to them.

One afternoon she went for her regular visit to Dr. Blanchard. He took her blood pressure, listened to her lungs and heart, asked her questions about how she was feeling. Then he took an instrument with a steel headband and a protruding ringlike device which he fitted around his head and into his ears. He bent toward her and pressed it carefully against her abdomen as she lay on the examining table. He listened with an intent expression, moved his head in the device carefully across her body. She felt his warm breath against her naked belly. When she started to say something he held up his hand.

"Wait," he said. Then he smiled. "Yes," he said finally, "I can definitely hear the heartbeat."

She grew thicker, wore her blouses out, left the bottom buttons open. When she could no longer zip her trousers she purchased a pair with a stretch front, and two smocks, a pink one and another with a pattern of blue and yellow wildflowers.

She was always hungry.

Another morning when she lay on the examining table Dr. Blanchard handed her his long-necked stethoscope.

"Here," he grinned. "You listen."

She fitted the instrument into her ears as he put the small round end of it against her abdomen, raising his eyebrows.

"Hear anything?" he asked.

"No," she whispered, listening intently.

He moved the piece and pressed it again. "What about here?" he said.

She shook her head, holding her breath and watching him. He moved it again. "Now?" he asked.

She frowned. "I'm not sure," she said. Then, disappointed, "No, I don't think so."

"Listen carefully," he said. "It's very faint."

Her body tensed with the effort to hear.

Very softly, almost in her imagination, she heard a rapid, whisking sound. "Butterflies," she said, looking up at him. "It sounds like butterflies."

He smiled and she felt tears stinging her eyes. "That's your baby," he said.

When he told her she was going to have twins, she tried to act surprised.

"Next month when you come in," he said, "I'll show them to you on the ultrasound."

"I'll be able to see them?" she said incredulously.

"That's right."

At her next appointment he moved the elaborate apparatus next to her as she lay on the table. While he pressed a plastic device onto her swollen abdomen she turned her head to look at the screen. With his other hand he pointed to a mass of undulating pinpoints and shadow, visible on the terminal.

"See this?" he said. "Here's the spine, this wavy toothpick thing. The heart—this small dark area that's jumping around—and the head, here's the head. The image is quite clear, do you see? That's one of them. Can you make it out?"

"Yes," she said, clenching her hands.

"And here's the other one, down here, not so easy to differentiate, it's behind and to the right . . ." He sounded as excited as she felt.

"Yes, yes, I see it!"

She watched the jittery electronic picture. "These are my babies?" she said finally.

"They certainly are. At this very moment, as we talk."

Later, when she'd changed into her clothes and sat facing him in his office, he asked her what plans she'd made for after their birth. "Do you have somebody to help you?" he said. "It's a big job for one person, especially if you plan to continue working."

"I know," she said.

"Ordinarily I'd say it's none of my business, but your case is unusual. You don't have anybody to help you. Your sister-in-law is in Portland, isn't she?"

Dorothy nodded.

"And you said she's having her own baby."

"Yes."

"So she won't be able to come and stay with you."

"No."

"Most women have family to help when the babies come."

His was an old-fashioned presumption, that women always had aunts or cousins or mothers-in-law to help them. As if there were no such thing as waking alone every morning.

"Before you know it they'll be here," he said.

"I know," she said, twisting her handkerchief.

"If you'd like," he said, "I can ask my wife if she knows somebody to assist you. I've told her about you, I hope you don't mind. She thinks you're very courageous."

"Why?" Dorothy asked, startled.

He looked embarrassed, as if doctors shouldn't talk to their wives about their patients. Dorothy was touched by his self-consciousness.

"You're thirty-nine, single," he said, adjusting the pen holder on his blotter. "You don't live with anyone. In your spot many women would have had an abortion, or arranged to give the baby away. Especially with twins."

"Oh, I don't think so," she said. "It was my choice to become pregnant." She cleared her throat, trying to stay close to the truth. "It was bad luck their father died. I miss him. I'm sorry we can't do it together, but that's the way it is. I'm not being brave, I'm doing exactly what I—what we

164

planned. I want my babies."

Surprised at her words, she opened and shut her pocketbook, then examined the clasp.

"I'll have my wife give you a ring if you want."

Dorothy nodded and looked up again at Dr. Blanchard.

She wasn't planning to give either of her babies to Elmo Shaw.

Chapter Twenty-Six

Early the next morning Dorothy sat at her desk at the library, studying her fists.

She'd heard her babies' heartbeats, felt them moving and growing inside her! In the dark moist places between her organs she was creating from her own mysterious secretions their flesh, their eyes, their fingernails and eyelashes. Their brains. She was fashioning muscle and bone marrow, tiny joints that bent and opened, fingers grasping and reaching, miniature hearts of gristle and tendons fed with rich blood rushing through intricate networks of thread-like vessels. At this moment she was readying them to burst forth from her, to breathe air and come to life.

She felt like God.

Since she'd first felt her babies inside her she'd been working up to this, when she'd face at last what was happening to her. She fit her fists together carefully, knuckle to knuckle. Yesterday, when she'd seen them on the ultrasound equipment, she'd finally surmounted her fear and decided to fight for them both.

Her chances weren't good. The only weapon she had was her brain. But it was a good brain. Surely if she used it properly the odds against her improved.

It gave her a sinking feeling when she considered that as smart as Henry had been, he hadn't been able to use the information he'd discovered. He'd panicked.

She'd lost her control too, rushed to Portland and endangered Jeannie and Spark.

Biting her lip, she reminded herself that at this moment she knew most of what Henry had known and she wasn't hysterical.

That was encouraging.

If she could find out more about Mr. Shaw—how he operated, with whom he'd dealt and what had happened to them in the last hundred years, then she might have a chance to thwart his wishes and break the contract.

It was her only chance.

She focused her thoughts on Henry. He'd been an excellent librarian and a thorough researcher—probably more thorough and better organized than she was. He'd had a talent for keeping centered when often she got sidetracked. But she was the more imaginative researcher. She'd depend on that because this search would need a healthy dose of creativity.

She had no idea where to start.

Clearing her throat, she wiped her upper lip and the back of her neck with a tissue.

In her years at the library she'd learned that the first part of every search consisted of asking good questions.

Wadding up the Kleenex and dropping it into the wastebasket under the desk, she picked up her pencil and licked its tip. On the legal pad squared on her blotter, she wrote:

What do I want to find out?

For a moment she looked at the question she'd written. Then, under it, she wrote:

Answer: How I can protect myself and my babies.

She fingered the pencil. Under the last sentence she added:

What my chances are.

Instantly she crossed this out. She didn't need to know her chances, knowing them would only frighten her.

She wrote another question:

Has anybody successfully opposed E. Shaw?

And another:

Has anybody kept both babies and lived?

She paused, gazing across at Henry's empty desk. Then

167

she looked back at the piece of paper in front of her. In the center of the page she wrote in capital letters:

P R E C E D E N T.

She underlined the word twice.

If the journal didn't ennumerate Elmo Shaw's actions through the years, perhaps another source would. Maybe somebody who dealt with him had kept a diary and it might even have ended up in the Literary Library, just as his had. It was a long shot, but it was possible. You didn't have to be famous or important to want to keep a record of who you were and what you were doing. All kinds of nobodies produced work that ended up in this place. It seemed to Dorothy much more likely she'd be able to find clues here about Mr. Shaw's other patients than in the more conventional research archives across town. "He's a bully," she thought. "He goes after the babies of people who won't make waves." She sighed. "Like me."

She opened the middle drawer of her desk and removed the note Henry had left for her the night he'd found Mr. Shaw's journal. She unfolded it carefully and read it for the hundredth time: "Dorothy—check out one of the 7 sisters. Historian? Geneticist?" Until this moment the message hadn't made any sense. But as her thinking became coherent she understood what he meant. He'd been searching for *two* documents. Mr. Shaw's journal and *something else*. The dim memory of cataloging the journal had sent him scurrying through the collection trying to locate it. But he'd remembered something else too, something about "7 sisters." He'd been asking himself other questions even as he dug into the cabinets and barrels. The memory of the other manuscript, record, journal—whatever it was—had occurred to him while he was looking for the first thing he remembered. But he'd jotted a note to her so she could begin a parallel search for whatever it was the next morning. He'd planned to discuss it with her, to explain what he meant. But he'd never had the chance.

Her jaw tightened. Why had he surrendered to the fear? Why hadn't he stayed searching for information that might have helped them? Or explained properly what else he remembered? And why had he been so secretive while she

168

was still in the office? Why hadn't he discussed the situation and his hunches with her while he was able to?

She sighed, releasing the anger. She'd done the same thing. She'd never warned him about the dogs, and she'd known perfectly well they were connected to her and her desire for a baby. And as soon as she'd found out who Mr. Shaw was she'd run away too. She couldn't blame Henry for doing what he did. He hadn't had time to calm down, as she'd had.

She walked to the water cooler and watched the bubbles rumble and ricochet as she filled a paper cup.

"The seven sisters are stars," she said quietly. "They're in a constellation."

She went to a bookshelf standing against the wall and removed the *A* volume of the encyclopedia. She placed the heavy book on Henry's desk and opened it to the "Astronomy" section.

The seven sisters, known formally as the Pleiades, were located in the constellation Taurus. They were named for the seven daughters of Atlas, turned by Zeus into stars when Orion—crazed with lust—pursued them.

She scanned their names. There was no indication any of them were twins. She stooped to pull a copy of *Goldfinch's Mythology* from a box next to her desk. Flipping to the index, she found a referrance to the Pleiades. One of the seven sisters was Electra, mother of Dardanus, the founder of the Trojan race.

Sipping the water and returning to her chair, she leaned against it and paged through the book. How old was Orion? Was he an evil old man? In another section he was described as the giant hunter who pursued the seven sisters and was eventually slain by Artemis, then placed in the sky. His age wasn't mentioned.

If Electra's son founded the Trojan race, she thought, perhaps legends of the Trojan war held the clue she was seeking. She pulled her chair to her desk, sat in it and read the terrible stories about the Trojan prince, Hector, killed by Achilles and tied to a chariot, dragged by his heels three times around the mighty walled city. She read about his wife Andromache, fleeing from the ruins of Troy with her child, caught and claimed as bounty by the murderous Pyrrhus.

She read too about Hector's sister Cassandra who saw the future but whose predictions nobody believed.

But there were no stories of twins in the myths of the Trojan War. Nor was there an old man who tempted with promises of great riches or eternal life.

She slammed the book and rubbed her forehead with her fist. Where was the connection?

She felt as if on a wild goose chase, no closer than when she'd started.

But this was the nature of research, she reminded herself. You didn't unearth information immediately, particularly when you didn't know exactly what you were looking for. She must be patient. Centering her notes on her blotter, and taking a long breath, she sharpened her pencils, put them in the holder ready for tomorrow. She returned the various books to their proper places, put on her coat, locked the door and went home.

Today was September 22nd. She had three and a half months.

PART TWO

Hallie

Chapter One

Hallie Lorena Crecelius, 71, was related to Dr. Emil ("Doc") Blanchard—Dorothy Kite's obstetrician. She was his wife's mother's sister. His aunt by marriage.

Tall and elegant, with blue eyes so dark they were almost purple, long arms and big bony hands, she was a professional musician who'd never married and never retired.

In 1990 she lived in an apartment in a residential hotel in midtown Manhattan. Her apartment was located on the same floor as the one where Robert Benchley once lived. Her windows faced the Algonquin Hotel, across the way on West 44th Street. In the 1920s and 1930s, Benchley and his friends at the round table had held court there. Hallie felt akin to the irreverant American ghosts and enjoyed living among them.

Her parlor was large and pie-shaped, cluttered with exotic possessions: a table from Istanbul with secret drawers and inlaid mother-of-pearl relief carvings of draped figures in turbans; jeweled boxes; a serpentine sofa from Portobello Road in London; Shaker boxes filled with earth and clumps of sweet-smelling herbs; a glass cupboard displaying jade figures—Samurai warriors on rearing horses, miniature Buddhas.

The hotel had been Hallie's home base for more than thirty years. When she was out of town the management tended the plants and kept the rooms aired and ready for her return.

The centerpiece in the parlor was the red mahogany grand

piano standing in front of the French windows, its heavy legs carved in an intricate pattern of leaves and grape clusters. Every afternoon, as the sun slanted through the filmy drapes, Hallie played the piano. Sometimes she chose a group of Chopin nocturnes, or songs by Schubert, Handel and Liszt. Often she selected pieces by Mozart and Beethoven. Mixed in with the conventional classics were, invariably, tunes by Stephen Foster, W.C. Handy, George Gershwin, Fats Waller. Sometimes she invited hotel personnel and other guests in to listen. She and the impromptu concerts were a prized fixture at the hotel.

For nearly fifty years Hallie had made her living playing in concert halls, cafés, living rooms, rinkydink saloons and nightclubs all over the world. She'd taught at the prestigious Mannes School of Music and at Juilliard, and once played a selection of songs written or made famous by American artists such as Scott Joplin, Robert Johnson and Henry Roeland Byrd ("Professor Longhair"), for Hallie Selassie, then Emperor of Ethiopia.

At the age of 62 she'd joined the Peace Corps and for two years taught reading, writing and music to children in the mountains of Peru.

Since childhood Hallie had been gifted with an ability to sense or foresee certain events before they happened.

Because these "visions" occurred only occasionally and most often centered on unimportant incidents, she didn't overestimate the ability. She believed information about the future was available in everybody's unconscious and scoffed when friends called her talent supernatural. "You can see what I see," she told them. "You just have to pay attention."

To her, the present melded into tomorrow and yesterday simultaneously, just as undercurrent moved out to sea beneath waves flowing irresistably toward shore. Believing time was a never-ending circle, like tides, she felt there was no reason you couldn't see what was going to happen with as much certainty as you saw what had already occurred. She believed that civilization and its technological recipes had interfered with this instinct but occasionally people like her came along to provide evidence that it still existed. If her friends didn't share her relaxed view of the phenomenon, she was unbothered. She regarded her prescience as an accidental idiosyncrasy, like being left-handed.

Just because she could sometimes see the future didn't mean she was special, merely that other people had forgotten how to do what she did.

Only once had the ability resulted in her taking action to avert tragedy. When her group of Peace Corps volunteers was nearly finished building a hut on the side of a mountain to house the community school, she insisted they move the shack to another site, well out of the way of a mammoth mudslide she clearly saw coming. Her colleagues argued that the place they'd selected was not only beautiful but located conveniently near fresh water. Hallie pointed out that the local people were already moving their homes as if they too knew what was going to happen. When the villagers said they would keep their children home if the school remained where it was, the team of idealistic but practical young Americans reluctantly moved the hut. The following morning an avalanche obliterated everything in its path, including the original place for the school. Afterward the Peace Corps workers regarded Hallie with respect and sought her opinion on every decision.

"Don't ask me," Hallie scoffed. "Ask the villagers. They know better than I do."

Since her return to New York her visions had become less frequent and when they occurred their focus was mundane. Somebody's hat blowing off and landing on the hood of a passing car wasn't important even when she could predict it. She was beginning to think advancing years were softening the focus of her ability, and she was secretly frustrated by this evidence of old age.

Recently, however, she'd been disturbed by strong recurrent and unpleasant images. She saw herself lying somewhere with her eyes closed, hands crossed on her chest and flowers strewn around an unfamiliar room, some set in a glass jar at her head. Outside were mountains of snow and swirling winds. She heard a woman screaming, saw a bloody baby, felt herself grasping the slippery infant in the darkened room and dipping it into a shallow container of liquid.

The pictures unnerved her but long ago she'd learned the

175

uselessness of questioning what she saw. Passing time would unravel the puzzle and reveal there'd been no reason to be afraid. She reminded herself of the joke about the blind man grasping the tail of an elephant and trying unsuccessfully to describe what he held. He said it was a broom. Knowledge was a matter of perspective. There were harmless explanations for what she saw even if she didn't yet know what they were.

One night she served coffee to her niece, Jane Blanchard, and Jane's husband, Doc, after a hilarious dinner spent in a West Side restaurant. The women sat together companionably on the sofa. Hallie was taller than Jane. Her long legs were crossed easily and her ankles, in dark stockings, were still slender and elegant. She wore no makeup, was dressed in a dark red suit with a chiffon scarf clipped at her shoulder by a gold brooch. Next to her, her niece moved with quick, impulsive gestures. Her mouth was small and outlined in a perfect bow with bright red lipstick. She wore a black Armani dress and sat curled up on the sofa next to Hallie, with her shoes off. The women paged through a dusty photograph album while Doc went behind the Japanese screen to the tiny kitchen to remove an ice tray from the freezer.

Hallie and Jane enjoyed looking at the family pictures neither of them had seen for years. Jane especially liked seeing herself young and carefree. "In another life," she laughed. "Who knew my mousy brown hair would magically turn blond by my fiftieth birthday?" she giggled.

Hallie talked about her days as an ambulance driver in London during the Blitz. "I was just twenty-one," she remembered, paging backward, looking closely at the snapshot of herself as a laughing young woman wearing a short flared skirt and a tailored blouse. Her hair escaped in rebellious wisps from under a jaunty visored cap, and she stood between two grinning young men with their arms around her waist. "Here I am on the day I flew solo the first time. I learned to fly in New Jersey, at some bumpy little airfield, in a rickety airplane with baby-carriage wheels.

176

Your mother took this picture, Jane, before I went up, in case I crashed, so they'd have the photo to remember me by. That's your father standing on my right."

Jane leaned forward to get a better look.

"I planned to join the war effort by ferrying bombers across the Atlantic," Hallie continued. "All my friends were gung ho about helping the British. The boys were all joining up. I wanted to do something brave and unusual."

"Always the star," Jane said.

"Always," Hallie agreed. "But no sooner did I climb down from the plane than I started throwing up, first in the bushes at the side of the field, then in the car on the way home—your father had to keep pulling over to the side of the road. 'Not in my car!' he kept shouting. Your mother wouldn't stop laughing, she thought it was all a joke. But I was humiliated. I mean if you're going to be brave then you oughtn't to throw up all over everything. My father thought I was afraid of flying—by myself—but I soon realized I couldn't stand the idea of delivering bombers, even to our side. It turned out I was a pacifist. So I went to England and signed up there for hospital work. I saw a lot of blood and guts there, believe me—I even delivered a couple of babies in the middle of the bombing." She paused thoughtfully. "I guess I wanted to prove I could be a pacifist without being a coward." She laughed. "Your grandfather thought I was crazy. I think I embarrassed him."

"Oh, you and he were always at it," Jane said. "But mother used to say you were his favorite."

"Only when I followed instructions."

"Which was rare."

"Damn right."

They continued turning the pages of the album, speaking of the children in the photographs, babies then, grown now. Their conversation ranged widely. There were relaxed silences signalling their ease with one another. After one such long pause Jane mentioned a patient of Doc's who was expecting twins. "She doesn't have a soul in the world," she said. She'd invited her to lunch one day next week.

Hallie asked why. Surely Doc kept his office separate from his home?

177

"There's something about her," Doc said, sitting on the arm of the sofa next to Jane. "I think she could use a friend."

"According to what she told Doc," Jane said, "everybody she's ever known—including her boyfriend—died within a week of each other. Which sounds pretty fishy to me." She sniffed. "She's probably Henry Kissinger's mistress, some awful person who's pulled the wool over Doc's eyes."

Hallie smiled at Jane's joke but felt herself tensing unaccountably. She turned a page of the album.

"Our Jane sees conspiracies everywhere," Doc said, sipping his Pepsi and squinting to study a photograph. "She even thinks our doorman is in the CIA."

He winked at his wife who smiled up at him. It still thrilled her to be married to the handsomest boy at the party. She'd fallen in love with him the first time she'd seen him, strolling across the dance floor at a mixer at Briarcliff Junior College, on his way to introduce himself to her and ask her to dance. He'd stood straight and slim then, hands in pockets and dark hair curling across his forehead—the impoverished medical student. She'd been looking for somebody rich but his Glenn Ford good looks and easy confidence won her heart. She'd never regretted it. He still made her feel beautiful and cherished, no matter how silly she sometimes felt. "He's always picking up strays," she told Hallie affectionately. Then she urged, "But I need you to come along when I take his patient to lunch. To keep me company."

Hallie rubbed her chin and flexed her fingers, relaxing them.

"He wants me to help her find a nanny," Jane said.

The notion of going to lunch was ominous, but Hallie didn't know why. She said she'd go.

"Oh, good," Jane said. "Then we can decide afterwards what we think of her." She turned the page and frowned. "What are you doing in this snapshot?" she said. "You look spooky."

Hallie took the album and studied the photograph. It showed her lying somewhere with her eyes closed and her hands crossed on her chest. There was a ghostly aura surrounding her which obscured the background. "That's funny," she said uneasily. "I don't know what this picture is

178

doing in here with all the family pictures." She explained that a friend had taken it eight years before, in Peru one afternoon when she was napping in her tent.

She was lying. It resembled another photograph, taken in Peru as a joke, but she knew it wasn't the same one. This photographic image was precisely the disquieting scene she'd been seeing in her mind's eye. It had nothing to do with the other photograph.

"It looks as if you're laid out for your own funeral," Jane said. "With the flowers in the background."

"Those aren't flowers," Hallie said brusquely. "They're shadows." She looked up, meeting Jane's bewildered gaze, then glanced again at the photo. At the head of the cot on which she lay stood an unmistakable vase of flowers. "Maybe it *is* flowers," she admitted. "The Indian women were always bringing us carnations."

Hallie and Jane looked back at the photograph. The waxy flowers curving delicately from the container next to Hallie's head were clearly lilies.

Doc bent and eyed the snapshot. "It's overexposed," he said. "That's why it looks as though you're surrounded with rings of light and you can't make out the flowers." He straightened. "Somebody should have used a light meter," he added helpfully.

Hallie slipped the photograph out of its corner holders. "It doesn't belong in this album anyhow," she said. "These are family pictures from years ago. I don't know how it got here."

She went to the desk where she opened a compartment and removed a film developer's yellow and black envelope. "It belongs in here with the other snapshots from Peru. I never seem to have time to make up an album for them." She removed several other photographs, picked through them on the blotter. "Yes," she said. "Here's one just like it." She showed it to them.

"There aren't any flowers in this one," Jane said dubiously.

"Maybe they're two shots of the same pose," Doc said. "Somebody brought the flowers for the second shot."

"That's it," Hallie said. "We had a good laugh about it,"

she added. "They put it up on the bulletin board. 'Hallie at work,' somebody wrote under it. Everybody thought it was a hoot."

"Perhaps that's how it got separated from the other pictures," Doc suggested. "And you stuck it in the album for safekeeping."

The album they'd been looking at had been in the bottom of the drawer since Hallie had moved into this apartment. She hadn't touched it in years. But she didn't say so.

"I don't think it's a hoot," Jane said. "It looks like it was taken at your funeral and it frightens me."

"You're just being melodramatic," Hallie said, returning the photo envelope to the desk drawer. She turned the small brass key in the lock and put the key in her pocket. "It seemed funny at the time." She sat again. "But I guess you had to be there." She turned another page of the album. "Let's look at the pictures of you as a teenager."

"Oh, yes," Jane exclaimed, eager to change the subject. She didn't like mysteries.

"Now, here's a fine pair of legs," Doc said, pointing to a shot of Jane waving gaily beside a 1959 Buick. "Looks like Betty Grable."

"Whoever she is," Jane said. "Must have been before my time."

Hallie looked at her guardedly. Had she ever seen herself dead? It seemed unlikely. Her niece was literal-minded and charmingly self-centered. Now she studied her own photograph with innocent conceit, stretched languidly and pulled Doc down next to her. They nestled together and continued paging through the album.

After a while Doc rose to put on another record. Jane continued turning the pages and commenting on the pictures.

Hallie looked toward her bedroom door and shivered.

Chapter Two

That night, long after Jane and Doc had left, Hallie paced in her apartment, reluctant to go to bed. The memory of the photograph haunted her. She retrieved it from the envelope in the locked drawer and tore it into flakes, watched them flutter into the trash basket. She carried the container into the hall and emptied it down the incinerator.

But she didn't feel better.

She turned on the radio to an all-night call-in show and switched it off irritably after a few minutes. For a while she watched television, a popular movie about a girl possessed by the monster in her own nightmares. Once Hallie had enjoyed the movies' flamboyant scariness but now watching the townspeople standing by helplessly made her impatient. Finally she flicked the television off too.

She stood in the center of the parlor, her neck prickling with exquisite self-consciousness. She rubbed her palms together. The creaking of the old building, the rattling of the windowpanes, were omens of impending calamity. She wandered from one room into another, fiddled with the papers on her desk without seeing them, moved away and behind the kitchen screen where she made a cup of cocoa. She carried it around without drinking it. Finally, a few minutes before three A.M., she turned off the lights and undressed, leaving her clothes in a heap on her bedroom chair. She removed a flannel nightgown from a hook on the closet door, slid it over head and climbed into bed, pulling the covers tightly and safely around her. But she—who never had trouble falling asleep—had trouble falling asleep. The clatter and jangle of street sounds bothered her and she flopped from one side of the bed to the other, covering her head with pillows, pretending she wanted to go to sleep but knowing she was afraid to. When she finally rose and padded across the room to pull the heavy drapes across the window, the stillness that followed seemed sinister. In her bed again she became even more agitated. Once more she rose, tiptoed to the window and drew the curtains open to readmit the light and noise. She moved back to bed noticing the soreness in her muscles and joints.

"Old age sucks," she said, her tone surprisingly loud and rebellious. She said it again. The tough words and the familiar sound of her voice reminded her she knew how to take care of herself. "Old fool," she added with satisfaction. Then, unaccountably comforted, she snuggled into the blankets, shifted to one side of the big bed and closed her eyes.

In an instant she was asleep, transported to a place where she moved cautiously ahead in a mist, unable to identify her whereabouts. She knew something essential to her safety lay just ahead, but she couldn't remember what it was or why she needed to reach it. An unpleasant sound engulfed her, as if she were in a small room, alone with someone breathing with difficulty. But she couldn't see who it was. There were long silences between each echoing breath. When the feeble inhalation started again it amplified gradually until it became so loud she wanted to hold her ears. It was as if she were *inside* the sound. She found herself breathing as fully and deeply as she could, reassuring herself it wasn't she who was making the frightening noises. Clearly the person she heard was near death. Each breath was an exhausted effort to ingest oxygen but the scratching and wheezing interfered, closed off the lungs, produced an asthmatic burbling at the shallow base of each breath. A rattle.

She peered ahead and saw a doorway. The sound of breathing followed her across the threshold into a huge warehouse room. The floor was gritty and cold. Candles flickered everywhere. She saw hundreds of iron cribs, each containing a motionless infant, radiating in rows away from

182

her—rays from a setting sun. Gradually she moved toward a long platform standing among the cribs. Candlelight illumined the black velvet that lay draped on the table.

She saw herself lying there, as she'd appeared in the photograph earlier in the evening. The same lilies stood in a glass vase at her head, her hands were crossed with identical tranquility. She stiffened and drew back, but something pulled her closer. She leaned toward the table and looked with dread into her own dead face. Some terrible impulse made her reach out to touch it. She felt cheeks as hard and dry as wood. The grey lips were twisted and tight, like rope.

As she stood there the corpse's eyelids clicked open and Hallie stared into the cold marble eyes of a china doll.

Turning frantically she saw that the babies in the cribs were all dolls. Each of them reached toward her with chubby wooden hands, their hinged mouths clacking open and shut, whining "Mama" in unhuman doll voices. She was surrounded by the dolls, engulfed by them, they groped toward her, pulled at her, insistent, threatening.

The terrible sound of breathing stopped and Hallie fell backwards, helpless and doomed, down a black well of silence.

It was she who was dead.

Later she sat quietly in the living room and waited for morning, contemplating the picture she saw of herself in death. The image flickered, clear, unavoidable, soon. She glimpsed herself—as in her dream—lying on a flat surface in the center of a cluttered room, her hands crossed on her chest. She was wearing boots and a thick pair of woolen trousers.

She felt herself letting go of life. Inside her chest her heart quivered, swelled, stopped.

There was an imploding sensation, a sucking—then nothing. Black.

There was no pain.

She wiped her mouth calmly with the back of her hand.

She was to grapple with an ordeal of spirit, a challenge whose details she was unable to predict. Somebody else would be involved. A stranger. Someone she must protect.

An arduous journey through cold.

And there was evil. A big room with mirrored walls, an enormous bed covered with red satin sheets.

Finally she rose stiffly, went to her desk and began putting her affairs in order. She would be ready.

Chapter Three

The following Wednesday Hallie and Jane met Dorothy Kite for lunch at a small restaurant in midtown.

Dorothy dressed carefully for the meeting. She chose a pair of cultured pearl ear clips—left by Madelyn—and a dark maternity dress lined in taffeta. It rustled as she moved, giving her a sense of elegance. Going to lunch with strangers meant she was venturing into a place where there might be new friends and new ways of thinking, so she wanted to make a good impression. She sensed that something essential to her wellbeing (and her babies') depended on the meeting's going well.

She might get help here.

Jane Blanchard had combed her blond hair back and artfully arranged it to give herself height. She wore a tight dark suit with large ceramic buttons which she unfastened as she sat down with Hallie at a table in the rear of the restaurant to wait for Dorothy.

When Dorothy approached their table behind the maitre d' Hallie knew her immediately. With excited curiosity she observed the young woman's nervous movements, the tense twist of her shoulders, her quick short steps, the way her eyes darted into the corners and probed each of the people she passed. Here was the key to her premonition.

Jane leaned forward to shake hands and introduce herself and her aunt. Dorothy's eyes flicked nervously toward Hallie.

The maitre d' hurried off and Jane sat back as Dorothy

pulled in her chair and settled herself. A busboy pushed past their table carrying a tray laden with wobbling towers of dirty cups and saucers.

"Clearly we're not the kind of people headwaiters make a fuss over," Jane said, nodding toward the kitchen door swinging shut a few feet away. "We can't all be honored statesmen like Richard Nixon," she joked. "Somebody has to sit near the kitchen."

Hallie pulled her eyes reluctantly from Dorothy's and opened the menu. She breathed deeply, beads of sweat appearing in a glistening arc across her forehead. As she paged through the large menu, her heart thumped. Her senses were acutely engaged in surreptitious study of Dorothy's smell, her look, the texture of her skin, her long-fingered hands and tapered nails, the tone of her voice.

Hallie wanted to memorize every crucial detail.

After each of them ordered, Jane broke a hard roll into three pieces and buttered each segment briskly. "I'm awful at small talk," she announced with a bright look at Dorothy. "So I'm just going to dive right in."

Dorothy smiled politely. She glanced again at Hallie.

"Doc wanted me to get in touch with you," Jane said animatedly, oblivious to the tension and electricity crackling around her, "because you were facing twins all alone. He felt you needed moral support. That's why I called. I thought you might enjoy some good old-fashioned girl talk."

Dorothy thanked her. She looked again at Hallie, wondering who she was, why the sight of her was so exciting, why she felt such a strong connection with her.

"Tell us about yourself," Jane told her.

Returning her gaze reluctantly to Jane, Dorothy repeated the story she'd concocted for Jane's husband: an automobile accident had killed her fiancé and his mother; her own mother, ill for years, had recently died; she lived alone. When she talked about her pregnancy her eyes shone with happiness. It was clear she didn't feel sorry for herself and wasn't asking for pity.

So Jane responded warmly, clucking in response as Dorothy spoke, her own eyes filling with sympathetic tears. When she finished, Jane told her not to worry, there were all

186

kinds of people who could assist her. For example, she knew of an employment agency specializing in nannies. "I often help Doc's patients find people," she said. "It's difficult to locate somebody reliable and the obstetrician's wife is in a perfect place to establish some kind of nanny network and follow-up." She grinned. "I'm thinking of hanging my shingle next to Doc's: 'I'll deliver a nanny after my husband delivers your child.'"

Jane fingered one of her gleaming earrings and frowned as the waiter set their plates in front of them. Her fruit salad was served on a large white dish. Slices of apple, pineapple, peaches, and red grapes were arranged around a scoop of cottage cheese set in a seashell of iceburg lettuce. She picked up her fork and poked at the pretty food unenthusiastically. She looked at Hallie's plate.

"Aunt Hallie," she said after a moment, "are you going to eat *all* of that huge piece of meat?"

Hallie speared her own steak, cut a large sliver from it and deposited the chunk on Jane's plate. "I suppose you'll give me all the cottage cheese I want," she commented wryly, carefully watching Dorothy's response to the joke. "Jane learned long ago how to get people to do what she wants," she explained. "The rest of us know what she's doing but we play along anyway."

"It isn't as if I forced you," Jane said, tossing her head coquettishly.

"True enough," Hallie said. She fell silent, looking again at Dorothy.

Dorothy put her fork down and cleared her throat. She had to learn more about Hallie. Why did she seem so important to her? But she felt awkward asking personal questions. She didn't know where to start.

"Hallie's a musician," Jane said, volunteering information innocently, dabbing at her mouth with a napkin. "She's lived alone so long she thinks she knows everything. There's never been anybody brave enough to keep her in line."

Hallie smiled. "Unlike you, I suppose," she said.

"What kind of instrument do you play?" Dorothy said. She was thinking of her father, of the piano he'd left behind.

"Piano," Hallie said.

187

Dorothy shivered, feeling a connection even more strongly.

"When I started out," Hallie added, "I played the trombone."

"No!" Jane exploded. "I never knew that! The trombone!" The unlikely image of her elegant aunt playing the trombone made her laugh.

Hallie nodded at her niece. "You see? You don't know everything either." She turned back to Dorothy. "That was when I was in elementary school. I liked the sound of the trombone. It seemed so—I don't know—*irreverent*. Those swooping notes. I wanted to play trombone in the marching band in high school." She sipped her glass of water. "By the time I got there, however, I learned that the trombone was only for boys. Girls who were music students were allowed to play the triangle and the xylophone, or freeze their bottoms being drum majorettes and cheerleaders. The prospects seemed pretty dismal, so I gave up both band *and* trombone. That's when I started seriously studying piano."

Jane shook her head. "Well, I'll be," she said. "I never knew. The *trombone*."

"Later I intended to play piano seriously, as a soloist with various symphony orchestras—"

"But you *did* do that," Jane interrupted. "All over the country."

"Yes," Hallie said, "but it wasn't enough. When people hear Mozart or Beethoven they sit with their hands in their laps as if they're in church. From my standpoint—as a performer—there was something missing. In concert I felt like a conduit, an interpreter. I didn't feel as if I was making *myself* heard. It's hard to explain. When you're a soloist, you want people to listen to *you*. Not just the person who write the words or the notes, but you too. It's the reason you get up in front of everybody and put yourself on the line, so they'll hear you and respond to you." She shrugged and grinned. "I guess I've got a stupendous ego." Then she paused, took a carrot from the appetizer plate and rolled it pensively between her fingers. "For years I'd been playing Fats Waller and Dixieland at home," she continued. "For my own enjoyment, with nobody else around. As if there was something wrong with that kind of music. God, classicists are such snobs. Then one night I went to an after-hours place with a friend of mine and there was this old upright in the corner. I jut sat down at it and started to play and sing. Stride. Rhythm and blues. Dixieland. Don't ask me what got into me, it just seemed like that was what I wanted to do. The place was packed, dark and smoky, people talking at little round tables. After a while I looked up as I was playing and saw everybody grinning, swaying and stamping and clapping along with me. I made them *move!* I couldn't believe the power I had, it was wonderful." She sat back.

"I never knew any of that!" Jane said.

"It made me think about that kind of music, the people—black people—who played it. It made sense to me, that people who were powerless elsewhere would invent that kind of strong music. Why, it had the power to arouse people, to make them jump out of their chairs and dance!" She took a bite from the carrot and chewed thoughtfully. "Imagine, not permitted to play the trombone because you're female! Is that dumb, or what?"

Dorothy nodded eagerly. Then, bravely, hardly believing she could surmount her shyness, she suggested, "Perhaps—since you hadn't been allowed to play the music you liked—maybe that's why you took to music like that," she said. "Playing it gave you—as a woman—power you didn't have elsewhere."

"It certainly gave me common experience with the black musicians," Hallie said. "We understood each other. And I could fool around with the music, inject myself. There wasn't just one set way to play it. Jazz musicians are very generous when they respect you."

Dorothy admired Hallie's experiences, and—even more—the perspective, the *wisdom* she'd developed by examining what had happened to her and how she'd behaved.

Dorothy wanted to learn how to be like her.

They looked at one another for a long time.

Jane pushed away her plate and signaled the waiter for coffee. She turned to Dorothy. "Doc says you don't have a partner for the Lamaze classes," she said.

Dorothy shook her head, no, she didn't. "But I don't

189

mind," she added stoically. "I'm used to being on my own."

"I can be your partner," Hallie said quietly, and Jane looked at her with surprise. She hadn't planned to become personally involved with Doc's patient—nice as she seemed. And she'd only invited Hallie to come along for the company, there wasn't any need for her to *do* anything. "Of course you have your own friends," she told Dorothy hurriedly. "You don't want us butting in, we just thought you might want to talk about it—"

"I think it's important to talk," Hallie told Dorothy quietly. "There's a lot we have to find out about each other."

Dorothy looked into her steady blue eyes and agreed.

"It was the strangest thing," Jane told Doc later. "They acted as if they'd known one another for ages. And I sat there like a bump on a log."

"I doubt that," Doc said, grinning. They were walking home from the movies. He took her elbow as they crossed the street. "You know how Hallie is," he added. "She's always fascinated by interesting stories and people who don't fit into categories."

"Well, it was Hallie who had the interesting story, if you ask me," Jane said. "She talked and talked. Why, she told Dorothy Kite all kinds of things about herself that I never even knew! You should have heard. Dorothy kept asking her things, and Hallie answered, telling all kinds of details. And you know she never talks about herself, not to us!" She frowned, searching for words. "It was almost like a job interview." She glanced into a darkened shop window, at the display of pocketbooks. "They were talking to each other past me, as if I had nothing to do with anything. As if the only reason I was there was to get the two of them together."

"Come now."

"I know it sounds crazy."

"It certainly does."

They walked silently for a while. "They went off together with their heads together and forgot all about me," Jane pouted.

Doc glanced at her. "I think you're jealous," he said.

"I certainly am!" she said. "I feel left out."

He put his arm around her shoulder and squeezed. "Look at it this way," he said. "You fixed up two lonely people. Thanks to you each of them has a friend she didn't have before."

"Hallie's not lonely!" Jane protested.

Doc squinted ahead. "Don't be so sure," he said. "She's getting old and her health isn't great. I know you don't like to think about it, but she doesn't get around with the same old zest. I think a new friendship, a new interest is just the ticket."

Jane thrust her hands into her pockets. "You're probably right, but the way they just sat there looking at each other . . ." She swallowed uneasily. "It was spooky."

"You're being melodramatic."

Jane didn't answer but she knew she was right. Something was going on between the two women, something mysterious. She'd keep an eye on them both.

Chapter Four

Hallie and Dorothy went together to Dorothy's apartment after they'd finished lunch with Jane. Busy with their separate thoughts, neither spoke in the cab. Dorothy studied the back of the driver's head and considered the peculiar attraction—it felt almost primal—drawing her to the accomplished old woman sitting next to her. She had experienced none of the adventures Hallie had, known none of the people she'd moved among, considered few—if any— of the issues Hallie had confronted. Yet it was as if Dorothy knew her already, as if there were strong historic associations between them, as if she'd located her after a long and painful absence.

It felt right to be sitting beside her, going home.

If only she could enlist Hallie's help for her own adventure. At lunch she'd sensed strength in her, and imagination. Grit. Dorothy needed these things in her battle with Elmo Shaw. She needed this woman to help her.

On her side of the backseat Hallie looked out the dirty window and watched a blur of storefronts as the taxi jounced on its way uptown.

Dorothy was the catalyst in her final adventure. With this recognition her fear had vanished. The clouded events she'd foreseen were about to reveal themselves in context and this certainty brought relief and acceptance. She'd soon learn Dorothy's story and her own part in it. It would become her story too. Her earlier incomprehension had produced the nightmares, the uncharacteristic feelings of despair. A relationship with Dorothy was the crucial piece of the puzzle and recognition of its importance fixed it in place with the strength of fate. She felt herself comforted and strangely excited by the approaching crisis and her role in its resolution.

She saw again she was going to die soon, but, curiously, she felt no fear or reluctance. She'd done everything she wanted in her life—made music, traveled, been recognized and rewarded, known interesting people and done interesting things. She'd made her mark, and was satisfied. Death was no more frightening—or mysterious—than birth. She glanced at Dorothy, sitting straight and tense beside her. A strong urge to protect her welled up in Hallie, and she reached across to take her hand. "It's going to be all right," she said.

When they finally arrived at Dorothy's apartment, she climbed the stairs slowly behind Dorothy, who unlocked the several locks on her front door, hurried inside and hung up their coats. Breathless from the climb, Hallie settled in the chair by the living room window while Dorothy moved into the kitchen to make a pot of tea. A ray of wintry sunshine slanted through the blinds to brightly stripe Hallie's curly gray hair. The narrow beam trailed from the top of her head, across her shoulder and onto the floor, like a ribbon. Dorothy brought the cups and saucers on a tray and set it down. Seeing how cluttered and confining the apartment was, she was suddenly self-conscious. The familiar furniture seemed dowdy and worn. She fiddled with a bowl of dried flowers on the mantel.

Hallie waited.

Finally Dorothy sat down, facing her across the coffee table. "Dr. Blanchard's wife thinks the world of you," she began, trying to talk small talk, holding her teacup with both hands to steady them. She wondered that even now it was difficult to call Jane Blanchard by her first name. She hated being so shy, it made her feel inept and inexperienced.

"Jane admires me because I have a career and never married," Hallie said. "She sees that as nonconformist. Now that she's in her fifties her heart aches because she never went around the world in a balloon or had an affair with an

Iranian diplomat."

Dorothy smiled, wondering if Hallie had done these things. "I like to read history," she ventured, "and I've learned that being sentimental about the past means you obscure the way things really were."

Hallie nodded. "When Jane came along in the fifties, not marrying meant you were an old maid. Being nonconformist or independent were euphemisms. These days when Jane yearns after all the glamour and mystery she supposedly lost out on she forgets that back then she wanted to get married. The alternative wasn't glamorous to her at all, not then." She set her cup and saucer on the coffee table. "I think she's satisfied with her life most of the time. But every once in a while she gets a galloping case of the if-onlys."

Dorothy mentioned the "old maid librarian" stereotype. "Loving history and making your living working among old books makes people think you're queer—if you're a woman. They think you should give it all up, just get married and make some man happy." She thought of Henry. "And of course if you're a *male* librarian, it's just as bad. People say 'why aren't you a captain of industry, out there getting and spending! Must be something the matter with you.'" She smiled hesitantly. "Here I go sounding like some radical."

"Noticing when people are treated unkindly is hardly radical," Hallie said. She looked around the room, focused on the upright in the corner. "Is your piano in tune?"

"I'm afraid not. It hasn't been played in years." Dorothy couldn't remember ever hearing it played. Since her father's departure it had remained in its shadowy place, silent testimony to both the fact and impossibility of better times.

"We'll have to get it tuned," Hallie said.

Dorothy agreed quickly. *We!*

They began talking simultaneously.

"I have to tell you—"

"I need to know—"

Hallie leaned back laughing. "Perhaps you'd better let me in on what's happening to you," she said. "I feel like a character in a whodunit. What's going on?"

Dorothy nodded, nervously straightening the antimacassar on the arm of her chair. She looked up cautiously to

194

study Hallie's face. She saw the clear eyes watching her. She wanted to be honest without frightening her away, so she started slowly, first admitting that the story she'd told her about her boyfriend and his mother was a lie.

"I thought it sounded a little farfetched," Hallie said.

Dorothy exhaled, hugely relieved, almost giddy. At last she could tell somebody the truth. She continued slowly, searching for the right words, trying hard to make the unbelievable events believable. She described her obsession with having a baby and the events leading to her pregnancy. With an effort she controlled her tone of voice. She didn't want to sound hysterical.

Certainly the story sounded crazy.

But Hallie didn't appear skeptical. She listened intently as Dorothy spoke.

When she described the artificial insemination procedure, Dorothy jumped up and hurried to her desk. She removed Elmo Shaw's journal and thrust it into Hallie's hands. "This is the man who did it to me," she said. "It's his journal. Read it."

Without a word Hallie took a pair of rimless spectacles from her handbag, fitted them carefully over her ears, positioned the ledger on her lap and began reading.

After turning on the standing lamp behind the chair Dorothy went into the kitchen and refilled the pot with water. She put it on the stove to boil, moistened a sponge and wiped the counter with it. Then she stood biting her thumbnail, waiting. She jumped when the kettle started whistling. When she reentered the living room Hallie didn't look up. Dorothy sat down opposite her. After several minutes Hallie closed the ledger firmly and looked at Dorothy.

"It's the same man, Hallie," Dorothy said. "The one I signed the agreement with is the person who started the journal in 1820. Elmo Shaw."

Hallie shook her head. "I usually believe anything but I'm not sure I believe that."

"If you saw him you'd know," Dorothy said. "He's so old! And after what happened to Henry—there isn't any doubt."

Hallie tapped her finger against her cheek. "What

happened to Henry?"

"He found the book you just finished reading. It was stored for years at the library where we work. I was at the doctor's—at Dr. Blanchard's—when he found it. Henry hadn't even told me he was looking for it. I had no idea anything like it existed. After he read it he was so frightened he went out and got drunk."

"I can't blame him for that," Hallie said.

Dorothy described the dogs gathering one by one outside the saloon, waiting for him. She told of his terrified flight up the street and how it ended. "They weren't ordinary dogs," she insisted. "They were trained—*commanded* to get him. That's why they could disappear afterward. Into the air."

Hallie shifted restlessly.

Dorothy reached across the table impulsively and grasped her hand. "Please help me," she said. With a start she remembered the woman under Jeannie's tree who'd made the same request of her. She told Hallie about the women in the old-fashioned clothes who'd appeared to her—reflected in the store window, on the plane, in Jeannie's yard. She was certain they were the ghosts of Mr. Shaw's other patients. They wanted her help.

Hallie asked her if she'd ever had any supernatural experiences.

"Like what?" Dorothy wanted to know.

Hallie described her own ability to see—sometimes—into the future.

"No," Dorothy said. "And I don't have ESP either. I never know what other people are thinking, I only wish I did!" She frowned. "But those women. I was the only person who saw them, I'm sure. They were there for *me* to see."

Hallie looked toward the window.

"I've always tried to be good," Dorothy pressed. "To do what other people want me to do, kind of design myself to measure up to other people's expectations, wait for things to happen *to* me. But now that I'm pregnant, everything has changed. I can't just sit by and wait for something to happen, for good luck to fall out of the sky. I have to take action! And time is getting short. That's why I'm asking you to help me. I don't even know what I'm asking you to do. But I know I

196

can't do it by myself. That's the first step, knowing that. Asking you to help me is the second step."

After a moment Hallie glanced toward the corner. "Do you mind if I play the piano? It helps me think."

She rose and went to the upright, lifted the cover and stood looking at the discolored keys. Dorothy watched as she gingerly tested a few notes, one at a time. They quavered, hoarse and out of tune. Then Hallie sat on the stool, wobbled on it thoughtfully, looking at the keyboard. She flexed and rubbed her fingers, then struck a series of ascending chords. Next she rippled a soft arpeggio. The sound reverberated in the silent room. Turning fully to face the instrument, she straightened her left leg at an angle toward Dorothy. With her other foot she pumped the peddle, setting a thumping, wheezing, wildly cheerful beat. She launched a series of major chords and began to sing.

"You can listen to temptation . . ." came her reedy alto. "You can even go astray . . ." She banged out the syncopation. "But if you listen to temptation, there's gonna be the Devil to pay!" She grinned, her big left hand striding up the bass by octaves, first the low note and a split second later the higher one. Simultaneously her right hand tinkled in the treble. Her song boomed somewhere in the middle. "You can go to church on Sunday," she continued. "Even wash your sins away. . . ." She shook her head threateningly. "But if you're only good on one day . . . there's gonna be the Devil to pay!"

As suddenly as she started she stopped. The stool creaked as she turned on it to face Dorothy. "I'm going to move in with you," she said.

"I can't ask you to do that," Dorothy said, resisting her excitement.

"It's what I want," Hallie said. "Until two or three weeks after the babies come. Until you're all safe." She paused. "Did you ever hear of yin and yang?"

Dorothy squeezed her hands together. "Opposites?" she said.

Hallie nodded. "Kind of. It's the Chinese concept of balance," she said. "As I remember it, yin represents one side of life—the dark, cold, wet side. Yang's the opposite—light,

197

dryness. Heat. The Confucians claim yin and yang are opposing forces in nature. When they're combined they produce harmony."

Dorothy frowned. "I don't see—"

"Maybe if we can find what exists in opposition to Elmo Shaw—the Yang to his Yin—maybe you have a chance."

"How do we know anything opposes him?" Dorothy said in a strained voice. "He's got exactly what he wanted for a hundred and sixty years."

Hallie shrugged. "Maybe so," she said. "But he's real, isn't he?"

"You mean flesh and blood?"

Hallie nodded.

"Yes," Dorothy admitted. "He's a real person."

"If he was born he has to die."

Dorothy shook her head. "Why? If he can live two hundred years, he can live forever."

"Not necessarily." Hallie looked back at the piano keys. "If something starts in history," she said thoughtfully, "it ends in history. Nothing is forever, especially not a human being, even one with magic powers."

"I wish I believed that," Dorothy said, shuddering. "But I don't think natural law applies to him."

"Natural law always applies."

"Try telling Henry that."

Hallie raised her eyebrows. Did Dorothy want to throw in the towel?

"Of course not," she said, stung. "But it was selfish of me to ask you to help. Maybe you shouldn't get involved."

Hallie crossed her arms firmly. "I'm already involved," she said. "I don't seem to have any choice."

"What if he tries to kill you?"

Hallie's expression softened. "I've already had a full life," she said, looking kindly into Dorothy's troubled face. "And in the last chapter it might be interesting to come up against old Scratch himself. Or his *employee.*" She grinned. "Besides, I'll die happy if the old bastard dies along with me. I think that's exactly what's going to happen. A fair trade— one old codger for another." She stood and moved to the window.

198

Dorothy followed her and they watched quietly as the rain pattered on the pavement around the street light below.

It was November first.

The following afternoon Hallie moved in with a suitcase, a briefcase jammed with sheet music, and a potted philodendron.

Chapter Five

For the next several days they talked endlessly. They went for walks, shopped, cooked and ate together, washed the dishes, talked and talked, their voices rising and falling until late at night when one or the other of them began nodding with exhaustion. In the morning they were up early, hungry for more talk. Dorothy tried hard to describe herself and the events which had shaped her. What she remembered most about her mother, she said, was missing her. Being with her, in the same room, even side by side—but being locked out, excluded somehow, on the other side of an invisible wall. When she reported the hurt, it overwhelmed her and she started to cry. Even though they'd lived together all her life, she'd never felt filled or surrounded by her mother's love. She'd felt herself an outsider who yearned for nurture she never received. She felt no different even now.

Madelyn hadn't been able to help it, she added quickly, wiping her eyes, defending her. Nobody had loved her either. She'd had no resources to pull love out of.

Dorothy told how she'd stayed behind when Spark left. She must have remained at home in order to win her mother's love at last, she said, to be filled with her warmth, surrounded by the safety and comfort of that loving place.

But it never happened. Madelyn died and left Dorothy still empty, still unprotected. At the base of her feelings was an ache that never went away.

The inheritance had been Dorothy's chance to free herself from the yearning that prevented her from facing the future and inventing her life. Her child, paid for by the legacy, was a present from her mother. Dorothy would forge a connection through her baby to Madelyn, complete a circle that could never be broken. That's why the pregnancy had been imperative, why she'd allowed herself to make the evil arrangement with Elmo Shaw after the clinic rejected her, why she'd gone ahead against Henry's advice and her own misgivings.

It was as if she'd become pregnant with herself.

"Does that sound crazy?" she asked.

Hallie shook her head. No, it didn't sound crazy.

Once pregnant, and with Henry killed, she'd understood she must keep both her children, not just one of them. She'd faced the prospect of waging a supernatural battle alone.

Hallie understood solitude. All her life she'd maintained a vigorous independence, chosen and fashioned her destiny without permitting the intrusions of others—no matter how well-meaning or well-loved. She'd had love affairs, of course—a summer with an Italian Count in a villa overlooking the Mediterranean, another several months in the Pyrenees with the aforementioned Iranian. But she'd always had to break it off, unencumber herself, turn her back and flee. She'd prized her autonomy and never questioned the impulse dictating this ultimately solitary journey through experience. Now, as she listened to Dorothy, a flash of unexpected insight revealed the life she'd chosen as curiously barren. She'd permitted others to love her but held back her own feelings. (She always had to hurry off to the next gig—pack her bags—leave.) She'd feared—without naming it fear—emotional entanglement.

But you have many friends, Dorothy argued.

Hallie disagreed, wondering that she'd never seen herself truly. Acquaintances. Not friends.

And since her twenties she'd rejected even the possibility of marriage—proudly, with a dash of braggadocio—but now she wasn't sure she'd reached her present state without giving up something valuable.

"Jane claims I like saving the world but have trouble with little things like including somebody else in my plans," she confessed.

Hallie suspected the success of this great adventure with Dorothy depended on their establishing a strong relationship. Yet these weapons of closeness and commitment were traits she'd done her best to avoid developing. At the age of seventy-one, her life's tools, flashy as they were, could prove inadequate for the task. She was unskilled at intimacy.

"I'm a loner, too," Dorothy said, remembering Jeannie's accusation. Jeannie must have felt that Dorothy's inability to ask for help meant she didn't love her!

"We have to help each other learn to reach out," she said quietly. It wouldn't be easy for either of them.

They continued talking, focusing on what lay ahead. They agreed it was necessary to learn more about Elmo Shaw. When Dorothy told of Henry's note about the seven sisters and her unsuccessful attempt to discover what he'd meant, Hallie said firmly. "The seven sisters aren't just stars. They're colleges too. Mount Holyoke, Wellesley, Smith. The rest of them. That's what he was talking about."

Dorothy clapped her hands. "Of course!" she said. Why hadn't she thought of that?

She'd go to the library and follow the lead.

Evil had been around longer than Elmo Shaw's mere two hundred years. Perhaps somewhere in ancient folklore there'd be a description of somebody like him, and maybe there'd also be stories about people who'd stood up to him, descriptions of the techniques—rituals or magic—they'd used.

"I'm a librarian, for heaven's sake," Dorothy said. "I'm an expert researcher. If there's anything written down, anyplace—I ought to be able to find it. That's my training."

The realm of metaphysics would be Hallie's source. If Elmo Shaw was a reincarnation of ancient evil, then she might have to learn ancient rites of exorcism to do battle with him.

"We're up against primal greed," she said. "We need all the artillery we can muster." She paused, then grinned disarmingly. "Hell," she added with a careless wave of bravado, "if I can learn conjuring, I might discover a whole new career."

Neither of them mentioned how pitifully inadequate—even fanciful—their plans were. But they had no other ideas.

Chapter Six

One evening Dorothy was waiting for the bus on her way home from the library. It was later than her accustomed time. Above her the sky was black and starless. The bus stop was located across the street from a vacant lot fronted by a six-foot-high metal fence topped with loops of barbed wire. Large pieces of the fence had been pried apart and stiff prongs, like hooks, curled outward. An abandoned car without tires listed against the curb on its axles. On both sides of the street dirty sidewalks stretched away, deserted.

She stood under a feeble arc of light from the street lamp. Occasional flurries of snowflakes as tiny and sharp as granulated sugar swirled and bit her cheeks, then dissipated without leaving a trace on the pavement. She watched a bundled person scurry around the corner, unrecognizable and mysterious behind a muffler and hat. His footsteps thudded as he vanished. Dorothy tightened her scarf clumsily with mittened hands. Nearby a ragged woman emerged from the dim area in front of a boarded-up doorway and slowly gathered her belongings from the pavement where she'd been sleeping. Carefully bending and straightening, she loaded her possessions into a flimsy shopping cart with crooked front wheels. She took the several thicknesses of newspaper which had made her bed, folded them with difficulty and pushed the bundle into the bulging basket already holding a rumpled shopping bag crammed with empty cartons and cans, a cardboard suitcase and a long fragment of awning decorated with a fringe of orange balls. The wind caught the awning and whipped it sideways until it streamed from the cart like a flag. The old woman ignored it, slowly moving back and forth. Her face was set with deep lines of sadness and experience. Periodically she paused to rub her hands and blow on them. She was dressed in several grimy layers of clothing and a plastic garbage bag, worn upside down with holes torn for her head and arms. A wool cap with a moth-eaten pompom was pulled low on her forehead. As Dorothy watched she finally finished packing and moved off, grunting with the effort of pushing the shopping cart uphill, across the broken squares of sidewalk and into the gusting snow.

Dorothy turned from her and leaned cautiously toward the street, peering downtown to see if the bus were coming. She was impatient to get home to show Hallie what she'd found.

Except for an empty taxi whizzing by with its headlights piercing the dancing snow, the avenue was empty. She turned again to face the vacant store, her back against the wind.

She tensed as a young derelict approached. Dressed only in filthy chinos and a fisherman's sweater unraveling at the wrists, he was rubbing his thin chest, clapping his hands for warmth, hopping from one lopsided square of sidewalk to the next. He wore no socks with his unlaced sneakers, which flopped open. His curiously flat eyes skittered and flicked as he neared her.

"Evenin', Mama," he grinned, focusing his gaze suddenly and nodding good-naturedly toward Dorothy's obvious pregnancy. Despite his bravado he looked cold and ill. Raising his shoulders with his elbows jammed against his waist and his wrists held loosely in front of himself, he kicked one long leg toward an invisible soccer ball, lowered a shoulder, swooped and bent his narrow torso into the doorway just vacated by the old woman. With a quick lunge he reached under a sheet of newspaper weighted in one corner with a brick, and pulled out a half eaten bagel. "Umm, umm," he said, taking a bite and squeezing shut his eyes. He brandished the dirty bun. "Now, that's *good*."

Dorothy turned from him as a towering bus, its windows

204

dark and blank—pulled up from out of the rolling mist and opened its doors. Steaming light poured onto the curb and she lumbered up the steps, deposited her token and squeezed through the crowded aisle, relieved at the noise and warmth of the people inside. A teenager stood and offered her a seat, which she accepted gratefully. She sat down, eased her back, and set her feet on the slushy rubber carpet, and turned to gaze through the window. The addict with the bagel had disappeared. She glimpsed the old woman pushing her cart stubbornly up a side street, bent into the wind. Dorothy wondered if she had known the boy was coming, if she'd hidden the food there for him.

It seemed unlikely.

As the doors of the bus opened at her stop, Dorothy stepped carefully down the steps. Her head snapped back from an unexpected blast of cold coming like a slap across her face. She made fists in her mittens and leaned forward, into the wind. Half a block from the entrance to her building she raised her eyes and met the gaze of an old man holding a pair of dogs on a short leash who was blocking her way. He bowed and tipped his large-brimmed black felt hat. "Good evening, Miss Kite," he said.

It was Elmo Shaw.

The leash he held split into two short leads attached to thick iron spiked collars fitted snugly around the dogs' throats. The large animals pranced impatiently. One of them sniffed and slobbered at Dorothy's ankle.

"How nice to see you," Mr. Shaw said. "You're looking well."

She stood rigidly, unable to surround her fright with words.

"I suppose by now you're eager for confinement," he said.

She didn't reply.

"My patients tell me pregnancy seems endless by the seventh month," he said, smiling conspiratorily. She stared at his eyelids, noticed the sparse lashes sticking out from the runny pink rims like bristles. "So much time has elapsed," he continued. "And so much time yet to come. But you look

205

radiant, my dear. Pregnancy always brings out a woman's true beauty."

She stared at a sore on his nose. The circle of putrid flesh oozed a thin green liquid which dribbled onto his cheek.

"You must be careful with yourself," he continued, paying no attention to her silence. "Take nothing less than ten hours of sleep every night, a long nap during the afternoon. Eat plenty of red meat, milk, cream, butter, cheese. Absolutely no exercise. You don't want to jeopardize the precious life within you." He smiled again. *He knew best.* "No thinking, my dear. No worrying. It's out of your hands, you have nothing to do with what's happening. Lie back and let it happen! You're a receptacle for god's greatest miracle—an oven, nothing more." He chuckled. "Try not to take yourself so seriously, Dorothy. You're getting dark circles under your lovely eyes. I'm afraid you may be losing your youthful radiance."

She stared at him. He was giving her bad advice. He wanted her to be fat and helpless, to care more about losing her looks than losing her children. He wanted her to believe she had no part in what was happening to her—that she was an *oven*—not somebody who could make choices and take action, someone who could protect herself and her babies.

The larger of the dogs lunged at her and Mr. Shaw yanked up the leash, causing the animal to yelp. It sat back on its haunches, turned it gray jowls toward him and curled its lip menacingly. Dorothy saw there were spikes on the inside as well as the outside of its collar, and traces of blood on the creature's neck where it had been rubbed raw.

She looked at Elmo Shaw steadily. "What you did to Henry—" she faltered as his eyes fastened onto hers again.

"A terrible accident," he said. "I read about it in the newspaper. Terrible."

"It wasn't an accident," she said.

He placed his hand delicately over his heart. He wore a cashmere overcoat with mother-of-pearl buttons, a crimson silk scarf loosely knotted at his scrawny throat. Specks of dandruff were scattered on the scarf, on his black velvet lapels and on his sleeves. His heavy odor pulsed around them in the cold air.

"Why, Dorothy—whatever can you mean?"

"You killed him." She swallowed. *"Elmo."* She spat his first name in response to his use of hers.

"There, there," he said, inching toward her and putting his hand on her arm. "You mustn't become distraught. It's bad for our babies."

She jerked her arm away. "They're my babies, not yours. And if I'm distraught, it's your fault," she said.

"Now, now," he crooned. "Pregnant women get the silliest ideas." He smirked insinuatingly. "Have you sent your companion out for strawberries and peanut butter in the middle of the night yet?"

Her stomach tightened. He knew about Hallie. But he wasn't going to make her lose her focus. "I'm not giving you either of my babies," she said. "I'm keeping both of them." The wind whipped around her shoulders, snapping her scarf into her face. She pulled it away.

"Don't be ridiculous," he said. "You agreed to the arrangement."

"I've changed my mind."

"My dear lady," he said. "You signed a contract."

"After what happened to Henry I've decided not to go through with it." She curled her toes tightly in her boots. "I'm sure it wasn't a legal contract anyway. There weren't any witnesses."

"Of course it was a legal contract," he said. "And whatever unpleasantness befell Mr. Small was his own fault. It has nothing to do with our agreement."

"It has everything to do with it."

He made a clucking sound. (How could she ever have thought him charming?) "You're getting emotional, Dorothy. Losing your judgment. Emotionalism is the major failing of your sex, I'm afraid. You must try to think rationally, my dear."

She shook her head emphatically, taking a step back. "You can't make me give you either of my children," she said. "I won't do it."

He sighed in a long-suffering way. "Of course I can make you give me one of your children," he said. "I'm sure you know that."

"Not if I refuse."

"Dear, oh dear," he said, adjusting one of the dog collars. "You're just being silly." He straightened again, knotting the leash firmly around his gloved hand. "But we'll ignore what you've said. I'm sure when you think it over you'll realize you can't avoid doing what you've agreed to do, that it would be *very* foolish of you to try and break our contract."

"That's for me to decide," she said in the strongest tone she could manage. "Let me pass."

She ducked her head and started forward on trembling legs. Her hands were clammy inside her mittens.

"By all means," he said, bowing and stepping aside in a burlesque of politeness. "I'll be seeing you in January, my dear." As she passed he added softly, "We live in a land of laws, you know. Your silly objections will never prevail in a court. The baby's mine, Dorothy, whatever you say. And you know it."

She pushed blindly past him into her apartment house and upstairs to Hallie.

Chapter Seven

She described the encounter while she put away her hat and coat. "Oh, Hallie, he's worse than I remembered," she said, leaning shakily against the closet door. "How could I have gotten involved with him?"

Hallie pulled her gently down the hall and into the living room. "You wanted a baby," she said. "You were willing to try anything."

Dorothy nodded miserably and sank into the chair by the window. Yes, and now she was caught by the consequences of her obsession. "How can we think for a moment we can defeat him?" The bravery she'd summoned on the street had evaporated. She felt vulnerable again, entirely helpless.

Hallie returned from the kitchen with cups and saucers, a teapot on a tray. She sat on the couch and quietly poured the tea. Dorothy bent over her cup and sipped thirstily, shutting off the memory of the sneering old man, his huge dogs with their bloody collars.

Hallie sat back and crossed her legs. She was wearing a bulky sweater with bright horizontal stripes and tailored woolen trousers. "What did you find?" she asked.

Dorothy looked at her blankly over the rim of the teacup. "Find?"

"At the library. You telephoned you'd found something."

Quickly Dorothy set down the cup, made an exasperated sound and stood. "Seeing him made me forget everything." She hurried across the room to retrieve her shoulder bag from the table by the door. "I mustn't panic," she said impatiently. "That's exactly what he wants, damn it." She frowned as she unfastened the clasp. "I found the book Henry was talking about," she said. "It was in with the Seven Sisters files—the *college* folders, just as you predicted." She pulled a slender blue volume from her bag. "A biology professor at Barnard wrote it in the fifties," she said, returning with the book to sit on the sofa. "She must have had it privately printed, I couldn't find mention of it in any of the usual references. It's an offshoot of a study she was conducting. I think this is the only copy of it in existence. Henry always said nothing was lost if you just knew where to look," she added. "But if he hadn't remembered something about cataloging it—more than twenty years ago—I never could have found it."

"He's still helping us," Hallie said gently.

Dorothy nodded, biting her lip. She missed him, ached to have him sitting beside her holding her hand and helping her through her fear. She swallowed, forcing back the yearning, and centered her concentration instead on the book in her lap. "In 1950, the author—Stephanie Williamson—was studying heredity versus environment in personality development," she explained. Henry's face quietly receded as she continued. "She was comparing personalities of identical twins raised in the same household and personalities of other sets of twins raised separately, without knowledge of each other. She wanted to see which traits were inherited, and which developed as a reaction to environment." She turned several pages of the book and began reading. "'While delving into scholarly data,' she says, 'I came across records of two sets of twins born in the last century to middle-aged New York City couples, both sets mysteriously separated at birth who grew up without knowledge of each other. In each case a "good" twin and a "bad" twin.'"

A whistling wind insistently rattled the windows. Hallie leaned forward to hear better as Dorothy continued.

"'They were, of course, perfect candidates for inclusion in my study because all four histories were well documented,'" she went on. "'But curious coincidences in the two sets of life stories compelled me to look further into the connections between the two sets of twins, even though such inquiry drew me outside my original assignment.'" Dorothy paused and glanced intently at Hallie. "'After examination of available records,'" she continued with careful emphasis, "'I found the birth of both sets of twins occurred forty-two years apart—on the same date, January 1st, in 1843 and 1885. The attending physician was identified on both birth certificates as Elmo Shaw.'"

"Oh, Jesus," Hallie said. She rose and went to the desk, where she removed Elmo Shaw's journal from the drawer and began riffling the pages.

"That's not all," Dorothy said, watching her. "Both mothers died five days later, on January 5th. Of 'childbirth complications.'"

Hallie looked up, her finger holding the place she'd found. "Just like his notations," she said. "What were the years?"

Dorothy looked back at the page. "1843 and 1885," she said.

"Yes," Hallie said, referring to the journal. "He has them here. Butterworth and Trask. In between—in 1864—were the Sloan twins."

"Williamson didn't find them—just Butterworth and Trask."

"It doesn't matter," Hallie said. "Her two cases jibe with his. That's enough."

On the mantel the clock ticked steadily with a muffled tin sound.

As Hallie sat down again, holding the journal tensely, Dorothy continued reading: "'When I examined various city records to ascertain the details of Elmo Shaw's professional practice, as well as other related factors (did he deliver other sets of twins? What happened to them?), I couldn't find any information about him. No one named Elmo Shaw was registered in any list of physicians in the State of New York or in New York City during that period. He didn't belong to any medical society. His name was nowhere included in any city directory of offices or residences, or on any tax roll. I was not included in the censuses during this period. I found no birth or death certificate issued in his name.

"'After this lengthy and fruitless inquiry I reluctantly put aside issues of Elmo Shaw's identity and looked further into

211

the histories of the twins he'd delivered in 1843 and 1885.'"

Hallie waited while Dorothy turned the page.

"'In both cases I found one twin raised in a prosperous home by a father in his fifties or older. The mother was in her forties at the time of their delivery and her death. Both mothers had been jubilant at the prospect of motherhood because their pregnancies came late. They'd thought themselves barren. In both instances the "bad" twin disappeared immediately after its birth and resurfaced a couple of decades later with another name and no apparent link to the birth parents. The fathers never revealed that the single babies they raised were twins.'"

Dorothy looked again at Hallie. "Why didn't the fathers try to trace their other children once their wives died?" she said. "Why didn't they suspect foul play?"

Hallie frowned thoughtfully. "They may not have recognized any connection between Elmo Shaw and the deaths of their wives," she said. "In the nineteenth century mothers died in childbirth all the time. Remember too that he took the babies when the fathers were most distraught, when their wives lay dying. And he could have told them they were participating in an illegal medical experiment. That would've kept them quiet, especially if they felt—as you did—that their cases were unique, even extralegal, that they were getting special treatment." She sighed. "By never telling about the other child the fathers kept their side of the bargain. There wasn't any reason for them to do otherwise. They'd made a deal, that's what businessmen do, that's what they understood. They were upholding the law by going through with the arrangement, as they and their wives had promised. Mr. Shaw counted on them to be upstanding citizens, and they were." She watched as Dorothy turned the page. "We may be the only ones who know the whole story, Dorothy. We know who Elmo Shaw is—they didn't. Knowledge gives us the understanding we need. It gives us the strength to break the contract and keep both babies." She added firmly, "We're going to protect you, too."

Dorothy felt the heaviness of her fear as it crept across her chest and moved coldly down her arms. "My babies don't have a father to raise them," she said. "Henry's dead. And

212

I'm going to die too."

Hallie leaned toward her. "We won't let that happen."

Dorothy smoothed the pages of the book. She repeated what Hallie had said, her voice so small and quavery the sound made them both smile.

"Why don't you read the case histories," Hallie suggested. They needed to learn more, to find some clue to point them in the direction of something that would cause Elmo Shaw to fail.

Dorothy cleared her throat and began reading again. "'Frances and Elsa Trask were born in 1885,'" she read. "'Elsa was taken from her forty-six-year-old mother (Marian Griffen Trask), at birth. The delivery took place at home as did most births then. Nobody knew there'd been a second baby.

"'Frances grew up uneventfully. The lack of a mother's presence wasn't unusual in those days of frequent childbirth deaths. There were servants and a nanny who cared for her until she was well into her teens. Frances's father, who had no other children, never remarried and doted on her. Very little is known of Frances's personal life but the remaining photograph of her captures the expression of a serious person without particular physical distinction.'"

Dorothy displayed a faded photograph of a solemn young woman standing stiffly next to a table draped with an oriental rug. She grasped a volume of poetry and frowned at the lens as the shutter clicked.

Dorothy returned the book to her lap and turned the page. "'After the death of her father, Frances used her considerable inheritance to open a home for orphans and she worked there diligently. She never married and died of heart disease at the age of forty-seven.'"

She turned another page.

"That's interesting," Hallie said. "Opening an orphanage."

"She may have felt an unconscious need to care for babies whose parents had died or abandoned them," Dorothy said.

"Maybe she was looking for her sister," Hallie suggested. "Without even knowing it."

"Poor thing," Dorothy said sympathetically. She looked

down to find her place again. "'On the other hand,'" she read, "'Frances's twin sister, Elsa Trask Shore, led a thoroughly corrupted life. Her early years aren't documented, but by the age of twenty-one she'd abandoned her husband, of whom nothing is known, and become madam of the most notorious whorehouse in New York City. It was rumored that her clientele included at least one member of every old New York family. Gossip held that a United States Senator and a Supreme Court Justice—both married, of course—maintained charge accounts with her establishment and that several young scions of old New York families made a habit of spending the evening with her and her "ladies" the night before they wrote their examinations at Columbia.

"'Her fortune was vast because of sumptuous gifts from businessmen who demonstrated their devotion to her by presenting her with stock certificates from various incipient American corporations.

"'Mrs. Shore became a millionaire many times over. This was due not only to client gifts but to her own acumen and cunning. However, despite her wealth she never abandoned the "calling" making her famous. It was said there was *nothing* Mrs. Shore wouldn't do for her customers, including permitting them to beat her with chains. She was rarely seen in daylight and wore a thick black veil at all times, supposedly to hide the scars on her face and throat. On Christmas Eve in 1931 somebody strangled her and hung her with her own silk stocking from the crystal chandelier in her parlor. Authorities speculated she'd gotten careless and when one of her sadistic customers went beserk, she wasn't able to protect herself. After all, official reports claimed she was "only a prostitute"—not a respectable person with normal desires and feelings. There was an assumption that she'd asked for it.'" Dorothy paused to glance achingly at Hallie, then swallowed and looked again at the book. "'Her murderer was never caught'" she read, "'though rumours abounded as to his important political position. The newspapers of the time conjectured that the investigation was cursory in order to protect him. But the outcry died down quickly. She'd been expendable, after all, and evidently in his position he wasn't.

"'An inquest was held and careful notes from it still exist. The coroner testified as to the condition of her body. Elsa was a little thing, just over five feet tall and for many years had been addicted to laudanum and morphia. Moreover, the ravages of venereal disease had befouled her sexual organs. In addition she was covered with bruises, some old, others fresh. One of her arms had been broken so many times it looked as if she had three elbows.'"

Dorothy closed her eyes and rubbed her chest. The room pressed around her as if the air itself had weight and evil intention. But she must continue, she must learn what kind of fate lay in store for her own child if her determination faltered. After a moment she turned to the second case history and began reading again.

"'Herman and Osgood Butterworth were born in New York forty-two years earlier, in 1843,'" she read tonelessly. "'They were born to a fifty-year-old couple who owned a small retail establishment later bought by Macy's. Osgood disappeared from the family home minutes after his birth and was never acknowledged by his father, who always claimed Herman was his only child despite the presence of the second name on the birth certificate. He insisted this was a clerical error, though—interestingly—it was never corrected.

"'Lillian Brynker Butterworth, the mother of the twin boys died five days after the difficult delivery without regaining consciousness.'" Dorothy met Hallie's gaze. "On January 5th," she said, reaching for her cup. The remaining tea was cold. She set the cup and saucer on the tray and brushed back a strand of hair.

Hallie asked if she wanted her to brew more tea.

Dorothy didn't think so. "I want to get through this," she said. Determinedly, she began reading again: "'Herman Butterworth grew up to found the first settlement house on the Lower East Side. He lived quietly and—from every account—virtuously, dying from natural causes at the age of fifty. He never married. On the other hand, Osgood Butterworth—his "bad" twin—resurfaced at the age of twenty-one with another surname—Schogh,'"—she pronounced it to rhyme with "log"—"'and no connection with his family of birth. He became president of the First American Bank of New York before his thirtieth birthday. After the Civil War he wielded great power in the nation's increasingly intricate financial networks. He lent money to the robber barons and took part in several shadowy schemes to defraud investors and to crush and ruin competitors. Because there were no laws at that time to prevent any but the most vicious of these practices, he was never brought to trial.'" She scanned the page. "'He had a man-about-town reputation and married late. After a few months of marriage he appears to have become unsatisfied with his bride for he beheaded her one morning before leaving for the office.'"

Hallie jerked upright. *"He what?"*

"That's what it says." Dorothy repeated the sentence and then finished the paragraph, her voice barely audible. "'After the murder Schogh carried his wife's head with him in a carpetbag to a meeting downtown with some of his Wall Street colleagues. There someone mistakenly opened the satchel and found its gruesome contents. The police were called and although the matter was quickly hushed up— many fortunes, old families and reputations were involved with him and at risk—Osgood spent the next year in prison. He was murdered there by inmates who ganged up on him and beat him to death. There were rumors his business associates paid to have him exterminated, to remove the troublesome figure from their otherwise exemplary lives. But these allegations were never proved.'"

As she listened a picture flickered in Hallie's mind's eye: Several solemnly bearded businessmen with watch chains glinting across their waistcoats sit around a shining mahogany table. One of them leans down to open a valise on the floor between his chair and his neighbor's. He starts, then stares in horror at the contents. Inside the bag in a mass of tangled hair lies a bloodied head, its mouth sagging open, the eyes rolling back and showing white . . .

Hallie blinked, dismissing the picture. She glanced across at Dorothy. "Are you all right?"

But Dorothy was frowning. "His last name," she said. "The bad one." She glanced at the text. "Schogh." She spelled it, then leafed back hurriedly. "The other one. The bad Trask twin. Her name was Elsa *Shore*," she said.

A siren sounded distantly outside.

They looked at each other, each struck with the same thought.

"You could pronounce *Schogh* as *Shaw*," Dorothy said.

"And New Yorkers often replace a *w* with an *r* at the end of a word," Hallie said.

The bad twins were both named Shaw.

"It shouldn't surprise us," Hallie said. "He raised them, just as he said he would in his journal." She shuddered. "He even *married* Elsa, if you can call whatever he did to her *marriage*."

Stephanie Williamson had discovered nothing about the other twins Elmo Shaw had listed in his journal, babies separated from each other at birth every twenty-one years. But it wasn't necessary for Dorothy and Hallie to learn what had befallen the others. The two bad cases she'd unearthed were enough to signal the fate of the rest of them. Whatever humanity the second twin might have developed or inherited was contaminated by twenty-one years in the house of Elmo Shaw.

Dorothy looked toward the piano. "He promised me the daughter I gave him would have an enviable life," she said. "The liar."

"He wasn't lying," Hallie said, then held up her hand as Dorothy sprang hotly to interrupt. "No, no," Hallie said. "Listen. He *hated* his wife, blamed her for his poverty and unhappiness. He thought all his problems would be solved if she were dead and he were rich." She shrugged. "As far as he was concerned, whatever else happened to Elsa and Osgood was beside the point. They were both rich. He thinks that's enough. He thinks that's enviable."

"Their lives weren't enviable!" Dorothy cried. "They were full of pain!" She pounded her chair's upholstered arms. "They didn't have anywhere to turn. He corrupted them when they were little and defenseless. They never had a chance. Of course they became monsters. Nobody loved them, not ever, not for a moment." Even their mothers had abandoned them.

Icy wind gusted around the trembling window sash and

the curtains flared.

After a moment Dorothy put the book aside and laid her palms on her abdomen. She gently massaged the rolling and shifting within herself. "I never had the right to give my baby away," she said, looking again at Hallie. "When I signed the contract I thought a mother owned her child, that she could sell her if she wanted, like a carrot from a bunch. But I was wrong. Babies aren't property. You can't trade them for something you want. And Elmo Shaw didn't have the right to buy my baby, no matter what service he performed, or what piece of paper I signed." Her eyes flashed. "You can't buy and sell people. After a child is born its mother is its caretaker, not its owner." She lifted her chin stubbornly. "It's an illegal contract. I don't owe him anything."

Looking angrily toward the window, she caught sight of her undulating reflection in the wavy glass and the blackness behind it. As the wind moaned steadily she felt a chill and pulled her sweater tighter.

Every twenty-one years since 1822 a desperate woman longing for a baby had been persuaded by Elmo Shaw to sign away her child in order to keep its twin. He hadn't revealed the lifetime of misery and brutality in store for the infant he carried away.

Nor had he told any of the mothers they'd die without even seeing their babies. Undoubtedly he was amused by the irony, his secret joke on the women he despised.

Dorothy was ninth in this line of women. Because she knew who he was she might be able to change the outcome of the story. If she did this, perhaps she could help the other mothers find peace, as they were asking her to do. And maybe the terrible story would never happen again.

But so far she and Hallie had learned only of Elmo Shaw's successes.

There wasn't much time to learn of his failures—if any.

It was December 6th.

Chapter Eight

One December afternoon a few days later Jane Blanchard came to tea bearing gifts. She was sitting with Hallie when Dorothy came home, her hair still wet from the shower after her swim. Their faces turned toward her as Dorothy entered the room and Jane waved gaily. "We thought you'd be home sooner than this," she said. "Hallie's already showed me around the apartment. I hope you don't mind. I wanted to see your cozy nest." She'd meant to come calling sooner, she said. But something was always interfering. "You know how it is. The holidays. This and that."

Jane had thrown her overcoat casually across the back of her chair and propped several bulky shopping bags on the floor against it. Each bag was stuffed with bright Christmas packages.

"I'm glad to see you," Dorothy said, smiling a welcome but secretly wishing Jane hadn't chosen this afternoon to visit. She yearned to curl up on the sofa and talk to Hallie without interference. But she smiled politely, good manners springing from some deep requirement.

As she settled awkwardly into the chair by the window, Jane, watching her, dropped her eyes and blushed. "I know I'm acting as if we were related," she said, gesturing toward the packages. "But with Aunt Hallie living here we're practically sisters." She tidied her hair with the palms of her hands and looked contrite. "I'll try not to be embarrassed at how wonderful I am to give you a one-woman baby shower if you'll just pretend we've known each other for ages." She regretted her characteristic impulsiveness. She shouldn't clomp in, spread out and take over, Doc would say she was coming on too strong. It was a habit she had—one not always appreciated. But she did so want to be included in what was going on here. She was determined to be charming and to make friends with Dorothy.

Slipping off her shoes and putting her feet tiredly on the hassock, Dorothy was reminded of her sister-in-law. Jeannie had had her baby—a nine-pound boy—in Portland the week before. Little Anthony, Jr., was delivered by a last minute cesarian section. Jeannie had told Dorothy she was disappointed because she'd wanted to be awake during the birth. But at least there hadn't been any complications and the doctor told her she could have a dozen more children if she wanted. "The baby has more hair than Spark!" she'd chortled. "And the incision is so little I'll be able to wear a bikini again."

As Dorothy watched Jane's expressive face she was struck with the thought it could be Jeannie sitting here grinning at her, demanding to be included and loved. So Dorothy smiled again at Jane—Jeannie's surrogate—this time with genuine warmth.

"I've been telling Aunt Hallie that twins are such a fascinating idea," Jane said, relieved. She and Dorothy would be friends after all, she wasn't going to be left out. "Two babies, conceived at the same moment, growing together squashed into the same tiny space. Listening to their mother's heartbeat . . . baBOOM, baBOOM . . ." She tilted her head. "Why every time one of them twists or bends her arm, the other one is affected." She lifted a heavy parcel with both hands from one of the bags she'd brought. "The first present is for you," she said eagerly, handing it to Dorothy. "Aunt Hallie told me on the phone you had a hobby of collecting obscure old books. I found this on one of those card tables across from Zabar's. Can you imagine—" she interrupted herself,—in this weather? Standing outside all day, hoping somebody's going to buy something?" She shook her head and watched as Dorothy unfolded the wrapping paper. "It's full of wonderful old photographs of bygone New York." She winked mischievously. "Maybe it'll

220

remind Aunt Hallie of her youth." She batted her eyes comically at her aunt.

Smiling, Dorothy put aside the wrapping and turned the large pages of the book. Jane came to look over her shoulder.

One photograph showed the old Pennsylvania Station with dusky beams of light slanting from the massive sky-lit ceilings that arched hundreds of feet above the girder-separated track-beds. On the next page a grainy view of the long-gone Grand View Hotel appeared, rising stolidly from the peaceful waters of Brooklyn's Lower Bay. It resembled a square, many-tiered river boat.

Dorothy thanked Jane for the present. Her fascination with bygone days had started in her childhood, she said. She had no idea what had precipitated the interest, but there it was. "This is very thoughtful of you," she repeated, turning a page and gazing at a picture of an elaborate Victorian mansion. The plane of its roof was interrupted with turrets, dormer windows, chimneys, a wrought-iron railing. The huge house was built of stone, with masses of ivy licking up the sides, tentacles creeping across several of the pointed windows to wrap around the leering gargoyles and gutter pipes.

Jane squinted to read the caption. "The Wash Castle," she said. "Overlooking the Hudson. It was torn down to make way for the West Side Highway." She straightened and looked toward the window. "It must have been located near here."

Dorothy continued paging through the book. As she did Jane commented on various photographs of long-ago landmarks. "Imagine living in one of those beautiful buildings with the high ceilings," she said. "Carved moldings, hundreds of fireplaces. Life was slower then, more civilized."

"There weren't any toilets," Hallie said. "No central heating."

Jane made a face. "Spoilsport," she said.

"Sentimentalist," Hallie grinned. Their banter was an old game conducted with obvious affection.

Dorothy turned another thick page, studied a photograph

221

of the glittering ballroom of the old Waldorf hotel. Elegantly gowned women with upswept hair and over-the-elbow gloves smiled flirtatiously at dancing partners who sported drooping mustaches, and wore white tie and tails.

A wave of gloom settled on Dorothy. All these vital, attractive people had died long ago. Suddenly she was not charmed by the past. Its jangling futility depressed her. She sighed and closed the book.

Noticing her change in mood, Jane hurried to the sofa. "Let's open the presents for the babies," she said. She plucked a square package from one of the bags and handed it to Dorothy, who put aside the book and lifted the cover from the slender box. She brushed back the tissue. "Oh, how pretty," she murmured. She displayed a white cotton bonnet with long silken ribbons.

"There are two of them," Jane said. "Where's the other one? Isn't it there?"

Dorothy looked into the box. "There's just the one," she said.

Maybe the identical bonnet was in another package, Jane said. Stores often did that with presents to make it look as if there were many gifts. "Open another one."

But the next present contained a lone dress decorated with a pattern of eyelets and embroidered flowers.

"Wait a minute," Jane said. She reached to open another gift herself, this one containing a tiny undershirt with snaps at the neckline. It was so sheer and delicate the red polish on her nails was visible as she showed them the shirt. "They've only wrapped one of these too," she said with irritation, folding the little garment and stuffing it back into the box. "I bought two dresses, two bonnets, two undershirts. Two complete outfits. Everything matched." She picked the last package from one of the shopping bags. "Here," she said. "There have to be two sets of these."

Dorothy took the gift from her and carefully unwrapped the pink and blue tissue. Inside the folds of paper she found a single pair of fuzzy booties. She held them up for both women to see.

"That takes the cake," Jane said crankily. "There aren't

even two pairs of booties! You just can't trust salespeople these days."

Dorothy glanced at Hallie, then back at Jane. Her heart was pounding. Elmo Shaw had stolen her twin baby's things. She put the boxes on the coffee table and wiped her hands on her skirt.

"But I wanted something for *both* babies," Jane wailed. "I don't understand what happened."

"It's a mixup," Hallie said, glancing worriedly at Dorothy, then at Jane. "Did you keep the receipts?"

"Well, of course," she said. "Even *I'm* not that ditzy." She dug into her purse. "Here they are." She waved several flimsy pieces of paper, then held them at arm's length to study the figures they contained. "Yes, yes," she said. "Each one says I paid for two items."

Dorothy closed her eyes and shrank further into the chair. By stealing the clothes for the second baby, Elmo Shaw was reminding her that one of her twins was meant for him and she was helpless to prevent it.

The mantel clock made a whirring electrical sound and struck seven blunted tones. Jane crammed the receipts into her bag and hurried to put on her coat. She hadn't realized it was so late, she had to leave, Doc would be wondering where she was, wanting his dinner. She patted Dorothy's shoulder and promised to telephone. "I'm mortified about this," she said.

Dorothy's gaze flickered toward Hallie's

"It makes me feel so stupid," Jane went on, oblivious to Dorothy's silence. She bent to zip her boots. "I'll straighten it out and come back with the rest of the things in a day or two," she said cheerfully, gathering the wrapping paper and boxes together, jamming them into one of the shopping bags. "I want to keep tabs on both of you anyway," she added, knotting her scarf, flinging her purse over her shoulder and picking up the bags with both hands. She started down the hallway to the front door. "This will give me an excuse," she called to Dorothy. "I'll be back as soon as I straighten it out."

She returned to hug Hallie and kiss her soundly, then she

223

hurried out the door and clattered down the four flights of stairs.

Hallie reentered the living room and found Dorothy standing at the window with her back to the room. "It was a slipup at the store," she said reassuringly, standing behind her. "That's all."

Dorothy shook her head emphatically. "No," she said. "Elmo Shaw did it. He stole my baby's things."

"He isn't that powerful," Hallie said. "It was an accident. You're reading more into it because of what you know."

Dorothy touched the soft fabric of the draperies, hid the cord in a fold and smoothed the bulge with her fingertips. "He's watching me right now," she whispered. Her eyes were glassy, unfocused. "He knows I'm trying to learn how to defeat him and he's laughing because I can't." She began to cry. "He's going to take my baby and I'm going to die. Like the others. I can't stop him."

Hallie led her to the sofa. "You're just tired," she said.

"He's too strong," Dorothy said. "He has magic."

Hallie went to the piano and sat on the stool. Music had a way of clearing the air, inexplicably energizing and uplifting. She banged a loose-wristed series of chords. After a minute she began singing loudly. "There's gonna be a change in the ocean," she sang, rolling her eyes heavenward. "A change in the sea," she thumped her foot insistently. "From now on there's gonna be a change in me." She grinned bravely at Dorothy, who looked at her with large frightened eyes.

Outside, after a futile search for a cab in front of the building, Jane lifted the bags and started up the snowy street. She tucked her chin into her scarf and hurried toward the lights on Broadway. She didn't notice the limousine parked at the corner with its engine idling quietly. One of the side windows in the rear was rolled down an inch. Even if she'd looked, and she didn't, she wouldn't have been able to make out the figure on the other side of the dark glass, an old man sitting quietly in the Packard's plush backseat next to a pair of sleeping dogs. He took a drag from a Turkish cigarette and watched her through slitted eyes as she squared her shoulders, hitched the packages and turned into the falling snow.

Then, breathing a thin stream of smoke, he tilted his head and looked up at the building she'd just left, at the brightly lit windows on the fourth floor front. He listened to the faint tinkle of saloon music as the wind enveloped it and carried it away.

Chapter Nine

Hallie and Dorothy put up cribs and laid away baby clothes in the nursery (once the dining room). They scrubbed the bathroom walls and unfolded the bathinette. Hallie cleaned behind the toilet with a wire brush.

The apartment smelled of lemons.

As they worked they talked about Elmo Shaw.

"His skin hangs on his face as if there's no connective tissue," Dorothy said. "His skull moves around inside the flesh like a rat under a sheet." She tried to describe his smell but only made herself gag. "It's disgusting," she shuddered.

Hallie wondered where he lived. Did he have neighbors? "Those dogs must make a lot of noise."

Dorothy remembered the complaints about dogs barking the night Irene and Marcus died.

"He keeps them someplace," Hallie said. "And somebody knows where. You can't hide that many dogs."

Every morning Hallie joined Dorothy in her floor exercises, and every week they went together to natural childbirth classes at the hospital on West 88th Street. There Dorothy practiced a relaxation routine and studied charts and photographs in the booklets they were given. She continued riding the bus to and from work, and swam daily. Her paycheck arrived in the mail regularly at the library and she deposited it in the bank on the way home every Thursday. Concentrating on the details of her preparation kept her anxiety manageable.

Hallie did the marketing and cooking. During the long

winter afternoons she sat quietly in the dark living room, meditating, her hands folded quietly in her lap. She focused her attention on a deep interior place having no connection with her surroundings, a secret shimmering pinpoint of a place holding images of life she hadn't yet lived, knowledge she'd never learned. She saw again and again the scene of her death, but it had become a familiar sight, an inevitable one. It didn't frighten her. She sought other, fresher revelation, enlightenment, new messages.

When nothing further appeared to her, day after day, she was patient. What she wanted would come.

Every night after dinner she and Dorothy sat at the kitchen table and read steadily through a pile of musty books Dorothy brought home. They were searching folklore for mention of an event or a story, some testimony to clarify what was happening, a clue to a history and future sweeping beyond Elmo Shaw. Something to tell them what to do.

It was slow going but they plodded on.

Jane telephoned a few evenings later to tell them the department store had indeed made a mistake with the baby gifts, the sales clerk had inadvertantly withheld the second little outfit, thinking it a duplication. "Damned fool," Jane said. "It was just as I thought. She wrote it all out on the receipt and then turned around and wrapped half the order."

Salespeople weren't what they'd been at B. Altman's.

She'd bring both little dresses, matching bonnets and booties over in a day or two.

Dorothy hung up, sighing, hugely relieved. She'd presumed Elmo Shaw could do anything, that he was able easily and magically to intrude himself into every corner of her life. Jane's comforting news gave her a sense that—perhaps—his power was limited.

When she sat down again her eyes wandered around the familiar kitchen. "You know," she said finally, "I'm making an assumption that Elmo Shaw has all the power."

Hallie looked up at her. "Yes?" she said.

"According to some of these books," Dorothy continued thoughtfully, "we women have neglected our power for so long we've forgotten how to use it. We've even forgotten it exists."

227

"What power?" Hallie said.

Dorothy paged slowly through one of the thick books.
"Magic?"

Dorothy didn't answer, but frowned, continuing to look through the book.

"Thousands of years ago women were worshiped," she said, finding the place and holding it with her finger as she looked up at Hallie. "They were goddesses and magicians. Life-givers. Healers. But as history evolved, other power—power connected with ownership, territory and expansion—male power—superseded the female power of birth and continuum. As that happened, the rules about what power was, how it should be used—and by whom—changed too.

Hallie ran her fingers through her untidy hair. "Go on," she said. Where was this leading?

Dorothy edged forward in her chair. "Elmo Shaw talks about power in his journal, remember?" she said. She glanced toward the ceiling and recited: "'Greed is integral to progress, the point of civilization has to do with the control of inferiors . . .'" She twisted a strand of hair and pushed it impatiently behind her ear. "He was talking about how the power he knew about had evolved. And he was accurate as far as he went. Greed drives expansion, nobody argues with that. And expansion and exploitation have defined history, at least in recent times. But that definition of power, that use of it, leaves out women. Our power is deeper, more mysterious than the power of greed." Dorothy struggled to find the words she wanted. "Down through the centuries, women became inferiors as we became property. Elmo Shaw made that assumption about his wife, remember? He talked about her as if he owned her."

Hallie nodded. "His daughters too," she said. "He didn't teach them to read because he claimed their husbands would take care of them. As if they had no prospect, no interest beyond matrimony."

Dorothy agreed.

"Property can't read."

"Or think for itself."

"Property is inanimate, it isn't greedy. It has no power."
Dorothy squeezed her hands together, concentrating. "As

228

women became property," she went on firmly, following her path of logic, "the birth process became something others controlled. Think about it. Why is a baby with an unknown father called illegitimate? Every baby is legitimate to its mother. It's only illegitimate when a man can't say for sure it's his."

Hallie smiled. "I never thought of that," she said. "You're right. Why would a mother call her own child anything but legitimate? Illegitimacy is about who owns the baby, not who its parent is."

Dorothy continued: "When I ran into Elmo Shaw the other day—when I told him I was planning to keep both babies—he discounted what I said. He just dismissed it, Hallie, he didn't try to argue or refute what I said. It never occurred to him that I might turn the tables on him. He's been in control for so long he's forgotten he doesn't come by it naturally. He doesn't know there's any power except his. The rules he's depending on institutionalize the power of the already powerful and leave me out in the cold." Her eyes flashed. "But those rules are made by a power derived from war, and greed, and death—not from life, Hallie."

Hallie nodded, following closely. "You're the one giving birth, Dorothy, he isn't. He *can't*. He's totally dependent on you to get what he wants. And on your side is the very force and power of nature!" She thumped her palm on the tabletop. "If you think of it from the point of natural law, Elmo Shaw is just a cranky old man who's used to having his way."

Dorothy shivered, and pulled her sleeves over her fists as Hallie went on excitedly. "Dorothy," she said, "I'm old and not afraid of death, so his threats don't scare me. You're pregnant, giving life—which he can't do himself. Think of it," she said, her eyes wide with the revelation, "he's *terrified* of dying. Why else would he have lived this long? He has all the money he wants but he still has to have you to get him what he needs to stay alive. He can't keep his bargain with the Devil unless you cooperate."

"I'm not going to—but he doesn't know that."

"And it's too late for him to locate somebody else to get pregnant. This January 1st will be exactly twenty-one years

229

since the last birth, according to his journal. He doesn't have room to maneuver. There's something magic about the date, something imperative. Perhaps there's some significance to the new year, but the reason isn't important. This time around it has to be you, he has no choice. He assumes he's got you where he wants because it's always worked for him and nobody's ever disputed him," she said. "So he's complacent. But he's totally dependent on you."

They were silent.

"Oh, Hallie," Dorothy cried, "if only we knew what to do!"

Hallie frowned,and looked at her hands. She wanted to tell Dorothy that things would work out, that their insight would lead to discovery of what they must do. But the words died in her throat. She still didn't have a clue.

One snowy afternoon a few days later, Hallie traveled downtown to a shop she found listed in the yellow pages under "Master Magicians and Products of the Occult." She carried with her a shopping list she'd compiled after her study of several of the old books.

The store was located at the foot of a rickety stairway in a Tribeca basement. She pulled open the door on creaking hinges and looked inside uneasily, blinking until her eyes became accustomed to the dim interior. Along one side of the room she saw a dirty glass counter holding a jumbled display of magicians' equipment—collapsible silk hats, dusty scarves, wands, dice, masks, card decks, sets of boxes within boxes. Shimmering crystals of many sizes dangled from the ceiling on silken cords sending tiny clusters of rainbows dancing along the floor and walls. Clouds of incense hung in the air. The smell was sickly sweet and stale. A tall wooden bookcase teetered across from the counter. Its crooked shelves were stuffed with astrology texts, thick books on the craft of magic, numerology and ESP, accounts of magicians, hypnotists and witches. Handwritten notebooks contained recipes for love potions or untraceable poisons.

There were no other customers in the shop.

The turbaned woman sitting in a soiled armchair by the

door continued knitting silently as Hallie moved past her to the back of the store and pushed aside a beaded divider. As she entered the room behind the clicking curtain a cat slithered frantically between her legs and vanished down a hallway. Startled, Hallie stood aside with her hand on the cool wall, frowning to get her bearings in the semidarkness. The only item of furniture in the tiny room was a battered cupboard with glass doors and shelves displaying grimy rows of bottles and jugs with homemade tags. She approached apprehensively to read the faded labels and discovered some of the jars contained an opaque liquid, others were stuffed with seeds and twigs, remnants of roots and crushed plants.

"Can I help you?" the storekeeper said. In her slippers she'd moved soundlessly behind Hallie, who jumped with fright at the sound of her voice.

Recovering herself, Hallie shook her head, no thank you, and—heart thumping—retreated through the beaded curtains, and hurried in a panic out the front entrance.

But halfway up the block she slowed her pace, then stopped. She couldn't return to Dorothy empty-handed just because she'd been frightened by a cat, a deep-voiced, stealthily moving proprietor and the unconventionality of the goods in a magic store.

After all, the place was listed in the yellow pages. It was a respectable retail establishment, no different from Bloomingdale's. She chastised herself for behaving foolishly.

So she crammed her hands decisively into her pockets and with long deliberate strides returned to the store, pulled open the door again and without preamble asked the storekeeper for information about the magical uses of herbs and the casting of spells. Smiling enigmatically, the woman put aside her knitting (it was something long and black, like a shroud) and asked Hallie for specifics. The two women talked softly for several minutes. Hallie gave her the list from her purse and the storekeeper looked it over, made one or two additions and deletions, then nodded and went again into the back room. Hallie awaited her restlessly.

Two hours later Hallie arrived back at the apartment with an armful of books the storekeeper had recommended and clusters of little paper bags stuffed into her purse. She spent the evening studying the marked passages in the books, underlining, starring paragraphs, taking notes.

She was still at the table and nodded without looking up when Dorothy said goodnight.

Lying in bed later Dorothy looked toward the window.

She couldn't fall asleep. At the Lamaze classes she'd learned ways to distribute pillows beneath her to help her relax. Before lying down she'd carefully laid them out on her bed to support every angle of herself—the backs of her knees, the bends of her elbows, the narrow curved place where her neck joined her head. When she'd been less huge this care had helped. But by now such precautions were useless. Her straining, swollen body responded only minimally to deep breathing and the slightest movement unbalanced her bulk and discomfited her.

Frightening images pierced the blackness whenever she closed her eyes.

So she lay still and forced herself to imagine flopping easily from one side of the bed to the other without first planning each move. She pictured herself sitting cross-legged on the bedspread, examining her toenails in the light from the lamp on the bedside table, as she'd done once. She saw herself sleeping in a spread-eagle position too, on her face, blissful and unperturbed. She remembered touching her knees to her chest merely by raising and bending her legs and pulling them toward her face. The madness of that act, its utter impossibility now, made her momentarily forget her other concerns. She remembered how strong and supple her legs had felt. Her ankles were puffy now. Her knees ached. She imagined her once-flat stomach, the lithe, effortless way she'd twisted and bent, as graceful as a ballerina, as heedless as a boy. She closed her eyes again and pretended her body was as she remembered.

But it wasn't.

She turned her head from the windows to watch the shadows on the ceiling. After a while she threw back the comforter, got up heavily and moved to the window. With a groan she collapsed into the old slipper chair. She peered through the frosted panes to see the snow whirling relentlessly, as it had been steadily all day.

On this night, curiously, the babies were quiet inside her. (She planned to name them Charlotte and Emily Anne, for the Brontës.) She was relieved at the inactivity. She didn't think she could face the kicking and jouncing that was their habit. The jutting wall of her abdomen was stiff and hard as bone. There was no movement beneath it. She explored this phenomenon with her fingertips, wondering what her companions were up to. But she couldn't find them, there was no answering flutter and roll, no comforting sense of other presence. For some reason they were lying low.

She put her palm against the pillow at the base of her back and leaned against it, momentarily easing the ache.

The bedroom door burst open and Hallie stood silhouetted against the light from the hall. Her unpinned hair hung to her shoulders and she held her robe together with her knobby hands.

"I figured out where Elmo Shaw lives," she announced. "We have to go there and steal something that belongs to him."

Chapter Ten

Hallie pulled Dorothy into the living room. The lights were blazing. "Look," she said excitedly, pointing to the book of photographs Jane had brought weeks ago. It lay open to the photographs of the Wash Castle.

Dorothy picked up the book and blearily examined the images of the old mansion.

"The Wash Castle," Hallie said excitedly. "Think about the name."

Dorothy carefully reread the caption and looked again at the photograph. "I'm sorry," she said finally, still baffled. "I don't know what you're telling me."

"Don't you think it's a strange name?" Hallie persisted.

"Lots of names are strange," Dorothy said. "Crecelius is strange."

"Sure," Hallie said. "Kite is unusual too. But Dorothy— Wash is something else." She paused, then said slowly, "Wash is another spelling of Shaw. It's an anagram." She indicated one of the photographs. "This is where he lived and saw his patients. The Wash Mansion." Her finger pressed into the page. "A dozen blocks from here. Until they tore it down."

Dorothy frowned. He couldn't still live there. The book said the mansion was razed in the thirties. Sixty years ago.

"But he does!" Hallie persisted. "They razed the mansion but they didn't bother with the basement. They just planted bushes and sod over it and left. It's under Riverside Park. Nobody cares about it, nobody remembers. He still lives down there! It's perfect for him because it's connected to an abandoned subway. The place he's made is huge, cavernous, built on several levels—there's even plenty of space for the dogs. When the city tore down the mansion to make room for the highway he went underground and he's never moved!"

She explained hurriedly: "At the time the West Side IRT opened in 1904, a large area was excavated for a spur to service the ferryboat passengers arriving from New Jersey at 120th Street. The plan was for this subway shuttle to run directly from the ferry landing into the main subway artery several blocks east, on Broadway at Columbia University. Complications prevented the spur from being finished on time and later it was decided the additional operating expense was too great. So the elaborate underground station was abandoned and eventually forgotten. The New Jersey launch had long since ceased running. But the old ferry depot at 120th Street still existed—boarded up and overgrown with a tangle of ninety-year-old vegetation—and so did the underground subway station and trunk connection. Much of it—three stories of corridors and staircases and vaulted rooms—lay beneath the still-existing basement of the old Wash Castle."

Elmo Shaw lived there!

"I've just been visiting it," Hallie said. "In my head. It's immense."

Dorothy frowned. "What good is knowing where he lives?" She leaned tiredly against the back of the sofa and crossed her arms. She hadn't put on her slippers and her feet were cold. "How does that help us?"

Hallie returned the book to the end table. "If we go there and get something belonging to him—a lock of his hair, a piece of his clothing—something he's touched recently or worn next to his skin," she said, her eyes shining behind her spectacles, "then we can put a spell on him. I think I know how to do it."

Dorothy looked at her, weighing the importance of what she was saying. "A spell."

"Yes, damn it, a spell!"

Dorothy laughed nervously. "Give me a minute to digest

235

what you're saying. You sound like a lunatic."

Hallie sank into the sofa. "You're right," she said, watching as Dorothy settled carefully into the easy chair opposite, stretched her legs and bent stiffly to rub her cramped calf. "Take a minute," she said. "Think about it."

Dorothy's eyes wandered around the room. "You want to cast a spell," she said. "A magic spell."

Hallie nodded. "Yes. I think I know how."

"We have to go there—where he lives—and steal something of his."

"Yes."

Dorothy closed her eyes. "I'm eight and a half months pregnant," she sighed. "You're seventy-one years old. Neither of us can run. I'm too fat to hide. And it's snowing outside, it's freezing. Slippery." She smiled. "You think we can go there, steal something of his and get back without getting caught."

"It's too late for either of us to behave rationally," Hallie urged. "We have to go with our instincts. We don't have any options."

"If he finds us, he'll lock me up and kill you."

"That's a risk, yes."

Dorothy snorted. "Some risk."

"We have to move beyond our experience," Hallie insisted. "That's our only chance."

The radiator thumped and hissed.

"We have nothing to lose," Hallie said, suddenly tired. "We're both dead if we do nothing."

At least they'd have a chance if they risked everything.

It would soon be daylight.

Chapter Eleven

Morning came, cold and gray. An inch of snow fell during the night and was still falling, quiet and steady, when Dorothy woke. Mercury in the battered thermometer attached to the outside of the bedroom window stood at eighteen degrees.

Bolstered by the dim eastern light and feeling slightly braver after a big breakfast, Dorothy donned her sweaters and woolen pants, pulled on her parka, scarf, hat with earflaps, and fleece-lined snowboots to follow an equally bundled-up Hallie downstairs and outside. She felt energetic, if clumsy and slow-moving. She hoped they were right about being at the peak of their powers. She certainly didn't feel powerful. She tried not to dwell even for a moment on the fact that Hallie was an amateur at mysticism. She claimed she'd learned such power and Dorothy had to believe her. She did have extraordinary ESP. Such sensitivity must lead inevitably to the ability to perform magic. It was the only hope they had.

They rode a nearly empty Number Five bus silently up Riverside Drive to 120th Street where they emerged in front of Riverside Church. Hallie led the way across the deserted street and turned into the park. Dorothy followed her down several winding sets of slippery stairs and through a graffiti splotched tunnel curving toward the river's edge. In the tunnel they passed a man who made his home there in an Amana refrigerator carton. He watched suspiciously as they hurried past his place, out of the tunnel and toward the river.

The Hudson had frozen across to New Jersey and the snow falling onto the ice gave the majestic waterway a curiously flat, empty look.

Except for the man in the box there were no people in the park on this dreary morning, and little sound of traffic from the West Side Highway, jutting behind and above them on mighty girders driven solidly into a towering wall of boulders.

Hallie squinted at the snarl of snowy trees and bushes rising on both sides of the path leading from the tunnel. "Keep your eyes open," she told Dorothy. "The entrance is around here somewhere, I'm sure of it."

She left the walkway and with difficulty made her way north into the heavy brush. Behind her Dorothy pulled thorny branches aside and hunched to avoid overhanging limbs, her arm in its bulky sleeve bent for protection across her face. Hallie crashed ahead several yards in front of her, turning, ducking, squirming sideways. She struggled through a clump of huge fir trees whose giant branches dropped to brush the ground and interlace, making passage difficult. The mighty trees allowed no light to penetrate and she felt her way along. "This way," she called.

Dorothy followed laboriously, pushing the branches aside when she could, bending and climbing through when they were too heavy for her to displace. Sticky needles scratched her face and she pulled them away with her mittens, inhaling a pungent pine odor as she did. As she inched forward, squeezing through the narrow openings, she gulped for breath. The exertion made her sweat and she stopped often to rest.

Nobody had been in this part of the park for years.

Hallie tilted her head alertly and listened. She grabbed Dorothy's forearm and supported her as she climbed across a tree stump choked with ropy vines. "It's not far now," she said, turning cautiously and looking ahead. "I can feel it. We're almost there."

Sinister quiet pressed around them.

Dorothy wiped the gummy pine sap from her cheek and squinted in an effort to see behind Hallie's shoulder. "What's that?" she said, blinking, rubbing her eyes, refocusing.

238

Ten feet beyond them, nearly hidden beneath a snowy thicket of roots and underbrush, they saw what appeared to be a hinged cellar door. A rusty padlock had been wedged through iron latches protruding along its base.

"That must be it," Hallie whispered excitedly. She hastened forward, reached to pull the lock. It held firm.

Straightening, she wiped her nose with the back of her snow-encrusted mitten. "Find a stone," she said. "Something heavy enough to break the lock." She squatted to rummage in a pile of dead leaves and branches. As she foraged in the rotting vegetation, a sour odor wafted upward. She choked and turned her face.

Dorothy staggered toward her carrying a huge rock in her arms. She stood over the padlock and dropped the stone on it, but it thudded away harmlessly. Hallie retrieved the boulder, grunted as she lifted and held it high above her head. With an enormous lunge she threw it at the padlock. This time there was a distinct clicking sound as the weight crashed to the ground. When she bent and attempted to pull it apart, however, she found the lock unbroken.

She hoisted the stone again. Once more she threw it down and this time when she examined the lock she found it crushed. But it still held firm. She looked at Dorothy. "It's not going to break."

"A lever," Dorothy said. "We need some kind of a lever to pull it apart."

Hallie agreed. "There must be a rod or a pipe around here somewhere," she muttered, getting up stiffly. She'd gone several feet when she heard Dorothy's frantic shout. Hurrying back toward the sound, she ducked under a low-hanging limb and climbed across a dead branch dangling precariously from a tree split long ago by lightening.

Dorothy was standing in a snowy tangle of brown grass at the base of the wall of granite supporting the highway. Thirty feet above her the iron girders of the roadway jutted up like pillars. Hallie could hear the faint wooshing sounds of early traffic passing overhead.

A doorway, half-hidden with moss and overgrowth, had been carved into the solid rock behind Dorothy. Her hand rested on the glistening knob of the small wooden door.

She'd pulled away the vines and opened it easily, as if by magic.

"It's like the secret garden," she said. "A door in a wall."

Hallie moved close to her. "You're right," she said, peering through the entry into darkness. "The other door was a decoy. This is the one I've been picturing. This leads to where he lives." The narrow stairway curved down into nothing. "It's black as pitch," she said, moving cautiously forward. "Be careful." She took a deep breath and began climbing down the cramped stairway winding crookedly out of sight. "Put your hands on my shoulders," she instructed. Dorothy gripped her as they twisted steeply downward. Gradually the light from the open entrance behind them disappeared.

The treads, carved from bedrock, were uneven and narrow. The women had to fit their feet sideways as they descended. Hallie groped along the damp granite walls. She paused to remove her mittens and stuff them into her pockets so she could feel the way more easily.

The cold air held a stale, putrid odor, as if it had hung there for years. Dorothy's stomach lurched sickeningly and she blinked without seeing.

Neither of them spoke.

After descending a long time Hallie slid her foot forward across a hard, bumpy surface. Earth. "I think we've reached the bottom," she said. She took a step. "Yes," she said, taking another cautious step, then another. She held her arms out to measure the dimensions of the room they were in. "We're still in a tunnel," she said, pressing outward with her palms against the damp stone surrounding them. The hallway was about three feet wide. Her fingers detected a slithery membranous substance covering the walls. She swallowed a wave of disgust. It was probably mildew of some kind.

Dorothy, still grasping her shoulders, squeezed her as she continued moving forward.

"Wait," Hallie said. "There's a door here." Her fingers rapidly traced the edges of the door and located the handle. She stood back gripping the handle. "Shall I open it?" she said.

In the dark Dorothy opened her mouth and closed it

again. Yes.

Slowly, slowly, so as not to make a sound, Hallie twisted the latch. When she'd forced it to the top of its arc she took a step back and, pulling with both hands, worked the heavy door toward her. It opened reluctantly, with a terrible creak and rumble.

A smoky beam of light made them flinch and turn their faces away. Then they blinked, accustoming their eyes to the sudden light, and leaned forward cautiously to see what lay inside. The door opened to a narrow wooden platform. A rickety staircase led from the platform where they stood to the floor of an enormous garage twenty-five feet beneath them. Its banister dangled unsafely.

Several vehicles were parked below them: a twenties-style limousine with open driver's seat upholstered in leopard skin, and a glass and enamel passenger enclosure with curtained windows behind the chauffeur's seat; a buggy with huge cast iron wheels and a twelve-foot-long whip protruding from the coachman's perch; a fringed surrey with two rows of red padded seats; a sleigh with immense curved wooden runners; a bright yellow car in the corner; a large black Cadillac of recent vintage. A canvas-topped Rolls Royce was pulled up in front of it, sporting white seats, maroon fenders and shining spoked wheels. A 1940 Packard with bright whitewalls and silver trunk handles was parked on a hydraulic lift. It hood ornament glistened.

Each vehicle was perfectly maintained but there wasn't a sound in the huge garage and no sign of people. Not even a horse to pull the surrey.

Dorothy gripped Hallie's arm. "It's every car—every carriage he's ever used," she whispered, awestruck. "It's like a museum."

"But nobody's here," Hallie said.

Where were the mechanics? The chauffeurs? The ironmongers and blacksmiths? There wasn't a soul around.

"They must use that ramp to drive in and out." Hallie pointed to an arched opening beneath them in the wall on their right, and a driveway slanting into it, curving upward and out of sight. "When we get down from here and explore the rest of the place we may have to use the garage exit

241

ourselves to get out." She reached toward the rickety banister and gave the rusty piping a shake. It rattled and clanked ominously. "This stairway doesn't look like it can hold any weight," Hallie said. "It's probably going to collapse as we climb down."

She stepped gingerly onto the first step. It sagged under her and she detected a slight shiver of metal. She jumped back to the platform.

"Maybe we should go back," Dorothy said.

"I can't go back," Hallie muttered.

"But there's no way we can get down this thing," Dorothy said. "It'll never hold." She pushed the aged railing and watched it swing sickenly into midair.

Hallie turned and gave her a fatalistic look. "I can't climb back the way we came," she said. "It's too steep. I'm too old." She'd known on the way down she couldn't return that way. "You can't either. We have to go down."

Dorothy looked at the vehicles parked below in orderly rows, as if on display. "I guess we've burned our bridges." But her eyes widened as she met Hallie's. "I've never been so frightened," she whispered.

"I know," Hallie said. "Me too." She turned and squinted to see across the huge room. "There's a door against the far wall. It must lead to his living quarters." She took a deep breath, preparing to enter enemy domain. "If we run down the stairs as fast as we can, we'll reach bottom before the whole thing rips away from the wall," she said, hoping she sounded more confident than she felt. She gripped Dorothy's hand. "Come on," she urged. "Before anybody comes." They crossed the platform, hesitated for a split second, then galloped headlong down the cast-iron stairway. A tortured grating noise followed them. Halfway down Dorothy held back, watching in horror as the structure buckled and undulated beneath their feet. "Keep moving!" Hallie yelled, yanking her, and Dorothy followed frantically. As they reached a few steps from the bottom there was a popping metalic sound. The remaining bolts burst from the wall of bedrock like machine gun bullets and the entire structure teetered sideways into emptiness. "Jump!" Hallie commanded. "Jump!" They leaped together off the edge of the heavy stairway as it crumpled and thudded behind them onto the floor, the thunderlike crashing sending up huge clouds of dust.

Despite frantic clutching Hallie lost Dorothy's hand as they landed. Her knees buckled at the jarring impact with the floor, and she fell, rolling out of control for several feet. She came to a stop with one leg twisted beneath her, her head cracking painfully against the gleaming spoked tire of the Rolls Royce.

The dust settled quietly. Hallie shook her head and with an effort pulled herself up by gripping the silver door handle. She straightened her leg slowly and wiggled her foot. Miraculously, nothing seemed broken. She bent to brush herself off.

Dorothy stood a few feet away next to the surrey, blinking. She cautiously examined her arms and legs, then looked up with relief. "I must have bounced," she said, trying to smile.

Except for the creaks and wheezes as the wrecked stairway settled onto the empty concrete floor behind them, there was no sound anywhere. "We have to get to where he lives," Hallie said. "We can't waste time here. Somebody's sure to catch us." She glanced at the driveway ramp. "But remember where that exit is," she said. "If anything happens to me."

"Nothing's going to happen to you," Dorothy said nervously.

"Of course not," Hallie said. "But memorize where the exit is anyway, just in case we get separated." She rubbed her throbbing shoulder and hoped her old body would hold up against further exertions. Already her lungs ached. Her straining rib cage constricted painfully every time she inhaled. She hid her discomfort from Dorothy, whose face was pale and worried. Hallie yearned fiercely to protect her—the daughter she'd never had—to lead her to safety through this awesomely dangerous place. She must forget her own vulnerability and use every sense she possessed for the dangerous journey. There'd be time to attend to herself later.

Indistinct images pulsed and faded in her mind's eye as she focused on the vision she'd had late last night of Elmo

Shaw's bedroom—a large square space, a mammoth fireplace with a black marble mantel. In the middle of the room a huge bedstead towered, its headboard made from twisted silver spikes. Instead of windows there were mirrors everywhere and in a corner facing into the room stood a red plush chair, tall and imposing as a throne.

Dorothy looked around guardedly. Miraculously, nobody had come running in response to the crash of the collapsed staircase. But they couldn't count on luck. As soon as someone returned to the garage he'd see what had happened and know strangers had entered the sanctuary. They wouldn't be undetected for long. "Let's get out of here," she urged. There was a steel door in the cement wall a few feet behind the lift.

Hallie pulled it open and looked inside at an elegant hallway. Its walls had been papered in red silk. The high narrow ceiling stretched away, glistening with a rich coating of black enamel. Brass sconces with blown glass holders containing thick black candles flickered every dozen feet. A soggy smell and a heaviness hung in the atmosphere, an unmistakable sense of being underground, a chill and dampness in air never warmed by sunlight.

Dorothy followed close behind. Under her clothes her belly felt tight and uncomfortable. She loosened her coat and unwrapped her scarf. Despite the cold she was sweating.

After they'd proceeded down the hallway for ten or twenty yards they came to an archway opening into a huge kitchen. An enormous black stove on delicately curved iron legs stood against the far wall between glass and steel cupboards reaching to the domed ceiling. A collection of modern kitchen appliances stood on the spotless counter tops and steam rose from a cast-iron pot set on one of the stove burners. An unfamiliar odor hung in the air, cloying and slightly rancid. The big room was empty.

"Something's cooking," Dorothy said, sickened by the smell. She covered her nose and mouth with her scarf, craned across the threshold to look further into the room. Two tomatoes, an onion and several long strings of grey and black funguslike herbs lay on a chopping block. A wide-bladed knife peirced one of the overripe tomatoes.

244

Silence hung oppressively.

"Let's not wait for the cook to come back," Hallie said, turning away. "We're not going to find anything in here." She wanted to get to the old man's bedroom. It was close by, she could feel waves of coldness surrounding them, ominously drawing them deeper and deeper underground.

And there was a sound, very faint, almost too slight to notice. Neither of them commented on the low-pitched hum. But it became perceptibly louder as they moved further into the mansion.

Ahead of them the hallway divided, the paths vanishing in two directions. In an agony of indecision, Dorothy looked at Hallie. Which way should they turn?

Hallie closed her eyes and rocked on her heels. Her jaw clenched with concentration.

But the whereabouts of the bedroom flickered tauntingly just beyond her consciousness. It was here but nowhere. Close by but inaccessible. She was bombarded with a series of tantalizing images but each of them flickered unrecognizably and then vanished, to be replaced by another fleeting obscurity, and another.

The hum was appreciably louder. It sounded human. Like a moan.

After taking several steps into the left fork, Hallie stopped uncertainly and focused on the tall door she stood facing. She laid her hands against its polished mahogany surface.

As she did this, the sound around them intensified. Dorothy covered her ears. The resonance penetrated her very soul and filled her with sadness and despair.

The icy cold from the door seared the flesh on Hallie's palms, made her pull back in surprise and blow on her fingers to warm them. Dorothy hurriedly resnapped her coat. Hallie put her shoulder against the heavy door and pushed. Surprisingly, it swung open on well-oiled hinges.

Inside, the windowless room—nearly as cold as the interior of a refrigerator—measured about twelve feet square. The stagnant atmosphere burned their noses like dry ice. The walls and floor were covered with squares of shining white tile. Brilliant light glared from several circles of florescent bulbs dangling on rigid chrome rods attached to the mirrored ceiling. A whirring remote control camera with a tiny flashing red light hung on a swivel apparatus and pointed toward the center of the room, where an empty iron crib stood. Clusters of leather straps and buckles dangled from both ends of the crib's thin mattress.

Everything in the sterile room was hard and sharp. And the air was so cold Dorothy could feel the blood shrivel and retreat from her fingers.

A set of baby scales rested on a glittering aluminum table against the wall.

"It's the *nursery*," Dorothy said. Her frightened voice reverberated eerily. She stepped inside, then recoiled with a frightened "Oh!" Against one wall crouched a huge dog, its teeth bared, red tongue lolling, hard yellow eyes staring blindly. But it made no sound at the intrusion. It stood motionless, ready to pounce, as if paralyzed.

"My god," Dorothy said. She crept closer to get a better look. "It's stuffed!" She removed her hand from her pocket and reached out gingerly to touch it. The glistening black coat felt hard and strangely slimy.

"Keep away from the camera," Hallie warned.

Staring in fascination, Dorothy moved away from the animal, inching backward until her back slid against the smooth wall. "It stands at eye level," she said. "Exactly where the baby in the crib looks. It's so *frightening*." She peeled her eyes away from the dog to take in the rest of the room. "This is Elmo Shaw's idea of childcare," she said. "A nursery that looks like an operating room. Freezing cold. A monster in the corner. Nowhere for nurturing, no softness, nothing but silence and cold. A perfect place to keep a baby barely alive, to train her to become a sadomasochist."

With the manacles attached to the crib, the baby would be held motionless, her little arms and legs rubbed raw, unable to do anything except stare at her own reflection in the mirror on the ceiling.

The television camera would permit others to watch her without anyone having to touch or comfort her.

And nobody would come when she cried.

It wouldn't take long for her to learn the futility of her need and her own abject unimportance. Within a few days, when nobody responded to her lonely cries, the little voice would falter, then fall silent. She'd lie quietly on the hard mattress, covered by the scratchy blanket folded neatly at its foot. The debilitating cold would turn her hands and feet blue.

He'd thought of everything.

Dorothy flushed with outrage. Why had she thought it reasonable to produce and then give away a child in order to decorate her life with its twin? How could she have been so naïve and selfish? A hundred and sixty years ago Elmo Shaw's wife—a woman who hadn't been able to read or write, whose name Dorothy realized she didn't even know— that woman had known the truth of his greed and grotesque ambition. She'd killed herself and her child to prevent such a thing from happening.

Dorothy vowed again to protect her children with the same dedication and spirit of self-sacrifice.

She closed the door and moved quickly into the hallway where Hallie waited.

Why wasn't anyone here? This emptiness wasn't right. They oughtn't to have such easy access. "It might be a setup," Hallie warned. "A trap of some kind."

Around them the atmosphere crackled with urgency. They sensed a flurry of electrical activity, a hubbub of energy bombarding them from all directions. There were voices too—excited, insistent—yet there was no sound anywhere. They were alone.

Dorothy looked at Hallie. "They're here," she whispered.

"Who?" Hallie peered intently into the dark but saw nothing.

"The other mothers," Dorothy said. "They're going to help us."

Instantly Hallie held out her arms. "Tell them to take us to his bedroom. I can't make out where it is."

As if in a dream, the hovering force animated their feet and gently propelled them along, skimming the floor, down steps, through archways, past closed doors, into shadowy windowless rooms and out again. They glimpsed massive tables in the dimness, overstuffed sofas and chairs, large-screened televisions, an entire gymnasium with up-to-date body building equipment, faded tapestries hanging on glistening silken walls, clotted swirls of dark paintings framed in squares of gold, marble statuary balanced on tapered pedestals illuminated with hidden pins of light. They moved across polished tiles, down dark hallways opening into abandoned waiting rooms with rows of dusty benches, down endless curving corridors. As they were pulled along, doors opened at the touch of their fingers, like toys, and closed quietly when they had passed through. They moved in the center of glowing warmth that dispelled the cold, radiated on their cheeks like sunshine. Murmuring voices surrounded and encouraged them. The soft words were unrecognizable yet the indistinct voices comforted and led them through the underground maze.

Finally, breathless, they found themselves facing a mighty door, larger than any they'd yet seen. Its granite frame arched fifteen feet above them. Several hinges, long triangles of hammered brass glossy with frost, gripped one side of the door. A curving black handle in the shape of a serpent protruded from the opposite side.

They'd reached their destination.

Identical cast-iron carriage lamps containing lit torches jutted on either side of the door which loomed above them like the entrance to a fortress. The cold air was acrid and smoky. Further down the hall the red light of a remote control camera blinked on as they approached.

The warmth and the soft voices subsided into the gloom and Dorothy and Hallie stood facing the door in an atmosphere of fearsome cold. It sucked and pressed against them, as seductive and dangerous as a black hole.

Hallie twisted the ebony handle with all her strength.

There was a loud clicking sound as the latch disengaged. She put her shoulder against the door and pushed. It creaked and opened. Inside she saw Elmo Shaw's bedroom, exactly as it had appeared in her imagining.

The great spiked bed stood on a platform in the center of the room, a crimson satin coverlet draped across the black silk pillows and cascading in thick folds down the fur steps to the stone floor. Blinding beams of light from the black crystal chandelier ricocheted as if shot by laser. The huge silver bedstead was reflected endlessly in the framed mirrors hanging everywhere. As Dorothy followed Hallie into the room she recoiled suddenly, horrified, until she realized the frightening presence she detected creeping toward her was merely her own reflection, framed in a shimmering rectangle of gilt across the room.

Clouds of icy vapor from their breath hung before them. The familiar stench—like rotting hamburger—was stronger than ever.

Hallie glanced around quickly. "Where are his clothes?" she said, covering her nose. "Do you see his comb or brush?"

Dorothy squeezed her mittened hands for warmth as her eyes darted from one side of the room to the other. A mahogany chiffonier stood against one wall. Relief carvings of snakes and doglike creatures crouched and coiled menacingly on its doors and drawers.

Hallie tiptoed to it and pulled open one of the tall doors. She gasped. "Look," she whispered, pushing into the crowded contents. inside hung a collection of clothes arranged as if awaiting a costume ball. There were embroidered coats with wide cuffed sleeves and velvet lapels, ruffled percale blouses from antebellum days. A pair of leather breeches with a buttoned fly hung next to a pair of silk knickers. Fascinated in spite of herself, Hallie smoothed the fabric of a knee-length frock coat with black satin buttons much like one she remembered seeing in a famous photograph of J.P. Morgan striding up Wall Street. "It's everything Elmo Shaw ever wore," she said, awestruck. There was a watered silk vest, a smoking jacket with tassled sash Noel Coward might have owned, a modern double-breasted suit, its Italian-cut jacket slightly and fashionably flared and two pairs of matching trousers hanging with it. There was even a bright kilt dangling a red purse on a cord.

Dorothy opened one of the drawers and frantically pulled out a crimson silk scarf. She was sure it was the one she'd seen Elmo Shaw wearing the other day outside her apartment building. It still held in its folds some of the specks of dandruff she remembered. The afternoon seemed long ago, when she'd walked on the surface of the earth, before she'd known of this evil place beneath its crust, where the richly furnished rooms echoed coldly without a trace of human warmth. Where the air itself had been imprisoned for more than a hundred years.

A spasm of fear caused her mouth to twitch and tighten.

The huge door slammed suddenly. They whirled to see what had caused the noise, and as they did the door burst open again, then slammed itself jarringly. The mirrors rattled and thumped against the walls and the drawers in the wardrobe opened and shut as if struck by maddened hands. The huge entrance door opened again, shut, opened and shut again, each time with a noise like a gunshot. A glacial cold settled around them, the icy, hopeless presence of evil. They began to gasp for air.

"Run!" came the voices, clear now, in unison and screaming. "Run!"

Dorothy stuffed the scarf into her parka pocket and she and Hallie raced in terror from the room.

A dog growled softly, close by.

They looked around frantically. From one direction they could hear snarling and claws scrabbling toward them on the stone floor. They turned and charged blindly in the opposite direction.

They felt themselves being pushed ungently down the corridor as fast as they could move. "This way!" came the voices, enveloping them with pulsing electricity. "Run!" The hallway widened as they hurtled around the corner. There was another noise ahead of them, an insistent roar. It sounded like the ocean and seemed to come for an opening in the wall concealed behind a wire grating. With a huge grunting effort Hallie ripped the mesh from the enclosure and turned back to help Dorothy climb into the hole. "Hurry!" she shouted.

Dorothy squeezed sideways into the tunnel, pinching her feet and pressing them onto the iron rings protruding from the stones inside. She bent and straightened her legs, pumping herself horizontally, squeezing her arms over her head to grasp the rusty rings and pull herself through the cramped space. She could hear Hallie pushing close behind her. Sweat blinded her as she scraped and twisted through the opening with immense effort.

In the circle of light behind them the face of a dog appeared, drooling and snarling as he clambered and pressed into the entrance hole. He tore at the soles of Hallie's boots.

Dorothy felt the outline of a wooden door above her head and she reached frantically to push it. It was tightly closed.

"He's got my boot!" Hallie screamed, kicking her foot wildly. Crouching in the narrow space, Dorothy planted her feet on the rusty iron rings jutting from either side of the enclosure. She straightened her body, thrusting up mightily through the space, using her head as a battering ram against the door. It gave way and clattered onto the cement floor on the other side. Hallie wrapped herself around Dorothy's leg, pushed and thrust with her. Together they erupted from the tunnel and thudded onto the floor on the other side.

The roar was loud in front of them and when they scrambled to their feet they saw they were at the dark end of a subway station. The noise they heard was the sound of a train pulling in. They ran for it, squeezing past people who looked at them with curiosity and then disapproval as they were pushed roughly out of the way. Hallie and Dorothy boarded the last car of the train as the door closed. Almost weeping with relief, Dorothy, rubbing the bruise on her forehead, wrenched to look out the window, at the station as it disappeared behind them.

Through the dirty glass of the subway door she saw Elmo Shaw's red silk scarf fluttering on the empty platform. A huge black dog stood over it, holding it with its paw, watching the train as it hurtled out of the station.

Chapter Twelve

That winter snow fell in New York City for nine days and nights. It did not melt. There were hours of respite when the clouds brightened. Eager and hopeful, people began digging out. Then the skies darkened and snow fell again. It was as if it would never end. Life in the city slowed and nearly halted. The temperature hovered around fifteen degrees, at night dipping below zero. Icicles formed on the insides of windows, even in elegant Park Avenue apartments. Lights went out everywhere. Uptown, in unheated slum dwellings, families huddled together to keep warm.

During the second week of the snow the wind increased. People heard it howling as they sat in their kitchens. They talked uneasily to one another, raising their voices over the eerie wailing which sounded like the moans of an inconsolable woman.

Schools closed early for Christmas vacation.

After a week, the governor declared the city a disaster area, but even the Red Cross couldn't get through to help. Manhattan Island was under siege. Commuter trains and the subways arrived and departed late, then stopped. Bridges, tunnels and roads closed down. The airports shut and employees found their ways home as best they could. Telephones didn't work. The stores closed. Piles of Christmas merchandise stood abandoned on darkened counters or, outside, in boxes under mammoth snowdrifts on loading docks. The Rockefeller Center Christmas tree, decorated with green and gold glass balls, remained unlit.

Nobody came to admire it anyway. Gradually the snow filled the ice rink in front of it and covered the tree's majestic branches, which drooped and cracked from the weight. After the first few days of the relentless snow there was little looting, except in grocery stores. Nobody could get around and survival became the primary objective.

On New Year's Eve an ornately decorated crimson and silver sleigh—the one Dorothy and Hallie had seen in Elmo Shaw's garage—glided and bounced through the snow. Elmo Shaw himself stood at its front, cracking a whip at the straining dog team pulling it. The team consisted of nineteen surefooted black hounds as large as St. Bernards, but crueler in aspect, and more menacing. Nobody was outside when the sled flew past. Nobody saw the old man standing high at the front of the mammoth sleigh, legs apart, black muffler wrapped tightly around his face and his cape flapping behind him. Nobody heard his shouts and mad laughter, nobody heard the frightening report of his long whip, the barking animals or the eerie tinkle of the bells on the straps and harnesses as the dogs plunged through the swirling snow.

Elmo Shaw was ready for Dorothy Kite.

Chapter Thirteen

All afternoon Hallie watched from her window as the snow fell and fell, piling in enormous drifts, blowing sideways and obscuring the other windows across the courtyard. That night, despite exhaustion brought on by their frantic mission in Elmo Shaw's subterranean fortress, she'd lain sleeplessly in bed awaiting the first weak light of dawn. She listened to the screeching wind and shivered at its relentlessness. In the morning she turned on the stove burners for heat and hobbled on aching legs to close the kitchen door so as to keep the warmth within the room. Dorothy slumped silently at the table sipping tea.

The date was December 31st.

With every hour Dorothy became more listless and depressed. Her dark eyes followed Hallie blankly around the kitchen. In spite of her throbbing limbs Hallie moved briskly, setting out the morning meal, making toast, trying to convey a confidence she didn't feel. Dorothy's face had lost its healthy color. She bent obediently to eat her breakfast but looked up again and pushed it away. She sighed and turned to stare out the window. "Why did I have to drop his scarf?" she whispered. "It's all my fault." She rocked in her chair, rubbing her arms to dispel a chill that seemed to come from inside herself. "We'll never be able to stop him now."

Hallie faced her with her hands on her hips. "Stop feeling sorry for yourself," she said firmly. This was no time for self-recrimination. "We have to think of a new strategy, that's all." She studied Dorothy's despairing expression, then poured more tea, thumped the pot onto the pad in the center of the table. Next she pulled out a chair and sat. "You can't lose your nerve now," she said. She took a dishtowel and wiped her forehead. The heat in the small room was making her sweat. Was this how her life would end? With surrender? And defeat? Dorothy was giving up—abandoning her—and it made her cruel. "They're your babies, not mine," she added roughly, baiting her, trying to make her angry. "You're the one who promised to give your child to that man," she said. "Not me."

Dorothy looked up briefly. For a moment Hallie thought she'd roused her. But her eyes wandered away again and she fingered the cream pitcher absentmindedly, pushed it against the sugar bowl and aligned them with the teapot. "I know," she sighed.

Hallie tried to think of something else that might wake Dorothy from her despondency. Her own helplessness frustrated her. She tapped her fingers against her mug. "Why do you think Elmo Shaw's list of births and deaths started in 1822 and ended in 1990?" she asked suddenly, inspired with a new idea. She leaned forward. "He didn't record any more dates after this year because there won't be any more victims after you. You're the one who's going to kill him."

Dorothy sighed again. "He ran out of room," she said after a moment. "The list is on the last page. That's why there isn't any date after mine."

Hallie pounded the table and the dishes jumped. "Bull!"

There was a shriek of wind at the window. Dorothy began to cry. She wiped her cheek with the back of her hand. "It's all my fault," she said miserably. "Putting a spell on him was our only chance."

Hallie was relieved to see her tears. "Don't talk nonsense," she said, her voice gentler. "You're playing into his hands if you give up."

Dorothy nodded slowly. She must keep strong and in control for the next few hours. It was ironic that at this time, when she felt least able to act, she must call on her greatest resource of will and commitment. The struggle hadn't even begun and already she wanted to surrender.

She thought of Elsa Shore, whose arm had been broken so many times it looked as if she had three elbows.

Elsa Shore could be her own daughter.

She blew her nose, making a noise reassuring in its ordinariness.

"Maybe he *was* out of paper," Hallie said, watching as Dorothy folded her handkerchief. "Or tired of adding twenty-one to twenty-one to twenty-one. I don't know. But it gives me hope. I think you're the one who's going to lick him."

Dorothy took a long sip from her cup and replaced it carefully in its saucer. She stretched and wiggled her fingers, smoothed the table cloth, looked back at Hallie. The leaden bulk of her abdomen pulled and tightened. A seed of an idea played on the fringe of her mind. "Maybe we can cast another spell," she said hesitantly, looking around the room.

Hallie waited for her to continue.

"On us instead of him," Dorothy said slowly, straightening in the chair as her thoughts focused. Could they make something to ward off evil spirits? Some kind of charm? She'd read about people doing that.

Hallie's mouth fell open in surprise. She'd allowed fear to limit her imagination. Elmo Shaw wasn't the only person they could enchant. They could cast a spell on Dorothy, make an amulet she could wear on a chain around her neck. The books Hallie had been studying contained recipes for all kinds of enchantments and the ingredients to put in such a locket were already in the house. She'd intended to use them casting the spell against Elmo Shaw. There was no reason they couldn't arm Dorothy instead of concentrating on him. This new approach might even work better.

Dorothy considered for a moment, then suggested they make two amulets, one for each of them. "Before the babies come you're in more danger than I am," she told Hallie. Afterwards we're both at risk." She had a locket Madelyn had given her on her sixteenth birthday. It held a tiny snapshot of her mother. She kept it wrapped in tissue in her bureau drawer. And Madelyn had treasured a locket containing pictures of Spark and Dorothy as children. Dorothy knew right where it was. She and Hallie could use

256

these lockets for the spell.

Hallie went into the living room and brought back a book with a worn binding. She opened it eagerly and put it on the table in front of Dorothy. They bent together looking for a passage which would tell them precisely what to do. After a while Hallie returned to the living room and brought back a stack of books. She cleared the table of the breakfast things and sat down to read.

Across from her, as she turned the thick pages, Dorothy became increasingly excited. The color returned to her cheeks.

They read to each other, considering and discarding ideas, discussing what must be done. The hours ticked by. Late in the afternoon Hallie made them sandwiches and they ate hungrily.

Finally, convinced they'd discovered the exact procedure they would use, they prepared the small room for the ceremony.

Carefully following the instructions in an alchemist's book of rituals, they emptied the kitchen of everything that wasn't built in. They carried the pots and pans into the living room, loaded a couple of boxes with foodstuffs from the cupboards, another carton with dishes and silverware. They packed the contents of the refrigerator in plastic bags and placed them outside, on the windowsills. Then they unplugged the refrigerator, tilted it awkwardly and alternately pushed and carried it into the hallway. Finally nothing remained in the room except the kitchen table. They took turns scrubbing its surface with a mixture of soapy water and alcohol, then dried it carefully and rubbed it with pieces of gauze. As Dorothy read aloud from the old book Hallie carefully placed several small items in the middle of the table. Next they put seven tall candles—three black, four white—in a circle of brass holders on the shining surface. By a few minutes before midnight they were ready, standing in the dark facing each other quietly across the table. They watched tensely as the iridescent hands of the wall clock moved to cover the hour. At that moment Hallie lit a match, holding it first to the candle next to Dorothy's right hand. She proceeded clockwise until all of the wicks flickered, casting unsteady shadows across their faces.

257

Hallie moved the match slowly back and forth in front of Dorothy's unblinking eyes, then her own.

"For our mother," she said quietly, and blew out the match. She reached to place the forefinger of her right hand on the tabletop, flinching in surprise from the electric spark the touch produced. Pressing firmly, she drew a circle around the substances arranged in a smaller circle in its center, then sprinkled iron filings from a small paper bag around the diameter she'd drawn to enclose the ingredients. "We ask for safety in the name of Al-mah, the moon and soul-mother, who protects us even as we sleep, who remembers who came before us and promises others will follow."

She straightened, placed her hands across her chest, closed her eyes and began reciting. "Here is the powder of the fireflower, which represents your essential love," she said. "The shredded leaves of the columbine drive away evil. Dried lotus blossom symbolizes the four basic elements of earth, water, air and fire, the gifts bringing life to your children and sustaining them"

She hesitated, frowning, looking at Dorothy, trying to remember what came next.

Dorothy watched her anxiously. "Mistletoe," she whispered.

Hallie nodded gratefully and closed her eyes again. "Mistletoe, which unlocks every door, even the hardened heart of Elmo Shaw." She finished the list of ingredients quickly: "Here are seeds from the rosemary plant, to strengthen the bonds between you and us. Powdered sage for wisdom, dried jimson to ensure longevity and the ability to act decisively. Garlic to prevent evil from intruding and harming us."

Carefully, moving with great care and deliberation, Dorothy reached to make the shape of a triangle inside the circle of iron filings Hallie had drawn. Then she drew a square connecting each corner of the triangle, again within the circle. "With the four corners of the square we call forth the male. Strength," she said in a small clear voice. "The three corners of the triangle represent the female. Wisdom. The triangle and the square united are seven, which is the number of completion, of Yin and Yang, of universal harmony."

Watching intently, Hallie waited for Dorothy to finish. Then she recited carefully: "The square holding the triangle forms two other triangles. Together they represent the girl, the woman and the crone," she said: "The shape of the triangle signifies the doorway of birth." She looked sternly above Dorothy's head, at the darkened room behind her. "All life lies with the circle. As we place these substances into the amulets we ask you to keep us safe as we wear them and to come to our aid when we need your help." She paused. Then Dorothy joined her in saying: "We ask for your love and protection *not because we deserve them but because we are alive.*"

They pinched a part of each small pile and sprinkled the ingredients into the lockets. Then each woman pulled a single hair from her head, selected a locket, placed her hair within it, and snapped it shut. They held the lockets over the center of the table with the chains dangling, their knuckles touching.

"We ask for your love to envelop these baby girls as soon as they are born, to keep them safe from harm," Hallie said. "You are their mother as you are ours, and *your love knows no condition.*" Then she blew out the candles. Counting to ten in a whisper, she moved to the doorway and after a moment of quiet, she switched on the light. Dorothy blinked at her.

"It's done," Hallie said.

Dorothy felt enormously tired and slightly dizzy from concentrating. She leaned against the wall to steady herself and studied her locket. Then she hooked its long chain at the back of her neck and let the amulet slip under her blouse. "I feel different," she admitted.

"If the charms work we'll never know it," Hallie said. "We'll only know if they don't work."

Dorothy lugged the box of plates back from the living room and thumped it onto the table. She patted the locket in its place around her neck.

"Happy New Year," they told each other gaily.

They felt they'd taken a great step toward safety.

PART THREE

Mother

Chapter One

Dorothy moved calmly around the kitchen putting things away, closing cupboards, shutting drawers. She and Hallie brought the refrigerator back and pushed it into place. Hallie reloaded it. The pots and pans went back under the sink, the herbs, spices, noodles and canned goods were restored to the cupboards. When Dorothy finished washing up she turned off the faucet firmly and glanced at the clock. It was a quarter to two in the morning. She felt ready to do what must be done.

She wiped her hands on a dishtowel and folded it neatly on the rack. "I can't go into labor here," she said, turning to Hallie.

"It won't be a picnic but I think we can manage," Hallie said. She knew the fury of the snowstorm necessitated staying in the apartment for the birth. Unfortunately, the phone was out so they were cut off from Doc and professional help. The prospect of going it alone was unnerving, but there was no alternative. They still had heat, water and electricity. They could cope.

She looked around the kitchen, figuring what they'd need. She hoped fervently there wouldn't be any complication. She reminded herself women had been giving birth to healthy babies—even twins—since the beginning of time, sometimes—often—unassisted. After all, nothing was more natural than giving birth. Invention of the science called obstetrics was recent in the long history of human reproduction. And she'd studied the process at Dorothy's classes and herself assisted in several births—in Peru, and long before that in London during the Blitz—without the intrusion of hospital technology.

But she didn't want Dorothy to guess how jittery she felt. It might frighten her. "You'd better get back to bed," she urged. "We've had a long day. You have to rest."

"I can't go into labor *here*," Dorothy repeated with careful emphasis. "It's too dangerous."

Hallie sighed. "What do you mean?"

"We have to go to the hospital."

Hallie frowned. "We can't go out in this."

They both looked toward the window. Behind the glass the snow was blowing fiercely, whirling and clinging to the trembling panes, collecting in frozen piles at the corners. Beyond the snow the black wind howled.

"The charmed locket will keep you safe here," Hallie said. "Why do you think we went through that rigamarole?"

Dorothy shook her head. "If the charm works we'll be safe even if we go outside," she said.

"No spell keeps you safe against *stupidity*," Hallie said. "Going outside in a blizzard is stupid."

"You know as well as I do we aren't sure the spell will work," Dorothy argued. "We're taking a chance on it. We're not witches, we don't have any experience casting spells. Maybe we did it wrong. And if the charm doesn't work when Mr. Shaw comes it'll be too late to do anything else—if we stay here. And he's sure to come. Snow won't stop him." She turned and strode from the kitchen.

Hallie followed her into the hall.

"We're helpless by ourselves," Dorothy said over her shoulder. "Just like all the other mothers he tricked." She opened the closet. "They stayed home—away from everybody except Elmo Shaw and their husbands—and look what happened to them. They played right into his hands." She pulled on her parka. Balancing awkwardly against the door jamb and reaching with difficulty across her bulky midsection, she yanked on her boots and fastened them quickly. "We have to go to other people so we can get their help." She looked at Hallie, her eyes dark with determination. "Without the phone there's no way we can contact anybody.

264

We're isolated, Hallie. Exactly where he wants us."

Hallie sighed again. That was true. But she continued to resist. It wasn't safe outside.

Dorothy reached encouragingly for her hand. "We'll be all right," she said. "Can you see some tough old nurse at the hospital handing over one of my babies to that awful old man? Or a doctor sending a newborn into a blizzard?"

"What about you?" Hallie pleaded. "If we go outside you'll freeze to death before we can even get to the hospital." In other circumstances a middle-of-the-night foray into a raging snowstorm was unthinkable. Tonight wasn't ordinary but Hallie didn't think they should try to reach the hospital anyway.

She was confused.

Try as she might she couldn't call up a vision of what was going to happen. She sensed the babies would be born safely, but maybe she sensed it because she wanted it so much. Was the slippery infant she saw herself holding up one of Dorothy's babies? She supposed so but she wasn't sure. And looking into Dorothy's stubborn face didn't help resolve the dilemma.

"You shouldn't come," Dorothy said. "You know I'll be safe until after the babies are born. But—except for the charm—there's nothing to protect you. So you'd better wait here until morning, to be on the safe side. Then you can come to the hospital—"

"And find your frozen body under a pile of snow along the way?" Hallie said. "No thanks."

"The hospital's only ten blocks from here."

"In this weather it's more like ten miles," Hallie said. "Use your head."

"We'll take a cab."

Hallie snorted. "My god, Dorothy, what's the matter with you? There aren't any cabs in this storm. Don't be crazy."

Dorothy started determinedly toward the door. "Then I'll walk," she said. "It's not that far. And I still have time before I go into labor. I'm feeling strong and energetic, the way Dr. Blanchard said I'd feel right before labor starts." She unlatched the door and opened it.

Hallie pulled her coat decisively from the closet. Dorothy

was her charge and she couldn't permit her to make the journey by herself. "You're not leaving me behind," she said, bent to pull on her boots, then straightened as she zipped her coat. "But can't we wait till morning?"

"Nothing's out there in the dark that isn't there in the daylight," Dorothy said, her eyes snapping as she thumped down the stairs. "And morning will be too late."

Hallie relocked the door and followed her noisily. "Wait up," she called, looking apprehensively into the common hallways. Their neighbors had evacuated the building, and probably the city.

She had to admit Dorothy was right. They must be with other people when Elmo Shaw came, and nobody else remained here to help them. There would be professional staff at the hospital and that's where they must go.

She pulled her scarf tightly around her face. Never had her involuntary ability to see the future seemed such a useless gift. It and their amulets were their only weapons. She felt grossly ill-equipped for the battle ahead.

Outside they entered a blind world of sharp-edged snowflakes and biting cold. They labored through a huge drift to approximately where the corner was and huddled there, looking up and down Broadway. Several unidentifiable vehicles, abandoned at the sides of the roadway, lurked beneath mounds of snow. The streetlights which might have guided them stood dark.

"Look!" Dorothy shouted triumphantly.

A checker cab was advancing regally up the avenue. Its dark windshield glittered in identical opaque arcs as the wipers busily whirred and clicked, pushing the snow aside with angry swipes. The numbered sign attached in the center of its roof was lit, signifying the cab was empty and looking for passengers.

Dorothy lunged into the street waving her arms. "Stop!"

The vehicle pulled up shudderingly, halting less than a foot from where she stood with her feet planted in snow that reached the ankles of her boots. She turned and grinned back at Hallie, feeling as if nothing could harm them. They hurried through the drifts to the side of the taxi. From the front seat the driver reached back to open the door and

Hallie got in, then helped Dorothy climb in after her.

"Boy, are we glad to see you," Hallie said to the back of the driver's head. She gave him the address of the hospital. "West 88th between Columbus and Amsterdam."

"See?" Dorothy said, settling into the seat. It was upholstered with a fur-like material, and she took off a mitten and rubbed her hand gratefully against its softness. "We'll be there in no time." She laughed giddily. "I told you, you can *always* find a cab in New York."

"I guess our charm works," Hallie said, reaching under her collar and gratefully fingering the amulet hanging on the cold chain around her neck.

The driver shifted gears, the motor engaged powerfully and the car rolled forward. Outside, snow danced and swirled in the beams from the headlights. There was no sign of people or other cars on the streets. The windows in the buildings they passed were dark. Corrugated metal barriers were pulled across most storefronts and giant snowdrifts hid many entryways. It felt as if they were the only people in New York City.

But it was cozy inside the cab.

"Your heater certainly works well," Hallie yelled to the driver.

Without answering he gripped and spun the steering wheel. The car rocked as it made a ninety-degree turn at high speed. Dorothy glanced at Hallie uneasily. "Why is he going east?" she said, puzzled, looking out the window again to get her bearings.

Hallie leaned forward and rapped loudly on the plexiglass partition separating the front and back seats. "Where are you heading?"

The driver didn't respond. Instead there was a roar from the motor as he accelerated.

"He's going into Central Park," Dorothy said, sitting up tensely and pulling on her mittens. "Stop him."

Hallie glanced at his hack license above the meter. "Oh, god," she said, looking frantically back at Dorothy.

There was no name on the faded license and the date read 1958.

Dorothy struggled to open the door.

"Wait," Hallie warned, holding her arm. "You can't get out. He's going too fast."

As soon as she'd spoken, the cab screeched into another turn, Dorothy lost her grip on the handle and flew out the open door, the force from the sudden turn drawing Hallie with her. Instantly the door slammed behind them and they landed with soft thumps, one after the other, in a drift that cushioned their fall like a giant feather bed. The taxi sped off in clouds of exhaust and snow, the chains on its tires making rhythmic clacking sounds. After a moment the noise and the rear lights vanished.

"He intended to do that," Dorothy said, using a branch to pull herself up. Big snowflakes melted quietly on her cheeks. "He meant to dump us in the middle of the park where we'd be lost." Hallie stood slowly and brushed herself off. Checker cabs were a relic from another time. She should have realized finding one on a night like this was too lucky to have been a coincidence. Worst of all, now that the memory didn't matter, a vivid image of the taxi parked in the garage at Elmo Shaw's mansion appeared in her minds' eye. She saw it clearly, pulled up behind the Rolls Royce. "The driver was supposed to leave us here."

"And I delivered us to him, damn it," said Dorothy. "On a silver platter."

But they didn't have time for recriminations. The temperature was in the teens and the snow was falling relentlessly. Around them landmarks were covered with it and the night was absolutely dark and silent. Even the wind had dropped ominously.

"We have to get out the way we came in," Hallie said. She pointed in the direction the taxi had disappeared. "That way." They had to hurry. Mr. Shaw would arrive at any moment. He knew where they were even if they didn't.

They started off. There were no curbs, no stone walls or traffic signs, no indication of the roadbed except for a relative flatness between drifts. But areas of snowy flatness existed in many places—the road could be anywhere. Dorothy squinted ahead. The taxi tracks were already obscured. "If we go in a straight line we'll come out somewhere," she said. They no longer knew which was was

268

east and which way west. But the park was a rectangle and if they traveled in a straight line they'd get to one of the boundaries sooner or later. "I'll go first, like a snowplow," she said. They pushed ahead silently for several minutes. The shallowest snow was knee-deep and every few feet it drifted into waist-high mounds.

"I think we passed this tree before," Dorothy said hesitantly, putting her hand out to a giant sycamore. "I remember the way the branches come out one side, like a W."

By now Hallie's cheeks were glossy with ice, her lids nearly frozen under a snowy crust. "Let's try that direction," she said, pointing and turning slowly in snow that reached her thighs.

Dorothy started out again, concealing her mounting panic, concentrating on maintaining steady forward progress. Hallie followed as closely as she could. At one point Dorothy slid into an icy hole, but Hallie's strong hands were under her arms instantly, pulling her out, and they went on.

After several minutes Dorothy stopped. "Oh, no," she said.

A thick tree stood directly in front of her. Three snow-covered branches emerged from the battered trunk to form a W. "We made another circle," she said, moving closer to examine the area around the tree. "I can't even find our tracks." They'd been here only minutes before but already there was no trace of them. She peered ahead fearfully.

Hallie moved close. "If we face straight ahead and keep the tree behind us, sight a bush or something, then reach it and sight something else in the same direction and aim for it—"

Dorothy nodded and moved away.

Pulling her cap over her eyebrows with both hands, Hallie glanced upward. "It looks as if the snow's letting up a little," she said hopefully.

Dorothy could see no change, but remained silent. She found she could hardly pick up one foot and put it ahead of the other. The snow was dense and solid, sucking around her aching legs and slurping like mud, but somehow heavier than mud, and freezing cold. The icy wet oozed into her clothes, down her legs, encircled and numbed her toes. Her soaked boots gripped her feet like shrinking bindings. With every step a steel ribbon of pain shot through her shins to her knees, up her thighs and into her back. The wind was picking up again. It beat against her and made her hunch forward. Her throbbing ears crackled with interior noise and when she ponderously moved her hand to pull her scarf across her face, she found that everything on her head was caked under a crust of ice. Her hat was indistinguishable from her hair, her ears, her cheeks and forehead. She thumped the sides of her head with her fists and bit her tongue, inducing vivid pain.

She looked back for a moment and saw Hallie moving with excruciating effort behind her, her face unrecognizable beneath its icy coating, her mouth fixed grimly under the frozen mask.

Dorothy thought suddenly of Henry, saw his impatient expression, his hands thrust in the pockets of his blue parka as if he were slogging angrily through the banks of snow beside her. She could almost hear him saying, "Why did you get me into this?" She wiped her nose with her sleeve and took another step, wishing she'd never made him agree to help her have a baby. His disapproving face seemed so clear and only inches away—she saw his frozen breath and the silky hairs in his eyebrows. Oh, Henry, she thought miserably, it's your fault too. If you hadn't stood by me none of this would have happened. You'd still be alive and I'd be home, lonely perhaps but alive and living out my life in whatever pathetic way I could. You were too good to me. You shouldn't have loved me. I didn't deserve it.

She was unlucky; she should have faced it long ago and made peace with her destiny, not dragged everybody else into hopelessness with her. Her hunger for motherhood had brought disaster, but she should have known it would. She'd blinded herself and refused to learn from the indisputable evidence of her lonely past. Now she was going to freeze to death without ever even giving birth.

A self-pitying tear spilled onto her cheek and froze before she could brush it away but deep inside her heart swelled rebelliously.

Henry had loved her and she would go to her grave grateful for it, no matter what else happened. Hallie was her best friend, the only friend she'd ever had. Surely love was a good thing, a lucky thing!

She crossed her arms tightly, pushed her face against her scratchy sleeves and looked ahead stubbornly.

Reproaches sapped her resolve and exhausted her. Elmo Shaw wanted her to hate herself. She mustn't give in to him. Her babies had to be born, they deserved life, Henry had died to give them the chance for it. She must guide them into it and protect them afterwards. As she struggled forward she was flooded with fierce feelings of yearning and love. She and Hallie must find their way out of the park to the hospital. She refocused on their goal and tried to shut out everything else. That was what mattered. Her babies. Her friend. Safety.

She halted, wanting to cry, staring at the now-familiar tree rising in front of her. They'd stumbled in another circle.

"Don't stop," Hallie warned. Her voice was barely audible behind the cloud of labored breath. She moved two or three feet forward and floundered. Dorothy twisted in her tracks to grab her. She turned again and concentrated on the gargantuan effort it took to raise one foot slightly and push it inches ahead of where it had been. She bent her knee and grunted with effort. But she couldn't lift her boot. It was hopelessly mired in the snow beneath her.

"What's that?" Hallie said, coughing, her lungs laboring to resist the icy air. Dorothy moved her eyes in the direction Hallie looked. She saw a light. It bounced and flickered for a moment, then vanished. They began shouting. The darting beam came again, closer.

"Somebody's coming!" With a desperate last surge of energy Dorothy started running drunkenly toward whatever it was. Lumbering behind her, Hallie fell sideways, righted herself, crashed forward.

A dog team and large sled emerged from the steady snowfall and headed for them. The driver stood on a platform above the dogs. The sled slid and jounced rapidly between the trees, the iron runners glinting as they cut through the drifts. The barking dogs strained and plunged through the snow as the driver cracked a whip loudly over their heads.

With a flash of recognition, Dorothy halted in her tracks. "No, no," she cried. "It's him. It's Mr. Shaw."

As Hallie swiveled toward the sleigh, Shaw leaned down and reached for Dorothy. His black hood slipped off his face and he smiled. Hallie saw the incandescent flesh around his mouth, the way it sagged and puckered with a thousand tiny lines, his corrupted lips the bright color of a decaying tomato; she saw the matted hairs encased in dirty icicles dangling from his nostrils. His insinuating smile revealed stumps of transparent teeth and the long pink tongue that flicked, serpentlike, between them.

She took a frightened step backward, pulling Dorothy with her.

"You're not the one I want, you old crone," Mr. Shaw yelled. With a contemptuous gesture he straightened, cracked his whip across her face and knocked her into the snow.

"Run!" Hallie shouted to Dorothy, rolling forward toward the dogs, raising her arms, twisting, tangling herself in their harness.

Dorothy stood riveted.

"For god's sake, run!" came Hallie's voice through the barking. The animals surrounded her and pounced hungrily.

"No!" Dorothy screamed.

Not Hallie too!

Dorothy lurched forward swinging her arms. "Get away! Get off her!" She turned toward the old man. "Call them off!"

He snapped the whip inches from her face. "Not unless you come with me," he commanded.

Dorothy grabbed Hallie's hand and pulled her free. With a snarl the lead dog leaped after her and knocked her down again.

"Run!" Hallie shouted again from the middle of the swarming pack. "Save yourself!"

"Free her!" Dorothy screamed.

Mr. Shaw leered. *"Forget her."*

Dorothy hit a dog in its face with her fist. It turned toward

272

her with a snarl, crouching powerfully between her and Hallie. She punched it again, with all her strength, and, reaching for Hallie, she screamed again. Hallie yelled too. The dogs yowled and the despairing moan of the wind rose, throbbing and humming. The noise was a hopeless, piercing cacophony vanishing unheard into dark.

Suddenly the lead dog wrenched back, turned its head and peered into the forest. With an effort Dorothy pulled Hallie up. As she got to her feet she sputtered and gasped. One of her sleeves was nearly ripped from her coat and dangled at her side. She clutched its torn edges around her arm. "Something's out there," she panted. "Listen."

Mr. Shaw turned too. He stood atop the sled, tilting away from them, straining to hear.

All of them heard the unmistakable sound of a motor gradually becoming louder. As soon as he identified the noise Mr. Shaw took control of the dogs and turned them in the opposite direction from it. He looked back at Dorothy with a warning. "Don't think you've escaped," he said, saluting her with the whip, then cracking it above her. "I'll be seeing you later today, my dear." The dogs threw themselves against their harnesses, heaved the sled into the gloom and disappeared.

Hallie and Dorothy began waving and shouting as a noisy skimobile skittered into sight, impertinent and anonymous as a remote-control toy.

"Hop on board," shouted its driver, pulling up and reaching toward them. Hallie pushed Dorothy into the small compartment in the back of the vehicle and hauled herself in beside her. The driver, in an aviator's helmet and goggles, grinned back at them.

Using her shredded sleeve to wipe her bloody nose, Hallie saw the congealed blood had carmelized with ice.

"We're going to precinct headquarters," the driver said. "Hang on."

The women clung together, their eyes teary with relief as the sputtering vehicle slid and bounced away across the snow.

Chapter Two

When they followed their rescuer across the main room of the police station a few minutes later, Dorothy looked around with amazement. When she'd passed through the space eight months ago (at the time she'd come to inquire about Henry's body) her footsteps had echoed on the glistening linoleum. Now the room was transformed into a crowded emergency shelter for blizzard refugees. Desks and filing cabinets were pushed against the walls and the air pulsed with the sour odor of wet clothes hanging on a crisscross of sagging clotheslines.

Aluminum cots were set up in rows and people lay on them staring at the ceiling or asleep despite the noise and activity surrounding them. A pandemonium of conversations in many languages resonated in the large room, and several preschoolers, too excited to sleep, frolicked and darted as if at a picnic. Their exhausted mothers huddled together, watching. Some dozed with slack jaws. In the corner a woman with pale braids fed a baby at her breast.

People made way for Hallie and Dorothy. A bearded man, lolling in a wooden arm chair, jumped up as they neared. "Sit here," he insisted, helping Dorothy peel off her frozen parka. He hovered deferentially as she settled into the chair he'd vacated.

The man who'd been sitting next to him widened his eyes in startled embarrassment as soon as he perceived her advanced pregnancy. He arose hastily and hurried into the crowd, pulling his friend with him. Hallie collapsed in his empty chair. Dorothy looked up gratefully at the young police officer who'd brought them through the storm on the skimobile. She asked him, "Is Detective Canaday around?"

He scanned the crowd. "He was here when I left a couple of hours ago," he said. "Do you want me to see if I can find him?"

She nodded.

As he hastened away, Hallie frowned. "Who's Detective Canaday?"

Dorothy explained he'd driven her downtown when Henry was killed.

"Now I want him to help us get to the hospital," she said.

Hallie's eyes widened with astonishment. "We can't go outside again."

"We can't stay here," Dorothy said firmly. "It's out of the question. I'll be giving birth in the next few hours." Her voice edged higher and she pulled nervously at her fingers. "I can't do it in this madhouse. Detective Canaday will understand. He'll get us to the hospital." She remembered how safe she'd felt with him. Surely he would take care of them.

Hallie tensed. Outside Mr. Shaw was gliding and thumping through the storm on his giant sleigh just waiting to get his hands on them again. They mustn't go outside.

This Detective Canaday—whoever he was—would understand how dangerous their leaving would be. Surely he'd refuse to allow it, even without knowledge of Elmo Shaw.

She unwound her scarf and wiped her cheeks with it.

"I'll be all right," Dorothy said, attempting to mollify her. "If I wasn't strong I'd be dead by now." She tried unsuccessfully to laugh. "I can still make it to the hospital. He'll get us there in the skimobile."

"But Dorothy, we're safe here," Hallie insisted. "I know it's not an ideal place to deliver twins, but—"

"I don't have much time," Dorothy interrupted, not listening. She looked down at herself, shifted uneasily, frowned, slid her hand under her leg and leaned on it.

Detective Sam Canaday loomed in front of them, clearing his throat and brushing crumbs from his rumpled cardigan. His eyes were bloodshot with fatigue. "You wanted me?" he asked brusquely, looking first at Dorothy, than at Hallie.

275

Dorothy could tell from his expression that he didn't remember her. She smiled brightly to hide her disappointment. "Detective Canaday," she said. "Hello."

He frowned impatiently. "Yes?"

"I'm Dorothy Kite," she said. "I'm the woman—" She paused. "The friend of the man attacked by dogs several months ago. You took me downtown in a police car . . ."

As her voice trailed away he stared at her, uncomprehending. Suddenly his mouth opened and shut in quickly concealed amazement. "Jesus," he said, glancing away quickly. "Dorothy Kite. I remember. How've you been?" He shook hands with her energetically, his face hot with embarrassment, still unable to meet her eyes. "I didn't know you were married," he added, taking a step back.

"I'm not."

"Oh," he said, reddening to the tips of his ears. He shifted his weight. "I thought—"

She apologized. "I didn't mean to embarrass you," she said.

"I'm not embarrassed," he said gruffly. "But—I remember making a mental note to call you sometime for lunch." He shrugged. "I never seemed to have the time."

"And now look at me!"

Their eyes met finally and they burst out laughing. Dorothy turned to introduce Hallie, who'd been listening with curiosity.

"I asked the patrolman to find you because we need somebody to take us to the hospital," Dorothy said.

"What?"

"We have to get to the hospital."

He glowered. "We can't take you," he said adamantly. "The skimobile's out rescuing people and bringing them here. We're not using it like a taxi."

"I wouldn't ask you if it weren't important," she said.

"You can't just get up and go to the hospital," he said. "You're lucky we got you here. A dozen people have died in the last twenty-four hours. Roofs are caving in, several parts of Manhattan are blacked out, a lot of places are without heat, whole areas are without telephones—there's no telling when we're going to dig out. Why, the snow's six feet deep in

276

some places and there's no sign of it stopping. It's the worst storm in history." He waved his arm grandly with the New Yorker's perverse pride in his city's capacity for gargantuan calamity. "This may not be the Ritz, but our generator is working and it's warm."

Her imploring eyes didn't waver from his.

"Ms. Kite, I can't take you to the hospital," he said, more quietly. "I'd like to, but we can't spare the equipment. We'll try to make you comfortable here. If you can just relax for a few hours, maybe tomorrow—"

She wobbled to her feet. "I can't give birth to them here," she warned.

His eyebrows shot upward. *"Them?"*

She nodded. "I'm having twins."

"It never rains but it pours," Hallie said helpfully, grateful to this sensible man for refusing to take them outside again.

"My water broke about a half hour ago," Dorothy told him.

He groaned.

"Please take me to the hospital," she pleaded. "The contractions are coming every three or four minutes. I don't want to go into labor here." She took a deep breath and exhaled slowly.

"I can't take you anywhere," Canaday said. His expression was sincere, beleaguered. "You have to understand that."

"I don't understand anything!" she cried, exploding finally with pent-up hurt and fury. He'd never bothered to telephone her even though he'd said he would, and now he was going to prevent her from getting to the hospital, where she'd be properly cared for. What was the matter with him? Why couldn't he help her? She wanted to have her babies in peace and safety, somewhere where doctors and nurses would look after her. Not in this dirty Bedlam of a place.

"Shh," Hallie said soothingly. "It's going to be all right. Nothing's going to happen to you." She placed her hands across Dorothy's abdomen and pushed gently. "She's as tight as a drum," she said, looking up at Detective Canaday. "You'd better set up a delivery room someplace. Right now."

He sighed. In the last few hours his professional mission of maintaining order and protecting the public safety had stretched unrecognizeably. And now that he was so tired he saw rings of light around people's faces, it looked as if he was going to have to help deliver a set of twins. His broad back sagged as he put his hands on Dorothy's shoulders. But he looked reassuringly into her eyes. "Don't worry about a thing," he said gamely. "I've delivered babies before—it's part of my job." He managed a weak grin. "Twins are more complicated, but they're in the manual too. Leave everything to me." He tried to look confident. "It won't be easy but we can manage," he said. "I'm afraid you're going to have to trust me."

Painfully, reluctantly, looking at Hallie and then up at him, measuring him, Dorothy realized she had to give in. There wasn't time to argue. She had to husband her energy for the ordeal ahead.

She had no choice.

Hallie squeezed her hand. "It's best," she said.

Dorothy lowered her eyes and sighed with disappointment. "All right," she said. "I'll have my babies here."

Instantly the detective straightened, spun on his heel and coralled a harried policewoman hurrying past with an empty coffee urn. They conferred urgently. Then the woman hurried off.

"We're going to put you in the boiler room," he said, turning back to Dorothy. "It's the only place that's vacant. We'll try to make you as comfortable as we can. Can you cross the room and make it down some stairs?"

"Of course," she said indignantly. "I'm not an invalid." She glanced proudly at Hallie. "We just survived a blizzard."

"And worse," Hallie muttered. She and the detective looked each other over nervously. Hallie wondered whether he'd been telling the truth, if he'd ever delivered a baby. No matter. She knew what to do. There wasn't any magic involved. Dorothy was fit and healthy. They'd get through it.

"Wait," Dorothy said, and they paused, supporting her for a moment as her head drooped. She let out a shuddering sigh. When she looked up and signalled she was ready, the three of them started forward majestically, Moses and the Jews entering the Red Sea. By now everybody in the room

278

knew what was happening. A way through the crowd opened for them. Hands reached out and patted Dorothy as she passed.

"Good luck, dearie."

"It'll be over in no time," clicked an old man with bright false teeth. "You'll be on the front page of the *Daily News,*" he added enthusiastically. "Probably get a lot of presents from shops in the area."

"Diaper service for a year," somebody else piped.

"A fifty-dollar gift certificate at the liquor store."

Dorothy was grateful for their encouragement. She tried not to think of what lay ahead. She sneaked a look at Detective Canaday. He appeared calm and able, just as she remembered. And Hallie would see to it nothing went wrong. They'd be all right. As she gripped their arms her heart swelled with optimism.

The policewoman awaited them at the bottom of a narrow flight of stairs. She took them through a doorway at the end of a hallway. The tiny room was stuffed with a jumble of cartons and folded tables, broken appliances, a sofa nearly hidden under stacks of bulging boxes, an empty refrigerator without a door, the sweating boiler. A sink with a single faucet tilted against the wall. Next to a tall casement window a battered steel door led outside, its lock rusty with disuse and caked with dirt, the access blocked by a plastic bag overflowing with bureaucratic trash and a tower of yellowing newspapers tied with twine. A rectangle of stiff wire mesh was tacked to the splintered window frame and outside, a small courtyard was barely visible. The brick wall enclosure and the stairway leading to the street level were entirely hidden under snow. The mesh screen quivered and clicked against the wall as the wind whistled around it. The police officer had detached its bottom portion in order to pack the window frame with rolls of blankets to keep out the cold.

In the center of the room she'd pushed aside some of the debris and pulled in a golden oak library table with fluted legs. An air mattress and a clean sheet transformed it into a delivery table.

A card table under the huge black window was covered

with paper toweling and held the electric coffee urn full of soon-to-boil water, a pair of scissors, a blue rubber dishpan, rolls of cotton, several packets of handiwipes, a bottle of iodine, a jar of vaseline, cotton swabs, tongue depressors, a small rubber hammer.

"What's the hammer for?" Hallie said.

The police officer grinned sheepishly. "Sam told me to empty the first aid kit," she said. "And add anything I could think of."

"I'm not sure about the tongue depressors either," Hallie smiled.

"Can the lights be lowered?" Dorothy said.

Sam asked why.

"When the babies are born the light should be dim," she said.

"We'll cross that bridge when we come to it," he said evasively.

"I mean it," Dorothy said with intensity. "Babies aren't supposed to explode into bright lights and loud noises. It's very frightening for them."

"Okay, okay," he said hurriedly. "We'll get a desk lamp, set it on the floor. Turn off the overhead when the time comes." He grunted. "You're lucky we still have electricity. It might go any time."

She looked toward the table under the window. "And later the rubber basin has to be filled with warm water," she said. "Body temperature."

Sam turned pleadingly to Hallie. "Now what is she talking about?"

"It's in a book we read," Hallie explained. "The babies should be swished around in warm water after they're born. It helps them adjust to their surroundings."

He shook his head, bewildered by Dorothy's requirements. "This isn't a maternity ward in a swanky hospital, you know. We'll do the best we can with what's available. What we have to offer may be primitive, but it's all we have." He sighed. "There's a blizzard going on, in case you've forgotten."

"I know," Dorothy said with a conciliatory pat on his arm. "It's very important, or I wouldn't ask, Lieutenant."

280

"Okay," he said. "A basin of water." He rolled his eyes comically, as if long-suffering. Then, "You'd better call me Sam," he said. "We're going to be good friends by the time this is over."

Dorothy agreed, shy again, then looked around nervously, trying to remember what else would be important. She told the policewoman—whose name was Rhonda Flannagan —not to leave them alone. "Somebody has to be here, with Hallie and me—all the time."

Sam promised that he or Officer Flannagan would be with them until after the babies were born. "You won't be able to get rid of us even if you want to," he said. "It's the law. In case you decide to sue us."

"Not likely," said Hallie.

He left as Dorothy got out of her wet clothes. Hallie and Rhonda helped her remove her clammy sweater, pants and longjohns. Dressed only in the big flannel shirt flopping to her knees and buttoned backwards, she sat on the edge of the makeshift bed while Hallie pulled off her boots, then stripped off her several pairs of socks and threw them into the corner. Dorothy lifted her shoulders, inhaling deeply. After a moment she looked at Hallie and said, "The contractions are getting stronger."

The women helped her settle herself. They piled her discarded clothes around her so her body was comfortably supported. Sam returned, closed the door softly, took off his sweater, folded and placed it under her head. "Sorry we don't have any pillows," he said, pushing up his shirtsleeves. His freckled forearms were thick and muscular. He offered her some water and a couple of aspirin tablets. She thanked him, sat up and sipped from the cup. "But I don't want any aspirin," she said. "It might make me throw up."

"I don't know how to tell you this," he said. "But aspirin's the only painkiller we have. Except for some bourbon."

She shut her eyes and shook her head. "I can't have that, either," she said.

"It'll help," he urged.

No.

He glanced at Hallie. "Now what's she talking about?"

"You have the shot of whiskey," Hallie told him. "You'll

281

need it more than she will. Believe me, Lieutenant, she has everything under control." She smiled proudly at Dorothy, who was lying back, breathing evenly. She placed her hand on Dorothy's abdomen. "Inhale," she instructed. "Push my hand up, the way we practiced. Slowly. Slowly. Fill your diaphragm. That's it."

Dorothy focused on Hallie's hand, now held two or three inches above her, and as the pain came again she concentrated on raising the wall of her stomach to meet it. After a few seconds she expelled her breath in short bursts.

Several times in the next couple of hours Sam, Hallie and Officer Flannagan helped her off the platform so she could totter around the room. Afterwards she climbed back onto the table and lay back with her eyes closed. Hallie helped her roll sideways, bending her legs. She moved her hands firmly against her lower back, massaging with a steady circular motion. As the contractions deepened, Dorothy held her hand and looked intently into her eyes, as if garnering strength.

There was a loud knock on the door and Sam went to open it. He whispered to somebody standing just outside, then turned back to them. "There's some kind of altercation between a couple of winos upstairs," he said. "Go take care of it, Flannagan."

With a worried look over her shoulder, the police officer hurried from the room, leaving Dorothy with Hallie and Sam.

Dorothy groaned.

Sam brought her a paper cup filled with whiskey. "You'd better drink this," he said sympathetically. "I don't care what the book says." He put his hand behind her head and pressed the cup to her lips. She turned her face, her lips clenched, and some of the whiskey spilled.

"She won't take it," Hallie said. "She told you. She wants to know what's happening."

"But that's crazy," Sam said. "Nobody goes through childbirth without something to dull the pain. This is all we have, but it's better than nothing. Jesus."

"I won't take any," Dorothy said. Then, explaining, "I have to be able to think."

"You don't need to think!" Sam said in exasperation.

"We'll do the thinking, damn it." He scowled, holding the cup inches from her face.

"You might as well drink it," Hallie told him after a few moments of impasse. "She's not going to."

Shaking his head, he poured the whiskey carefully back into the bottle, set it down with a thump. Then he looked at Dorothy. In his face impatience struggled with admiration. "If she can stand it, I guess I can," he said.

The intensity of the labor increased. After three hours the wrenching bone pain deep in her back made Dorothy moan steadily.

"Don't resist it," Hallie said. "Give into it, ride with it. Yell. We don't care. Breathe through your mouth," she told her. "Fill your lungs. Let the air out slowly. Relax. Feel the gravity making your legs and arms heavy. Lie back. Let go."

The sensations filled and pulsed into every corner of her consciousness and she had no ability to climb beyond them. She wallowed, gasping. She forgot the snow outside and where she was. All that existed was in this ugly room, the onset and release of crushing pelvic spasms, each worse than the last, unmerciful, relentless . . .

She had no thought even for Elmo Shaw.

The contractions built into searing crescendos that ripped through her, splitting her. She felt like a living chicken being torn apart by a sadistic butcher.

She cried out and clawed at Hallie's arm.

Hallie soothed her. "This is the worst part, remember? Only five or six more contractions, that's all."

"I can't stand it!" Dorothy gasped, pulling Hallie toward her, then pushing her away, writhing sideways.

"Yes, you can," Hallie said firmly. "It's almost over."

Dorothy felt it would never end, that she would die from pain.

They helped her stand and she leaned against the table. Sweat streamed down her face, her arms, between her breasts. She flexed her numb fingers. She mounted the table again, rocked back and forth on all fours. She flopped back, rolled on her side, hunched, elongated, spread her legs, brought them together, gripped Hallie's hand in a grip that left bruises. Sam sponged her face with a damp paper towel.

Intervals of relief shortened to seconds, barely enough time for her to lie back and close her eyes.

The lower area of her spine began quivering with tremendous pressure and she began to shout. Hallie pulled her forward and Sam lifted her so that she could lean against him, which she did for a moment, then twisted away.

In some deep place she wondered why she didn't burst, fly apart, spew pieces of herself against the walls and ceiling, explode out of her body.

She lurched onto her side and clung to Hallie with both hands. She called for her mother. She yearned to lie in her arms, warm, protected, free from pain. It would never end.

Hallie helped her lie back again and pressed a wad of shirt against her lips. "Here, bite this," she said. "We're almost home."

Sam turned away to wipe the sweat from his eyes.

With suddenness Dorothy dug her heels convulsively into the wadded clothes at the foot of the improvised bed. She arched her body. The excruciating sensation squeezed, a new power prevailing to wring her innards as if she were a balloon being popped. She ground herself downward with all her strength, grunting, attempting to expel an enormous object—a watermelon, a basketball. She bellowed behind gritted teeth. Struggling upright, she moaned something Hallie understood. She turned to Sam. "She wants to squat," she said. "Let's help her up."

Dorothy's eyes fluttered wildly to the ceiling.

"And the lights," Hallie said. "Turn off the lights."

Sam rushed to switch off the incandescent tubes overhead. The room fell instantly into shadow, illuminated only by the weak beam from the lamp on the floor behind some boxes.

Hallie held Dorothy firmly around her shoulders and helped her squat forward.

"Come on, Dorothy!" Sam shouted, standing in front of her, bending toward her, putting his big hands, palms together, under the moist warmth of her body. "We can see your baby's head!"

"It's almost over!" Hallie yelled. "Pant! Pant!"

Dorothy breathed rapidly, rasping through her clenched teeth, gripping Hallie's hands, then straining prodigiously, her eyes bulging. Suddenly there was a burst of white pain, a huge expulsion, and then she felt a weaving and fluttering, as if she were pushing a long thick spinning thing out of herself.

"It's coming! It's coming!" Sam cried, reaching in to catch the red and white streaked infant as it slithered toward the tabletop. He pulled, twisted and lifted it forward tenderly, placing the naked baby across Dorothy's abdomen as Hallie helped her lie back again. "It's a girl," he said.

The redfaced infant took a long, quavering breath. The throbbing umbilical cord, supple and twisted as a peppermint stick, gradually fell slack. Hallie tied it in two places, cut it carefully with the sterilized scissors.

Sam blinked and grinned, his eyes bright.

Hallie took the baby and cradled her, walking quickly to the table holding the coffee urn and basin. She tested the water temperature with her elbow, then immersed the infant in it cautiously. As she slid into the warmth the little girl's sticky eyelids opened and she looked around slowly, up at Hallie, then sedately and curiously, into the room. She took another deep, steady breath.

Sam stood behind Hallie, grinning and waving. "I think she can see me," he announced. "Hello there, little girl. It's your Uncle Sam." He rocked in his heavy shoes and cleared his throat, making a loud harrumphing sound.

Twenty minutes later Dorothy delivered the other infant into Hallie's waiting hands. While Hallie coped with the discharging placentae, Sam swished the second baby in the warm water and dried her off. Then he placed her next to her sister in Dorothy's encircling arms.

"They're big," Hallie announced. "I'd say between six or seven pounds apiece."

They helped Dorothy sit up. Her hair was wet and matted around her forehead. Hallie brushed it back for her, behind her ears. A baby rested in the crook of each of her arms. She looked into their faces. "Well, now," she whispered with a shiver of happiness. "Let's just see who you are."

Chapter Three

Rhonda Flannagan brought in an empty filing cabinet drawer to serve as a bassinet. In a burst of munificence Sam asked her to fetch his good tweed jacket from his office closet. When she returned and handed it to him, he folded it meticulously so the silk lining faced up. Then he squatted to pad the drawer with the garment, carefully positioning it so the drawer's sharp edges were warmed and softened with its bulk.

Meanwhile Hallie dressed the babies in the little clothes that had come as presents from the displaced mothers upstairs. During the hours of Dorothy's labor, the women—conferring excitedly with one another about what was happening in the boiler room and what would soon be needed—dug into the hastily packed suitcases and soggy paper bags they'd brought to the shelter and pulled out garments meant for their own babies. They insisted they didn't need the clothes and wanted to share them with the newborns. Downstairs Hallie fastened the infants into the shirts and diapers, then laid the sisters side by side in the padded drawer. She tucked a large square of flannel around them. The blanket was soft from many washings, decorated with faded duck decals. She wondered whose patient hands had long ago hemmed the edges in tiny stitches.

Sam hoisted the drawer onto the lumpy cushion next to Dorothy. The sofa had been cleared and served now as her bed. The drugless birth had left her clearheaded and exhilarated. She peered delightedly into the drawer as he

286

placed it beside her.

A few minutes later he left them to climb the basement stairs, looking forward to announcing the birth. Tired and bleary-eyed as he was, he was proud of what he'd done. He and his wife had never had children, a piercing hurt between them for thirty years. For them the wistful phrase "if only . . . " had secretly modified all their life together, blunting and limiting even the happy times. Now his chest swelled with unexpected joy, his steps lightened as if he were coming home after a long absence. He felt like the new father.

His eyes swept the big room with professional thoroughness as he entered and made his way to the front. Clearly these people could use some good news. More of them had arrived since he'd last been upstairs. There must be nearly fifty people jammed into the space, which rocked with noise. He asked a policeman standing near the front entrance how the weather looked. "Seems like the snow's never going to stop," the officer yelled over the din. "The drifts keep getting higher and higher, and they don't melt. We can hardly get in and out any more." His young forehead puckered with worry and he jerked his head in warning toward the crowd. "They're getting stir crazy."

Sam knew the sheer number of refugees represented a safety hazard. Tempers were bound to flare, and once that happened, keeping order would be impossible. There were only six cells in back and he didn't want to use any of them, but he would if he had to. He fingered the key ring hanging from his back pocket. Nearby a man pushed away a teenager angrily. Sam's hands shot out and he separated the two as the boy responded, raising his fists and pressing forward. "Let's keep our tempers," Sam warned. "The last thing we need is a fist fight." With a contemptuous look at Sam the boy turned and swaggered away. The other man sullenly returned to a woman who sat crosslegged behind him on a mat, watching.

Some of the people had been here since the day before, and the space they'd marked out for themselves and their families was being threatened by newcomers who didn't have anywhere to sit with their own belongings. Supplies of food and water wouldn't last. If only Sam had some idea of how much longer . . .

He climbed heavily onto a desk and spread his arms for quiet. As he gained attention the noise level lowered until he could hear only a few whispered conversations, and they quickly stopped. Everybody watched him expectantly and he could feel the mood of the crowd lift and surge as he spoke. At the news of the babies born downstairs a huge cheer went up. Twins born in a blizzard—at noon on New Year's Day! It was a miracle.

He described how Dorothy had courageously undergone the ordeal without so much as a swallow of whiskey. People were incredulous. When he finished talking he jumped down from the desk and a group immediately surrounded him, clamoring for more information. Also they wanted to visit Dorothy, to see for themselves she'd really done it. They needed to look her over and study her face. Was she beautiful? They wanted her to be beautiful, like a princess, but few could remember what she looked like, she'd been upstairs for only a short time and it had been the middle of the night, when many of them were asleep. Sam assured them she was a fine-looking woman and then, surprised at the quickness of his reply, decided with a wave of pleasure that yes, it was true. She was a fine-looking woman. He remembered especially her steady dark eyes.

People needed to see the babies too, make sure they were real.

They felt themselves witnesses at an inspiring event of history and wanted to tell Dorothy of their admiration, celebrate her grit by rewarding her with presents. The children demanded to be taken to look at the brand-new twins. Did they look *exactly* alike?

On of the police officers unlocked a storage closet and found boxes of red, white and blue plastic flowers, left over from a Fourth of July street carnival. The bright flowers were distributed to the children so they could take them to Dorothy.

Nobody considered that permission to visit her might be refused.

But Hallie opposed letting anybody in. "It's too chancy,"

she told Sam when he returned to the basement.

He assured her he'd keep order. "We won't let anybody touch the babies."

"No," Hallie said, crossing her arms resolutely.

"If it's a question of germs—" Sam began. But Hallie shook her head. It had nothing to do with germs.

Dorothy studied Sam's expression, saw deep inside his eyes a wary look that was almost fear. She wondered at its source. Shifting her attention thoughtfully to her newborns, she noted again the miracle of their delicate nostrils and tiny blossomlike ears.

"The room's too small," Hallie said.

Dorothy unbuttoned her shirt and picked up Emily Anne, who'd wakened, crying, and put the baby to her breast. The infant pulled and sucked insistently—without instruction. Even though she knew her milk hadn't yet come in, Dorothy was warmed by this strong indication of her baby's survival instinct. She cradled the infant in the bend of her arm and watched the budlike mouth working energetically. The tiny fingers fanned out and pushed against her with a steady rhythm. She knew Emily Anne's eyes, closed now and protected by luminescent lids fringed with curving lashes, were a deep blueblack. Charlotte's eyes glistened with a slightly bluer tint. She had a tiny dimple on her upper lip that danced when she suckled. She slept soundly, hadn't waked crying and waving her little fists as Emily Anne had. Even now she lay studying her surroundings without making a sound, as she'd done when Hallie bathed her in the basin of warm water after she'd been born. She was a quiet, thoughtful baby. Emily Anne was already a person who yelled and stiffened and resisted—she was going to be a handful; Charlotte was different—serene and deep. After only a short time it was easy for Dorothy to differentiate her babies. They were identical twins but there was nothing identical about them, not to their mother. How could she have thought she'd be able to give one away? The idea was grotesque.

She looked up at Sam. "Why do you think it's important for the people to visit us?" she asked.

Hoping for her support he turned quickly to her and said

that the birth of the babies had taken people's minds off the blizzard and the fact they were its hostages. "You never know what a crowd this size is going to do," he said. "They're irritable. Insecure, rootless. They want to go home but they can't. They're easily worked up."

"That's too bad," Hallie said. "But if they're near hysteria it's even more important we don't allow them down here. The last thing we need is a riot." She frowned impatiently. Why didn't he see the danger? Whose side was he on?

Dorothy looked into his face too. The heavy creases at the sides of his nose formed drooping parentheses around his mouth. There were bags under his eyes, squint wrinkles radiating from the corners. His double chin wobbled and there were smudges of ugly stubble on his cheeks and under his nose.

As his eyes sought hers she saw passion and concern too, and was moved.

She glanced away for a moment, considering.

Sam Canaday wasn't the enemy. Neither were the people upstairs.

She looked at Hallie. "I think we should let them in," she said. "A few at a time."

Hallie shook her head vehemently. "No."

Dorothy studied her friend. If there were a crush of people in this tiny room the old man might easily sneak in among them and steal one of the babies. Hallie's fear of this happening was legitimate. But Dorothy guessed her resistence went deeper, into secret places Hallie herself was only dimly aware of. It was possible that by preventing anybody else from coming into their little room she was really preventing anybody else from entering their lives.

But Dorothy suspected that human connection would save their lives.

In their long conversations Hallie had described her life as a magnificent Christmas tree glistening with ornaments of adventure. This seductive glitter—independence—had dictated that she live on the edges of other people's families and never establish one of her own, a price she'd gladly paid because she'd been enjoying herself. In their discussions, however, she'd come to see that in this pursuit of autonomy

290

she'd always avoided emotional engagement and finally, at 71, she regretted it, with surprising fierceness. This brilliant life she'd lived—in its very glitter and variety—wasn't enough. She'd come to need Dorothy's voice in it and that made everything different. She was making plans for herself which included Dorothy and the babies. She'd never needed anybody else before. The new feeling frightened her.

As she realized she'd lost control of what would happen in the next few hours, she resisted the new emotion. She was caught by a bewildering and unaccustomed helplessness. She was uncertain. Shaky. Was this how *mothers* felt? Hopelessly dependent on their children's behavior and judgement? Losing control like this? How terrifying.

The prospect of opening the boiler room door and letting strangers flood through made her heart stiffen with foreboding. Why couldn't Dorothy see the danger? Hallie glanced resentfully at Sam, blaming him for widening their dilemma. Surely security lay in being well defended—not in the exhuberant letting down of barriers.

Once, not getting her way would have spun her on her heel and she'd have walked away. But in the last weeks she'd pushed beyond her history and now she wasn't sure what she should do. Every possibility seemed like a terrible risk.

Sam leaned quietly against the wall, his arms folded. Although he quietly listened to their argument, he was extremely curious. He observed Hallie's alarm and wondered what danger they were discussing. He guessed that in some way their trouble was connected to what had happened to Henry Small months ago—but he didn't know how. He listened, trying to piece together the story.

In his years on the force he'd learned people were apt to talk more openly in front of him if he acted as if he had no interest in what they were saying. So he stood quietly. He sensed Hallie's hostility toward him without being able to identify its cause. They had cooperated well during the labor and delivery and he didn't understand the conspicuous change in her attitude.

"We have to keep them out," Hallie said.

"We have to let them in," Dorothy responded, her voice just as loud. "I'll ask them to be godparents, all of them." She looked toward the window. "Last night," she said, "Mr. Shaw intended to kidnap me while I was still pregnant. He had the cab driver dump us in the middle of Central Park so we'd be defenseless. He planned to rescue me so I'd have the babies at his mansion. You were the only person preventing it and he intended to let you flounder and freeze to death in the blizzard."

Hallie nodded grimly. "I nearly did."

"But when the skimobile appeared he had to change his plans and let us get away." She leaned forward. "That shows he isn't all-powerful. Things we do can change what he does, just as you said. You told me so when I lost his scarf, don't you remember? When I was so depressed. You said we could still make choices—take actions—to defend ourselves. You said we could still beat him. Oh, Hallie, you were right! We've had good luck ever since we cast the spell." With an emphatic movement she grasped her locket on its chain and pulled it out from the fold of her shirt. The gold glinted in the dim light. Sam bent imperceptibly, taking a look.

"There's probably no connection," Hallie said quickly. She didn't want Dorothy to wave her locket around in front of Sam. He'd think they thought they were witches. That was the last thing they needed.

But Dorothy wasn't at all self-conscious. "If we wall ourselves in I'll lose my child," she said with finality, sitting back. She cleared her throat. "And we have to tell Sam," she said. "He has to know so he can help us."

Hallie gasped and an unreasoning thud of jealousy hit her with the force of a blow. Her mouth went dry as she looked at him, then back at Dorothy.

"Tell me what?" he said pleasantly.

There was a thump behind the black window and a resistant groan from the wooden frame as a drift of snow fell against it.

Rhonda poked her head in the door. "They're waiting in line all the way up the stairs," she said expectantly. "When can they start coming in?"

Hallie looked at Rhonda, then at Dorothy, finally at Sam. She was outnumbered. Her pulse hammered in her ears as she forced herself to accept this, and, inch by inch, to back

292

away from controlling the decision. She mustn't feel abandoned and jealous. That was an infantile reaction. After all, responsibility for the babies' safety was Dorothy's, not hers. She saw she couldn't have her way even though she believed Dorothy's way was dangerously wrong. Being right wasn't enough. Her focus must center now on how to help, not on proving Dorothy wrong. God, she thought with a wave of dizziness that made her grab the wall for balance, it was *hell* being second banana. She had no practice for it. "Okay," she said finally. The little room was very quiet. "But no more than three people can come in at a time. And I'll scrutinize everybody at the door. They can have five minute visits, that's all." Her watchful stance and scowl would serve notice nobody could stay long.

As she positioned herself next to the door Dorothy shot her an intense look of understanding and gratitude. Hallie smiled weakly in response, and sighed, her chest knotting as if she'd just run up several flights of stairs.

Dorothy borrowed Sam's comb and readied herself to receive the visitors.

When they came they were surprisingly quiet and well-mannered. The children in each small group carried a bright plastic flower. They set them on the floor by Dorothy's couch or on the table against the wall, then asked to be lifted to see the babies. Their parents brought other things too, gifts hastily improvised from possessions they'd managed to bring from their homes. One young mother tied her little boy's white flowers with the velveteen bow from her own ponytail. She congratulated Dorothy shyly, tugged at her child as he tiptoed to set his jar of flowers on the table. After peeping at the soundly sleeping infants, she and her son left, squeezing past the long line of people who waited patiently just beyond the door, along the hallway and up the stairs.

A man in greasy trousers carefully placed a photograph of a Hawaiian beach, creased from years in his wallet, in Dorothy's hands. He told her he'd carried the picture ever since he'd been stationed there in the army. "It's the most beautiful place I've ever seen," he said. "I want you to have it. Put it over their crib so it'll be the first thing they see when they wake up." He straightened, and for a moment he gazed at the twins. He clicked his teeth and glanced again at Dorothy. There'd been a betting pool on the exact hour the babies would be born, he said. A teenage boy had won. Later the boy himself shuffled in and presented his prize—several coins wrapped in a grimy hankerchief. "You keep it, ma'am," he said. "Use it toward their college education." His earnest generosity touched her and she accepted his gift with a promise that he could visit the babies whenever he wished.

"I'd rather somebody sawed off my leg than have a baby without anesthetic," the old man behind him said. His companion, a middle-aged woman with grizzled hair and unbuckled galoshes told him sarcastically that since he was well past the age of motherhood he could make any wild claim he liked. The old man slapped his thigh good-naturedly. "Ya got me there!" he croaked, a wide smile revealing his toothless gums.

After a long time Emily Anne woke and began crying in her explosive newborn voice. The last visitor finally left and Hallie shut the door behind her. As Dorothy tended to the baby, Sam told them he'd sleep on a cot just outside in the hall. They could talk in the morning. He was too tired now to deal with whatever the complications were. All of them were exhausted, well beyond the ability to discuss anything. He didn't want to cross swords with Hallie, whose eyes flashed whenever their glances met. He felt himself at a disadvantage. A good rest would help. There was plenty of time to straighten things out.

Dorothy let him go. Her own mind was spinning with fatigue—she'd tell him about Mr. Shaw later, when she wasn't so tired.

When Sam left, Hallie pulled a chair close to Dorothy.

In a few hours January 1st would be over, she said.

Dorothy smoothed the baby's soft hair, then returned her to the drawer and looked around the room, rubbing her chin. Had they thought of everything?

"Go to sleep," Hallie urged. "I'll keep watch."

Dorothy realized her lids were heavy and she was having trouble focusing. "We have to tell Sam about Mr. Shaw," she said. "As soon as he finishes his nap."

"Yes," Hallie said. "We will. But now you have to sleep,

so you'll be strong."

"I'll just rest my head but I won't go to sleep," Dorothy said.

Despite her intentions her neck relaxed against the scratchy horsehide and her head fell back. She was asleep instantly. Hallie pulled the blanket over her, then pushed her chair across from the door which leaned open, slightly ajar. The dark hallway was quiet. She sat, crossed her arms and tipped the chair until its back touched the wall. Her adrenalin pumped furiously. She would save them from Elmo Shaw. She felt strong and ready. She knew she could protect them.

The old man would get in over her dead body.

But she was having trouble breathing.

Chapter Four

Urgent whispers filled Dorothy's ears.

She stood uncertainly and looked into swirling mist. "Who is it?" she called.

The insistent sounds continued, coming from several directions at once. They flickered unrecognizably at the edges of her consciousness, warning her, filling her with foreboding.

She stretched her arms imploringly. The icy vapor clung to her fingers. "I can't hear you," she pleaded, pressing forward, shivering, the cloying moisture adhering to her calves and ankles, filling her lungs, crystalizing into slivers of ice that coated her nostrils and the corners of her mouth.

The chorus of whispers came from places on the other side of the mist. She was in danger here. Her shoes were lost somewhere and she stood barefoot, clenching and unclenching her frozen toes in a puddle of ooze. There was warmth and dryness where the voices were but she couldn't reach it.

"Please," she said. "Where are you? I don't know how to get to you."

She knew she must get to the safe place where the voices were—was it home?—but the sounds were receding like ebbing tide. When she tried to twist and pull herself after them, she stood paralyzed, as if her legs had taken root.

She became frantic with a desire to move, to run, to escape, but even as she groaned with exertion, nothing happened. Inside an unmoving crust she jumped and pushed wildly but her imprisoning body remained motionless.

Suddenly a voice separated from the others and came clearly, like a knife through the air: "Wake up."

It sounded like Hallie. Was she here? Dorothy looked around. If Hallie were here everything would be all right. The sharp command came again: "Wake up!"

As she pulled herself from sleep into wakefulness Dorothy rubbed her eyes and blinked at the place where Hallie was sitting, expecting to see her beckoning. Instead she saw her familiar shape curving in the chair, a long S. Her fingers curled delicately around the length of pipe she held poised in her lap—ready to do battle—but she lay quietly and her eyes were closed. Her head lolled back on the chair rest, chin sagging and mouth slightly open. Her legs were thrust in front of her with her feet, in big boots, angling upward.

The voice that had waked her couldn't have been Hallie's. It must have been part of the dream.

Debilitating cold settled on Dorothy like a blanket of ice. She squinted at the luminous dial of her watch. Only a couple of hours had passed. It wasn't quite midnight.

He will arrive any minute now.

She looked around the room, accustoming her eyes to the dark, grounding herself by studying her surroundings. The boiler was the hulking cylinder in the corner, squatting hugely with its tubes and pipes elbowing out and upward, branching powerfully through the walls, into the ceiling, a giant scarab with undulating metal arms. Periodically it hissed and rumbled, but it was silent now. The window was the shuddering black rectangle high on the wall next to it. The wind whistled behind the rattling panes.

Dorothy swallowed nervously and leaned to tuck the covers tight around the sleeping babies in their drawer. Then she straightened and reached to squeeze her locket with trembling fingers. It felt cold and impersonal, unrelated—even irrelevant—to anything that had happened or might still happen. A hard lump of fear rose tightly in her throat and she swallowed again. "Please keep us safe," she whispered into the dark, gripping the locket. "Please."

Her senses seemed to stretch and quiver with apprehension. Even the roots of her eyebrows and the pores on her cheeks ached from concentration. Fully awake now, she was experiencing an anxiety that swooped and soared inside her but showed no external sign except in her frightened eyes.

She looked toward the door. She could hear Sam snoring on the cot he'd set up just outside in the hall, great long shuddering exhalations, each ending with a little explosion. Except for him, and the old building's night sounds—tinkles and creaks—everything was silent.

She pulled the blankets tighter and told herself there was no way the old man could get through to them. He'd have to force himself past the crowd in the upstairs rooms, and even if he managed it—and how could he?—he'd still have to find his way down the stairs, make it through the police officers stationed in the corridors, and finally past Sam. And hadn't Sam promised to keep them safe and posted himself outside their door to watch out for them?

They were his special charge. He'd see that nothing happened to them.

But Sam was alseep. Should she wake him?

She should have insisted on telling him the truth before they went to sleep. He didn't know the danger. If he knew, he wouldn't be sleeping, he'd be sitting here with her helping her keep watch.

She realized her jaw was clenched to keep her teeth from chattering and she was holding her breath. With an effort she opened her mouth, exhaled, moved her tongue cautiously behind teeth as frigid and unfamiliar as tiny cubes of ice. Her breath was a recurring cloud that vanished into the dark.

Cold crept through her despite the pile of blankets she crouched beneath. It seemed to freeze her heart in her chest and brought with it an overpowering sluggishness. This new lethargy pulled her down into motionlessness and further, into nothing.

For a long time she sat passively and stared ahead.

She was thrown backward by the force of a sudden icy blast that slammed her violently against the back of the couch and caught at the papers in the trash bag, whipping them into the air. The rubber dishpan skidded off the tabletop and smacked against the wall, caught by the shrieking onset of wind. She fought to snatch the babies' blanket as it billowed and snapped above them.

What was happening?

The door to the hallway slammed with a deafening crash.

The boxes in the corner toppled noisily, scattering objects that thudded and smashed against the cement floor.

She felt the couch rise and fall beneath her with great thumps. The covers blew past her and swirled into the center of the room, mixing with the column of trash papers, spinning and tangling together.

She reached frantically to grab the drawer holding the twins as it wobbled and bounced away from her. Her hair blew across her face, momentarily blinding her.

There was an explosion of shattering glass and Elmo Shaw burst through the casement into the center of the room, his snowy cape flapping about his shoulders, his terrible odor radiating from him in a pulsing ring of light. Behind him the wire mesh screen clattered to the floor. Papers and blankets whirled around him as though he stood at the eye of a hurricane. Laughing madly, he swooped toward Dorothy and before she could react, grabbed one of the babies from its place in the drawer, flung it roughly over his shoulder and started again toward the broken window.

There came a vivid flash of light and he was silhouetted against it, leaping onto the windowsill and crouching there. He looked at her over his shoulder, cackling, smacking his lips, grasping the wailing baby and preparing to exit the way he'd entered, like a giant crab swiftly climbing the snowbank just outside, to his waiting sled.

Next came a deafening crack of sound.

Instantly the old man convulsed. Dorothy saw him relax his grip on the baby and in that instant she flung herself after him and grabbed the baby's naked foot. She pulled the infant from his weakening grasp and twisted away from him, holding her tight, using her own body as a shield between them.

"I'm shot!" he screeched in astonishment.

There was a crackling sound—like fire—and overpowering waves of a rancid, sulphurlike odor. The old man lost his balance, tottered and fell backward through the broken window in the snow bank. There he writhed and twitched, trying to turn himself onto his stomach in order to crawl up

299

the snow drift and escape. His long fingers clawed at the air in frantic spasm. "I'm shot," he screamed again, sliding back impotently. Then, stiffening, flinging out his arms, he gasped: "I'm dead!"

Dorothy clung to her baby and backed away from the window as Sam pushed past her with his revolver smoking in his hand. "Don't look," he shouted, though there was little to see. Mr. Shaw had fallen into the blackness and Dorothy could barely make out the outline of his body against the snow.

The room was suddenly full of police officers. She picked up the other baby and hugged both of them against herself, shaking, hardly knowing what she was doing or what was happening. A policeman pulled her through the crowd and into the hall.

She was bewildered and looked back into the room.

Was this how it ended? The whole terrible ordeal? So quickly she didn't even know what had happened? The cement was cold under her bare feet and both babies were twisting in her arms and crying. She held them tighter, knowledge gradually warming her like radiance from the sun.

Sam had killed Elmo Shaw.

He'd never come back.

Her babies were safe! She and Hallie had triumphed.

The terrible old man would never again tempt some frightened woman into giving him her baby.

The two-hundred-year-old nightmare was finished.

She wanted to shout with the joy of it. Her babies were safe.

The old man was dead.

It was the locket, she was sure of it. It—and Sam—had saved them. Thank god for their lockets. Thank god for Hallie's research into the supernatural. Thank god for Hallie's imagination.

Thank god for Hallie.

The policeman led Dorothy to a bench against the wall under a bright bulb swinging on a long cord. She smiled blissfully up at him, wanting to throw her arms around his broad shoulders and kiss him.

She turned to watch as Sam closed the boiler room door and came to her. He knelt stiffly on the floor next to her and put his hands on her arm.

She looked for a moment into his sad eyes and then jumped up.

"Where's Hallie?" she said.

He stood too. "I'm sorry," he said. "I'm afraid she's dead."

Chapter Five

He said Elmo Shaw hadn't killed her. She'd died peacefully, sitting in the chair. He guessed she'd been dead for about an hour.

Dorothy stared at him, uncomprehending.

It had been time for her to die, he persisted. She hadn't suffered, he said. After all the exertions her old heart muscle had tired of beating, and stopped. She'd died quietly, while they were all asleep.

The attack of the maniacal old man had had nothing to do with it.

As he continued talking soothingly Dorothy jerked away from him and returned to the boiler room doorway. She held the babies tightly against herself and looked into the room.

More than once Hallie had described her own death scene—herself laid out in a dim place on a table with flowers at her head. And here it was, exactly as she'd predicted. The police had placed her body atop what had served as the delivery table only a few hours before. A mason jar crammed with plastic lilies brought to celebrate the birth of the twins now stood cheerlessly at her head. Her hands were crossed on her chest and her face bore an expression of serenity, even acceptance—but it wasn't Hallie's face. Dorothy choked to see this tranquil impostor and turned away with a stifled cry. Where was Hallie? The corpse's face could belong to anybody—it might have been stamped on a piece of wood at a manikin factory, identical to a hundred others. It had nothing to do with Hallie. There was the familiar sharp line between the heavy brows, but there was no humor in this face, no hint of laughter, no music—the dancing eyes were closed, hidden under eyebrows as thick and heavy as if molded in bakelite. There was no grin, no raised eyebrow. Where was the quick movement of her big hands, the impatient energy, the anger, the stubbornness? None of what had consituted Hallie was preserved here. They could stand this thing in the corner and put a lampshade on its head if they wanted to, it wouldn't make any difference. Hallie herself was absent. Dorothy had lost her only friend.

They'd never even said goodbye.

She slumped into the corner of the sofa. Rhonda came to her and unpeeled her fingers from around her babies, returning them to their drawer. Dorothy's eyes followed her movements but she saw nothing.

It felt as if she'd lost her mother again and this time the pain overwhelmed her. She saw Madelyn's cloud of cotton-candy hair, her brown eyes and short upper lip, the small crooked teeth and dimple in her chin, and her heart broke.

What was this life she'd wanted, rushed toward, embraced? Struggle and sweat, that's what it was, useless, unceasing effort culminating in an instant of achievement wiped away with the force of a foot in her stomach, knocking her back again into waves of yearning, loss and emptiness.

She wanted to be the way she'd been before she'd decided to have a baby. Then she'd looked out from behind her eyes without touching or being touched by anyone. She'd been numb, a porcelain teacup wrapped in cotton. Why had she sought with such tenacity a "normal" life? What did "normal" mean? A life of disappointment, dashed hopes, cruel anxiety and failure, that's what "normal" was. Suffering was what happened in a normal life, it was the natural consequence of connection and love. And she was tired of it, she'd had enough, she didn't want to be normal any more. She wanted to stop striving, she wanted to stop expecting anything, she wanted to be left alone. Even the bitterest loneliness was better than this hell of caring.

Of losing whatever it was you loved, every time, without fail.

From the first afternoon when Hallie had said she was

going to die, Dorothy should have believed her, she should have protected herself from pain by sending her packing. She never should have permitted her to move in. What good was having a friend if—by definition—sooner or later you'd lose her? Who needed closeness if loss was its inevitable component?

As Sam directed two young police officers to put the body into a large zippered bag and remove it, Dorothy watched, rocking and moaning.

She couldn't bear it.

Emily Anne woke with an angry bellow and Dorothy looked at her without seeing her little red face and pumping fists. She was vaguely aware of a sharp pain in her breasts, a fullness, a tension that increased as the baby's cries grew louder.

Her milk was coming in.

At the other end of the makeshift bed Charlotte's eyes fluttered open and she began shifting and moving too, though she didn't cry.

Dorothy watched, hardly hearing.

Rhonda bent toward her. "Your baby," she reminded her. "She's awake."

Dorothy looked at her blankly.

"She needs to be fed," Rhonda said, and lifted her from the drawer. "I'll just change her, get her ready for you."

The baby continued crying loudly as the police officer unpinned her diapers. Her little arms and legs jerked and straightened, quivered with outrage. Dorothy felt herself becoming interested—as if returning from a distance—and she moved one of her hands across her chest absentmindedly, to ease the bursting feeling.

Rhonda handed the baby to her.

"Your shirt," Rhonda said, and indicated Dorothy should unbutton it.

She bent obediently and unbuttoned her blouse, took the baby and put her to her breast. Emily Anne caught at her ferociously, sending a piercing sensation through her breast and into her arms. The baby wriggled and scowled nearsightedly as she locked into a steady sucking rhythm.

After a while Rhonda picked up Charlotte and, crooning softly, tended to her.

Dorothy sighed and her eyes filled with tears.

She and Hallie had talked often about memory and experience. How something in your past could burst upon you with all the immediacy and sensuality of the moment, called up by something as simple as a smell or a strain of music. Hallie said there was no time in the unconscious. Deep inside people, yesterday—with all its confusion and excitement—was as present as today. In those secret places inside you nothing was ever forgotten, nothing ever faded away. There everything was stored carefully so you could take it out and feel it again whenever the moment was right. The influence on her of her past feelings would continue until she herself was dead.

Until a few hours ago she'd thought that outsmarting Mr. Shaw would solve all her problems. Now she understood that life was far more complicated, that it took more than one thread to weave a life.

She watched herself feeding her baby and remembered longing for motherhood. She'd never been numb. She'd ached—always—for this small person who now lay within her arms. She couldn't go back to a time when she'd been without pain, for that time had never existed. She couldn't give up now. This was what she'd wanted. All her life. Hallie had helped her reach this place and she'd hate it if Dorothy gave up now. She must be here for her babies, must care for them and bring them along. She was their mother. They were connected to her through a mysterious biological bond, and her yearning for that connection was the reason she'd undertaken this long and painful journey. Giving in to misery would negate everything that had happened, all the pain, all the stretching and joy, too.

She sniffed. In her cynical way Madelyn had often said life was a bucket of worms—but it was life, all Dorothy had, and here were these babies she'd wanted so desperately. She must take care of them, worms or no. She hadn't bargained on the agony, she hadn't known these extra feelings—once felt and acknowledged—would be so powerful, battering and wringing her relentlessly. But here they were. She had to learn how

305

to cope with them.

And she was afraid! How could she be a mother—by herself—without Hallie to guide and support her? She wasn't competent to raise children by herself.

She wanted Hallie. She wanted her mother.

The pain would never go away. It was part of her.

Chapter Six

They were home. Sam brought them during the night in the skimobile, made sure they were settled and then left, promising to return soon. He told Dorothy he felt a strong obligation to see that she and her newborns remained healthy, at least until the snow subsided and life returned to normal. When he came upstairs after examining the furnace—he reported it was chugging away efficiently despite the building's eerie emptiness—his eyes twinkled. He confessed that his concern over their well-being was more than professional obligation. "It's personal," he said, smiling broadly and reminding her these were the same words he'd used on their first meeting.

Dorothy's expression softened.

"I'll be going," he said. "You're safe now." He reached to shake her hand firmly with both of his. He'd be checking in on them often.

Later, after she'd fed the babies and tucked them into their cribs, Dorothy found she was unable to sleep. She lay on top of her bed, still dressed, nervously clasping and unclasping her hands. For the first time she could remember she was frightened to be alone. Whenever she closed her eyes they opened again instantly. She flopped from one side of the coverlet to the other but couldn't get comfortable. Toward morning the moonlight slanting through the window faded and disappeared, replaced by a noncomforting dawn. She rose, checked the babies, then wandered into the hallway.

The familiar rooms consoled her, and she moved through

them quietly, reestablishing herself in her surroundings. She stood in the center of the room that had once been her mother's, then Hallie's, and felt an overpowering sense of emptiness. Nobody lived here anymore. The bed was still made with the sheets Hallie had slept in, her things were scattered around and hanging in the closet, but she wasn't coming back and this finality was imprinted by profound silence.

Dorothy remembered how the room had lost its identity of thirty years' duration immediately after Madelyn's death, even while her characteristic smell still hung gently in the air.

She sighed. How quickly space reclaimed its anonymity after somebody died.

She wondered if all traces of her would be neutralized as quickly after her own death.

Why not? She was only human, after all. Once she died other people would move in, replace the furniture and take over the place. After a while there wouldn't be anybody able even to remember where the piano had stood.

She shook her head. She mustn't think these thoughts. They made her edgy, depressed. Her head ached.

She moved out of the room, forcing herself to think of practical tasks. She must call Jane Blanchard. The phone was still out of order so she could postpone it for now. She rubbed the goosebumps on her arms, planning what she'd say to Jane, how she'd break the news of Hallie's death. She dreaded doing it. She'd never before told anybody about the death of a beloved friend. What words did you use? How could you prepare somebody for such news, or give comfort afterward?

She herself remained uncomforted. There was nothing anyone could say to her which would help. Perhaps—over the long run—sharing sadness with someone who cared as you did weakened its hold. She hoped so. Then she and Jane could ease—if not remove—one another's pain.

Perhaps they could even become friends.

And she longed to talk to Jeannie. She needed to hear her voice, feel her warmth and love. Dorothy pictured her frowning, standing in her own kitchen, talking on her own phone with the receiver squeezed between her shoulder and her ear, freeing both hands so she could energetically scour the frying pan as she talked. She saw Spark sitting in his chair at the kitchen table, looking up at her, his expression interested and concerned.

She wanted to see their new baby—her nephew—hold him in her arms, feel his solidness against herself, discover his face, the color of his hair, who he was.

Even with her babies she felt alone. Her solitude had never seemed so hurtful and unfulfilling.

She walked from Hallie's room across the hall to the kitchen where she stood at the sink and let the water run, then filled a glass and sipped from it. The building was quiet. An occasional creak or woosh of snow falling from the fire escape across the back wall was the only sound she heard. She looked down from the window above the sink, across the backyards hidden beneath many feet of snow, at other windows, sightless and crooked behind manila paper shades. Everything was gray, cold, still. The snow had stopped at last. She noticed that the resourceful superintendent of the building across the way had dug out from the morass already. He'd built an unsafe-looking tunnel leading up from his cellar door, like a mineshaft, bolstered its walls of snow with brooms and mops and telescoping pipes from a vacuum cleaner. There was a trampled path leading from this makeshift entrance, between the buildings and toward the street, past half-hidden windows she knew to be a dozen feet off the ground.

There was no sign of anybody at this early hour, although some hardy soul was walking his dog. She heard the sound of barking.

She set the glass, with a click, on the counter. A smudge from her lips remained imprinted on the rim above the design of braided forget-me-nots. The tumbler was the last of a set Madelyn had bought while Dorothy was in high school. Its familiarity gave her a pang. She paused at the kitchen table and flicked away a crumb, then stood looking into her hand for a long time, feeling cold creeping up her legs like ice climbing the marrow inside her bones.

There was a sound from the babies' room, a faint rattle and thump, but she didn't move in response. She stood still, shivering slightly, staring at the lines in her palm without seeing them.

In her shoes her toes shriveled with cold. She moved her eyes heavily toward the radiator. Had the furnace stopped? She placed her hand on one of the painted iron surfaces, then jerked away quickly, licking the tips of her burning fingers.

Heat pulsed up from the furnace.

Why was it so cold?

Was a window open somewhere?

A baby started to cry lustily and she moved automatically toward her bedroom, where the cribs were.

But the cry came from the opposite direction, from Hallie's room.

Her head turned quickly toward the sound, and she hesitated, momentarily confused.

The babies were in her bedroom, she'd tucked them in only minutes ago.

But the cries came from down the hall in the opposite direction.

Dorothy started running toward her baby's cries.

The door to Hallie's room stood ajar and as she approached she glimpsed a sight that froze her heart in midbeat.

Under the open window leading to the fire escape crouched one of Elmo Shaw's huge black dogs, its coat glistening with flakes of slime. The edge of a yellow blanket dangled from its jaws. On the floor in front of the creature Dorothy's baby lay on the carpet where she had unrolled from the blanket. She was kicking and waving her small arms, crying fiercely.

With a shout Dorothy flung herself toward her child, then pulled up as the dog growled. It placed its great paw in the center of the baby's chest as if daring Dorothy to come closer.

At a wild laugh behind her she whirled to confront Elmo Shaw. He was standing in the doorway holding her other baby and grinning at her. "I've picked the one I want," he said. "You can have that one." He indicated the baby on the floor and added, "If the dog is willing, which I doubt." He laughed again to see her horrified astonishment.

Elmo Shaw was dead.

She'd seen him die herself!

He'd tricked her.

She'd let down her guard and now she was alone and there wasn't anybody to help her.

"No human can kill me, didn't you know that?" he said. "Even your middle-aged friend with his big gun." He leered at her, licking his cracked lips suggestively, laughed again, then turned and hurried away. In the hall he pulled open her front door. "Goodbye," he called. "Perhaps we'll meet again."

She couldn't go after him, even though he was carrying away her baby. Its twin was here, but the dog was ready to pounce on her if she attempted to pick her up. If Dorothy were killed there was nobody to save either one. They'd both be doomed. She didn't know what to do. As it watched her the dog shifted its massive shoulders and pressed its huge paw against the infant, whose wails increased in protest. The dog snarled, pulling back heavy folds of muzzle, revealing strings of bloody drool and locked yellow fangs as large and dangerous as tusks.

"No," Dorothy yelled stoutly. "No! Get away from her!"

She heard the receding thumps of heavy boots as Elmo Shaw departed down the stairway.

He was going to escape.

With desperate invention, Dorothy grabbed a large container of scented bath powder from Hallie's dresser, tore off its closely fitting round lid and jammed the nearly full container onto the dog's face. She moved so swiftly the dog had no time to react. Instantly a huge cloud of talc wafted benignly into the air. The beast jerked violently, its nostrils clogged, and began rasping and choking repeatedly. Quickly blinded, it became frantic. It was unable to breathe, and it writhed and rubbed its face on the carpet, gagging, turning and clawing in an ever-tightening circle under the window. The baby was forgotten.

Without hesitation, and holding her breath against the white cloud that lingered in the air, Dorothy grabbed the baby, rewrapped her in the blanket and raced from the room, slamming the bedroom door behind her as she ran into the kitchen. She opened the freezer and pulled out a bag of pork chops. Then she spun and sped from the kitchen, down the hall, out the door and down the dark stairs after the old man. As she ran she held the package of meat with her free hand and bit at it frantically, spitting the plastic into the air, ripping it open with her teeth.

Two floors below she heard the front door slam behind him.

"Oh my god, oh my god," she said, ignoring the skidding thumps of her heart, half falling, crashing down the dark stairs after Elmo Shaw. "Please don't let him get away." Then, louder, stronger: "You son of a bitch! You murderer! You can't have her!" She rushed to the front door. "Do you hear me?" She flung it open and set herself squarely on the crest of snow that led from the building's entrance. The stoop and stairway had disappeared under it. She squinted into the weak morning light, looking for him. The air was solid with cold; she could almost see it, frigid and sparkling with supernatural energy.

She narrowed her eyes against the cold and held the warm bundle of baby tightly against herself and turned toward the sound of barking. She saw the great sled parked several feet away, its curving runners pointed uptown, the team of dogs facing her breathing clouds of steam, prancing and jostling each other, all of them poised and ready to haul the sleigh away and out of her life. There were nineteen dogs, big as ponies, straining and yelping as they waited eagerly for a command from Elmo Shaw. He was at this moment pulling himself into the coachman's seat. She watched as he dropped the baby roughly on the leather cushion beside him and yanked the whip from its holder.

She lurched forward into the cold.

"You fucking son of a bitch, you murdering bastard," she screamed, running toward him. "You're not going to get her, you fucking shit." Outrage rose like a scalding fountain within her and she pounded toward him, through drifts that reached her thighs.

The buildings around her rose, half-submerged and unrecognizable in unfathomable depths of snow. It was a sinister, unfamiliar place of doorless structures with windows gaping above her like broken teeth. Her frantic shouts vanished, unheard by anybody except the evil old man who stood at the front of his perch, the whip high above his head. "Out of my way, you miserable female," he screeched. Then he laughed. *"They'll match, just like bookends,"* he whined, imitating her. He brought down the whip and cracked it across her face. "You betrayed the child yourself," he said. "It's not my fault." Then, wielding the whip again, "Get out of my way."

She twisted away to protect the baby she held, and, hunching, backed toward the sleigh again, into the dog team. She'd block their passage, prevent them from moving.

She took a pork chop from the bag and threw it up, above the dogs. One of them leaped into the air and caught it in his mouth. Instantly its harness mate jumped upon him and pulled the meat away. The first dog, snarling in response, crouched sideways in its chains and snatched back the morsel. They rolled together, snapping ferociously, fighting for possession of the meat. Using their claws to rip and gouge, they slashed each other as they gripped with their teeth and yanked back and forth. Neither dog gave up its corner of the food. Blood mixed with sweat and ice smeared their dark coats. Dorothy threw the rest of the pork chops, one by one, into the air. The other dogs jumped wildly after them, biting and trampling each other in a frenzy to get there first.

The dogs were starving. But she'd brought no more food. In a moment the chops were gone and the angry dogs had turned their attention back to her.

"How foolish of you, my dear," Mr. Shaw said. "These are *hungry* dogs."

Help me!

She yelled. The incoherent sound came from her toes, it erupted from her as loud and as angry as the roar of a lion. The snowbound street reverberated with it. She shouted again and took a step toward the sled. Her arms were tightly crossed across her chest, covering her baby. She never took her eyes from Mr. Shaw's.

Help me god!
Forgive me!

313

Elmo Shaw didn't care what she was screaming. He swiped at her, pushing her back with his whip, cracking it in her face and across her shoulders, driving her off. She blinked and winced under the onslaught and took a first step backward and then another. He was beating her back, there were ribbons of blood on her cheek from the whip, and scalding pain.

She cried out again, half sobbing, surrendering to the knowledge that she was helpless to prevent the old man from taking her child. She couldn't stop him by herself—and there wasn't anybody left who could help her. She was alone.

Or was she? She rubbed her arm across her eyes and blinked to focus. Something was moving across the empty vista of snow. Wonderingly, she saw an old woman limping toward the sled, dragging a misshapen burlap sack. She was dressed in slippers that flopped open like moccasins and she had a ragged blanket around her shoulders.

What was she doing here, Dorothy wondered wildly—this crazy old woman, dressed in rags and half frozen? Mr. Shaw turned on his perch, following Dorothy's gaze.

The excited dogs became ominously silent. They milled around in their chains, nudging and nipping at each other, making worried little sounds, circling, watching warily as the old woman approached them. One of the dogs started to whimper. Mr. Shaw turned with an oath and cracked the whip across its shoulders. It wriggled and jerked away, snarling.

Dorothy recognized the old woman. She'd been huddled in a doorway near the clinic the night when she'd been impregnated.

And later, after the dog attacked the derelict, when Dorothy had chased it off, this woman had come along and lain beside him. She'd shared her newspaper, made a blanket with it to cover them both. She'd called Mr. Shaw's dogs "the hounds of hell." As if she *knew*. She'd warned Dorothy, too. "Vigilance," she'd said.

Weeks ago she'd left the half-eaten bagel for the drug addict under the newspaper in the doorway. Dorothy remembered the way he'd loped along, swooping down to retrieve the food as if he'd known precisely where it was hidden.

And when Dorothy and Hallie arrived at the police station the night her babies were born, this same woman had been sitting there on the floor, patiently giving herself a bath with a square of paper toweling and a dixie cup full of water.

Along with Elmo Shaw she'd been with Dorothy all along. Watching. Waiting.

"Nice dog." The old woman spoke to one of the huge black creatures. It sat back clumsily on its wide haunches as she stroked its forehead.

Mr. Shaw spat on her. "Get out of the way," he sneered.

Unperturbed, the old woman worked her dirty fingers carefully along the purple jowls of the lead dog, massaging, tenderly wiping away the bloody saliva, making a clucking, concerned sound. She smoothed a place between the dog's eyes. "There, now," she crooned.

"Move on," Mr. Shaw said impatiently. He cracked the whip across her narrow back.

She didn't flinch.

"Please," Dorothy said, putting out her free hand, touching the old woman's shoulder. "He'll hurt you."

She looked back at Dorothy kindly. "Get behind me," she said in a warm, soft voice. "I will protect you."

Dorothy felt surprising strength in her shoulder and obeyed her.

As Mr. Shaw watched in astonishment, the old woman moved forward among the snarling dogs. Her bony hands and wrists, streaked with grime, poked pathetically from her sleeves. One of the dogs lunged toward her, but it wrenched back and halted, rolling its eyes, without touching her. The old woman knelt beside it in the snow and undid its harness.

As she stood again the animals milled ineffectually around her. One of them snapped at her outstretched hand but came away sheepishly, with nothing between its teeth. It gazed at her and began to wag its tail.

Dorothy cowered into the snowbank with her arms wrapped around her baby and watched the old woman as she moved among the dogs, making a singsong sound. She

315

unfastened their chains and dropped them into the snow. At first the dogs yelped and backed away from her, their ears sliding back, frightened. In the next moment they were puppies, bounding after her, playful, unmenacing, freed.

Through the cloud of snow churned up by the cavorting dogs Dorothy recognized a millennium of suffering in this small hunched figure, in the bend of her back, the set of her drooping shoulders, the comic bow of her spindly legs.

Like her mother, she'd come in answer to Dorothy's cry.

She'd come to forgive, and her forgiveness was unconditional. It came indiscriminately, with the force and inexorability of nature.

She forgave Elmo Shaw as well as Dorothy—not because either of them deserved it but because they were alive.

The old woman waited beneath him, looking patiently up at Elmo Shaw. He stood high above her on the sleigh, screeching with rage. His dogs had run away. He raised his arm, preparing to strike her again with the terrible whip. In his fury he seemed unable to perceive his loss of power.

As Dorothy watched, blinding light pulsed and radiated from the weapon. There was a violent flash, a simultaneous crack of thunder. The earth under Dorothy's feet seemed to roll and pitch. She grabbed the snowbank to steady herself and saw the smoldering whip slither like a living thing out of the old man's frantic two-fisted grip and drop into the snow, sizzling and hissing through it—a flaming snake.

A moment passed. Shaw's milky eyes were round with fear. Abandoned by his dogs and without the whip, he leaned down, frightened and bewildered, sucking his fingers. He seemed slowly to shrivel and sag against the front of the sled as he whimpered.

Finally, with a convulsive shudder, he reached tremblingly toward the old woman. Thin tears oozed from the corners of his eyes, and slowly, slowly, he crumpled from his high place on the sled and slid down its steps and into the old woman's waiting arms.

"I'm tired," he whispered. "Take me home."

He lay within her grasp, small and withered, as helpless as a cradled baby, his fearsome powers gone.

"It's time you rested," the old woman told him quietly.

"You've had enough." He nodded, sighed with exhaustion, and closed his eyes.

Then she glanced back at Dorothy, who felt her cheek touched with fingers of infinite tenderness. "Take yo~ baby," she said.

The world behind the old woman darkened a~ Dorothy could see was her face, brightening and shr~ as if at the end of a lengthening tunnel. She felt the ~ her other baby being placed in her arms and then~he the comforting sound of many women around~her chuckled and laughed. Dorothy was engulf~ warm, happy sounds of mothers. Their love~ among them and soothed her. Finally her~ faltered entirely and she fainted into the s~

When she woke she found herself in h~e'd got there, into her babies' crib. She didn't know~The quiet in the but there was no sign of what had hap~ny was studying room was peaceful, not ominous.~ coverlet, the pink Emily Anne's hand, which lay open~postage stamp. She square of palm hardly bigger th~feline wrapping itself examined the delicate tracing o~to the fat wrist. As she around the little thumb and le~t seemed to her that they stood looking down at her chi~rib, under this window in had always lain together in~smelled this fragrance and this room. As if she'd al~room had never known any known these sounds. As ~ever would. inhabitants but these. A~whispered, running her finger

"You're safe now," ~eek, watching her silky eyebrows down Charlotte's sof~n, when the snow melts, we can go furrow, then relax. "~alk. I'll show you our neighborhood outside for a lovel~ ~ive in the city with us." and the people w~

She heard a kn~k at the front door. Giving a last look at the sleeping bab~s, she went through the living room to see who it was. Sh~looked through the peephole and saw Sam Canaday star~ing on the other side of the door in his dirty parka with ~e hood pushed back.

There w~s no sight so handsome, she thought, or so

317

vulnerable, as this man, freshly showered and pink, his hair combed neatly back with water.

He was holding a bunch of violets.

"Where can he have found those flowers?" she wondered.

Smiling a welcome, she unlatched the door and invited him in.

Epilogue

A pretty ending for the story of Dorothy Kite.

But you don't see the Devil crying into his beer.

Why should he worry? Nothing has changed.

Tomorrow he'll tempt her again and she'll leap at what he offers. Stupid woman, she's learned nothing.

No sooner does she get one thing when she tosses it aside and reaches for another. Next time she may offer "anything" to cure a sick child. Mothers have been known to do that.

She'll beg and cry and carry on. And the devil likes the sound of weeping. *Oh, all right,* he'll sigh dramatically, and return his scabby hand to rummage through his bag. *Is this what you want?*

He sets his price again, smiling to himself as she eagerly agrees.

He knows there's no restorative that lasts.

Then later, when she's playing with what he brought her, he'll come careening from around another corner, unexpected, jarring, knocking her off balance and laughing at her helplessness, shouting at her wooden-headedness, demanding his payoff.

The astonishing thing is she deals with him repeatedly. It's as if she and he have no history together, as if each encounter is new.

And what of the old woman who watched Dorothy as the story unfolded, and rescued her this morning in the snow? Will she return to help her again?

And who is she, anyway?

She's not nearly as famous as the Devil. She's as old as he is—in fact they were born together, in the same instant—but she has no bag of tricks, no glamorous outfit. She doesn't look prosperous the way he does.

How does Forgiveness dress on Halloween?

She offers no treasure except relief, an underrated benevolence unless it's needed. Nobody is afraid of her, so she commands no attention.

But she's there, looking over her brother's shoulder even while he's making his latest bargain. You can catch a glimpse of her sometimes waiting patiently in the shadows.

Where you find him, you'll find her—if you're willing to look. But because she's not nearly so pushy or conceited you often forget she's there.

He knocks you down, pushes your face in the dirt. She helps you up.

Good and evil, sin and redemption, hope and despair, yin and yang, since the beginning, playing off each other.

Twins.

It's the maddening story of life, and there's no end to it.